PLAY THE LAST CARD

Contents

For Grace, who met Ivy & Scott first and fell in love with them.
Thank you for not letting me forget them.

Chapter One

Ivy

Fingers tap against the rounded edge of the bar. Despite the large hands and the long fingers, the tapping is soft, and gentle, and completely out of rhythm. It makes the hairs on the back of my neck stand up. A slight shiver trickles down my spine as I eye the man who seems to be studying the bar top with great interest.

The tapping stops and he lifts his head. With the cap pulled low over his eyes, a shadow falls across his features and I can't quite make out the color of his eyes from my spot by the beer taps. I force myself to look down, eyes back on the taps as I twist my wrist and switch out the glasses in my hands. A steady stream of beer flows eagerly and the second pint glass fills to the top.

"Won't be a moment," I call out, my eyes falling on the man again. He hasn't called me over since sitting down, nor has he really shown any indication that he is ready to order, but I call out anyway. Still, there is something in me that can't resist trying to get his attention. He gives a slight nod without meeting my gaze and his fingers take up tapping again against the lacquered bar top.

The man's disinterest bothers me.

Why?

No idea. But it does.

"Here you go, Doug." I push the two overflowing pint glasses in front of the older gentleman.

"You should pour yourself one, darlin'. On me and the boys," he replies as I add the drinks to his tab.

"You know I can't drink on shift, Doug. Stop trying to get me in trouble."

He laughs, heartedly and with his whole body. He gives me a fake pout and shakes his head, telling me, "I'm just waiting for the day you quit this place and run away with me. You know that."

I can't help but laugh right along with him. Doug is good natured, sweet, and madly in love with his high school sweetheart. I've heard the stories about him and his wife enough times to know that he is only kidding about running away with him.

Doug is my favorite regular customer by a mile. I'm only here casually to help out but during the quieter hours when Doug and his buddies are the only ones around, they like to regale me with stories, talk nonsense, and dissect any football game that happens to be playing on the bar's televisions. I remember the time I'd asked Doug if he'd ever played before—a passing comment after I'd first started working shifts at the bar—and the rollercoaster of a story that had followed ended with him breaking his ankle in high school and ruining any chance of him going pro. I laughed, commenting that it was a damn shame because he looked like he could have been an American All-Star. That had earned me the brightest smile from Doug who'd been quick to agree.

That story remains my all-time favorite of his.

"You're a gem. Thanks, Ivy." Doug is missing a tooth but his grin hasn't suffered from it. The faded, over worn Broncos jersey stretches over his large beer belly. I can't help the smile that grows again and I wave him off.

When I turn, the man in the cap has raised his head a little and I can see more of his jawline. Sharp. So sharp.

He's been watching the exchange with Doug but when our eyes meet, his gaze drops and his fingers resume their out-of-rhythm tapping. I approach, moving slowly down the bar to his seat.

"Hi," I say, resisting the urge to clear my throat first. My mouth is suddenly dry and I practically feel my nerves pulsing under my skin. Why the hell am I nervous? "Can I get you something to drink?"

"Water." He pauses as his chin lifts slightly. His rough voice raises goosebumps on my arms when he adds in a low grumble, "Please."

"Sure. Nothing else?" My hand is already moving toward the chilled glasses in the fridge next to where I stand.

"Just the water. Thanks," he adds quickly.

At least he has manners. I fill his glass with ice, eyeing him as he whips the cap off his head and runs a hand through his hair.

My stomach turns over with a pang of familiarity.

I know him.

He looks so familiar, it's as if I recognize some of the features of his face but can't place them clearly in my mind. It's a blurry, pixelated version. My mind screams at me, positive that I have seen this man before. I try to school my features though; I don't want to scare him off while my brain tries to put the pieces of this puzzle together.

"You from around here?" I ask before I can stop myself, letting my easy and well-rehearsed customer service smile slip into place. I slide a coaster under the glass of water and place it in front of him.

Green. His eyes are green.

My gaze drifts over his strong jaw, and up to his hair, taking note of the way his hair curls at the ends after being trapped under his cap. I glance down, following the trail of corded muscles down his arms. His biceps stretch the cotton, the t-shirt he wears hugging his shoulders, his chest, his stomach. I swallow. I would bet good money that he has an eight pack under that shirt of his. My gaze darts around his impressive form and my fingers twitch, wanting to reach out to feel how solid he is.

God, I need to get a grip.

Finally, he meets my gaze. Another small shiver rolls down my spine as a chill spreads up my arms and I fight off the urge to shake them out.

"No."

"So, you just moved here?" I ask, studying him. My eyes linger on the shadow of a beard growing. I wonder what he looks like with the beard fully grown out? I imagine it only adds to the appeal. The ruggedness of him. A tall, wide man with a full beard. I think he would look good with a full beard. Although, it would probably hide that jawline of his, and that would be a shame.

His eyebrows crease, long lashes framing the green of his eyes and deepening the color just a little. He cocks his head to the side and frowns, clearing his throat.

Shit.

I'm staring.

"Yes. That would be the definition of me not being from around here," he replies in the same low, gruff tone.

"You could be just visiting." I shrug. I could walk away, I *should* walk away. There are a few glasses that could go through the wash, missing bottles of beer to be refilled in the fridge. I have things to do before we close. I don't have to stay and chat with this guy.

Yet the puzzle pieces still aren't making sense and I can't shake the feeling that I know him from somewhere. I hesitate for a second. "You look familiar."

It's his turn to study me and with his gaze the beginnings of a flush burn at the nape of my neck. I take a subtle deep breath, willing the heat to stay off my face. The corners of his eyes begin to tighten, fingers reaching to clutch the untouched glass of water in front of him before he says, "Hazard of the job, I guess."

"Oh?" I shuffle through my memories, searching for him. He isn't a teacher at the school. Unless he is new? No, I don't think they've hired this year for the junior school. I haven't seen him around the bar before, nor around the hospital and I don't spend my time anywhere else these days. I press on, my curiosity winning out over my politeness.

"What do you do?"

"I—" He goes to answer but something in his eyes shift as if he's only just realizing what I'm asking him and a gleam of joy flashes through the small cracks of his stoic mask. "Nothing important. I work across the road."

"For the Broncos?" I lean on the bar toward him, wanting to figure him out and trying my best to do so before I scare him off.

I'm curious. Sue me.

He's a mystery and the only thing I want at this moment is to figure him out. Eagerness be damned.

"You could say that," he answers. My heart skips a little as his fingers drum along the bar top again.

"Oh, well, you'll be a new regular then I expect. They all come over here during the week from what I'm told. And during home games, the bar is packed with fans." I wave a hand lazily around the bar.

"You're told? This is your first shift?" he asks. I bite down a smile. Good, I've got him curious too. Curious about me, maybe. Hopefully. My stomach flips and something flutters lightly in my chest.

I ignore the feeling though, tugging the cloth from my back pocket to run it over the bar.

It's cliché as hell but whatever.

I need a distraction from the butterflies suddenly roaming around inside me.

"My friend's parents own the bar. I only really work on weekends when they need help." I drop my gaze to the mahogany bar top, the flush creeping even higher up my neck without permission. "I'm actually a kindergarten teacher."

"Bit of a change. Toddlers to drunk adults."

"You'd think so, but not so much in my experience." I curl my fingers into the cleaning rag, sweeping it across the bar top again. "They're more similar than you'd think."

As if on cue to prove my point, a bunch of rowdy guys stumble through the door. One of them wears an off-white, stained with beer wedding dress. The others don t-shirts with a drunken photo enlarged—of what I assume to be the groom—and printed on each one. *Great.* I drop my head, rolling my shoulders back. So much for an easy, quiet afternoon. I was hoping for a story or two with Doug, an opportunity to pull out my school work and plan some lessons for the kids so I was well and truly ahead before the school year starts.

"Ah." The familiar man's eyes follow mine, his jaw tightening as he watches the group loudly decide on a round of shots. He shoves the cap back onto his head, pulling it as far down over his face as it will go. "I'll leave you to it."

"Oh." My chest tightens. I didn't want him to go. "Well, it was nice to meet you ..."

"Scott." He fills in for me.

I beam, holding out my hand across the bar. "Ivy."

Scott stares at my hand for a moment before wrapping his fingers around mine. His hand is calloused, rough, and uneven. It dwarfs my own. Yet as I settle into the shape and feeling of his fingers curled around mine, it's as if the two fit perfectly. As if each is carved out purely for the other.

He drops my hand, brows pulling together and a frown tugging at his lips.

"See you round, Ivy."

Despite the fact there isn't a hint of a smile on his face and his features are still set into what I'm beginning to think is probably stone, his eyes flash with something else. The green of his eyes swirl under the shadow of his cap. They're intense but a spark takes hold and lights a small fire in the pit of my stomach.

I swallow the lump in my throat, losing the war with the unwanted flush heating up my face. I give him a small wave, calling after him, "Welcome to Boston."

Chapter Two

Ivy

"Stop fussing, Ivy. It's fine."

I roll my eyes and continue my task of fixing the corners of my grandfather's hospital bed, a hand swiping beneath the mattress to smooth out the fold. If he isn't allowed to come home then the least I can do is make sure he is comfortable.

"You would think they would know how to tuck in the corners properly at least. Nan was the head nurse here for, what? Thirty years? She'd be disappointed at the slipping standards if she saw them today," I huff out, running my palm over the sheets again.

"Or, she would tell you to relax. Ivy…" I lift my head, meeting Pops' concerned gaze. The edges of the harsh blue, the same exact shade of my own, soften before I drop my gaze back on the perfectly tidy bed corner that I'd just undone only to re-do. "Will you sit down?"

I huff again, tucking in the last section of the hospital sheet before falling into the chair at his bedside.

"How was the bar the other day?" Pops asks.

"I don't want to talk about the bar," I grumble.

"Well, I do. Look at me." I find his gaze again. "You heard what the doctor said. It's time we think about the end now. I need round the clock care. I am not putting that on you. When we find a nurse, I will come home. For now, I am here."

"*I* could take care of you at home." My voice barely registers louder than a whisper. Pops leans over to cover my hand with his.

"Ivy, you're young. You're smart, beautiful, and you have an entire life ahead of you. You should be out living your life. Not caring for an old man two wobbly steps away from death."

I shake my head, tears stinging my eyes. "Don't."

William 'Billy' Booker was an American All-Star. From high-school football, to college, and on to the pros. Pops' career had been what most would consider hall of fame worthy. Drafted out of college, he played for the Packers, the Chargers and, finally the Broncos over a fifteen-year career. He gave it all up when he and Marie Booker—the love of his life—had their son, Matthew.

My dad.

Nan used to tell me stories about the birth of my dad. He'd been their miracle baby, the one they were told would never happen. The way Nan would tell it, they had finally settled into the knowledge that the dogs would just have to do. So much so, that she hadn't even realized that she was pregnant until she'd been four months along.

The miracle baby that had put an end to one of the most consistent and greatest careers in early American football.

Pops gave it all up in a heartbeat.

I'd never forget those stories, about how my dad had grown up with Pops at home and Nan working as a nurse at the hospital downtown. Nan had been a football wife for fifteen years. Once my dad had been born, she'd insisted on going back to work full time and Pops had been thrilled to stay home. A football in his hand since before he could walk, my dad was slated to be the next great American All-star.

Or so says Pops.

Pops coached his little league team. Been there to take him to his junior pro games, every weekend of the season, all over the east coast. Had sat in the bleachers yelling at the referee with all the other football parents through high school. Had done the same when dad had played for Harvard in college. Would have done the same when he'd gone pro.

Would have.

Matthew Booker died at the age of twenty-two as the rumored number one draft pick for the Boston Broncos, husband to my mom, Sara, and father to a growing toddler—me.

A few months after my third birthday, my parents were driving back from New York. Nan and Pops had given them a weekend away as an early Christmas present. My dad had been travelling for football, on the road for a string of away games before the break. Mom drove down to meet him but they decided to come home early. Dad hadn't been home properly between games and classes for a few weeks by then. He wanted to come home and start his break early, with his daughter. So they'd left, ignoring the weather warnings, eager to get home to their baby girl. Eager to get home to me.

Snow had been falling for hours, covering the ground. The fog had been dense. From the way the truck driver had told it, no one should've been driving in that kind of weather.

I still wonder if he meant himself, too.

Mom and dad never made it home.

"I want to see you living, Ivy. Really living. Not taking care of me, or planning lessons for four-year-olds, or spending your weekends talking to old geezers like you do at the bar." I tighten my fingers around his.

"I am living." It's a weak defense at best. I know I'm not. I know Pops is right.

"Playing cards with me on a Sunday and watching old reruns of *Friends* is not living. You need to have fun!"

I smile weakly, the corners of my mouth twitching as I grip his hand in mine. His skin is wrinkly and sun damaged but his hands still show signs of the hard work he did years ago on the field. Scars that haven't healed quite right. Bones distorted just slightly after being broken over and over again.

I sigh. "Playing cards with you is fun."

"Oh Ivy. I've let you down if you think that is fun. I worry about you."

Again, I huff, the laughter in my chest bubbling a little. "I worry about *you*."

Pops shakes his head at me, smiling as he says, "You are so much like your mother. It still surprises me, even after all these years. She always hovered over you and Matty like you were about to break any minute."

"I know. And dad would say: *you need to live a little.*"

"He'd tell you the same."

"I just want to make sure you're okay."

"I'm old, Ivy. It happens." He smiles sadly at me, his thumb running over my knuckles as my hand sits tightly in his.

Nan and Pops did their absolute best to raise me. They never made me feel like a burden. They loved me, gave me anything I'd wanted in life, cheered me on as I achieved my goals and picked up the pieces when I'd failed. They never second guessed the decision to raise me after my parents had died. And they had never hidden them from me either. The house is filled with memories of my mom and dad.

I had never not been able to ask questions. I knew what their life was like, their quirks and their habits. My grandparents had painted as vivid of a picture as they could for me growing up.

I knew them as well as I could.

But those memories aren't my own and the hole in my heart still gapes. It feels as though parts of me are missing and so far, I have had no luck figuring out where to find them.

Though I've long since learned how to live with the pain.

I had clung to Pops when Nan passed away a few years ago. It was my freshman year of college. I'd been living in the dorms, partying a bit too hard but studying even harder, when I'd gotten the call. I moved home the next week and hadn't left again.

Pops is all I have left.

"Don't say things like that. I need you to live forever." I try to give him my most convincing watery smile.

He laughs in his low chuckle, reassuring me, "I'll do my best kiddo."

The door to his hospital room creaks and a blonde nurse pops her head through the gap, eyeing the two of us softly. "Sorry Ivy, visiting hours ended a while ago and they'll have my head if they find you here."

"No worries," I reply. I turn back to Pops, getting to my feet before pressing a gentle kiss to his cheek. "I'll see you tomorrow, okay?"

"Ivy ..."

"It's Sunday. We have to play cards. It's tradition."

"Fine, but come in the morning. That will leave your afternoon free to go out with some friends."

"Pops, I—"

"No buts. School goes back soon, then you'll be too tired out from those rambunctious toddlers you teach. Promise me?"

I sigh, meeting his gaze and allowing the sea of blue to wash over me. I lift a shoulder in defeat.

"Fine. I will see you in the morning."

I wave to the nurses behind the station, their large coffee mugs steaming as they prepare for a long night ahead. Pops was admitted two weeks ago after a stroke. They're still monitoring him daily and ensuring he takes his medication. He's so forgetful these days. If only I was able to be home more he'd probably be able to come home. But Pops won't let me quit my job as a teacher or take a leave of absence.

So, we decided to compromise.

He stays in the hospital and I get to huff about it.

We'll find the right nurse, eventually. Nan gave me high standards when it comes to his care, being a nurse herself, and candidates that will be professional and not pry too far into our life are few and far between. For now, he'll have to stay under the care of the doctors.

My attention waivers at the buzzing in my pocket. I pull out my phone.

Katie: Where are you?

I sigh. The back-to-school celebration drinks planned at Pats has been sitting in the back of my mind for days now. I don't really want to go.

You need to live a little.

The voice in the back of my mind isn't Pops', although I like to imagine that they may sound the same if dad had lived to grow older. As hard as I try, I can't remember my parents all that much. I don't have any memories of dad talking to me, just the interview tapes that I watch on repeat and the home videos I obsess over. It's his voice, the one from the tapes in the back of my head urging me to just suck it up and go for a drink with my friends. It's always his voice that pushes me to do things, like he knows I'm likely to hide away for the rest of my life. I listen.

It might only be my own subconscious manifesting as his voice but I always listen.

Ivy: Leaving the hospital now. I'll come for one drink.

Katie: More like five, please and thank you.

Ivy: Two, tops.

Katie: Make one a shot and you have a deal.

Ivy: Fine. Deal.

Katie: Yay! See you soon, Booker.

Katie was my roommate for the three months I'd lived on campus in freshman year. We had just been getting to know each other, the tentative path to friendship forming when Nan passed.

She hadn't questioned the three in the morning phone call, hadn't questioned the flurry of movement, the rapid tears falling down my face.

She had simply slipped her shoes on, took the keys from my hand, and driven me to the hospital. She'd stayed till the next night, giving me a shoulder to cry on. She'd never asked questions, or for an explanation when my parents had never shown up, or when the nurses all knew who I was the moment we walked in.

She'd been a friend. Never asking or needing to know more than whether I needed something to drink or eat. She didn't pry or get curious—something I've come to learn must have been difficult for her because she truly loves gossip—and we've been attached to one another ever since.

The bar I walk into is a far cry from the one I closed up just a few nights ago. Then I was shuffling out the loud bachelor's group just after eight in the evening, now it's practically bursting. You wouldn't think it's the same bar.

Music makes the windows shudder with the deep base. I take a breath as I tug open the door to prepare myself. I recognize most of the people crowding around the bar. Most are teachers from the school, some with their partners, some without.

I force a smile at the office administration girls huddled in a booth by the door, heads close together clutching cocktails tightly in their hands. 'Girls' is probably the wrong word for the four women in their late fifties who only ever come to these things so they can learn the gossip firsthand, then spread it later.

Making my way to the bar, I spot Katie behind it, drunkenly pouring herself a beer.

"You aren't supposed to do that anymore." I laugh as I tuck my small bag and jacket behind the bar for safe keeping. A perk of being best friends with the owners' daughter.

Katie flicks off the tap, her smile glowing as she looks up at me. "You came!"

"I told you I would," I yell over the music.

"I never know with you, though. Half expected you to bail at the last minute."

I frown. "I'm sorry. I've been a shit friend lately—"

"Don't. I know you've got stuff going on with Billy." She throws her arms around me, squeezing me in a hug. "It's okay. I just miss you. Let's drink!"

Katie pushes the newly poured beer into my hands and watches eagerly as I take a large gulp, laughing as a trickle of beer escapes down my chin. Her laughter is infectious and the heavy weight that has been sitting on my chest since arriving at the hospital earlier today begins to lift.

A rush of fresh air flows through the bar as the door opens. The hair on the back of my neck stands. A shiver trickles down my spine. Chills skim over my skin. I look up, my breath catching. The butterflies in my stomach take flight and I can't help but stare.

Chapter Three

Ivy

He stands taller than everyone else. Did I notice that a few days ago? Did I realize how tall he is when he walked away from me?

I easily remember the way his hand felt in mine. Easily remember the way his eyes seem to change color, sliding from one shade to another with the slightest emotion.

"Fucking hell," Katie says following my gaze.

Scott scowls at the number of people in the bar, hesitating by the door. I watch as he scans the crowd, his cap still pulled low over his face. A black t-shirt similar to the one he was wearing the other day stretches over his shoulders. His jeans are tight across his thighs, falling atop a fresh pair of sneakers. He clutches a jacket in his hand, knuckles almost white at the grip.

Maybe he doesn't like crowds?

My gaze travels up those gorgeous arms finding his face, his eyes. They just happen to be boring right back into mine.

The blush is inevitable. This is the second time in as many encounters that he's caught me staring. *Damn it.*

I need to get it together if he is going to continue frequenting the bar.

A few eyes follow him as he crosses the crowd toward us. There's talk and whispers as he passes but as he walks toward me, no one calls out to him like they know him and no one stops him in his path. I knew I didn't know him from school. My gaze flickers to the table of over-fifties gossip queens as they watch with wide eyes.

The blush deepens so much my cheeks are in danger of going up in flames as Scott stops in front of me. The mahogany bar top separates us and I swear there is a hint of a smile on his face as he leans over it toward me. "You allowed to drink on shift now?"

Katie looks between the two of us, shock evident in her eyes but a mischievous smile plays on her lips.

"What? No," I reply, shooting a quick look over my shoulder at Katie before making my way around the bar. Coming to stand by Scott's side, he turns toward me. I can only just see over his shoulder.

Yep. I definitely didn't realize how tall he is.

I gulp, clutching the glass tightly in my hand. Waving my hand behind me, I introduce my friend. "This is Katie. Her parents own the bar."

"Ah," he replies. He nods a little in Katie's direction as a greeting.

Katie jumps forward. "We haven't met. You are?" She leans forward, hand extended, but Scott keeps his gaze firmly on me.

"Scott. New to town. Not just visiting," he tells her without looking away from me. The heat positively burns in my cheeks as his eyes rake over my face, dropping down my body. I shift my balance from one foot to the other, and back.

Is it getting hotter in here?

Someone should crack a window or something.

I take a long sip of my beer, hoping to soothe the nerves jolting through my body.

He orders a drink when one of the bartenders that are actually working comes around our side of the bar. Another water, this time with some lime. Katie disappears into the crowd, her eyebrows wiggling suggestively at me as she walks backward behind Scott's back.

I want to say something, anything.

The need to prolong his presence as long as I can steals through me and tightens my chest. "Settling into town okay?" I ask. He frowns, shaking his head, brows pulling together tightly.

"What?" He leans in and asks, voice raised. He can't hear me over the music.

I laugh, taking another sip. The beer in my hand is almost drained now and my head is a little fuzzier for it. Resting a hand on his shoulder, I push myself onto my toes to close some of the distance between us. What I can't close, he does himself, dropping his head.

Another shiver runs down my spine and my grip on his shoulder tightens. As I guessed, he's made of solid muscle.

Damn.

I need to stop reacting to him like this. I don't even know him.

"I said, are you settling into town okay?" I repeat. I feel his nod, face so close to mine if either of us turns our heads we'll be less than a breath apart.

His words fall over my ear, warm and deep. It causes yet another shiver. *Goddammit.* "It's been fine. I've never really liked Boston so I guess it'll be an adjustment."

"If you don't like it here, why did you move?" I ask.

"Work."

He pulls back, a lull in the music making it easier to hear as I reply, "Oh. That's right, you said you work for the Broncos right?" I try not to miss the feel of his warm breath on my ear.

I'm given another nod.

"You do?!" Katie's excited squeal makes me jump. Oh good, she's back.

He keeps his face neutral but the shift in his eyes, the slight crease between his brows, hints that he doesn't like the interruption anymore more than I do. My heart thumps harder in my chest and I will myself to relax.

"What do you do over there?" Katie cries, rocking on the balls of her feet excitedly. I cringe. Katie is a football fan.

Well, her boyfriend is a huge football fan so that makes Katie a football fan by default.

"Um—" Scott shifts uncomfortably.

"My boyfriend is a huge fan. He's around here somewhere. You guys should meet," Katie babbles, her eyes darting around the room looking for Grant.

I sigh, my eyes dropping to the floor as I try to discreetly take a deep breath. I like Grant, I really do. But I hate talking about football.

I hate watching it.

Hate anything to do with it really.

"You wanna make an escape while she's distracted?" The deep voice purrs quietly into my ear, spoken so closely that the words are just for me.

I raise my head, meeting his gaze. Still no smile. But my heart clenches at the thought of saying no and before I know what I'm doing, mysterious man Scott is following me toward the fire exit out the back.

The small table and chairs in the alley are normally for staff. Half the kitchen chefs smoke and like to come out here every thirty minutes to kick stuff around as they complain about whatever is pissing them off: the quality of the fish delivered, the long hours, Doug sending back yet another steak dinner because it isn't cooked just how he likes, even though it probably is.

Scott sits across from me, legs outstretched, bright yellow socks peeking out from the hem of his jeans. I sit cross legged on my chair, the empty glass rolling between my hands on the table.

"She's intense," he comments, breaking the settled silence between us.

I huff out a laugh. "You've no idea."

"I haven't seen her before." I feel my brows raise in surprise at his comment. He waves a hand at the back door. "Around here, I mean."

"You only came in for the first time a few days ago." I cock my head, studying him. I am so curious about this man. Has he come here often since we met? Does he look for me?

I kind of hope so. Even though that thought has me wishing I worked more shifts.

"I've come most days since then too. I live in the apartment building next door." He nods his head to the new sky rise built on the next block over.

"Ohhh, so you're rich rich," I reply, following his gaze to the high-rise building.

This almost pulls a laugh from him. I can tell by the twitch in his lips and the tiniest shake of his shoulders. And his eyes shine, the green shifting shades the slightest bit. I will crack him. I'm determined.

"Because of the apartment I live in?" he asks.

"It's brand new. And I remember the walk through. They were selling for millions. Right near the stadium, a building with a rooftop pool, a gym, and a theatre. This whole area is going to be developed. Or so says Doug, I guess." I shrug.

"Right. Well, it kind of came with the job."

"They're paying for you to live there?" Now it's his turn to shrug. "Woah. That's a pretty decent perk."

"I was a tough sell," he says slowly.

"Because you don't like Boston?" He nods, fingers twitching before they start the same out-of-rhythm tapping that he'd done the day we met.

Silence falls between us. A comfortable, easy silence. He continues his tapping and the glass continues to roll between my fingers. Our eyes meet, catching a few times as I sneak glances at him, and every time they do my stomach does somersaults.

The third time it happens, I hold his gaze. Curiosity rises in me again. "You just look so familiar. I just don't know where it's from."

"Do you like football?" he says as if to answer the question.

My shoulders tense. Eyes dropping as I set the glass upright. He stops tapping, sitting a little straighter in his chair. I let out a breath. "Uh, no. I don't. I'm not really a fan of it. At all."

"You ... you *hate* football?"

I pull my bottom lip between my teeth, nodding. "Well, hate is a strong word but I guess, yes? I *hate* football," I reply, holding two fingers on each hand up to emphasize the word *hate*.

"Have you always hated it?"

This catches me off guard. I cock my head to the side. "No. I guess not. My Pops took me to games as a kid, when I was five or six maybe. But ..."

He waits for me to continue on my own but when I don't he presses on, eagerness slipping between the neutrality of his voice. He *wants* to know. He's interested. Interested in *me*.

"But?"

"I dunno ... I guess overtime I just lost my enthusiasm for it and as I grew up I realized that maybe if football hadn't been a thing, my—" I stop myself, pulling my bottom lip back between my teeth and chewing. I was about to unload my family history on this guy. On a guy I've met twice. On a guy whose last name I don't even know.

"It's just not my thing." I finish, lifting a shoulder.

He nods, expression guarded and unreadable. Damn, I was making progress and now it's all gone to shit.

The football talk definitely ruined it.

I swallow hard, trying to clear the lump forming in my throat like it did whenever football is up as the topic of discussion. "I guess working for a team, you must like it?"

He hesitates for the briefest moment before answering. "I love the game. It's ... it's a safe space for a lot of players and I respect that."

"Are you a psychologist?" I ask, throwing out a guess at his job.

His lips twitch. That hint of laughter is back and my heart soars at the small victory. "I majored in psych in college, yeah."

"You must know a few players then?"

"A handful." He studies me before asking, "Do they ever come into the bar? Have you met any?"

"Me? No. I would run the other way," I say shaking my head.

"You don't even like the players?"

"The game is ..." I pause, rolling the right words on my tongue before saying them aloud. "Intense. The people that play it, the rules, the fans. You get involved, even just a toe dip, and you're thrown into this world where between September and February, everything revolves around which team plays when and who wins and why didn't they win and the ref is blind and it's always the other players fault …" I smile, a memory churning in my mind. "I went through a stage in high school where I got back into it, sort of."

"Let me guess, you were a cheerleader and you were forced to watch from the sidelines?" Scott leans back in his chair, smiling. I relax into mine a little as well.

"Ha. No. Although, I think it killed my Nan a little that I didn't want to try out for the squad," I say.

"If you weren't a cheerleader then …"

I sigh, cringing a little as I admit, "I dated the quarterback. For a very long six months of my life I was dragged to game after game, practice after practice, trying my best to get into a sport I hated. He would get so annoyed that I didn't give a crap about his stats or his throws."

"So you dated a douche?" Scott says with a smirk.

"In high school." I smile. "I hear he's very respectable now."

"Did he go on to play college ball?" Scott leans forward, resting those beautifully sculpted arms on the small table between us.

"Truthfully, he wasn't very good. I didn't keep track but I suspect he wouldn't have made a starting line-up." The corners of Scott's mouth twitches upwards and I mark another tally, almost winning on the imaginary scoreboard.

There is a beat, and then he says, "You're honest. I like that."

"Am I?" I ask.

"Mm. Not a lot of people would live in this part of town, work in a sports bar so close to a stadium and have the balls to admit they hate their Super Bowl winning team with everything they have."

Laughter bubbles up and spills over. He takes off his cap and threads his hands through his hair, smirking. He waits for my laughter to die, watching me intently, before speaking again. "So you wouldn't date another football player?"

"I'm a bit past my college boys phase." I try to laugh the question off. "But no. Probably not. Athletes just remind me too much of my—" I stop again, changing directions. "It's easier to just veto them all together."

"I see," he says with a nod. Silence settles again, this time thicker than before and less easy.

"Wait, you didn't say what you actually do for the B—"

"Ivy?" Katie pushes open the door to the alley, the thumping beats of the music pouring out after her and filling the quiet alley. "It's our—" she hiccups, giggling. "It's our song. Come on!"

I smile at her, getting to my feet. When she disappears back inside, I turn to Scott. "She'll kill me if I don't get in there."

"You best go then. Wouldn't want you to end up dead on my account."

Something stops me, one hand on the door, the other now being tugged relentlessly by Katie trying to get me to follow her. "I'll see you 'round?"

He smiles. A real smile, not just a hint.

Yes. Another point to me.

"Hope so."

***

The sunlight filters through the cracks of my bedroom curtains. The red glow from the time on my alarm clock illuminates through the room.

It's half past nine in the morning. Good god, I never sleep past nine.

I try to sit up. My empty stomach growls and the shots from last night pound against my head, reminding me of the terrible decision I made to stay and dance with Katie after my talk with Scott.

He had disappeared into the night and I hadn't seen him again. At least, not until I'd stumbled home and into bed. My dreams were filled with his green eyes, that sharp jaw and those small lines that appeared near his eyes when I'd almost made him smile.

The dream had played the night over again, except every time Katie had interrupted us, I'd told her to fuck off and Scott had pushed me against the wall. Dream me had relished his hands on my body, in my hair and between my legs.

I groan, the dream slipping from my memory the more I try to remember the way his fingers had darted over my skin.

Fuck.

My phone chimes from where it lays on the floor next to my bed, along with the shorts I'd been wearing. I can see my bra hanging on the chair across the room and my shirt from last night is near my bedroom door. I'm honestly useless when I'm drunk. Once I decide it's time to go to bed, nothing can stop me.

My skin hates me for it because I never remember to take my makeup off before passing out. Luckily for me, it's rare that I ever drink. But I still pay for my one-track mind with a break out.

I swipe my phone from the floor and drag myself to the bathroom, setting it on the vanity as I turn on the water.

My mind screams at me as I splash the cold water over my face. My phone chimes again. Blinking through the water still dropping from my lashes, I tap the screen to life.

Katie's replies to my '*home*' text last night are first. Then a message from another of my colleagues this morning, asking about what day I plan to go in to set up my classroom. But the last two are from my Uncle Jeff.

He's not really my uncle. He coached my dad when he was playing football in college and then moved down the street from us. His daughter is a few years older but we practically grew up together. She is one of my best friends.

Uncle Jeff: *Hi kiddo, wanted to check in and see how you were doing with Billy still being in hospital? Do you need anything? Cathy is making lasagna this week for dinner, want to join us? No pressure but would be good to see you. Also, found this picture of you with your mom and dad at a game we played against UCLA. If I'm remembering right, this was the first road game your mom brought you out to. Same game your dad set his passing yards record. He showed off for you, kiddo. Thought you might like to see it. Love you. Come for dinner. Uncle Jeff x*

Uncle Jeff: **1 Attachment**

I stare at the picture that now fills my phone screen.

No older than a year, I sit on my mom's hip. But while my mom is smiling brightly at the camera, the Harvard football jersey she wears hanging off one shoulder, my dad stares down at me and I up at him.

We have the same eyes. Back then mine weren't as defined and the color not as dark but they changed as I grew. I glance up at my reflection and then back to the screen in my hand. My hair color is the same as his, but the rest of me is pure mom.

I study the picture on my screen. Dad has sweat drenched hair and the black paint under his eyes is smeared down his cheeks but his smile is so wide, so bright. The edges of his eyes are crinkled. One hand is on the arm my mom is using to hold me, tight against my mom's body as he holds us both close to him. The other is thrown up above his head.

I can imagine him trying to wave his hands around, trying to get me to smile for the photo, but I can't remember the day. I can't remember if I'd been tired and crying or excited and laughing through the game.

I can't remember and I can't ask.

Everything in me wants to know the story. I can probably ask Uncle Jeff.

But I won't. I can't.

I type back a text agreeing to dinner and thanking him for the photo.

Stepping under the hot spray of the shower, my mind is still reeling. My newest photograph of my parents and I takes center stage of that chaos. I pool water between my hands to wash my face. I lean my head back under the spray and let the water run freely through my tangled hair. Over and over again. The picture plays like a memory in my mind. My chest tightens. I feel the air in my lungs become heavy. I try to swallow yet fail. I gasp, trying to catch some air but water just runs over my dry lips, chasing down my neck.

Damn it.

I don't need this while I'm hung over. I close my eyes, holding them shut as tightly as I can as I will myself to hold back the tears that sting behind my eyes.

The cruel reality of it all is that football makes me feel so connected to my dad. Every time I catch a glimpse of a game, of a play, I wonder if he'd ever run a play like that. Anytime I see a post on Instagram about a player and their stats, I wonder what it all means and if my dad's stats had been better or worse. I have questions yet the only person I want the answers from is gone.

In the end, I can't stand the reminder of what I lost. Every time I am, I'm thrown back into all the pain and the hurt and it feels as if it consumes me for days. The cycle repeats over and over.

So I avoid it.

The tears come despite my efforts and I let them. I allow myself to forget where I am for just a little while until the water starts to run cold. When my skin wrinkles and my eyes finally dry, I step out.

I wrap the plush towel around my body, swiping my phone off the vanity. Heading back to my room, I throw on some clean shorts and a t-shirt. I grab my keys, pulling my shoes on before heading downstairs and out the door.

By the time I get back from seeing Pops, a shorter visit due to the hangover and unexpected emotional overload thanks to Uncle Jeff, I'm exhausted.

I strip off my clothes and pull on some clean pajamas. Scrolling back through the messages, I save the photo from Uncle Jeff into the hidden folder on my phone and then connect it to the TV sitting in the corner of my room.

Scrolling to the beginning of the album, I press play on the first video.

My mom's laughter fills the room. Squeals of delight from my younger self and a badly mimicked roar of a lion coming from my dad follows. On the screen, I watch them smile, and laugh, and live.

This is all I have left.

CHAPTER FOUR
SCOTT

I'm obsessed.

Obsessed with something other than football. Moping around my apartment for the first forty-eight hours in Boston had been ineffective and bad for my health so I'd gone for a walk. I hadn't meant to go in. I don't like bar food. I don't even drink. But something caught my eye through the window and when I'd moved in for a better look, I'd been captivated.

Somehow her hair morphs between a honey brown with hints of chocolate to almost looking blonde when the light hits it just right, before darkening again when she shifts away and is shrouded in shadows. I'd watched—creepily, now looking back on it—through the window as she had smiled shyly and ducked her head talking to one of the other staff members.

My feet had a mind of their own, walking me into the bar, sitting me on a stool not too far from her. I'd pulled my cap down further over my face after spying the group of older men wearing tired football jerseys as they drank heavily at three in the afternoon.

She had spoken to me, leant across the bar as she poked and prodded for information. She may have just been being polite, or she may have found me as fascinating as I'd found her. Whichever, it doesn't matter. I don't care. Her polite conversation, spurred on by curiosity or not, had given me the perfect excuse to stare at her, up close.

Ivy.

I've committed everything I learned about Ivy that first time to memory.

Why? No idea, but it's taken up space in my brain.

Her eyes are almost a navy shade of blue, endless pools I've been dying to dive into since staring into them that very first time. I want to slide my fingers into her hair, want to twist the strands around my fingers, play with them and watch them change color in the light. Even her rehearsed customer service smile captivates me, haunts me. I'd been listing all fifty states in my head trying to keep my dick from getting hard after getting a glance down the front of her shirt when she leaned forward over the bar.

I'd never wished to be an ass man more than in that moment.

I haven't stopped thinking about her since.

Ivy told me she didn't work there all the time. I remember that because I also remember that she said she's a kindergarten teacher. That did something funny to my lungs. Sucking the air out of them and making it harder for me to breathe. At first, I thought it was because I'd been annoyed to find out she didn't actually spend forty hours a week in a bar that was less than a hundred meters from my house.

Easy access to her I'd thought, stupidly.

I'd thought my chest had tightened because I'd been disappointed. Later, when I'd been staring up at my bedroom ceiling and thinking about her, the image of her with a bunch of toddlers floating to the front of my mind, caring about them and actually wanting to be around them, caused it to happen again. I'd had no choice but to admit it might have been because it meant she'd have to be really good with kids.

Back when I was younger, before football took over my thoughts and my life, I dreamt of having kids one day. Maybe.

I still do. Some day.

Still, the knowledge that the bar is only a side gig for her hasn't stopped me from going back every day since.

See? Obsessed.

I've been back to the bar, looking for her every time. I'd had no luck. Until the other night. Restless and thoughts wandering, I'd decided to take a walk.

Naturally, I passed the bar. The music had drawn me in, the thumping music and the distinct sounds of a crowd gathered inside caused my pulse to skyrocket, but my feet drew me inside anyway. It's like I felt her or something.

Ivy is funny, mysterious, and drop dead gorgeous. She's got curves for days, soft looking hair that is practically begging me to run my fingers through it, and a smile that threatens to crack my chest in two. I didn't see a downside to pursuing her when I spotted her by the bar Saturday night. I still don't.

Something about her screams adventurous, and fun, and sexy. Screaming at me that she's in a complete other world then the jersey chasers I tend to settle with when I get tired of my right hand. The biggest tell of them all, the best if you ask me, is that Ivy seems to have no idea who the fuck I am.

Fuck, but I love that.

I've been playing pro ball for almost seven years. Sat on the bench for the first three of them after college, called up every now and then when the win was assured. Then, the starting QB sustained a career ending injury and suddenly I was in. For the last four years, I've worked my ass off to make 'Scott Harvey' a household name. I'm one of the most well-known athletes in the league. I am building my legacy. I train seven days a week. I take care of my body. I eat well and get eight hours of sleep. I watch old game tapes. I study my mistakes, and I correct them. I live, sleep, breathe the game.

And Ivy has no clue who I am.

On top of that, she's not a fan of football.

She doesn't even like the game.

***

My fingers flex around the metal bar, elbows locking with the weight as the bar reaches full height and I grunt through the resistance coursing through my muscles. With every rep, the bar gets heavier and the weight of Ivy's admission—*i hate football*—is the culprit.

It's playing on my mind. Running through my head. Taking over my thoughts.

How am I supposed to get her wearing my number if she doesn't want to look at the jersey!

"You good, man?" Flynn's hands hover under the bar, floating up and down with every press, ready to catch it if I fail.

I only grunt in response, mind still on the shy smile and pretty hair that I desperately want to touch. My muscles release, arms failing, and the bar drops dangerously close to my chest.

Fuck.

Flynn catches the bar and we rack the weights. I heave myself into a sitting position as Flynn walks around and sits on the bench across from me.

"I know Boston isn't your favorite place in the world but hey ..." Flynn gestures around the state-of-the-art weight room. This training gym is easily one of the nicest I've ever been to. "We made it. All those dreams we had back in college ... going pro, playing on the same team, getting those championship rings together. This is the place to do it. You made the right choice."

I only nod.

Have I?

Sure, the Broncos were almost unstoppable last year. They got a new head coach, Jeff Brady who switched up their game and got them to the playoffs. They were so close to the Super

Bowl. It should have been an easy acceptance. Would have been for anyone else. Not me though. I vowed to never step foot in Boston unless for an away game. Even then, I preferred to pay for my own flight out early if the team was lingering. I've been fined for it before but I continue to do it. Boston isn't the place for me.

"I'll get over it."

"You should come out with us; me and the guys. You need to bond with the team."

I shake my head. I can't think of anything worse than going 'out' in Boston. Not when my past is somewhere in this city.

I know what it looks like, what she looks like.

I know her name. Where she lives. Even where she works.

The odds of running into her are slim but I'd rather not chance it.

I took a chance coming here. I made a promise to myself that coming to Boston won't drag a past I want nothing to do with, into my future.

Football players, professional football players, draw attention. But I'm only here to play ball. To build something. My contract is for one season and I'm here for Flynn, here to get the ring. Attention isn't part of the deal.

Unless it's Ivy's it seems.

It's the offseason. The team's players are spread across the country with families on vacation, taking time for themselves before preseason starts. I wanted to put off moving as long as I could and had been planning to wait until just before camp but

Flynn returned from his Europe trip early—thanks to the nasty breakup with his girl of the month in Greece—and begged me to come to Boston before I originally intended.

I begrudgingly agreed and here I am.

Pre-season begins in a month. I'll be back on the road and playing football. That's going to be my focus, not worrying about bumping into a past that I'm rather keen on avoiding.

Did *she* even know who I'd grown up to be? I doubt it.

Did I want *her* to find out? Absolutely fucking not.

Boston has been off limits ever since the adoption records became public. I tracked her down, of course, but I have no desire to meet her. I want to keep it that way. A one-year contract means a one-year contract. I didn't even bother to sell my house in LA. I packed a few boxes and some suitcases.

I'm here to play football. That's it.

Although now that I've met her, I can't say no to a little bit of a distraction while I'm here.

A distraction with endless blue eyes, and hair that changes in the light, and a smile set out to physically hurt if I stare at it too long. I could use something to fill in my sparse free time. Something smart, witty, fun. Something—*someone*—like Ivy.

So no, I can't be bothered to go anywhere with the other guys on the team but I can be bothered to go and sit myself at Pats across the road from the stadium and pray to whoever is above that Ivy walks in today. Then, if I'm lucky, she'll smile at me and I can fall asleep thinking about her instead of my past, or the season, or the pressure. Just ... her.

I shake my head as I reply, "I'm good. Thanks."

"Come on." Flynn throws a friendly fist into my arm. "You signed the deal. You're here now. Let's make the most of the rest of the break before the season starts and we're too tired and too busy to remember our own names."

I wipe the sweat off my face with a towel.

"One drink?" Flynn asks, sounding hopeful.

"I don't drink." I scowl at the floor. Throwing the towel toward my gym bag.

"You *hardly* drink. I still remember that time in college that you almost pu—"

I look up at Flynn, defeat dropping my shoulders. "Fine." I stand, slapping a hand across my friend's shoulder. "Fine. One drink, *one*. I mean it Flynn."

"Done." A boyish grin takes over his face.

"Let's just go across the road though," I suggest. Maybe she's working today. School isn't back, it's still summer. I stretch, my muscles groaning at me for a hot shower and my couch. "I'm too dead on my feet after this morning's pick-up game to go too far."

One smile from Ivy, my little football hater, will make my body hurt less.

Flynn follows me to the showers. "Wherever you want man."

***

Pats comes into view, neon signs lighting up the window even though the early evening sun still hangs low in the sky, and my heart speeds up. Walking past this bar is my favorite part of my evening routine but nerves still shoot through my body.

I hate the feeling.

But I also kind of love it.

It's been a long time since I felt a buzz of excitement at the prospect of seeing a woman.

I want to see her. I really, *really* want to and I don't even know her last name. I should've asked for her number the other night.

Or her last name.

Or both.

Definitely both.

Why didn't I ask her?

Oh, that's right.

Football.

It's the thought of the pre-season, of being on the road again, of being away more often than I'm at home that held me back the other night. I'd pondered our prospects after she'd left me in the alleyway. She doesn't like football, fine. She's not interested in the game, no problem. But it's a huge part of my life—the biggest part—and any sort of relationship is surely going to be impacted by the fact she can't stand my job.

Am I thinking too far ahead? Maybe.

She probably doesn't even like me like that.

Doubtful.

Besides, the thought of breaking the routine I've subconsciously created—the one where I search for her between the dusty blinds behind the front windows and scan the bar for a glimpse of her honey brown hair every night while walking pointlessly around the neighborhood—makes my lungs constrict.

I'm not an idiot.

Ivy.

I don't know anything about her, not really. Just that her smile reaches her eyes and she has this endless wonder shining back at me whenever our eyes meet. With a simple look across that tiny table in the back alley, she'd been begging for a glimpse into my soul and I'd be damned if I hadn't wanted to give her one.

"I love this place. The atmosphere on a Saturday night during the offseason is epic," Flynn comments as I hold the door open for him, trying to hold off glancing into the bar.

I can practice a bit of constraint.

I think.

"Burgers are alright. Had one the other week," I reply, still avoiding the bar in the middle of the room.

"I could go for a burger. You want me to order?" Flynn asks looking around the bar and grinning.

I run a hand through my still damp hair, finally glancing around.

I'm about to say yes, wanting to slide into a booth and sulk because Ivy isn't the one behind the bar, but as my eyes roam to who *is* behind the bar, and the girls' eyes flash with recognition whilst they dart between me and Flynn, I change my mind.

"I'll get it." I nod for Flynn to sit down, making my way to the bar. Her name is ... Ivy's friend's name is ...

Shit.

I replay the memories from the other night, trying to sort through the noise. Naturally, my memory of anything but Ivy's soft looking hair, deep blue eyes, and distracting curves are blurred and irrelevant. I apparently retained no other information than *Ivy*.

"Mystery man." The friend smiles. "You're out of luck. She isn't here."

"I see that." Shit. Shit. *Shit.* What's her name?

"You'd probably know that if you had given her your number," she replies and I don't miss the accusation in her tone.

"Uh ..."

"You guys sat out there for a good thirty minutes and you didn't even make a move. She thought something was in her teeth."

I falter, Ivy's smile filling my head. It makes my dick twitch in my pants. "I—"

"I assured her you were probably nervous." She narrows her eyes at me. "She works again on Sunday. You can come back then. You know, to right your wrongs."

"Ah." Sunday. *Sunday.* Four days away. "Or ..." I tap my fingers along the rounded edge of the bar. "You could give me her number and I could right that wrong now?"

The words fly out of my mouth before I can stop them.

Damn it.

I'm in Boston to play ball. That's it. I don't want—don't need a relationship. I signed on for a year with the Broncos, hoping to take them to the Super Bowl, to get my ring, then to head back west and as far from this city as possible.

I'm not supposed to be actively chasing a girl.

I just *had* to walk by the bar when she'd been working. Had to forget how to think and find myself inside, to let myself talk to her. Two meetings—*two*—has me asking for her number like I'm planning to actually text her.

The fucking kicker? I know I will.

Can't wait to.

Before, I didn't mind a one-night stand when I needed it. Didn't mind sinking into someone willing to let me use them for the night but I haven't actively pursued a woman in ages.

Ivy is different. Feels different.

And without even realizing it, I've been pursuing her since I saw her.

I really, really want to text her.

To take her on a date.

To say or do anything to make her smile.

Fucking hell.

"Tell you what, lover boy." The friend's eyes flash, darting back to where Flynn is sitting and playing on his phone. "You get me Flynn Reed's autograph and you have yourself a deal."

This seems much too easy. I frown. "That's a low price for your best friend's number considering Flynn loves a bit of attention."

"It's just the right price for me to give her your number though." She smirks, pulling two chilled pint glasses from the fridge and heading for the beer taps. "Are you having a drink?"

I pull my lips into a tight line. "Whatever's on tap and mid-strength."

She nods. "You can write your number on a coaster and I'll pass it on, if you like. Otherwise, Sunday is your best chance."

"Right. I'll—" She flips her hair over her shoulder before switching the glasses under the stream of beer and her name floats through my mind. I roll my shoulders. "I might just do that. Thanks, Katie."

"You remembered!" She smiles brightly, pushing the pints toward me and holding up a couple of cardboard coasters. "Brownie points, mystery man. You truly looked like you might have popped a blood vessel when you first came up."

I don't reply, taking the cards from her before picking up the beers and moving back to the table with Flynn.

Steading my hand around the glass, I glance up at Flynn. "The bartender wants an autograph."

Flynn's head jerks up, eyes shining as he eyes Katie behind the bar. He smiles widely. "Wouldn't want to deny my fans."

Before Flynn can make his move, I fish a marker from the bottom of my gym bag and toss him one of the coasters. He signs the coaster and shuffles sideways to get up from the booth but I snatch the small piece of cardboard from him and stand up. "I'll give it to her."

He eyes me, his bright smile flattening into a sly smirk. I hold his gaze.

Ivy doesn't like football players. I am a football player. Katie is Ivy's best friend.

If Ivy is going to find out I'm the very thing she hates and swore never to date again, it's going to be from me.

But I'm going to snag a date before she does.

I shrug, trying to look convincing. "You don't want to break that mystery air, do you? Play a little hard to get, my man." I nod toward the bar, taking a slow step away from Flynn and towards my ticket to a date with Ivy. "Come on, I thought you were supposed to be good at this."

He barks a laugh as I back away toward the bar.

When I turn, Katie is staring at me with her brows raised. "How do you know him?" she asks. "Ivy said you worked across the road but didn't say what."

I scribble my number on another coaster and pass them both over. "Uh, I work with the players," I tell her tapping a finger along the bar.

Not technically a lie.

"Nice." Katie takes the coaster smiling. "My boyfriend is going to freak out."

"Uh-huh." I eye her as she looks over the coasters. Somewhere in the back of my mind, a red flag raises at the fact I just gave my number out to a total stranger but it's the beautiful face that makes me forget all the risk.

Katie clears her throat. "You know, Ivy hates football."

"She told me." I nod.

"And you work for a football team."

"Uh-huh."

"She won't watch games, not even on TV. She won't talk about them, won't listen to you talk about them either," she says. Katie waves the coaster with my number like a fan in front of her face like she's waiting for me to ask for it back.

I frown. "Football isn't my life."

Lie. Total lie.

Football is my life. My whole life.

Well … football and my parents.

Katie hums, pocketing the coaster with a quick tap of her pocket. "I'll pass it on, lover boy."

"Stop calling me that," I grumble. Katie just laughs and shakes her head, taking my food order before I slide back into the seat across from Flynn. I pull my cap from my bag, shoving it down over my eyes.

My phone burns in my pocket.

I hate waiting.

***

(Unknown): I did not think I had something in my teeth.

I laugh. A proper, out loud laugh.

My phone had been on the edge of the couch, the volume on the television on low as an old game tape played. I left the bar a few hours ago, Flynn getting his one drink before he matched with some chick in the city on a dating app and promptly leaving me there. I'd been more than happy to let him go. Darkness fell, I drew the curtains across the large floor to ceiling windows in the penthouse and settled on the couch in the living room.

I'd kept tapping the message icon on my phone, double checking I haven't missed a message even though the volume was fully up. The battery on the phone was completely depleted and when a notification popped up on the screen telling me that I'd only had twenty percent left, I'd realized I've been staring at the screen mindlessly for over ten minutes. So I'd banished it to the end of the couch.

It chimed and I dove for it.

At least Katie gave Ivy my number. I keep reminding myself that we've only met twice. We've had one proper conversation so if she hadn't texted then that was fair enough. The thought of Katie withholding the coaster anyway also crossed my mind. She seems to have the overprotective best friend role down pat and would probably find it funny to watch me sweat.

> **Scott:** I'm beginning to think Katie isn't the best source of information.

Ivy: I think she was testing you. I'm not working on Sunday.

Scott: She like this with everyone?

Ivy: She's protective.

Scott: I picked up on that, funnily enough.

Does she think you need protection from me?

Ivy: From anyone, really.

I lurch forward, feet dragging along the polished wood floors and elbows coming to rest on my knees. I can feel my heart thumping against my chest. Staring down at the text message, I wonder what she might need protection from. Maybe Katie is just a loyal friend. Maybe, most likely, there's a story there.

I want to find out.

I want to be the one doing the protecting.

I've been in Boston for three weeks. Three weeks, and already some woman has made her way into my head, sat herself down and is refusing to leave. The scariest part is I can't bring myself to care. I want her there. Invited her in myself.

> **Scott:** She gave you the coaster. That's something.

> **Ivy:** She said you earned brownie points and then flaunted Flynn Reed's auto-graph. Did you take a player to the bar?

> **Scott:** Flynn's a friend from college.

> **Ivy:** He's a big deal around these parts … you got a lot of friends in high places?

All my life, I've done what I could to avoid this kind of thing. The flirting over texts. The dating. The relationships. Sure, I had a girlfriend in high school. She'd been a cheerleader and I'd been a football player. It'd felt more like we'd had to date, less like we'd actually wanted to. We didn't last. In college, my one and only focus had been football. The hook-ups I'd had were mainly when riding the high of a win. Jersey chasers, sorority girls, study group partners. Not one had caught my attention for more than a night or two. We'd have fun before I'd get up the next day and go to practice and that would be it. When I'd gone pro, I couldn't tell who was there for me and who was there for the spotlight and free seats, so it had just been easier to not bother. So, I haven't.

I'm not celibate. I'm just not dating.

Ivy caught my eye through the window. That was three weeks ago and I'm still thinking about her. I itch to know more, to know everything. This isn't high school and it definitely isn't college. Whatever this is, I haven't felt it before and fuck if that doesn't scare me just a little.

> **Ivy:** Kidding … it was nice of him to sign the coaster for her, she's very happy.

My fingers hover, motionless.

Football starts soon. Ivy doesn't like football. I'll have to tell her and she probably won't want anything to do with me after that.

Maybe that's it. Maybe she's caught my attention so keenly because she *isn't* throwing herself at me immediately. It's probably because she has no idea who I am and that hasn't happened to me in a long time.

So better to get her out of my system right?

That's if I can even get a girl like her out of my system.

Yes. I'll get her out of my system. A date—maybe dinner and a drink, maybe two drinks … what do people do for dates these days?—and then out of my system. Once I know more, once I know enough to satisfy the low burn that seems to simmer beneath my skin at just the thought of her, I'll be able to focus.

Right?

> **Scott:** Ivy?

> **Ivy:** Scott?

> **Scott:** Do you want to have dinner with me on Sunday?

I watch as the conversation bubble appears at the bottom on the screen. It disappears, and appears once more. I feel like throwing something. What if she was just being friendly?

I remember the easy smile that slid across her soft lips when she asked where I'd come from, the practiced curiosity in her voice that comes from being in a job where she has to talk to people for a living.

I remember the way her wrist would twist when she poured a beer.

The small crease that appeared in her forehead when she'd been talking to one of the chefs about a meal that had been returned to the kitchen.

The way her shirt had lifted up her back, just slightly, when she'd reached up on her toes to replace a bottle on the top shelf.

With all of it, I remember the curves of her hips in the jeans she'd been wearing and the way her shirt had hung low as she'd leaned toward me across the bar. I'll be damned if I ever forget the pale pink lace of her bra. I feel like a bit of a creep, remembering it all, but she's hard to forget.

Ivy: I'd love to.

Chapter Five
Ivy

For a moment—when my keys are still hanging in the door and I can feel the strap of my gym bag slipping from my shoulder—the low chatter of the TV presenters travel down the hallway to greet me and I forget that no one else is supposed to be in my house. I forget that Pops is in hospital, I forget that he won't be sitting in his recliner with the blanket Nan knitted for him thrown over his legs when I round the corner.

My bag finally slips from my shoulder as I toe off my sneakers but as the realization washes over me that it can't possibly be Pops in the living room, I manage to catch the strap before the bag crashes against the tiles.

Pops is in hospital, a twenty-minute drive away, and the knitted blanket is with him. My stomach turns over, the delayed disappointment squeezing my lungs. I press a hand to my chest, feeling the expansion of my lungs and focusing on the deep breathing exercises Nan used to have me do whenever I felt overwhelmed. The shaky but controlled breathing works and the disappointment fades to a dull throb, setting my lungs free.

It still takes me by surprise at times that Pops isn't waiting for me whenever I come home. That he isn't sitting at the kitchen counter doing his crossword, or sitting in his chair watching something likely football related, or listening to music from the fifties while flipping through a years old car magazine. It makes my chest ache that this 'temporary solution' could become my new normal, that he may never come home again.

No. I close my eyes and take another deep breath in. He'll be fine.

I refuse to think about a time without him, regardless that it could be right around the corner.

If denial is a place on earth, I'm living smack-bang in the center of it.

And that is fine by me.

I don't want to lose anyone else. Especially not Pops, not yet.

A familiar laugh floats down the hall and my shoulders automatically relax. Katie's laugh.

"I gave you a key for emergencies," I call out as the plush white couch in the center of the open living room comes into view and so does the sprawling blonde hair of my best friend. Some sports panel show is on the television that sits over the large fireplace and Katie's bare feet are propped out in front of her on the ottoman we use more as a coffee table. I feign a scowl as I drop my gym bag onto the bench. "*Only* emergencies."

"This was an emergency," Katie tells me, raising an arm and waving it around in greeting. Her eyes are glued to the TV. I glance up, my fake scowl turning real as I watch a football highlights reel play on the screen. At least Katie had the decency to turn the volume down when I walked in.

"Oh? And what would that be? You forgot to pay your cable bill?"

Katie laughs, finally turning around on the couch to face me. "I was out of bagels." A smile breaks out on my face as she holds up half a bagel in her hand, generously smeared with cream cheese.

"So sorry, can't imagine the distress that must have caused you." I slap a hand over my chest nodding sarcastically.

"You have no idea."

"Do you want coffee?" I ask. My eyes drift to the TV again. The Broncos logo flashes on the screens behind the panel of presenters and it makes me think of Scott.

Tall, handsome, jaw chiseled sharp enough to cut right through my heart, Scott.

Damn him for being tied to football.

It makes me curious. About him, about what he does for work, how he's tied to the stupid sport. I hate that I'm curious about that world again.

I busy myself with the coffee machine, taking Katie's silence as a yes. It's always a yes when it comes to coffee. It's the first thing we bonded over when we became friends in college.

"How was the gym?" she calls again over her shoulder as her eyes are still glued to the TV. The volume is low enough that when I turn on the coffee machine, I can barely hear the presenters anymore. Still, something builds in my chest and I struggle for a moment to take a breath. I force myself to take a sip of water, eyes darting back to the TV. They're showing college reels now, some feature on a player it looks like as they've blurred most of the screen to single out one man on the field. It's the quarterback. I can tell from the two seconds of film they show. It runs in my blood even if I wish it didn't.

I decide that they must be showcasing some fresh talent that's either being watched or has already been drafted and while I could probably put up with it, the film switches games and the distinct difference between University of California, Los Angeles' blue and gold clear against the bright red of Harvard fills the screen. The memory of watching similar film reels when I was younger, late at night wrapped in my bed covers and clutching my favorite stuffed bear, clouds my mind and the echo of my dad's deep, happy laugh fills my head.

Ouch.

"Go home to watch football, you're ruining my morning," I say, my eyes burning as I watch the steady stream of coffee pouring into my mug.

"Spoil sport," Katie remarks, yet she still turns the channel over—Bravo, much better— before turning her body around on the couch to face me. She flicks her hair over her shoulder. "So, did you hear from mysterious football man?"

I smile, still not facing her in the hopes she won't catch it. "I still cannot believe you told him I thought I had something in my teeth."

"You did!"

"I know, but you aren't supposed to share those kinds of things with *him!*" I take her mug out from under the coffee machine before picking up mine and joining Katie on the couch. My legs curl underneath me as I lean into the corner of the lounge, and after Katie takes her mug from my hand I wrap both my hands around my own mug.

Coffee, in my opinion, saves lives. Mine especially.

"So ..." Katie says as she waits for me to finish savoring my first sip.

"I messaged him. He messaged back. I saved his number." I lift a shoulder, trying my absolute best to come off easy, confident.

I conveniently forget to mention the nervous pacing and many, *many* drafts of a first message I'd written out before sending the one I settled on.

She rolls her eyes at me and completely crushes any delusions I have of coming off cool, calm and collected. "Oh, please. You were probably a nervous wreck sending the first message and we both know it."

"I appreciate your confidence in my ability to date."

"If you had any ability to date, you'd have been snapped up the moment you walked on to campus that first day of college. You're a smoke-show." She grins behind her mug at me. "You're just too modest to admit it. That's why you have me."

"What? To remind me I have shit dating skills but follow it up with telling me I'm hot?" I ask resting my head on the back cushions of the couch.

"Yes." She nods. "And to steal your bagels."

"I know you have some at home. Grant buys them for you especially."

"You get the better ones. He's too cheap to go to an actual bakery for them."

It's my turn to roll my eyes, I bring the coffee mug back to my lips. "That's what you get for dating an accountant."

"Grant isn't boring."

"I never said he was."

"Your face did."

"Stop reading my face then." I poke my tongue out at her, nudging her nearby foot with my toe. I love her and she tells me all the time how happy Grant makes her, and I believe her. I do. But I also can't help but notice the frustration when he doesn't listen to her when she tells him about her day or the way she becomes quiet when he tells her she's being dramatic about something. He's nice but my best friend deserves more, better and bigger than just *nice*.

Katie goes quiet for a moment before shaking her head and plastering a grin on her face. "Can't help it, you truly would be so shit at poker. Promise me you won't ever play."

"Promise." I laugh, letting an easy quiet fall over us as I contemplate whether I should share the details of the texts with Katie. I sink back into the couch a little more before telling her quietly, "I agreed to go out to dinner with him." I keep my eyes focused on the dwindling amount of coffee left in my mug.

"You did?" Katie jolts forward, shock sinking into her features.

"Don't sound so shocked. I go on dates."

"I know that, but you don't—" She pauses, her head cocking to the side as her words turn softer. "I didn't think you'd be interested considering he works for the Broncos. I thought that you'd maybe find it too ... painful."

Sadness creeps into my chest, blurring the memory of the brooding man a little.

I sigh. "I guess. I mean, he's not actually a player, right?" I meet her gaze waiting for her to tell me the bad news.

"Not that I know of. I tried to drag Grant over to meet him but by the time he detached himself from his phone, you guys were gone and then he left instead of coming back inside with you."

"Surely we'd know his face if he was a player. He would've been recognized." I lean forward, placing the mug on the tray that lives permanently on the ottoman.

"To be honest, maybe Grant could but I certainly don't think I could pick them out of a crowd. Sure, some players would be super recognizable. The ones that have been around for ages or have been in the shit for some reason or another. But if he's quiet and keeps to himself, we might not." She rolls her mug gently between her hands, obviously trying to remember if she has seen Scott before.

"No. We were at Pats. He's come to the bar a few times. The place is always crawling with die-hard fans. There is no way he plays professional football for the Broncos and could get away being there without being recognized." I nod more to myself than to Katie, settling on my decision that there is *no way* Scott is a football player.

"Did he say anything about what he does over there?"

Truthfully, after one shot and a beer I'd practically sculled before heading outside with Scott to try to calm my nerves—not to mention the many drinks that came after he'd vanished—I couldn't remember exactly what he'd been saying. "He mentioned he did a psych degree in college … I think."

"You're such a lightweight." Katie laughs gently.

"Maybe he's an accountant or something in their finance department." I shoot her a wink before uncurling my legs from underneath me getting up from the couch. "It would kind of cancel out the whole football thing if he was as boring as Grant is."

One of the decorative pillows hits the back of my knees as I reach the bottom of the stairs. I laugh, calling back to Katie as I head for a shower. "Are you hanging around today? I could use a hand with some stuff for work if you are."

A groan sounds from downstairs and it makes me laugh again. Her reply filters up to me as I reach the top of the staircase. "Sure. Why not? My cutting and pasting could use some improvement since the last time you made me help you!"

***

It's funny how time seems to slow down when you're waiting for something to happen. My date with Scott looms closer and closer yet Saturday seems to drag on forever. After Katie helped me prep countless name tags and cut outs for my classroom set up day next week, she called Grant to drop over wine. We ordered pizza and got stuck into the latest season of *Housewives* on Bravo. It's escapism at its finest but I was desperately avoiding staring at the quiet text chain between Scott and I.

Like people say, a watched pot never beeps ... or something like that.

After my run on Sunday morning, I stuff a new pack of UNO cards into my bag and head for the hospital. The entire drive over I fidget and fiddle, tapping my fingers against the steering wheel. I play with the volume on the radio. I go from singing half-heartedly along with the song to chewing on my bottom lip.

I'm nervous today.

I love playing cards with Pops. We play all sorts: Gin, Canasta, even Go Fish. UNO is our favorite though, our Sunday morning ritual. We started playing after I stopped wanting to go to football games with Pops. His way of us spending time together every week. It started when I was eight and never stopped. Even as a teenager and hanging out with my friends was the main event on a Saturday, the tradition held up. No matter how late the party, no matter how long I'd stayed out on a Saturday night, I always got up on Sunday morning and played cards with Pops. Even during my college years.

It's our thing.

But today, I'm nervous. No need to dig any deeper into why. The text sitting unanswered is the exact reason why.

Scott: Looking forward to tonight. I'll pick you up around 7?

I didn't answer. *Hadn't* answered. Yet.

Part of me thought he'd definitely cancel, maybe even hoped for it a little bit. But even so, a bigger part of me is over the moon that he hasn't. Katie has brought up our date more times than I can count and each time my cheeks heat and my face goes a shade of red I've never seen before.

I'm nervous about seeing Pops, I'm nervous about what will happen after seeing Pops.

Dating isn't my specialty. I went out with guys in high school, had my fling with the football world before shutting that down for good. During college I'd gone to my fair share of parties and had the odd hook up here and there. Truth is though, I never really cared. I'd gone along because the movie they'd suggested had been one I wanted to see, or the food at the restaurant they'd asked to go to had been raved about and I was keen to give it a go.

Even with the few short-term relationships I'd had, the spark had fizzled and my interest dimmed after a while. They'd never made me nervous, or breathless with a smile, or curious.

I felt all of that as soon as I spoke more than two words to Scott.

He makes me nervous.

I try to focus on the board as I order Pops and I breakfast at the Starbucks drive through. A treat for us both and a distraction for Pops. Even Nan used to say the hospital food sucked.

The grateful smile on Pops' face when I walk in carrying his black coffee over ice and the smeared bagel relaxes my shoulders a little.

"You're my favorite grandchild," he tells me, his eyes tracking my movements closely as I set the coffee tray on a nearby table.

"I'm your only grandchild."

"I lucked out."

I smile, handing over the coffee. "Mhmm, sure."

His eyes roll into the back of his head a little when he takes his first gulp. I laugh taking a seat on the edge of his bed, sipping on my own. They filled a third of the cup with whipped cream this morning and I could honestly not be happier about it; future sugar crash be damned.

Pops whispers closely to his coffee, telling it over and over that it contains some sort of magical powers. He's so dramatic.

Nan used to roll her eyes and scowl whenever he did anything like this—act like his life was a soap-opera or something—but there was always a smile on her lips and she'd indulge him anyway. Every time. He has a childlike optimism about the world that I love.

That fact only makes my chest hurt more whenever I find myself thinking about losing him.

"So, how was your Saturday night?" he asks me, coffee cradled against his chest like he's scared one of the nurses might try to pry it away from him.

"Usual. Katie and I had wine, watched Bravo and fell asleep by nine."

"Ivy." Pops shakes his head. "You're twenty-three. I want stories about you dancing on tables and doing shots off a bartender somewhere."

I throw him a look. "Any other parent would be ecstatic to learn their twenty-something was being responsible and not partying their brain cells to death."

"I'm not just any grandparent though." He shrugs and meets my eyes. "I'm a cool grandparent."

"I should never have let you watch mean girls."

"Regina's mother is an icon. You cannot tell me otherwise."

I laugh, shaking my head in disbelief as Pops readjusts himself on his pillows, sitting up a little taller. He takes another sip of his coffee before putting it beside him and rubbing his hands together eagerly. "What are we playing today then?"

"UNO." I retrieve the cards from my bag and drag the hospital table over with me before settling back on the end of Pops' bed. "I got a new set to leave here with you. You can play with the nurses during the day when I go back to school."

I watch him as he shuffles the new set of cards and the urge to savor the moment sits heavily in my heart.

Sundays, playing cards and drinking coffee, will be what I miss most when he's gone.

The thought feels like a truck running over my heart and lungs all at once. Cutting off my blood supply and ability to breathe. I tell myself he'll be fine but when I really think about it, I'm lucky he's even still here.

He survives for me.

I know that. After Nan, he was devastated. I'd heard one of the nurses talking about us once, just after Pops was admitted a few weeks ago. She'd worked with Nan pretty closely and taken over from her when she retired before passing. She'd had this sad look on her face when she'd told another nurse that if my parents had still been alive, Pops would've followed Nan pretty quickly. I'd really looked at Pops after that, really *really* looked. He's sad, even after five years. He's so sad and he misses her. He's tired too. He hides it from me but it's unmissable when you look long enough.

He survives for me. He is all I have left and even though we've both been heartbroken after losing Nan, Pops won't leave me to grieve alone.

Suddenly, his annoying backwards parenting behavior—all the pushing for me to go out and meet people and date, even—makes all the more sense. It's that thought that makes me set my coffee aside as he deals a hand of cards to me and say, "I have a date tonight."

Pops stills, eyes meeting mine, jaw dropping just a little before he clutches his heart and takes a set of sharp breaths.

I stand, rushing to his side. "What?! What's hurting? Oh god, I'm sorry!" With shaky fingers I press the call button beside his bed and the morning nurse, Carol, rushes in. "What's wrong with him? He just clutched his chest suddenly!"

"It's alright, Ivy, don't worry. Step back for me," Carol tells me calmly, her eyes on the heart rate machine that I always have trouble reading as she picks up Pops' wrist to check his pulse. She waits for a beat before dropping his wrist, scowling.

"Billy Booker, you prankster. Can't you see you've terrified the girl with your little joke?"

My brows furrow, eyes darting between Pops and Carol. Pops is grinning like a cat now, reaching for his coffee. He grins as he says, "Worth it. Carol, my little Ivy is growing up. She has a date!"

"Pops!" I say, stepping back to his seat and swatting at his arm. "Don't. Do. That."

"Couldn't resist." He waves me off, winking at Carol as she retreats from the room. "Sit down and pick up your cards, Ivy. I want to hear about my future grandson-in-law."

"Don't be dramatic, it's one date."

"What's his name?"

"Scott."

Pops looks thoughtful. "Strong name. How tall is he?"

I narrow my eyes, glaring. "Tall. Very tall. Why?"

"You can't carry on the great Booker legacy without doing your best to breed with a D1 athlete, Ives! That would be a waste of all my efforts with your dad, and with you."

"Oh my god." I bury my head in my hands, Pops' booming laughter filling the room.

"I'm just teasing." He starts the game by picking up from the pack between us. "I'm excited to hear all about it, sweetheart. I am."

"He seems really nice." I can feel my face going red. "And he is really tall. So your legacy of a family line full of D1 athlete dreams seems safe." I smile, throwing out a card in my hand, a sense of calm washing over me as we settle into the game.

Time with Pops does wonders.

I swear, he jokes about it a lot but I think he might actually have magic powers.

"Bye, sweetheart. I'll see you soon."

"Are you sure you're okay? You barely ate lunch." I tilt my head, watching him closely. He was fine most of the day but barely ate anything, pushing his lunch away claiming he wasn't hungry. His color has paled a little as well as the hours flew past.

He waves me off. "I'm fine. The food here is barely food, you know that."

"Hm. Okay. Well, call me if you need anything."

"Not tonight though. You've got a date."

I shake my head. "You're ridiculous. It's one date. Stop thinking he's my soulmate."

"What if he is though?"

"I doubt it, Pops." He laughs with me but it's quieter than before, like he's struggling to keep something in. "You sure you're okay?"

"I—" He coughs a little, "I'm fine, Iv—" Before he can finish, a burst of coughs takes over him and I rush back to his side to help him sit forward. I watch, helpless, as he reaches a shaky hand into his pocket for his handkerchief, covering his mouth.

"Pops?" I ask, the coughing continuing.

He pulls his hand away, his face a little red but still devoid of any real color. There's blood on the white cloth and I feel my whole body start to shake. I don't hesitate this time. "Carol!"

***

Carol promises me before she leaves, handing over to the evening nurses, that Pops is fine. She tells me that it's nothing to worry about, that his body is just tired and a little bit of blood is perfectly normal. I insist she bring in one of the overstuffed, uncomfortable night chairs. Pops protested but once he fell asleep I overruled him anyway. He's been sleeping for over an hour but I refuse to move from his side.

I check my phone for the time. It's a little after five. Scott will just have to wait.

> **Ivy:** I need a rain check. I'm really sorry. My pops had a medical emergency, he's in the hospital.

The reply is instant.

> **Scott:** Of course.

Is he okay?

Ivy: Not really.

Scott: Can I do anything for you?

The band that appeared around my heart the moment I laid eyes on the man cinched a little tighter.

Ivy: That's okay. I just don't want to leave him alone.

Scott: I understand.

I can't bring myself to reply so I don't. I lay the phone on the table next to me and sink back into the uncomfortable chair. The blinds are down, blocking out the afternoon sun. I pull the blanket covering my legs up under my chin and focus on Pops.

He'll be fine.

He'll be fine.

I say it over and over again in my head in the hopes that if I say it enough, it will become a reality.

Pops wakes up sometime around ten and kicks me out, promptly ordering me home and not taking no as a response. The drive is slow and silent. My knuckles are almost white against the steering wheel as I argue with myself to not cry. My body is heavy as I pull into the garage and I don't have the energy to make it upstairs so I head for the couch, stopping by the freezer for the pint of ice cream stashed in the back. I'll have to run an extra mile tomorrow to make up for it but I can't bring myself to care.

I curl into a ball in my corner of the couch, blanket pulled over myself and ice cream resting against my curled knees. I flick through Netflix, pretending to be interested in the new shows before settling on watching *Friends*. Half way through a second episode and half the pint of ice cream, my phone chimes.

Scott: How's your pops?

Ivy: He's okay … they said it's normal. Old age, I guess.

Scott: Ah.

I'm sorry, though.

For what it's worth.

Ivy: Thank you. I'm sorry for cancelling.

Scott: Let's go with rescheduling … I want that date.

For the first time in what seems like hours, a small smile curls up my lips.

Ivy: Someone's keen. Haha

Scott: You have no idea.

Ivy: I'll be needing it after the first week of school that's coming up.

I watch the three little dots appear on the screen, before they disappear and appear again. He's writing and then deleting whatever he wants to say. It makes me laugh. He's tall, dark and handsome but I can feel his nerves through the phone. It makes me feel better about my own, knowing he's right there with me.

Scott: I'll be out of town this coming weekend, but make it the Saturday after and you're on.

Ivy: Done.

Chapter Six

Ivy

I'VE NEVER BEEN SO addicted to checking my phone than I have been this last week.

Since Pops' health scare had me canceling our dinner date with promises to reschedule, Scott and I have been having one long, continuous conversation. I'd learned so much about him. He spent more hours awake than asleep—a fact I knew because whilst I did my best to stay up talking to him each night, I still failed and woke up to not one but two texts from him from the night before and then from earlier that next morning.

I'd learned his parents were both incredibly intelligent and from family trees littered with political powers and scholars. I'd learned that he'd finished a psychology degree and graduated top of his class at UCLA. He loved going to the gym. Hiking. Peanut butter toast. The colorful socks his mom buys him every year at Christmas time.

I'd also learned that he didn't like to talk about his job, the only time he'd bought it up was when he mentioned that Flynn Reed was a friend from college. Before I could pry further, he'd changed the subject. He also didn't respond well when I asked why he'd moved here. He'd answered a short *no* when I'd asked if he liked Boston yet and then changed the subject again.

He is so open about everything else that I just left it. Despite his closed off attitude when it came to his work and Boston, Scott has me smiling at my phone every single time his name appears on the screen.

I may as well build a huge, flashing arrow pointing directly at me and illuminating the path to my heart for him. Catching feelings is inevitable and I don't even care.

Katie's been giving me shit about it all week.

It's because of her constant pestering and jokes that I opt to relieve her of her best friend duties of helping me set up my classroom. School goes back next week and the principal allows us to get into our classrooms the Friday before to get organized. Bless him for trying, but one day isn't enough for me to get my bare room ready for a new round of kindergarteners.

Last year, I hadn't tried that hard and the amount of comments the parents made got on my nerves. So, over the thanksgiving weekend, Pops had helped me deck it out with color and posters and pretty much any learning tool I could get my hands on at the time. The kids had been amazed walking in after the break.

Their tiny faces, the wonder and the excitement in all of them, is why I'll do it again. From the start of the year this time though.

I reach up on my tip-toes, stretching my arm into the corner with one end of the banner's string in my hand. "Damn it," I huff, dropping my heels back onto the chair. It wobbles beneath me and my hand slaps against the wall in an attempt to steady myself. Falling off and landing myself with a broken bone just in time for school to go back would be the worst-case scenario.

I'm starting to regret relieving Katie of her duties.

I got a jump start on decorating and have been in the room since seven this morning. My stomach is threatening to begin growling if I don't feed it and I could probably use a coffee—with a hit of sugar, of course. I jump down from the chair, heading for my bag to dig for my phone when it chimes loudly, as if it knew I was coming for it.

Scott: What's your coffee order?

I smile, and then try to smooth my features. Fight back against the smiling and maybe I can protect my heart from completely falling in love with the man before we even have a first date.

I'm so done for.

Ivy: Something too sugary for you, Mr. -I-workout-seven-days-a-week.

Scott: Maybe I work out because I have a huge sweet tooth I have to counter …

Ivy: Do you?

Scott: No.

Ivy: I do love to be right.

Scott: Coffee order, if you will.

Ivy: Can I ask why?

Scott: Coffee is your second love. You've said that every morning for the past week.

I wanna know what specific coffee I'm up against here.

Ivy: … cheeseball.

Scott: Please?

Ivy: Venti iced latte with two pumps of vanilla, a pump of sugar syrup and extra cold foam.

Scott: I hope you're covering the walls of your classroom with something soft.

You'll be bouncing off them with the amount of sugar you inhale.

Ivy: Helps me stay on the same level as the kids.

How was your morning?

Scott: Good, just spent it in the gym for a work out.

I text back a reply asking him what he did in the gym, and push my phone into my back pocket before eyeing the chair and the corner of the banner that is now lying on the ground. My stomach growls as I walk back over to the banner and try—and fail—to muffle the sound with a hand.

I'll put the banner up and then go for coffee. Scott asking for my go-to order now has me craving the sugar hit. With my venti iced coffee in mind, I step back up onto the chair with the end of the banner in tow.

It takes me another eight sweaty minutes to secure it to the hook in the corner and by the time I'm done with it, I'm cursing my decision to go into kindergarten teaching and not something that doesn't require so many colors ... like middle school teaching. Middle schoolers aren't impressed by anything. I wouldn't have to work so hard to impress their parents with my colorful posters and educational knick-knacks lying around the room.

I step back from the wall, hands on my hips, admiring my work.

My thoughts begin to drift towards the venti iced latte I'd promised myself earlier—surely I'm deserving of a muffin now too—when a low, appreciative whistle comes from the doorway of my classroom behind me, interrupting my thoughts.

"Looking good." I whip around on my heel, trying desperately to keep myself from blushing as I realize who's interrupted my self-admiring. "Very ... colorful."

Scott.

Freaking Scott, in the flesh and not just over text.

In my classroom.

Surrounded by the hand drawn posters I spent hours over the summer making.

Oh. Shit.

He's more attractive than I remember. Why was I such a lightweight? My single shot and a beer induced mind had dampened the memory of his looks. But now, with him standing in front me, still as tall and as broad as ever there is no way I'm ever going to forget this.

He stares at me, his cap pulled low over his eyes again and his hair beneath it curling at the ends. It's damp. He must have showered after his workout.

Images of him in a towel, seeing exactly what all those workouts are doing to his body plagued me. He probably has a six pack ... no, an eight pack.

Most definitely a pack.

"Are you drooling over me or the sugar drink in my hand? I can't tell."

The heat I'd been trying to suppress crawls up my neck and I'm sure my ears are bright red by now. I give myself an internal shake and zero in on the coffee in his hand.

"Heaven," I whisper loud enough to earn a laugh, and move closer to him.

"The drink then," he says. "Damn, this is my tightest t-shirt."

I take a sip of the iced latte, glancing up at him through my lashes as the heavenly liquid slides down my throat. "Oh no, it's working for you fine. But this right here." I take another small sip. "This is pure, unadulterated, heaven. Takes a lot to get on this coffee's level."

This earns me another small laugh and I pocket it just as I do all the others I get.

I pat his chest, moving past him to set the coffee down on my desk. "Don't worry big guy. You'll get there one day. Maybe."

If I'm being honest with myself, he's probably already there but he doesn't need to know that.

"I like your classroom." He stares at the posters I put up, the banner that hangs from one end to the other, the name tags that sit on the desks already.

"You're about five minutes too late to make yourself useful. I was struggling for ages with the banner and getting it hooked up on the corner over there." I wave my hand around, sinking into my chair and sipping from the sugary goodness he brought me.

"I can stay and help if you like. I've got nothing else to do today."

I look up from the drink. A mistake. It had been a mistake to sit down in his presence. It only makes him look bigger. Taller. More imposing. More attractive.

Get. It. Together.

"I don't ... that's nice but ... I mean, you don't have too."

He shrugs, looking around at the boxes scattered across the floor. "This looks like a lot for one person."

"Usually Katie helps but I relieved her of her best friend duties today."

He cocks his head to the side. "Why?"

Shit. "She's annoying and persistent. But really you don't have to stay. Thank you for offering but it's really fine. I can do this. It's boring, and a lot of me changing my mind on where things need to go. You don't want to be on the receiving end. I can be annoying. Really, it's—"

"Where do you want this one?" He cuts off my rambling and I finally force my eyes to refocus on him. He's holding the birthday balloon chart I drew—a balloon for each month of the year with all the kids' dates written in so we wouldn't forget to celebrate.

My mouth opens, closes, and then opens again. This man is really standing in the middle of my half ready classroom, on a Friday—which is surely a work day for him, although I won't ask—offering his help.

Katie will murder me in broad daylight if I turn him down.

So I don't.

"Over by the door, on that pin board." He nods, following my instructions, and carefully pinning up the poster. He even smooths it out with a hand when he's done.

And it's decided.

I'm done for.

***

The first week back at school always kills.

It's like I forget every summer just how brutally tired I am at the end of every day and just how I'm supposed to manage the energy to come back and do it all again the next day.

The kids are the most emotional that first week too. It's their first school experience. They're leaving their parents for the first time, all day, and meeting all these new people. It takes longer to calm them in the morning, they're weary of the teachers and the other kids.

Safe to say, between the teachers and the kids, the first week back is a rollercoaster filled with more tears than laughter. Thankfully it gets easier as the semester goes on. But god, the first week kills.

This year though, I have a new secret weapon to keep a smile on my face through the drop off tantrums and the 'I don't know how to share' arguments my five-year-olds are experts at.

Scott.

He'd stayed the whole day with me in my classroom, helping me get through my set up faster than I ever have before. We ended up sitting against the wall at the front of the class talking for almost two hours before I had to call it a day and get to the hospital to see Pops.

I'd hoped that Scott might ask to reschedule our date for last weekend but he'd told me that he would be out of town. Sure, I'd been disappointed but I hadn't pushed.

He'd turned up at my classroom with coffee and muffins and spent the day sticking up color posters. I'm not about to get sulky over the fact he had to work. Besides, he still texted me with what must have been every free moment because every time I've looked at my phone in the past week, his name has been front and center.

My favorites are the morning texts.

I told Katie by Tuesday that even if whatever was going on with Scott and I fizzled out, he'd raised the bar when it came to morning texts.

Over the weekend it had simply been a '*morning*' but when I woke up on Monday and checked my phone, there was a good morning and a request from him.

> **Scott:** Morning. First day back to school. A big one. What's your 'first day of kindergarten' outfit? Has to be good in order to set the tone for the whole year.

No pressure of course.

This is more of an excuse to get another glimpse of your pretty face.

I'm not ashamed to admit that I squealed and kicked my heels up when I read it. The smile on my face had been so wide and unmoving, I'd had to take a few deep breaths before taking a picture of my outfit for him in the mirror.

He'd told me that I made a good choice and that I looked amazing.

Cue more squealing.

He's asked for one every morning since and every morning I've obliged.

Even on Thursday when I had to dress in my gym leggings and the school branded polo top because my kindergarteners had their first official gym class on the school field. Those morning messages managed to keep a smile on my face throughout my entire day no matter what the kids threw at me.

Friday afternoon I kick my shoes off inside the door. A sigh of relief leaves my mouth and I feel the stress of the week float from my body. My phone chimes as I reach the kitchen, setting my bag down on the nearest stool.

Scott: Home?

Ivy: Just walked in … my feet are killing and the couch is calling my name. How's work?

He'd told me yesterday that he was away for work again. The curiosity of what he does is starting to eat away at my insides. I really want to know what the hell he does that has him moving to Boston for work but traveling every other week.

I sink into the couch as his reply comes in, rolling onto my stomach to read it.

> **Scott:** Home this morning. Was fine though. Work is work.

I decide it might be best to steer clear. I want that date and bringing up his work, as I've learned, causes him to shut down faster than a kindergartener being questioned for taking their friend's toy, rather than sharing.

> **Ivy:** Well, I'm exhausted. First week is always a killer.

> **Scott:** I imagine it would be. Everyone survived though. I call that a win.

> **Ivy:** Everyone survived, yes. Barely, but we made it. Haha.

> **Scott:** What are your plans this weekend?

> **Ivy:** Not a lot … standing morning date on Sunday with Pops but that's about it.

> **You?**

> **Scott:** Reckon you'd still be able to fit in that date with me?

My breath hitches and my heart skips a beat. *Finally*. The date.

> **Ivy:** I reckon I might be able to pencil you in.

> **Scott:** Free around one tomorrow? Send me your address, I'll pick you up.

I let out another squeal and kick my heels up. I'm doing that a lot lately and really, I don't want to stop.

***

Scott's black car pulls up two minutes to one and I am not ready.

"Shit," I curse under my breath, throwing my Converse sneakers at the front door and heading for the kitchen. My perfume is stashed in my work bag—still sitting on the stool where I dropped it last night. God, I really need to clean this thing out. I find the small bottle, spraying lightly on my wrists and dabbing my neck. I also spray behind me and step back into the light mist of scent. A habit I picked up from Nan. She used to joke that it was how she got Pops to follow her everywhere. I was so young I don't remember if I believed her or not but now it's a habit that makes me think of her every day.

I drop the bottle of scent back into my work bag and head to the door.

The doorbell rings. I stare at the closed door knowing Scott's the one on the other side and force myself to take a deep breath.

One … two … *stop smiling so wide Ivy, god* … three.

"Hey." I smile up at him in his signature cap and black t-shirt. I hope it's a good, natural looking smile. I hope my nerves aren't plastered all over my face.

His lips twitch up. His eyes gaze down my body before they meet mine again. I'm not sure how impressive I am in denim shorts and a white t-shirt but I feel like melting under his gaze.

Then he grins. "Hi, ready?"

"Yep. Just need to pull my shoes on. Come in."

He hesitates in the doorway before stepping inside. "This is quite the place," he says, glancing down the hallway behind me.

"My grandparents bought it in the sixties I think. Family home, renovated a couple of times over. Pops was bored after retiring."

He simply nods and I pull on my shoes.

"Am I dressed okay for wherever we're going?" I ask holding out my hands and turning on the spot. The action gets me a quiet chuckle. Deep and rumbling and soul soothing.

"Yes. Come on, I've booked so we don't want to be late."

"Are you going to tell me where we're going?" I ask him. My curiosity is eating at me.

"Nope. You'll see when we get there."

"Is it far?"

"Not really."

I close the door behind us, triple checking it's locked before throwing my keys into the bag across my body. The black Mercedes SUV doesn't necessarily stand out amongst some of the other cars in the street but it certainly makes my red Toyota pale in comparison.

"Nice car." I smirk a little as I follow him toward the street.

"Job perk. I prefer my truck but I left it in California."

"Why?"

He studies me for a second, hand reaching for the door as he goes to open it for me. I climb into the passenger seat as he answers. "Wasn't planning on staying in Boston long term."

I sense the same shut down I get whenever work comes up in conversation so I switch subjects as he rounds the car and slides in beside me. I let him pepper me with questions about my first week back at school. I'm mid story—recalling exactly when I'd discovered which kindergarteners weren't exactly toilet ready for the school year—when Scott pulls the car into a large parking lot.

"Mini golf?" I squeal excitedly. I jump down from the passenger seat as soon as Scott pulls the door open for me. The brightly lit sign shines even in the sunshine. Scott comes up behind me, his chest just brushing against my back. I stop myself from leaning back into him. Probably too soon.

"Do you not like mini golf?"

I smile, my inner child cheering for what's about to happen. "I haven't been since I was a kid."

"We can go somewhere else if you want," he says. I turn my head to stare up at him. His green eyes are filled with worry and it makes something in my chest tighten. He's nervous. Boy, do I like that he is. It matches my own nerves.

"No. I love mini golf." Now I do lean back into him a little, smiling up at him as his features shift from doubt to relief. I smirk. "I'm very competitive though. Hope you're ready to lose."

I step out of his space but reach behind me, taking Scott's hand to drag him to the entrance. The inside of the building is as bright and lit up as the outside. There's two staff members leaning against a bench behind the counter and early two thousand pop hits play loudly over the speakers. Other than the two staff members and us, the place is completely empty.

"Are they closed? Didn't you say you booked?"

"I did." I slow down at the empty venue as he nods. His fingers tighten around mine, tugging me along. "I booked out the whole place."

"You ... you what?!"

"Mr. Har–" One of the staff, the manager according to the title on his name badge, greets us.

"Scott is fine," Scott cuts him off with a small smile. "Thanks for doing this."

"Of course." The manager smiles widely and hands over two putters and golf balls for us to use.

"We open back up to the public around four so you have until then."

"You booked this place for three hours?! That's ... that must have cost a small fortune." Scott just shrugs before taking the putters from the counter in one hand and reaching for my own again with the other. He pulls me away from the counter and towards the archways that lead off to the courses.

He stands me in front of them, my back pressed against his chest again, holding out the putters and the balls in front of me to choose from. I take the neon pink ball and the shorter of the two putters.

"Which one first?" His words are quiet, said in a low drawl, his breath against my ear. If I was to turn my head slightly, tilt to look at him, our lips would be centimeters apart.

Would he kiss me?

Did I want him too?

God, yes.

Instead, I keep my eyes trained ahead and study the entrances to the course. After I allow myself a minute to enjoy his presence, I step away. Turning to face him, I walk backward toward the jungle themed course and flash him a smirk. "You're going down."

He laughs, eyes shining under the brim of his signature cap. "Bring it on."

***

"Wow, you really are awful at that."

"Putting is not my strong suit. I'm better at driving." We both watch the small ball slowly come to a stop. Scott's golf ball, mind you. I'm winning.

"Uh huh, interesting. You know, you can just admit that I'm a better golfer," I say as I swing the golf club gently next to me.

"This is *mini* golf and that seems like admitting defeat."

I nod in agreement. "It is."

He leans against the giant wave modeled around the eighteenth hole feigning a thoughtful look. "Nah, I don't think so."

I roll my eyes. Over the last two hours I've probably permanently etched a smile into my features and my cheeks are starting to hurt from laughing so much. The butterflies in my stomach are raging and even though I'm doing my best to feign confidence in his presence, my hands are definitely shaking a little every time he watches me take a putt.

I'm still winning, though.

I line up my shot, pull my arm back a little and let loose. Just enough for the golf ball to bounce off the angled wall and head straight for the hole.

I watch as it slows, crawling toward the edge. "Come on ..." I whisper, watching closely. Scott's eyes are on the ball too. We both watch it teeter before finally falling in. I drop my putter onto the fake green and lift my hands above my head in victory.

"Yes!"

Scott groans, shaking his head as he collects my dropped putter. "Damn."

I laugh. "Told you. Admit it, I'm a better golfer."

"Mini golfer," he corrects. I drop my hands and rest them on my hips, raising a brow, and wait. He sighs. "Fine … you're better. I admit defeat."

I throw my head back and laugh again, but this time his laugh joins mine. I'm about to tell him that he shouldn't have doubted my skills in the first place when he steps into my space, face hovering above mine. He's so close I can see the detailed, clean lines along his jaw where he trims his beard. He smells like soap, and cinnamon, and something else I can't quite place. He smells delicious. I feel myself rising on my toes. His lips are right there, hovering so closely above mine.

It would be so easy.

I stare at the gold flecks embedded into the forest green of his eyes. His cap casts a shadow and when he tilts his head slightly, the golden flecks shift and swirl. They're captivating. He's captivating.

He's staring at my lips. My eyes flicker down to his.

In the background, a door slams. I jolt. My heels drop back to the floor. I shoot up a hand and take the cap off his head. The moment's gone.

"I'm taking this. As my prize."

He continues to stare, gaze dragging between my lips and my own eyes, and back again.

"All yours."

Chapter Seven

Scott

With every drip of sweat making its way down the side of my face the same phrase turns over and over in my head; I should have kissed her.

I should have kissed her next to that stupid plastic wave and I should have kissed her when I dropped her off. She seemed to shrug off the *almost kiss* easier than me. I thought about it as I'd driven her to a park nearby where I'd organized a taco food truck to meet us for dinner. I'd thought about it as I watched her put away no less than six tacos, only four less than myself, and I'd thought about it as she laughed at my story about the time my mom had interrupted an exam in my final year at school because I'd forgotten to wear my lucky pineapple socks.

When I dropped her home, I'd driven five miles under the limit just to prolong my time with her. I practically tripped over the bonnet of my car trying to open her door for her and I had to bury my hands in my pockets in an effort not to touch her. I stood on the porch in front of her door and I studied her soft looking lips down to the exact shade of pink.

When I leaned down, my hand finding her hip and my fingers splaying across the fabric of her shorts, I hesitated for the smallest moment and gave her the chance to turn her head. My lips met her cheek and my pride had plummeted.

I'm a fucking idiot.

At least, when it comes to Ivy I am. My performance on the field is better than ever. She's in the back of my mind but my focus is on the team and it's showing. My teammates and I are starting to click. The running backs are learning my quirks, I've finally started to mesh with the offensive line after the center and I got on the same page. Flynn is my tight end but it only took us half a practice to get back into the rhythm of things. It's like playing in college with him again.

I'm getting comfortable.

Thank god for that.

Summer may have turned into autumn, the leaves have started to change their colors, but the sun is still beating down on our backs during this morning's practice. Flynn strolls up next to me, ripping his helmet off and lifting his practice jersey to wipe the sweat building up on his forehead.

"Honestly, fuck this heat." He lifts the water bottle, squirting it into his mouth. If only the jersey chasers could see him now. Flynn has always been good looking, but in college it was more of a baby-face-innocent look. My mom would squeeze his cheeks after wrapping his large frame up into a hug whenever we'd go to see my parents.

I shared a wall with the guy in college. He is anything but innocent.

He lost his baby face just before senior year. Now, he's all straight jawlines and abs. Before I moved to Boston, he had hair longer than his shoulders. He called it sex appeal but I just had the urge to cut it off with scissors. Thank god he did it himself before the season started.

Flynn shakes out his hair, sweat drops flying from the short strands.

I turn my eyes on him, leveling him with a stare as I drag a hand down the arm closest to him. "Gross."

"I'm allowed to be sweaty. I work hard," he replies while running a hand through the sweat soaked strands.

"Go be sweaty somewhere else."

I go back to watching the defensive team drills. Once they've finished up we will be heading for the showers before breaking off for meetings and film. It's going to be a long evening.

"Why are you so cranky today? Did your date over the weekend go badly?" he asks as he shoves my shoulder. I keep my stare ahead but it doesn't stop the inevitable replay reel starting over in my head, torturing me with the opportunities I missed to get a real taste of Ivy.

I scowl. "Shut up."

"Hm." I can practically hear the smirk forming on his face. "You know, I've been to Pats a few times since we went there."

This gets my attention. My eyes snap to him, my helmet slipping through my fingers and hitting the turf with a thud. "You what?"

"I wanted to get a look at the girl that has you all twisted up and smiling like an idiot at your phone," he says as he shrugs. He stretches his legs, lunging forward as he turns his face up to me. "Never seen you like this about a woman before. It's refreshing."

My chest tightens. Ivy is different. There were girls in high school, a short-term girlfriend here or there, and in college if I had needed to let off steam then I'd always found someone willing. But since going pro, I've been careful. Selective.

As in, I haven't selected anyone at all.

I'm committed to the game and my attention isn't wavering from that.

Well until now.

Ivy's undone all of it with a glance my way and a smile.

"Have you ... did you meet her?" I ask. I try to school my features into a look of disinterest, to feign some sense of not caring all that much that he was snooping around Pats trying to get a look at her.

But who am I kidding? I care a whole lot.

Pats is a sports bar. Not just any kind of sports bar but one that is across from the Broncos training facility dedicated to Boston's sports teams. It plays classic football games all day long. Flynn has been playing with the team since being drafted out of college. Any Boston football fan worth their salt would know who he is.

If Ivy is there, if she asks him how he knows me, he will tell her. I'll be outed.

"Na, she's not been there," he says and relief washes through me. "Met her friend, though. The one I signed the autograph for. Katie." There's an accusation in his tone and my stomach drops.

"Shit," I curse. "Look, I—"

He holds up a hand. "You're in deep shit if you confirm this. Please tell me the woman you're all twisted up about knows who you are? Please tell me her friend was just having a moment and didn't ask me if you were the team's psychologist or something?"

My guilt is written all over my face.

Flynn curses. "Are you insane?"

"I know." I rack a hand through my hair. "It's fucking stupid, and risky, and I'm a dick."

"No, but you are a franchise quarterback worth a few million dollars and trying to date a girl who doesn't know who the hell you are just before the season starts. This will never, ever end well man. You have to tell her."

He's right.

Damn it, I know he's right.

I'd known when I met her that she hadn't recognized me. I'd known it when she'd told me she hated football without hesitating like she might offend me. I know it every single time I field one of her questions about my job.

"I caught on pretty quick when Katie mentioned her friend had gone out with someone who 'worked' for the team." He lifts his fingers, air quoting himself. "What the hell made you not disclose you are *the* quarterback for the team?!"

"She hates football," I sigh, my head dropping.

"What?" Flynn stands straight, his stretching forgotten.

"Ivy, the girl I went out with, hates football. Like with a passion. Wants nothing to do with it. Doesn't watch the games, the coverage, not even *SportsCenter*. She has no idea who I am and I loved that at first," I admit, the word vomit hurling out of me. Ivy's smile blossoms in the front of my eyes again. "It was like we met and instead of seeing the giant flashing arrow pointing me out as a quarterback, she just saw some poor guy wallowing in the fact he's moved to a city he hates for work. She's determined to get me to like Boston."

I suppress a smile as I remember her listing off her top ten favorite things to do in the city over tacos.

Flynn shakes his head again. "You're such a sucker. You know that, right?"

"It was nice." I run another hand through my hair, tugging at the ends.

Across the field, Coach blows his whistle signaling we can hit the showers and eat. Flynn and I grab our helmets and head toward the change rooms.

"Look," Flynn starts. "I know that with who we are and what we do, there is a risk to meeting someone and them not being genuine but you still should probably tell her before someone else does. Just because she hates football might not mean she has her fucking head buried in the sand completely. If you like her, like properly like her and want a shot, you gotta tell her man."

We file into the change rooms, heading for the lockers where our bags sit.

"I will. I will tell her. I just ... it's been so nice."

Flynn stares at me, studying me as something like curiosity flashes in gaze. "Man, you're done for already."

"Shut up."

"You are though! This girl has you so twisted up." He grins, picking up his phone. "You know, this might be good for you. Dating a girl that hates football and doesn't give a shit that you're the best QB in the league right now. Very humbling."

I ignore him, digging around in my own bag. I sent Ivy a message this morning as I pulled up for practice. I wanted to see what she was wearing today. Her outfit of the day pictures are my favorite messages. Her clothes tell me a lot about her as a teacher. Sneakers, so she can be as active as the kids but still comfortable. Pants, always. Light colors even though she tells me she's spent a fortune on learning how to get paint out of her clothes since starting.

She wore denim cut off shorts on our date and converse sneakers. She hadn't cared about wearing heels or a dress, I'd told her to dress comfortably and that's what she'd done. She'd smiled, and laughed, and ate as many tacos as she'd damned well pleased.

Flynn's hand waves in front of my face, breaking me out of my Ivy induced hold. "Scotty, what's her last name again?"

"Huh, who's?"

"Your girl's, duh."

"Oh ... uh," I strain my memory. I vaguely remember her signing her name on the score cards at mini golf. "Booker, I think."

I look over at Flynn tapping away on his phone. He pulls up Instagram and in less than a minute, a picture of Ivy's smiling fills his screen. "Got her."

He holds the phone up to me proudly.

"You're a creep, you know that? You found that way too fast," I say to him as I take the phone.

He pouts, reaching behind him to pull off his practice jersey.

"What? So girls can be literal FBI agents when finding a guy's profile but I can't?"

I glance at him. "What the hell are you talking about?"

He sighs, taking his phone back. "Never mind. You're such an old man." I watch him scroll through her profile. "You know, Booker sounds familiar."

"Does it?"

"Yeah. I know that name. Just can't think where." He scrolls further down her feed, pulling up picture after picture. Summer holidays, in a swimsuit, to a photo of her on graduation day, to another of her at a college hockey game wrapped in a giant scarf and beanie. Another of her and Katie standing on the bar at Pats, drinks in their hands. Ivy's head is thrown back, her laughter caught on camera.

Flynn zooms in, studying her face a little closer so I lean over and lock his phone. "You can stop thinking of her altogether."

He sticks his tongue before tossing his phone back into his bag and heads for the shower. "You're no fun."

I shake my head, following him to the showers and pushing all thoughts of Ivy out of my head.

***

I take my seat in the back of the small theatre room. The coaches sit in the front and the rest of the guys spread out around me. Flynn drops down on my right, legs outstretched in front of him. He tugs his hood up and over his head and his arms fold over his chest. He is most definitely planning to fall asleep.

As the lights turn out and the game tape starts to roll on the screen—Coach's red laser pointer highlighting whatever player he wants us to be focusing on—my thoughts turn back to Ivy. This week, trying focus on the start of the season and on football has been torture.

While running drills on the field, or throwing the ball down the line ... damn my mind should be on practice but it's not. Her face is right there, the forefront of my brain.

I can't get the girl out of my head.

Might not be affecting my game but it's beginning to affect my sanity.

I'm still deflecting any work-related questions she throws at me. It's clear she has no idea who I am and Flynn has confirmed her friend doesn't either. It isn't that I want to keep it a secret forever but considering how she feels about football and considering my job, I just want time.

I want time to show her I'm more than a football player, more than a quarterback.

But she knows I work for the team and I want an excuse to talk to her. She has not sent a reply since this morning. I gathered this morning it was because she was wrangling children but it's now just after seven. She'll be home now.

I lean back, turning the brightness on my phone all the way down and snap a picture of my outstretched legs with the screen clearly showing the game tape we are watching.

Scott: *1 Attachment*

I wait, phone in my hand, eyes watching the screen whilst my mind replays the almost kiss for the millionth time over. Next to me, Flynn shifts further down in his seat.

Ivy: Looks like my worst nightmare.

Scott: And mine tonight …

Ivy: Tired?

Scott: You've no idea.

Ivy: I just got into bed, Friends is on and I'll be out any minute …

Jealous?

Scott: That sounds like a dream

Ivy: *1 Attachment*

Her room is bathed in shadows. A lamp must be on next to her, lowly lit. There is a small lump in her bedding where I guess she must have her legs curled up. As promised, the TV plays an episode of *Friends*. I've learned it is her comfort show and, even when she's watching some other new series, she is always watching *Friends*.

When I asked how she could watch the same show over and over, she'd told me that sometimes she just needed the background noise. And she likes that she knows how it all ends: happily.

I glance toward the front of the room at Coach. He is focused on the screen, laser pointer in his hand and red dot furiously moving across it.

When I look back down at the picture, I study her surroundings. White furniture, what looks to be a light pink color on the walls—although it is difficult to tell when the picture isn't all that well lit—a few pillows scattered on the floor in front of her bed.

Her room is all soft edges and comfortable landings.

Just like her.

> **Scott:** I like your room.

> **Ivy:** Ha! I haven't changed it since high school.

> But thank you.

I hesitate. The almost kiss replays over and over, melding with the moment she turned her head at the end of the night and my lips had landed on her cheek. *Her cheek?*

She'd turned her head so I'd caught her cheek, for fuck's sake.

When did my ability to 'woo' a woman go to shit?

I type out the question that has been burning inside my chest since I'd pressed my lips against her soft skin for the first time.

> **Scott:** Why didn't you let me kiss you the other night?

> **Ivy:** Um, not sure, actually.

Christ...

> **Scott:** You're not sure?

Maybe I'm wasting my time. I am taking the gamble that she might not hate football as much as she says she does anyway.

Maybe, even though I've become ridiculously obsessed with her in such a short time, she doesn't see me the same way. Maybe she sees me as a new in town, Boston hater that she'll try to change the mind of. Maybe I am being ... my phone vibrates in my hand.

Ivy: Scott?

Scott: Ivy?

Ivy: Will you try again next time?

Fuck.

"Coach?" The words are leaving my lips before my brain even processes them. "It's been a long day. It's hot as fuck out. Let's call it for the day. I'm sure the team would appreciate the early night."

Coach pauses the tape before getting to his feet and turning to stare at me in the back row. His eyes flicker to Flynn, who is curled completely into himself and sleeping quietly beside me. I nudge him with my elbow and he jerks awake, sitting up before running a hand over his face.

"We're playing the top of the division come Sunday," Coach huffs out. He glares at me, I glare back. "But Harvey's right. It was tougher than we anticipated out there this afternoon. You're dismissed."

I move before anyone else.

Flynn calls my name but I'm collecting my bag and out the front doors of the training facility before he even hits the locker room for his own.

I have to act on this now before she takes it back.

Before I lose my nerve.

Ivy's place is no more than fifteen minutes from the facility. I park in the same space outside her place as last weekend, my feet travel the same path as they had when I'd knocked on her front door and listened to her shuffle around behind it cursing my early nature.

I knew I should've waited around the corner a little longer than I did.

I'd been a full ten minutes early to pick her up for our mini golf date but forced myself to wait before pulling up to her house.

Her small red car is sitting in the driveway in front of the closed double garage door. For the first time since I'd seen her message, I hesitate, but it's only for a second. There's no porch light on, no light coming through any of the front facing windows. She's either adverse to leaving a hall light on or already asleep.

I take the chance anyway and ring the doorbell.

When there's no movement—knowing full well it's been no more than thirty seconds—I lift my fist and knock.

A light appears at the top of the stairs, shining through the curtains over the front windows that frame the door. Then another light, a shadow of someone moving down the stairs.

Then the porch light.

The beat of my heart slows as I wait.

Something clicks, likely the lock on the door, and Ivy's face comes into view as she pulls it open gingerly.

"I know it's only just after seven but I did say I was in bed already," she says, her voice sleepy and quiet.

Even her shy smile is beautiful.

Her soft features are free of makeup, her hair falls over her shoulders in loose curls and the pajama shorts are surely not legal; they're that short.

I focus on the blue eyes I think about so often. They swirl with confusion, amusement, and curiosity. She's wondering why I'm here. Why I left what was obviously work for me to see her. I have to eventually tell her what I do, especially now that I'm here to cement that I definitely didn't want her to be just a fucking tour guide.

"Scott? Is everything alright?" Her gaze flickers to the quiet street behind me.

"Can 'next time' be right now?" I step forward, hand resting on the door, pushing it open a little further so I could step my body directly in front and in line with hers.

"I– huh?"

"I'm going to kiss you," I say. Her eyes widen. I lift a hand to cup her cheek, thumb stroking along the edge of her jaw.

"You're ... you're going to..."

"And this time, you're not going to turn your head." I take her face between both my hands, cradling her gently as I step further into her space. There's a faint blush rising up her chest. It clashes with the soft pink silk of her pajamas.

My gaze drops to her lips. Her tongue darts out to wet them and I lean forward. "Okay?"

"Okay."

I dive in.

She tastes better than anything I could've dreamt up on my own. Strawberries, and something else sweet. Her lips are gentle and soft against mine. She's timid and shy at first but when I stroke a finger down her throat and run my tongue against the seam of her lips, silently asking for her to open, she does so and my whole body goes up in flames.

Her tongue tangles with mine as she rises on her toes, arms snaking over my shoulders and locking behind my neck. Her fingers drag through the hair at the nape of my neck, tangling amongst the strands and tugging.

Fuck, but I love that.

I drop my hands, curling them around her body and pulling her harder against me. I pull her bottom lip between my teeth and she whimpers.

Forget flames, her noises will have me in a pile of ashes at her feet.

When she pulls away, out of breath and blushing, I drop my forehead against hers gently. Her eyes close, a gentle smile appearing as she chews on her bottom lip.

I smirk, lifting a thumb to her lip and pulling it from between her teeth. She opens her eyes, watching me. I drop another kiss on her lips.

"Did you leave a meeting at work to come here?"

"Sort of."

"Will you get in trouble?"

"Well, no. I asked to be dismissed."

"To come here?"

"Yes."

"To kiss me?"

"Yes."

As if to prove a point, I kiss her again.

She pulls away. "Why?"

"Because I should've fucking kissed you on that stupid mini golf course and I've regretted it ever since."

She hums. "Yes. You should've." Her lips curl, a gleam sparkling in her eye. She rises on her toes. "But this is good too."

I meet her half way, knowing that I can likely spend the rest of my days kissing this girl and die a happy man.

Chapter Eight

Ivy

I'm running late.

I laid in bed for an extra thirty minutes this morning, fingers tracing the outline of my lips gently, thoughts stuck on the events of last night. Jesus, I am so far gone already and I don't even know his last name.

Careful not to spill my coffee all over the front of myself, I take the front steps two at a time. One hand blindly searches my bag for my car keys while my jacket hangs off one shoulder.

My concentration waivers for a single moment as my focus snaps towards something shifting in my peripheral vision but before I can center myself, my instincts have already forced me to flinch, glancing over my shoulder to try and get a better look at whatever is there.

I only have a second and half to take in the tall form wearing his signature black baseball cap and running shorts when I feel my coffee slip from my hands and my bag fall from my shoulder. I try to save it all at once, over correcting myself.

It's too late.

I'm falling.

Or I would've been falling.

Two large hands find themselves wrapped around my hips as Scott keeps me the right way up.

"Woah." His fingers dig into my jeans, steadying me. I give in, leaning into him and watching as my coffee pours from my keep cup and onto the pavement.

"You okay?" he asks.

I sigh. "Yeah."

My poor coffee.

He laughs quietly, one hand loosening as the other curls further around my waist. He lifts my bag from where it's hanging off my wrist, his breath skirting my skin as he leans down. My attention is drawn away from the wasted coffee when his lips gently press into the stretch of bare skin at the base of my neck. His grip on my waist tightens, and he presses another into my skin.

The coffee is no longer important, time is suddenly irrelevant, the school day completely forgotten.

I turn in his arms, lifting my chin and meeting his eyes. His cap keeps them in shadows despite the rays of sunshine that peek through the trees lining my street.

"Hi," I say quietly leaning up on my toes.

He nudges his cap up before dipping down, kissing me softly. "Good morning, Ivy."

He doesn't pull back very far, keeping me tightly wrapped in the one arm that was around my waist where the other holds my bag beside us. "Are you okay?"

"Running late. I had a lazy morning and now I'm paying for it."

"Lazy morning, huh?" he asks.

"Laid in bed with my thoughts for too long." I elaborate, lifting a hand to fix his cap as thoughts of the blistering kiss from last night fill my head again. I already know that the same soft smile that I've been sporting all morning is spread across my face again. I can't bring myself to care. Not when I am wrapped tightly in this man's arms. Not when our mouths are so close. Not when the intoxicating smell of him fills my nose and makes me light headed.

"What were you thinking about?"

I don't hesitate.

"You."

He hums, a smirk curling his lips up. "Me too." He leans down, kissing me again. And again. I press myself against him.

I could do this all-damn day.

But with my hand pressing into his chest and gently pushing him away, I know that I can't. "I'm already running late. This isn't helping."

"Sorry," he murmurs. He kisses me again, swallowing my answering sigh when he does. He pulls back, further this time, untangling himself from me. "I just wanted to see you before you went to school."

This man.

"I'm sorry you spilt your coffee." He eyes the coffee-stained sidewalk.

"It's okay. I can make another at school." I take my bag from him, finally fishing out my keys.

I turn away and make my way to ward my car, unlocking the doors and shoving my bag into the back seat. I slip my jacket on properly.

When I turn back to him, expecting him to be behind me, I find him closing his passenger side car door. He's got a Starbucks cup balanced in one hand, a small brown paper bag hanging from his fingers. My heart skips a beat, possibly two and I feel my jaw drop.

"Luckily, I come bearing sugary gifts." He holds them out to me but I don't—can't—move.

What the *fuck*.

"Who are you?" I say, my eyes bouncing between the coffee in his hand and his face, the sheepish look he's sporting utterly adorable.

"Huh?"

"No man is this good. No man does this. Not anymore." I shake my head in disbelief. "Haven't you heard? Chivalry died. Ages ago."

This makes him laugh, a smirk replacing the sheepish expression. He crowds me again and I don't protest. He reaches behind me, placing the coffee cup and the bag on the roof of my car.

"Hm. Sounds like a challenge." He cups my face angling my face towards his. He tilts, the sun peeking under his cap and brightening his eyes. "Me. I'm this good."

I forfeit.

He wins.

As long as he keeps kissing me and bringing me coffee, I've got all I need right here.

"Can I take you out tonight?" he murmurs. His lips hover above mine again.

Something in my chest jolts, probably my heart skipping yet another beat.

"What's your last name?" I say, my heart slowing to a dangerous pace.

He freezes. Caught off guard? Maybe. Or, surprised?

The emotion flickers and disappears so quickly from his face that I don't have time to decipher it.

"Harvey."

"Scott Harvey." I roll the name around on my tongue. Smiling, I look up at him. "Mine's Booker."

"I remember," he tells me. I feel my brows pull together in confusion. He clarifies, bringing a thumb to gently smoothly out the crease between my brows. "From mini golf. You signed your full name. So, Ivy Booker, can I take you out tonight?"

The way he remembers a moment so insignificant. Something as small as signing my name. A contented sigh leaves my mouth as my smile widens and I lean up on my toes, kissing him. "Yes, please."

"What time will you be home from school tonight?"

"I have to go to a pep rally at the high school this afternoon after class. First one of the year and all." I'm a kindergarten teacher yet they still require me to show up. Show some school spirit. The downside to the school having all three campuses in one. "But I'll be home by six."

"I'll pick you up at seven then?"

"Okay."

He smiles and kisses me again. "Okay."

"I have to go," I say. Scott makes no move to let me go. I don't move either. He just keeps kissing me, stepping me back a little until we're leaning against my car and making out like teenagers.

From somewhere in my car, probably lodged deep in my bag, my last alarm of the morning rings out and breaks us apart.

"I really do have to go now."

"Okay." He places a final kiss against my lips before opening the driver side door for me to slide into the car. I take the coffee and the small bag from the roof of the car and slide in. Tapping the push start button in the car, I press down the window and gaze up at him. He leans down, his cap securely back on his head. "I'll see you tonight."

I nod. "See you."

He backs away from the car and I back out of the driveway.

The twenty minute drive to the school is mostly spent sitting in traffic, completely unaware of my surroundings and, once again, my finger tracing my lips with a soft smile.

***

I give up on trying to teach the kids about numbers before lunch. After this morning, I've found it difficult to concentrate on anything but Scott Harvey and his lips. The kids won't stop giggling, the grey clouds have been threatening me with a lunchtime spent inside the classroom and as soon as those first drops of rain run down the windows I officially call it.

The paints come out, the kids are dressed in multi-colored protective plastic smocks, music plays on the speaker, and I slowly trail between the bunches of desks, eyes roaming over the finger paintings they are creating.

I asked them to draw their heroes in an effort to try and make it semi-educational. But as I justified to myself after a lunchtime spent indoors, they are five-year-olds and everything they do is educational.

"Who are you painting, Macy?" I ask bending down to her level. Macy is a quiet girl who sits on a table full of boys. When I'd let them pick their own desks at the beginning of the school year a few weeks ago I found it strange at first, mostly because they all think the opposite gender have cooties at this age, but when I finally met her dad during the first week of school, I understood.

Four older brothers, raised by a single dad and her uncle. Her mom had died a few months ago. Breast cancer. She takes comfort in being surrounded by the boys; they remind her of her brothers.

"It's my daddy," she tells me, her little fingers tracing the outline of the stick figure she drew. There is another next to him, smaller, with yellow hair. I know who it probably is, but I ask anyway.

"And who's this?"

"My momma," she tells me, chin tucking into her chest.

I twirl some of her hair around my finger, waiting for her to look up. "She's very pretty. You have the same hair."

Macy gives me a small smile. "My daddy says I look just like her. He says she was beautiful."

"I reckon he's probably right."

Macy nods in agreement and goes back to her painting. I look around at the drawings of her table mates.

Like Macy, most look to be drawing their parents. An ache spreads through my chest. A memory of my own parents, happy and alive, clouds my mind and for a second I can hear the echo of my dad's voice in my head. Explaining plays, talking to my mom, talking to me. Words I heard over and over whenever I poured over the home videos they made.

I close my eyes for a moment, inhaling and exhaling a few times.

When I open them, blinking away a tear, I look at the boy next to Macy.

Connor is only painting one very large figure in the middle of his page. The figure has what looks like brown hair, although Connor's mixed it with the blue he's used for the figure's shirt so I can't quite tell.

"Who's this, Connor?" I squint, leaning my head side to side, trying to make out the emblem he's drawn on the figure's shirt.

I realize it's a Broncos logo. It makes me laugh. "Do you know a football player?"

I tap my figure lightly on his page, drawing his eyes to the emblem. Connor shakes his head, brow furrowed as he continues to work on the figure's hair. Connor, I've discovered, isn't very chatty.

"Do you have an older sibling who plays football?"

"No, Miss Booker," he replies. His tongue is now poking between his teeth as he works on the figure's shoes.

"Who are you painting then?" I ask again.

"My favorite football player ever." He sits back in his chair. I lean back on my heels, still squatting beside their table. "He just got traded to the Broncos. Grandpa says he'll take me to a home game before Christmas. I'm gonna meet him."

"And what's his name?"

"Harvey. He plays quarterback. I'm gonna play quarterback one day." Connor nods, probably more to himself. So young yet so determined. It makes me laugh quietly.

These kids. I love how their dreams have no limits; nothing is out of reach for them at five. I fiddle with the ring around my neck, turning it between my fingers a few times. I know Connor is probably just dreaming big and that it's unlikely he'll play professional sport. He might only be five years old but I've seen him try to throw a ball at lunch time.

I may not like football, but I do love my kids so I lean in and say quietly, "You know, my dad was a football quarterback." Connor's head whips around, his eyes wide as they meet mine.

"Mhmm. He was good too. Was an American All-Star in college."

"Woah."

"I bet, though," I lean closer whispering now, like it's a secret just between Connor and I. "If you train really hard, you'll be even better than him."

"Really?" He stares at me with wonder.

"Yep." I pull back, moving to stand up so I can check on the other tables.

"Wow," Connor whispers, staring down at his own painting like he's now imagining it's actually him and not his favorite player, Harvey, in a Broncos uniform.

Scott's face invades my thoughts. I wonder if he knows this new quarterback that shares one of his names. Just the mention of his name has me thinking about him showing up last night and then again this morning, coffee in hand, pastry in the other, and the feel of his lips invading my mind.

He is a really good kisser. Like, really *really* good.

I had to sit in my car for an extra five minutes when I'd parked at school just to calm down. I wonder what it would feel like to have his hands exploring my body like his tongue did my mouth.

His tongue exploring my body ... him hovering above me ... fingers pressing into my bare skin ...

Fuck.

I force the images out of my head and take a deep breath. I cannot, will not allow myself to get hot and bothered whilst in the classroom.

As I move around the table, I tune back into the kids and hear Macy say, "Three of my brothers play football."

"That's cool," Connor says. "I don't have a brother."

"You can have one of mine if you want. I have four."

"Do you play football with them? I'd want to play football with them."

"Sometimes. When my daddy lets me."

At least football brings joy to some people.

***

Scott is on my front door step at seven o'clock sharp. The pep rally threatened to run over so I'd snuck out. Katie was all for it once I'd brought her up to speed with last night's, and this morning's activities. Her smug smile had grown wider and wider as I told her about how Scott had showed up last night just to kiss me. She practically fell over when I mentioned he'd shown up this morning with a coffee and pastry, just because.

So I left early, racing home to shower and change. I am slipping my feet into a pair of my favorite heels when the doorbell rings through the house. Just the thought of seeing him has me smiling like an idiot as I head down stairs and throw open the door.

"Hi."

He smirks, leaning against the door frame, hands tucked into the pockets of his dark gray dress pants. I barely get a proper look at him—black button-down shirt, sleeves rolled to his elbows, forearms on display—before he's swooping down to kiss me.

He pulls away and I'm left swaying slightly where I stand, light-headed from a simple hello kiss. "Hey, you. Good day?"

I nod. "Mhmm. It rained over lunch and the kids had to stay inside, so I gave up on teaching and we did finger painting."

His quiet laugh sends an electric current through my nervous system. "Sounds like a productive day."

"Yeah." He takes my hand, stepping onto the porch and waiting for me to close the door behind me. I check it's locked before sliding my keys into my bag. "Where are we going?"

He leads me to his car, parked in the same spot as it had been this morning. He squeezes my hand. "You like Italian?"

"Are you kidding? Pasta is one of my five food groups."

He rewards me with another laugh. "Good. You'll love this place then."

The restaurant is on the outskirts of the city. Scott parks in a small alley, rounding the car to open the door and holds out his hand. I take it and he doesn't let go as he shuts the door behind me.

He leads me into the small restaurant, my hand encased in his as he walks a step ahead. It's a dimly lit, hole in the wall, only a few tables, authentic Italian restaurant. It smells like fresh bread, and red wine, and pasta sauce.

My eyes flutter close as the aroma takes over my senses.

Nan used to make fresh pasta on my birthday. The flour would be everywhere and by the time we were done we'd end up eating in the middle of the mess.

This place smells exactly like home.

It's also completely empty of any other patrons.

"Mr. Harvey! Welcome." An older man, white mustache and balding head, comes towards us. Scott pulls me into his side.

"Big Al, good to see you." When I look up into Scott's face I'm surprised to see his smile is wider than I've ever seen it before. So much so, there are small wrinkles forming next to his eyes.

Whoever this Big Al is, Scott seems to adore him.

"How's Annabel?" Big Al claps Scott on the shoulder, laughing as he leads us to our table.

Scott squeezes my hand. "Still married, Big Al."

The older man looks at me, winking. "His mother is the one that got away. I always told her that I was better for her than Mason but alas, she claimed she loved him." He looks back at Scott as he shakes his head and says, "Your father can't even cook!"

Scott pulls my chair out and I sit, laughing at the exchange. Big Al tells us he'll bring over some wine and menus.

"So." I lean my elbows on the table, dropping my chin to rest on my hands. "Big Al?"

"This is my parent's favorite restaurant in Boston. They eat here every single time they're in town, even if the only time they have available is three in the afternoon."

I'm in serious danger of heart failure if he keeps saying things that make it skip beats. "Oh. That's ... well, that's adorable."

Scott hums and nods, eyes roaming over my face. He lifts a hand, stretching out to tuck a stray piece of hair behind my ear. "They'll probably drop dead from shock when I tell them I brought you here."

Another skip, this time accompanied with something lodging high in my throat. I swallow, staring at him. "You've told them about me?"

"I told them I met a girl in a bar."

"You've probably met a hundred girls in bars."

"Sure. But none that I've told my parents about."

Cue melting.

Cue me becoming a puddle on the floor, at his feet.

I lean over the table and take a sip from my water silently begging the heat in my face to calm down. The way he said it. The intense sincerity of his words. I completely, wholeheartedly believe him.

I stare at him, the green swirling in his eyes as the rest of the room blurs around us. It's becoming a habit of mine, blocking out the world when he's around. Pretending that no one else exists apart from him and I whenever he stares at me like this.

I break away from his gaze, watching as Big Al navigates the small number of tables in the space carrying our wine.

"What are they like? Your parents?" I ask him.

He doesn't hesitate. The smile on his face is brighter than I've probably ever seen it, reaching his eyes and creating those little crinkles in the creases. His love for them is written all over his face.

It's different to most men. I can see that instantly. Most men would shy away from showing so much emotion in the first few dates but not Scott. He's proud of his parents, of being their son.

It's so blatantly obvious it couldn't be more clear if I was hit over the head with it.

"They're great. They're—" He takes a deep breath, eyes falling to his lap for a moment before meeting mine again. "I'm so grateful for them, they're the best people in the world."

Something curls around my heart, aching deep in my chest coming to the surface. Not for the first time, questions on whether I would be saying the same of my own parents crawl up my throat.

A longing for them—to speak to them, to see them, to have them see me now—pulses beneath my skin. I suppress it.

"They sound wonderful. Well, your mom does if we take Big Al's word for it." I take the wine glass, now filled, and have a large sip. It dulls the ache.

"I'm adopted."

The wine lodges in my throat.

"Oh." I shake my head a little, completely caught off guard. I look up to find his eyes and it feels as though he is staring straight through me and into my soul. "Sorry, you caught me off guard."

He nods, the smile on his face still there. "I can tell. I guess that's why I love them so much. Because they didn't have to choose me but they did and I'm grateful."

"Do they live here? In Boston?" I know the answer is no, seeing as he hates it here so much.

Like I suspect, he shakes his head. "Nah, they're back in LA."

"Is that where you grew up?"

He hums. "Yeah. Since I was five. Grew up in the same house they live in now even though it's far too large for them both since I've been gone. But they're the sentimental type so they refuse to move."

He shakes his head, smiling and remembering whatever memory that's popped into his head. I smile along with him as I imagine a small dark-haired toddler running around a garden. It is harder to reconcile the large man in front of me with the images in my head but it works.

"Will you tell me about your childhood?" I take another sip of my wine.

"Sure. What do you want to know?"

I look up at him. He is so genuine, so honest about his parents. So open about being adopted. Yet I sit here not wanting to share anything about mine because how do you admit that your childhood was spent angry, and upset, and confused as to why your parents weren't there on the first day of school. Why my grandfather turned up to the daddy-daughter days at school, or why my grandmother was the one to get me my first bra (although I'm not sure I'd share that story with Scott anyway).

I avoid the subject of his job and where he works. I don't want to talk about football or anything close to it. I don't want to have to battle with the emotions that arise anytime I do.

There's a chance if we get into his job, and he actually talks about it, we might get into my connection to football. Getting into my connection will drag up the past and I do not want to think about it.

I shake my head a little, almost as if I am physically trying to stop the spiral I'm about to go down and focus back on Scott.

Chapter Nine

Scott

Three weeks, three more official dates.

More than three nights on Ivy's couch, popcorn or chips between us and a movie on the TV. Many, many more than three kisses hello ... and goodnight ... and just for the hell of it.

I've never felt more like a horny teenager. Even when I was one. Ivy has me wrapped up in her orbit like no other woman before. If I'm not on the field, I am with her. If I'm not in the gym, watching tape, sleeping (still in my own bed) I'm with her. Or I'm thinking about her.

The week after our dinner at Big Al's, I took her bowling.

I rented out the place again during the lunch hours on a Saturday because I had to fly out for a game that night. She slaughtered me in all three rounds, devoured half the pizza we'd ordered and celebrated every pin bowled down like she'd just won the fucking Super Bowl.

She might hate football but she is a natural at sports.

Though I'll never admit that to her.

Mini golf, bowling. I have a feeling she could pick up anything easily. Not for the first time, I've questioned whether she had some sort of athletic blood running through her.

I'm itching to take her out on the field. Get to throw a ball from the fifty-yard line with her right next to me. Watch her marvel from the middle of the field. See her in my world. There is something in me that just knows that she belongs there.

It's instinctual.

But she won't entertain a conversation about sports longer than to ask me briefly about work and then she'll move on. I don't push. I know I have to tell her the truth about my job. We are way past 'it just never came up' territory.

The more I find out about her, the more I know, the less I want to taint it with the whole 'by the way, I play the sport you seem to hate so much and I'm kind of a big deal playing it' topic.

So I steer clear hoping that when the time comes, she will know enough of who I am without football to not care who I am with it.

Since taking her bowling, I've spent most nights on Ivy's couch, her curled up on my chest and rewatching *Friends* or trying to stay awake for a whole movie.

Something she has so far only managed once.

The other times I've gently lifted her into my arms and carried her to bed.

No matter how much I want to get in beside her, I've made a promise to myself that before we go any further than making out like horny teenagers she needs to know who I am.

Blue balls be damned. My left hand would have to do until I work up the courage to confess.

The week after bowling, I took her back to the Taco truck.

I paid the owner a little extra to post on their socials that they would be closed so we could be alone. They played some slow, acoustic music from the truck and I'd done something I've never done before—I pulled her up from the table to slow dance under the stars.

Her head rested on my chest, her hand intertwined with mine. I held her tightly against me, fingers buried in the fabric of her dress.

I never, ever imagined pulling that move with anyone. I've seen it in movies I watched with my mom and while she'd gone all gooey at the scene I always questioned the authenticity factor. I hadn't believed a moment like that would ever present itself in the real, living world.

Yet there I was.

A woman sitting across from me and a plate of tacos between us when the music drifted around us like a light breeze. I'd moved without thinking. We came together without saying anything. She'd let out a quiet gasp when I pulled her to her feet and into my arms but the sigh of contentment that came when she was safely fitted to my chest was all I needed to know that I made the right move.

We danced, swaying from side to side, for the better half of an hour before she leant back in my arms, tilting her head up and pushing up on her toes.

I've come to learn this is how she silently asks me to kiss her and I always, *always* oblige.

Tonight, I'm taking her to the movie theater.

I called ahead, asked for their quietest session time in the evening and booked two tickets to the romantic comedy she's been talking about wanting to see. I have the tickets on my phone and my cap is as low as it can be as we walk into the building.

I look like an asshole wearing my cap so low inside while checking for paparazzi every few minutes over my shoulder.

But her hand is tucked into mine and she walks as close as she can without tripping. I've learned that she likes physical affection, Ivy. Not too much PDA but she prefers to always have some sort of connection whether it be holding my hand or having my hand on her back or around her shoulders when walking. When we lay on the couch, her legs are always twisted into mine and her head sits comfortably between my shoulder and my collarbone.

Luckily, my research has paid off and the movie theater is pretty much empty.

"I'm just going to use the bathroom before we go in. I can get the popcorn when I get back, because you paid for the tickets," she says playfully, picking up the discussion we were having on the way over about her paying for the candy.

I simply nod, knowing full well that I am going to buy it while she's in the bathroom. I watch her walk away from me for a second before I make my way to the kid standing behind the counter.

His bored expression brightens into amazement as soon as I get close enough, "Holy … holy shit. You're Scott Harvey."

That is exactly what I'm afraid of.

"Sure am." I throw a quick glance toward the bathroom before leveling the kid with a serious look. "I'm here with my girl tonight, trying to stay low key. Can you help with that?"

Thankfully, the kid is more than eager to help. He hurries to get the popcorn and M&Ms I know Ivy wants but won't ask for and I pay. Spotting a pen on the register, I reach over to grab it and one of the napkins that is sitting on the counter. I scribble my signature, sliding it over to the kid. "Appreciate it."

He nods, taking the napkin in his hand like I just passed over a hundred dollar note.

I meet Ivy before she can make it to the counter, worried she'll question why the kid is watching me so closely looking like he might cry, and steer her toward the theater.

Tonight might be too close of a call.

Still, when she lifts the armrest between us about fifteen minutes into the movie and then proceeds to curl into my side the anxiety of the kid outing me seeps away.

Just like any negative emotion tends to do when Ivy is touching me.

She sighs and laughs, and brings a few M&Ms to her mouth every so often, but she never leaves my side. After the movie, I keep her tucked into me as we walk back to the car and I lead her to the passenger side, opening her door to the SUV and helping her in.

When we get to her house, I kiss her against her front door for at least thirty minutes before letting her slip inside.

***

Just thinking about the flavor of Ivy and her lips has me itching to see her again.

"You have a dopey ass look on your face, man. Thinking about Ivy?" Flynn's voice cuts through my thoughts and the towel he throws hits my shoulder before falling to my feet.

"Shut up."

He grins. "No way. You're so into this girl, I've never seen you like this before."

I reach into my bag for my phone, glancing at the notifications and pretending it doesn't bother me that Ivy hasn't texted me back yet.

"So ..." Flynn smirks, glancing around the locker room at the few dwindling teammates left after the game. We won but it was a hell of a game. A few of the wives had flown in to watch the game so most of the team were headed out for dinner with them all. The perks of playing a Sunday afternoon game. "Have you told her who you are yet?"

"Yes." I have. Technically. She asked my last name and I told her.

Flynn raises an eyebrow. "Oh? And?"

"She was ... fine."

"And you sealed the deal finally?" he questions. I scowl as I pick up the towel he threw earlier and pitch it back at him.

Smug bastard.

Flynn's smile only grows wider.

He studies my expression for a beat, and try as I might he's known me since college and knows when I'm hiding something or lying.

He used to tell me to 'go get some' whenever I started being too harsh on the field or in practice because he could tell I needed to relax and work out some frustration.

The bastard is annoyingly perceptive for such a man whore.

His eyes shine and seeing that look on his face makes me groan. He knows. I turn away because I'll be damned if I have to face whatever fucked up comment he's about to come out with.

"Woah. This Ivy must be some girl." I can practically hear his smile widen. I hope it stretches his face and gives him wrinkles. "Imagine knowingly dating one of the number one quarterbacks in the country and still not having sex with him. What's wrong with you, Scotty? Trouble downstairs?"

His own laughter fills the now empty locker room, and when I glance back at him over my shoulder I see him doubled over and wiping tears from his eyes.

At least he makes himself laugh.

"No, you asshat." I grab another towel lying on the bench, twisting the fabric in my hands while Flynn continues to be

doubled over, distracted by his own laughter. "We're just …
taking this slow."

"Taking … taking things slow?" he says through bursts of
laughter. He looks up at me, wiping under his eyes again.

"Yes." I keep the twist in my hands ready.

Flynn's laughter sobers up. He regards me for a second and
then his eyes narrow.

"When you told her who you are … did you tell her who you
actually are or are you trying to get off on some technicality?"
His questions suddenly become serious.

I swallow, the towel pulling taunt in my hands. "I told her …
my last name."

He groans, standing up so he's eye to eye with me and before
I know it, he slaps the back of my head. I flinch but release the
towel, slapping it against his thigh.

"Bro. Ow." He rubs his leg and backs up. "You *have* to tell
her!"

"I know. I know."

"You know that before you can go any further with her, you
need to come clean. Because if you sleep with her, and then tell
her, she'll be like mad, mad."

I drop my forehead against the locker, eyes closing and as if
on cue, Ivy's beautiful and perfect face fills it.

"I know."

Fuck.

***

I can hear her shuffling down the hallway, probably annoyed that someone's gone ahead and interrupted her night. Not that I care. We flew in this morning and I don't have training tomorrow. I want to see her.

So damn it, I'm going to see her.

I've started to think of my life before coming to Boston as *before Ivy*. Not before the Broncos, not before moving, but always *before Ivy*.

A Monday night off before her was spent firmly sitting on the couch and watching the Monday night football game like the rest of the football crazed nation. It's much too early to admit that life is starting to revolve around her but I can't seem to stop it happening.

The door in front of me cracks open and her beautiful, confused face appears in the gap.

"Scott? What—" She pulls the door open further and I drink her in.

She wears sweatpants that are at least two sizes too big, rolled at the waist and dragging along the floor. Her tank top crops at her stomach and I'm caught off guard by the powerful desire to wrap my fingers around her waist just to feel how soft her skin would be under my rough hands. It's softer than butter. Her voice pulls me out of my thoughts.

"What are you doing here?"

"I got back this morning, went to the gym, and then was sitting at home." I lean my forearm against the doorframe, towering over her and into her space. She's taken over every inch of my mind lately, only fair that I try to take over hers. "But I didn't want to sit at home. I wanted to see you."

"Oh." Her lips form the perfect O shape, the word coming out soft and breathy. God, this girl.

"Yeah, oh."

"You wanted to see me?" she clarifies.

"Sure did."

I watch her throat as she swallows, as her tongue wets her lips. I follow the movement as she pulls her bottom lip between her teeth. I lift my free hand, leaning further into her space and tug it free.

"Hi." I breathe, my lips inches from hers.

This gets me a small smile. "Hi."

She leans forward, just the tiniest bit but it's all I need. My lips drop onto hers and I take her next breath as my own, kissing her until her hands are curled into my hair and my hands curl tightly around her waist.

When she pulls back from me, she is breathless and her eyes close for a moment. She looks up at me asking, "Come inside?"

"I was hoping you'd ask that." I let my hands drop to my side, grazing against her stomach a little as I make my way inside. When my fingers skim across hers, I tangle them together and pull her with me down the corridor.

She trails behind me, allowing me to easily pull her along as she rambles. "I was just watching *Friends* but we can watch something else, if you want."

I think about the list in her phone, the one I tried to memorize so I can bookmark all the movies on there. "We could knock another movie off that list you started."

"How did you know about the list?" She narrows her eyes.

I laugh. "Oh, so there is a list?"

"Well … yes."

"Then let's watch one of those?"

"How do you know about the list, Harvey?" Glaring playfully at me as I fall back into the couch, pulling her with me. I want her wrapped around me. I want to be wrapped up in her.

"I saw you adding to it the other night when we were at the movies. You saw two romantic comedy trailers and opened it up to add them." I dig my fingers into her sides gently, loving the way she squirms in my grip before I let up and she just relaxes back into me. "I'll go see those with you, too. If you want."

Ivy turns her head to stare up at me for a moment, a soft smiling settling on her lips as she arches a little, stretching back to kiss me. I met her halfway.

When she sits forward, Ivy opens her phone.

"*Murder Mystery*," she says quietly like she's confirming with herself. She finds the film on Netflix and settles back into me.

She curls, shifting her position so she's tucked more into my side rather than leaning back against my chest. Her leg goes over mine and she stuffs a hand into my hoodie's pocket before laying her head on my shoulder, the movie titles rolling.

"I'm glad you didn't want to sit at home," she whispers.

"Me too."

Somewhere toward the second half of the film I feel the fist that is still tucked in my hoodie pocket clench, scrunching the fabric between her fingers. My eyes are focused on the screen but I can't tell you what is going on in the film. I've been reciting the starting lineup for the Celtics for the last ten minutes trying to keep my hard on from growing any further.

I swear, it started as innocent touching. I rested a hand on the leg that was thrown over my own. Then my thumb moved, tracing the soft fabric of her sweat pants. It was about then that I'd stopped paying attention to the movie.

Ivy's body is a dream. My hand follows an invisible path from her thigh, over the curve of her ass. My fingers splay over the fabric of her sweat pants, digging into the soft flesh a little. I love the way my hands feel on her body, that she's got more to hold, more to touch.

I run a hand over her ass again, not being about to resist giving it a playful, but gentle smack.

"Stop it. You're distracting me," Ivy whispers. I don't need to look down at her to know there is a smile on her face.

Who gives a crap about what Adam Sandler is doing when I know just how soft the skin is under my hands?

Jennifer Aniston has nothing on Ivy Booker. Not to me.

Fuck.

I meet Ivy's eyes. Her fist is still clutching the hoodie but I don't move the hand that has drifted up her leg to the crest of her ass. I look down at her, eyes flicking between her lips. Her tongue darts out and wets her lips. I can't help it.

Movie be damned.

I lean down and capture her lips with mine. The kiss isn't slow or teasing. It is hard and messy and desperate. This girl has me wrapping my free hand around the nape of her neck, pulling her up my body and closer to me. I dig my fingers into the soft curve of her ass and tug. She falls completely across my lap and I keep tugging, not stopping until she settles there.

A groan rumbles from deep within my chest as she rolls her hips against mine. A small, delicious whimper escapes her mouth as I pull away. I lift my hands, running my fingers through her hair. It's so damn soft.

Everything about her is soft.

Her skin, her body, her lips, her hair.

Her.

I run my mouth along her jaw. She arches in my lap, her large breasts pressing into my chest. I curse my decision to wear a hoodie because if it wasn't for the thick fabric, I'm sure I would be able to feel her hard nipples against my chest.

Another whimper comes from her throat and my hands fall to her hips, fingers slipping under the fabric of her sweatpants and digging into her skin. I move her against me and she responds instantly, grinding down on my lap.

"Fuck," I murmur into her neck. Her hands press into my chest, resting back a little.

I meet her eyes to find the challenge written as clear as day in them. She smirks, her hands fisting the fabric of my hoodie again and tugging. I don't hesitate, reaching behind my head and yanking the fabric off my body.

My t-shirt goes with it.

My hands slide up her waist. My fingers splay out, dipping under the crop top she's wearing. My thumbs brush the underside of her breasts, curving over the swell of them and to their peaks.

Ivy smiles.

I circle a thumb around one hard nipple and press down. Her mouth falls open a little and she sighs, the pleasure radiating in waves of heat from her skin. Fuck, but I want to suck on her tits so badly. I want to map them out with my tongue, not just my fingers. She falls forward, her lips coming back to mine.

I let her nibble and suck and take control. My hands explore her body, content with mapping out her firm, full breasts.

Another whimper, another groan. She rolls her hips against mine and there's no way to hide the hardness now.

My hands slip, fingering the edge of her sweats. I pull back from her mouth, kissing the corner once more, and catch her gaze.

"Can I?" The rasp in my voice is deep and I lick my lips in anticipation. Fuck, did I want to taste her. Have her shaking, and moaning, and calling out my name beneath me.

A small voice, sounding oddly like Flynn, suddenly breaks through.

Tell her first. Stop and tell her.

But then with the pull of her bottom lip between her teeth and a definitive nod from Ivy, the voice dies. A smirk lifts on my lips and I dive into her neck, sucking and nipping at the skin. I inhale, fingers dipping under the waistband and between her legs.

She's so fucking wet.

My fingers slip through her as I coat them, gently caressing her. I swear, I could get high on just her alone.

A loud ringing breaks us apart. Ivy jumps in my arms, flinching at the interruption. I pull my hand back, just a little, finding the soft crease where her hip meets thigh. She hesitates for a moment, adjusting on my lap as she leans back. Her fingers scrape down my bare chest as she hovers over me, eyes on her ringing phone, lighting up on the side table.

I lift my hand, trailing my fingers up her side to stroke her cheek as the expression in her face shifts from heated to fearful.

"What?" I ask, fingers stroking her soft skin. "What is it? Who's calling?"

Ivy crawls from my lap, not answering me. She snatches her phone from the side table, bringing it to her ear. "Hello?"

The muffled voices drift out from her phone and I stiffen, sitting up beside her. Ivy slumps as she listens. "What do you mean?"

Another pause, more muffled voices.

"How ... how did that happen? Is he ... yes. I'll come now. Thank you." The last of her words are nothing more than choked sobs. I watch as she slumps, the hand holding her phone to her ear slumping by her side in defeat, her eyes filling with tears.

"Ivy?" I ask her, worry and panic filtering through me as I sit up, reaching for her. I lift my hands, and place one on her cheek and the other on her collarbone trying to get her attention.

"I–I'm sorry but I have to … go," she hiccups. Then she's scrambling. Falling over her feet.

I stand and steady her, my hand wrapping around her elbow.

"Hey, hey, hey." She tries to get herself free, tears filling up her eyes. My heart aches as I tighten my grip. "Ivy, look at me."

She stills, her chest heaving, but she looks up just as the tear finally rolls down her cheek. Everything in me breaks for her. I wipe it away, asking quietly, "What's happened?

"My pops. He–he fell in the shower … they said he lost con-sciousness … that he wasn't breathing for a bit …" she sobs. I pull her into my chest. Her next words are muffled sobs against my chest as I run a hand up and down her back, trying to calm her a little. "I can't lose him. I can't."

Her panic seems to settle something inside me and I take control. I press a kiss into her hair before peeling her away from my chest. I don't let her go as I move us down the hall, picking up my shirt and hoodie from the floor as we go. In the entryway, I sit her on the small bench that has a number of pairs of shoes lined underneath. Taking a pair of tennis shoes that I've seen her wear before so I know they're hers, I kneel down onto my knee.

She clutches my shoulders, leaning her weight into me as I slip each of the shoes on one at a time.

Tying off her laces, I look up at her asking, "Where's your purse? Do you need to take anything specific with you?"

She looks at me without saying anything. Her eyes watery and her fingers trembling as they clutch the fabric of my shirt. She shakes her head.

I'm searching my brain desperately for a way that I can make this better for her, that I can reassure her but she doesn't talk about the health problems her Pops has. He's a frequent figure in her stories and her memories that she shares from when she was younger but she never really touches on why he's in hospital.

I look up into her face, tucking a piece of hair that fell loose across her face behind her ear, and whisper, "Let me help."

She sucks in a breath, holding it in her chest for a beat before finally, she nods.

CHAPTER TEN
SCOTT

THE AIR IN THE car is stifling. Ivy is curled up in the passenger seat.

She doesn't speak. I don't try to make her.

Halfway to the hospital I reach over and splay my hand across her knee. My thumb gently rubbing against the soft fabric of her sweatpants.

I turn into the carpark and she directs me to the best place for us to park. As soon as we are stationary, I walk around the car and pull her door open. She slowly uncurls her body, stepping down from the car and into my side.

I leave her for a moment. Opening the back door of the SUV, I rifle through my training bag and take out the spare Broncos sweatshirt before slamming the door shut again.

I pull it over Ivy's head, shutting the car door behind her as she threads her arms through it.

Putting my arm around her shoulders, I tuck her small body into mine and guide her towards the main entrance of the hospital.

It is late. Visiting hours are obviously over and the only people in the halls are the staff. Most cluster around the different nurse stations we pass. Ivy gently guides our path to the elevator. When the doors chime open on the fourth floor, I drop my arm and let her step in front of me so she can lead the way now.

She doesn't get more than a few small steps before she pauses, her hand flying out behind her. She reaches for me. I catch up in one stride and thread my fingers through hers. Her grip tightens around my hand as she leads us to the room her grandfather resides in.

I have never really liked hospitals. I've been injured a few times throughout my career and the heavy bleach scent that clings to the air always makes my nose itch and my eyes water. I wonder how Ivy can possibly handle this, sitting in a brightly lit room for a whole day. But then, I've always been the patient. My parents' parents all passed when I was little. My parents themselves were healthy and any minor procedures they've had never required me to be at a hospital with them for long.

I glance down at Ivy as she slows her pace. I watch her chest rise and fall with each deep breath as she gulps down air. I squeeze her hand, pulsing our fingers together once and then twice. We reach the end of the corridor and Ivy pushes through the last door on the left. The bed is empty and only half the lights are on. A man in a dark blue scrub set stands, writing notes on a whiteboard that sits below a TV mounted on the opposite wall to the bed.

"Dr. Bryden?" Ivy's small voice echoes through the silent room.

The old doctor jerks back from the board, inhaling as if we surprised him. "Ivy. My god, sorry sweetheart but you scared me." Bryden looks to be in his mid-fifties, closer to sixty. He has white hair and wrinkles litter his face. The way he looks at Ivy with sympathy brewing in his eyes tells me that they are well acquainted with each other. This must be her Pops' regular doctor.

"What happened?" she asks, her voice shaking.

"Sit down, Ivy." He replies with another kind smile. "Who's this?" Bryden looks at me. He scans my face and a small flicker of recognition flashes in his eyes. I send up a silent prayer that he keeps whatever questions forming about me and who I am to himself.

Tonight is not the time for that particular conversation.

Ivy moves over to the bed, pulling me with her by our intertwined hands. "This is Scott. He's ... uh ... a friend?" She stares up at me as I sit next to her. I can't help the smirk that stretches across my mouth. Just by looking at her I can see the wheels turning, the questions that have nothing to do with her pops or why we're here racing in her head. A momentary distraction from the awful to fret about who she is to me.

Who I am to her.

This girl doesn't even know what she does to me.

A friend? Sure.

None of my other friends make me impossibly hard the way she does by just pursing those perfect lips of hers. None of the other friends I have kiss me like they're trying to steal every last ounce of air from my lungs the way she does.

No, I'm not just her friend.

But again, now is not the time for that conversation.

"Scott Harvey," I say, getting up from my seat next to Ivy's and holding my hand out to shake Bryden's. His eyes widen and his jaw drops, just a little. I quickly take my seat back on the bed and snake an arm around Ivy, pulling her close again. I redirect the topic to the reason we're here. "Can you tell us what happened?"

Dr. Bryden sighs, leaning against the blank bit of wall next to the whiteboard he was writing on when we came in. There's tiny writing of red letters, *O-R-7* written across the top and then three other doctors' names below.

"Billy was taking a shower earlier this evening. Something he's been relatively independent at so far. The nurses have told me that apart from the first day he was here, they haven't needed to assist him in going to the bathroom or showering more than helping him out of bed and getting his things set up in the bathroom," he explains.

Ivy leans further into me, her head resting against my shoulder as she listens. I tighten my hold around her shoulders.

"We think he slipped on some water getting out of the shower because the water hadn't been running when the nurses found him. He wouldn't have been out more than a minute, less even.

The girls check on his room pretty regularly. They love him." He offers Ivy another one of his smiles before continuing. "The fall caused a small brain bleed and he broke a rib or two upon landing. He was being rushed to emergency surgery as we called you in. He'll be in there a few more hours but I'm confident they'll stop the bleeding."

Ivy sniffles beside me and I shift my attention to her face. A few tears roll in tracks down her cheeks. My hand lifts, a thumb brushing them away.

"Is he going to be okay?" Ivy asks in a small voice.

"I suspect he will be just fine. Rattled, but fine." Bryden pushes off the wall and comes to stand in front of us, placing a gentle hand on Ivy's shoulder.

"But," he says, taking a deep breath like he's preparing for a fight. "Ivy, we've talked about this before. Billy is old. He's getting more and more fragile. This is simply the latest incident in a long line of them. You need to start making plans for long term, end of life care."

She starts to shake her head furiously, back and forth, pushing herself away from Bryden. Away from me. She stands moving around the bed and over to the window, arms wrapping around herself. When she turns her back and her shoulders start to shake with the silent sobs wracking through her body, I stand too.

"Ivy," Bryden continues, "I wouldn't say this if it wasn't true. I've been Billy's doctor for a long time and I know he hates to show it, but he's old. He's dying. It's time to come to terms with that."

She doesn't turn around and she doesn't answer. Her phone buzzes a few times as she turns it over and over in her hands. The way that Bryden looks over at her, the way his eyes soften and his sad smile is still stretched across his mouth tells me he's had this conversation with her before. He sighs again. "I will let you know when I have more updates. You can wait here if you're going to stay, otherwise if you want to head home I will call you when I know more."

"I'll ..." she hiccups. "I'm staying."

"Okay. Let me or one of the nurses know if you need anything. I'm going to stay until the surgeons have given the all clear."

Her phone buzzes for the fifth time in less than a minute. She glances at the screen and types out a reply before setting it back on the side of the couch.

I know it's probably Katie again. Ivy's best friend has been messaging non-stop since she let her know that we were coming here. Katie has been messaging her nonstop.

Should she come to the hospital? No, Ivy had replied.

Are you alone? Also, no.

Is Pops alive? Yes. Barely.

I stand quietly behind her. She's still shaking.

"Ivy, baby," I whisper in her ear. I take her shoulders and pull her gently back toward the couch. "Sit down."

She doesn't protest and lets me pull her down to the couch. Her body curls into mine and her head rests easily on my shoulder.

She's quiet for a while. I keep thinking she might fall asleep but then her phone buzzes and her eyes peel open. I wish I could tell Katie to knock it off. My girl needs sleep. She's strong as hell but she's tired.

We haven't heard anything about how the surgery is going yet and it's been over an hour, at least. My legs are stiff. The arm that's wrapped around Ivy has gone numb and the fingers that draw small, gentle patterns on her arm works automatically. I flex the fingers on my free hand in an effort to keep them awake.

Even in the moments when her eyes are closed, the tears still leak from beneath the closed lids. I lift my free hand to gently brush them away whenever they do. Every so often her body will start to convulse and she'll gasp for air, like she stopped breathing but didn't notice and it suddenly catches up with her.

She hasn't said a word since Dr. Bryden left us here alone. The nurses rotate in every so often, checking in on her when they can. She doesn't respond and I just say a quiet "no, thank you" for her whenever they come in.

Her phone buzzes again and I instinctively want to reach for it first so I can tell Katie to shut the fuck up with the texts but the buzzing keeps going. Someone is calling. Ivy lifts the screen so she can see who it is and I glimpse the name. The air empties from my lungs and an invisible band tightens around my chest.

Jeff Brady displays across the screen accompanied by a photo of her standing beside my coach. My head coach.

What the fuck?

Ivy swipes a finger across the screen, answering the call before putting the phone to her ear. "Hi, Uncle Jeff."

What.

The.

Fuck.

Uncle Jeff?

Why the hell is she calling Coach, Uncle Jeff?

Are they related? Fuck, this is bad. This is so bad. How did I not know there is a connection between them?

Jeff has picture frame after picture frame of his family in his office. I remember studying them intently the day I flew into Boston to discuss terms of my deal with him. His assistant had let me wait in his office to avoid being seen and to avoid the news that I was chatting to other teams being leaked.

I waited for a full ten minutes for Coach and while I waited, I had nothing better to do other than study the photos that littered the large bookshelves lining his office.

Not one of those photos was of Ivy. Not one. I would remember.

At least, I think I would remember.

"I'm okay." Her whisper down the phone breaks me from my mental spiral. "He's still in surgery."

Ivy's gaze wanders upwards and locks with mine. Her eyes are red rimmed and watery. The blue is impossibly deep. Like the infinite depths of the middle of the ocean. A storm brews in the form of another wave of tears as she nods along with whatever Jeff is telling her on the other end of the line.

Slowly, she unravels herself and stands from the couch. The nerves in my body ripple and the limbs that were numb a moment ago are assaulted with the feeling of pins and needles. I ignore the feeling, my gaze watching Ivy as she paces from one end of the room to the other. She stares at her feet with the phone still pressed against her ear.

"Damn it," she sighs, her shoulders slumping. "How did they find out?"

She's silent again as she listens, her head tilting toward the ground as she tucks her chin and stares at the floor. As I watch, her eyes close and a few new tears roll down her cheeks. I move to the edge of the couch, stretching out my legs. Ivy nods her head again asking, "How long do you think until they surround the hospital?"

She lifts her head. Our gazes meet and she stares, an apology written all over her face. What the hell is she sorry for? What is Coach saying?

I almost lose my mind and tell her to put him on speaker. Instead, I clench my jaw and keep my mouth firmly shut.

"Okay, thank you for the heads up." She sucks in a breath. "I will let you know as soon as I know. Thanks, Uncle Jeff."

Uncle Jeff.

Again.

I wait for a beat before speaking. She tucks her phone back in her bag that sits on the floor and I use her momentary distraction to unclamp my jaw and swallow the lump in my throat. She straightens, turning back to me.

"Who was that?" I ask, feeling like an absolute dickhead for asking even though I know exactly who was on the other side on the line.

"My uncle. Well, he's not really my uncle." She crosses the room, coming to stop in front of my seat on the couch. Her foot taps mine. I open my legs a little further and she moves forward to stand between them.

"Not really your uncle?" I press. My hands land on her hips when she gets close enough and I can't help but slip my fingers beneath the fabric of her sweatpants that cling to her hips.

"I have to tell you something." She chews on her bottom lip. Her fingers lift to skim across my shoulders and an apology is written all over her face. Another time—one that isn't plagued by this hospital trip and the fact my coach just rang her—I'll remember to tease her about how easy she is to read.

"My family is sort of ... football royalty."

As if the sound is delayed, her words hit me late and my brain turns them over a few times. And then, it's running a million miles an hour.

Shit.

"You're ... you're what?" I ask her, my brain reeling from the football sized bomb just dropped. If she is 'football royalty' as she put it, how does she not know who I am? How could she possibly be oblivious to my job? My part in the team?

"My pops was a quarterback for the Broncos, years ago but he is kind of a legend. He's been inducted into the hall of fame and everything. Billy Booker? I'm sure working for the team you've probably heard of him." Her fingertips press into my shoulders, like she doesn't want me to get up or leave her while she explains.

Billy Booker is familiar.

I know the name. I know who she's talking about. A framed picture of his Super Bowl winning team hangs in the corridor at the training facility.

"Billy Booker is your pops?" I'm not sure why I need the clarification but my brain can't seem to string more than that sentence together.

"My dad was a D1 athlete too. He died before the draft happened but it was rumored he would've been picked up by the Broncos too. It's why I don't like watching football. It ... it just hurts watching and knowing he missed out. And, that I missed out on him."

"Matty Booker is your dad?" I ask. A faint memory of my parents taking me to a college ball game in LA when I was younger hits me. I saw him play. I saw her dad play.

"I ... wow. Okay."

"I'm sorry," she whispers. "I should've told you. Now the press knows about Pops and that he's in surgery. They'll be turning up at the hospital within the hour to cover the story.

Uncle Jeff said he's going to try and call someone to clear them but it's only going to get worse before it gets better. My family's story is going to be everywhere. Anytime something happens with Pops they bring it all up again and I have to avoid the TV for weeks." She twists her fingers into my hoodie's fabric as she rambles.

My lungs feel like they fill with lead and I suck in a breath that hardly helps. Shit. She feels bad and my lie is way worse.

I know that I should probably use this time to tell her who I am. We're talking about football for the first time since that time in the alley at the bar. I could just … tell her. Easy.

But the way she stares down at me, tears once again threatening to spill over, stops me.

Soon.

Not yet.

"Hey." I stand up, taking her face between my hands and thumbing her cheek to wipe away the fresh tears. "You have nothing to be sorry about. The paps don't scare me. The fact you're Boston football royalty doesn't scare me."

She nods. "Okay."

"Jeff is Jeff Brady, right?" I ask, wanting to confirm my suspicion that Coach is the one she was talking to. She cocks her head, eyes burning with the question of how I know that. I shrug. "I work for the team. I know who Jeff is."

"Right," she whispers. She lifts a hand to wipe at her cheeks but I beat her to it, smoothing the skin under a gentle caress of my thumb. Even when glistening with tears, her skin is smooth and soft.

My dick twitches in my pants. Fucking hell. Obviously my brain forgot to send the message that now is not the time.

I sigh, dropping my forehead to hers and closing my eyes. She takes a few deep breaths. I trace my fingers gently from her cheeks down her neck, over the curve of her shoulder and down her arms. I can't help but notice the way my fingers sink into her soft waist. It's automatic for my hands to land here. I love the feel of her under my touch.

All of me loves it, it seems.

In my head, I start listing my teammates and their positions as I tell her, "It's going to be okay. He'll be fine."

"I hate when they bring it all up again," she tells me quietly. "They camp outside the house hounding me for quotes about Pop's and my dad, and they even want comments on the current team. Like I give a rat's ass about a bunch of players I don't even know."

My body convulses, a small shake ripping through me as I choke on a laugh. Even with the tears on her face freshly dried and the shivers of her body only just subsiding from her grief, she's fiery. Determined.

I like her more than I should for someone I've only known for a few weeks.

"What about Jeff?" I ask before I can stop myself. I have to know how she's related to him. I don't know all that much about Coach's family life, haven't really found myself caring all that much about football so far this season thanks to the bombshell currently in my arms, so all I know is that he's married with some kids.

He could be her real uncle.

Fuck, was I dating Coach's niece?

Shit.

"—my dad's old coach from college. Practically family." She finishes, pulling away from me. She barely takes a step away from grasp before I reel her back in.

"Huh?"

She cocks her head, lifting an eyebrow. "You asked a question and then didn't even listen to the answer."

There is a small smile teasing her lips so I smirk, lifting a shoulder in a shrug. This time, she giggles and I swear that half the weight I've been carrying since she started to cry lifts instantly.

"He used to coach my dad in college and his kids are around the same age as me, older though. He was really there for my parents when they got pregnant with me in their freshman year of college, lived on the same street for ages and then, he ended up getting the Broncos coaching gig. He was always begging to have Pops over for barbecues when I was growing up. Started because Uncle Jeff mainly wanted to pick Pops' football brain but they ended up becoming really close."

"So he's family?" I ask.

"Yeah. He's family."

Well, at least they aren't blood related.

Sounds like he is a pretty big part of her life and regardless, the moment she tells him about me, I'll be outed.

Keeping my identity a secret was becoming too risky.

Still ...

Looking around at the hospital room—the dimly lit bathroom with its door just ajar, the bed in the middle that is piled with colorful blankets obviously brought from home by Ivy, the sad couch in the corner of the room we've been sitting on—I can still convince myself that today is not the day to tell her that I am one of the football players she doesn't give a rat's ass about.

So, I let myself be convinced.

The silence envelopes us once again but neither of us move from where we are standing. Ivy leans into me, head resting back on my shoulder and my arms pull tighter around her. She fits against my body like a glove. Like ...

Like she is made to fit me. Just me.

Ivy's phone buzzes on the table and she barely glances away from the hand of cards she is holding. In the last hour, I've discovered that there is probably nothing she is more competitive about than UNO.

After forty minutes and multiple hands, I'm starting to fear for my life every time I win. My girl is determined like nothing else to outsmart me during a hand of the children's card game.

We were sitting around, waiting to hear more news of either her Pops or the paparazzi frenzy beginning to populate outside when Ivy sighed and got to her feet. She got the card game from one of the drawers, pulled the roll away table between us and dealt out a hand.

Before today, the last time I played UNO was when I'd been a kid but I haven't laughed like this in a long time.

It is too hard to not laugh.

Every time I play a reverse, or a skip, or a draw four card, Ivy's little scowl burrows deeper. The crease between her brows drawing them closer and closer together, her eyes darting between the deck of cards between us and the ones in her hand furiously as she thinks about her next move.

Every time she gets to her last card she knocks so rapidly, so loudly on the roll away table between us that I'm scared it might collapse between us.

That doesn't mean I'm not afraid to give it my all when it comes to winning. It takes a few rounds at first but eventually my memory of the game catches up to me and I give her a run for her money.

Her eyes narrow, the phone still buzzing next to her as she watches the single card left in my hand with disgust. She is going to lose; she knows it and she hates the thought.

I am loving it.

Reveling in her competitive nature and riling her up, I glance at the phone and then back to her, meeting the hard gaze she's fixed me with. "You going to answer that? Saved by the bell it seems."

I wiggle my single card between my fingers, showing it off.

She scowls grumbling, "You wish."

Slowly, as if the card she's playing is made of glass, she puts the green five on the pile. She retracts her hand slowly, eyeing me.

I let my face fall with shock, trying to mix in a hint of disappointment and close my eyes slowly. For effect, I mutter under my breath, "Damn."

When I look up, Ivy has a look of triumph and elation on her face. Her eyes shine with victory and she knocks on the table in quick succession. "Uno," she calls out.

I shouldn't be toying with her but it's proving to be too much fun and making her laugh has quickly gone to the top of my priority list. I lift my free hand, reaching for the pack of cards facing down that we draw from each round. As she begins to beam, watching my hand as it draws nearer, I slap the draw four and color change card in my other hand down on the upturned pile, winning the game and crushing my girl's victory in its wake.

"What? No!" She looks back and forth between me and the card in disbelief and I can't help but laugh. Her face is as beautiful in defeat and confusion as it was just moments ago when she thought she was going to win and end my streak.

I mean, I like her, obviously, but I'm still a professional athlete.

You can't win Super Bowls by letting the other team win.

"Sorry, baby." I lean back in my seat, stretching my arms behind my head. "You should've seen your face though. You really thought you had me there."

"I did have you! I can't believe this." She shakes her head at me, a smile peeking through.

I lean across the table, swiping her cards and catching her gaze. When her navy eyes meet mine, I smirk and throw her a wink. "Maybe next time."

Her phone buzzes again, this time with a text. She sighs. "Great."

"What's wrong?" I ask, shuffling the cards in my hands.

She shakes her head. "I love him. I do. But Uncle Jeff wants to come here and it's only going to make the media circus brewing outside worse."

I stiffen. If Coach comes here, if he sees me with Ivy, it's over. Before I can think of something to say, she is already replying back, typing a message across the screen and setting her phone down.

She nods to the cards in my hand. "Okay, one more round before he gets here."

A lump forms in my throat, the cards still in my hands as I stare at her phone. Shit. Fuck. Shit, fuck, shit.

I'm screwed.

I have to tell her. It will be better coming from me now rather than Coach outing me when he gets here.

I swallow hard, licking my suddenly dry lips and gaze back at Ivy. I open my mouth, ready to tell her when a small knock sounds at the door. One of the nurses that has been checking in every so often peeks around the corner. "Ivy?"

"Yeah?" Ivy's head snaps up to the nurse.

There is so much hope in her voice as she looks at the nurse. I hope like hell that there is finally some good news. My confession is on the tip of my tongue but I wait, watching Ivy as the nurse speaks.

"Your pops is in recovery now. Would you like to see him?"

"Yes." Ivy jumps out of her seat; the cards forgotten. I follow her, grabbing my own phone, keys and wallet from where I left it on the couch.

The nurse nods. "I'll take you up now."

"Ives?" I say, my hand reaching out for hers before she can race after the nurse. "You go see your pops. I'm going to head home." It is the shit thing to do but this nurse is giving me an out. And I'm taking it. Like a coward.

"Oh."

I rub a palm over my chest. "Unless, you want me to—"

"Sorry, but it's family only in the recovery room." The nurse gives me a sad look, and then turns back to Ivy. "I'll be at the nurse's station when you're ready."

"Okay, thank you," she replies softly. Turning back to me, the disappointment from mere moments ago has lessened. "Thank you for coming with me."

I nod, stepping in closer to her and breathing in her scent. "You call me if you need anything, okay?"

She drops her head to my chest and my arms lift automatically to pull her tighter against me. "Okay."

It is a muffled word said into my hoodie. I drop a kiss into her hair, inhaling. When I pull back, so does she, raising her chin to look up at me. She lifts a little on her toes.

I kiss her goodbye and hope once she knows the truth, she doesn't hate me. Because right now, I'm hating myself enough for the both of us.

CHAPTER ELEVEN
IVY

"Ivy."

I fuss with the bed corner again, mumbling under my breath as I sweep a hand beneath the crisp sheet. They changed the sheets on Pops' bed whilst we were having a short walk around the hospital floor yet they still couldn't get the corners right.

I furiously swipe my hand along the crease, tucking the sheet between the heavy metal frame and the mattress.

"Ivy."

I'm ignoring Pops and his insistence on talking about last weeks' news cycle. I'm sick of seeing my face on ESPN. I'm sick of seeing Pops' face on ESPN. Mostly though, I'm sick of seeing my dad's.

The news had broken that Pops had gone into emergency surgery thanks to an old timer that was staying in the same ward. He'd been a big fan back in the day. He and Pops are roomed next door to each other and had apparently become friends. The old guy had seen Pops and called his daughter about the legendary Billy Booker going into surgery, she'd told her husband, who happened to be a reporter at one of the local papers.

It snowballed from there.

Soon enough, ESPN were knocking on the door and asking for comments from 'the family' left, right and center.

The 'family' being me. Just me.

"Ivy, stop it," Pops says again, leaning forward in the bed to brush my hands away from the already perfect sheet corner. I glare at him before smoothing out his blankets anyway and moving toward the couch where a basket of fresh laundry is sitting. I pick up a t-shirt, holding it up to fold it when Pops' voice rings through the room again, loud and harsh.

"Put the shirt down, Ivy Grace. Now."

I flinch. It is the same voice he always used when I'd gotten into trouble at school albeit, it wasn't all that often that I'd had to hear it.

"You should fold these so you don't get them mixed up with the dirty ones." I try to keep my voice light, calm. He wants to rehash the past and I am not in the mood for it.

"Come sit here," he says again, not as loud but still as scary as ever.

I sigh, dropping the shirt into the basket. I move over to the bed, sitting beside him as he settles back into the pillows. He leans over to the bedside for the remote, flicking on the television to *ESPN*.

Great.

"I want to talk about this week. You've been on edge and we both know why."

"I haven't been—" The look he gives me has me swallowing hard and my shoulders slumping. I change directions. "I don't want to talk about football. Not now. Not ever."

"I know you don't sweetheart but I think we should." Pops gives me a small smile. "This week has been intense. Have you been watching the stories on the news much?"

"It's been hard not to." I cringe glancing towards the screen.

It's Friday and the highlights they are playing look to be from last night's game. For once, my dad's face isn't glaring back at me.

It started after the news broke of just rehashing Pops' career. They dug up game highlights and old tapes. They talked about his impact as a quarterback in the sport and then in Boston. The local news picked up the story and, on what seemed to have been a very slow news day, they had decided to feature a two-night special just on the football legacy that was my family.

I love watching the local news. I like recognizing the places I've been to on the TV and I like keeping up to date with what's going on in the city that I live in. I often sit in front of the six o'clock news with a glass of wine and a pile of work, making my way through it while the newsreader does feel good stories on local activists or small business owners.

However, they ruined my nightly ritual last Monday when the opening story had a cover picture of my family; Pops, Nan, me, and my parents.

Where had they even got the photo?

It looked to be one that had been taken in my dad's sophomore year in college. I was a baby in my mother's arms. I suspect someone had sent it in from the university.

It definitely wasn't one of mine, not from the box I keep tucked safely under my bed.

The newsreader had deep dived into Pops' career with the Broncos, talked about his family life and raising his son. About raising me. They even touched on the lesser-known fact that Pops had a small ownership in the team, something I didn't even think was public knowledge but the station had done their research well it seemed.

Then after they'd played a five-minute-long highlight reel of Pops' games—similar to the one ESPN had played the night after Pops' surgery—they moved onto my dad.

Pictures of him in his high school football uniform had been splashed across my TV. Him holding a state trophy, him scoring a touchdown, him posing for the team picture surrounded by the team. A picture of him and my mom at the senior prom. They had been laughing on stage, the crowns of their prom king and queen awards sitting lopsided on their heads.

I have pictures of them at prom. I have one framed on my dresser.

But I didn't have that one.

When the picture came across the screen, it felt like a hand reached into my chest and squeezed my lungs.

There I was. Watching the evening news on a random Monday and seeing a picture of *my parents* for the first time along with the rest of the world. Tears welled in my eyes. My heart was beating violently in my chest and for some reason, I felt a surge of anger flow like voltage through my veins.

I almost threw my glass of wine at the TV.

It isn't fair that the rest of the world gets to see a piece of them I never have.

The newsreader interviewed an old teacher of my mom and dads' and she'd described them as still the most loved up young couple she'd seen in all her years of teaching. She spoke about my mom's dedication to learning and the ability she had to pull my dad's focus from the one thing he loved most: football. She'd told a story about them I'd never heard and it made the hole in my chest, the one that had been there since I'd been old enough to understand they were gone, ache for days.

The anger surged again and I turned off the TV, throwing the remote across the room.

The TV remote is still somewhere across the room. I haven't been bothered to retrieve it.

It's been a week.

A little dramatic?

Maybe, but I won't be forced to dwell on those emotions.

And I certainly am not going to be forced to talk about football.

Pops' hand squeezes mine, bringing my attention back to him. My eyes focus back on him and he sighs, seeing straight through my false calm expression.

"You saw the local piece then," he says.

"Why do they care so much about them? Why do they have to bring it up?"

"Because like you, your dad grew up here. He went to the high school you did. He went to college here. He made a big name for himself in high school and college football. The local news covered him all the time and some of the people that still work there remember him. They remember me. So when things like this happen to me, they want to comment."

"They don't have the right," I grunt.

Pops laughs lightly, his thumb rubbing across the back of my hand in comfort.

"They do though. Freedom of speech and all that. Besides, I thought the piece was nice. They said some lovely things about your mom and dad, your dad's career—"

"I hate football for making him famous."

Silence falls like a blanket of freshly fallen snow around us after my words. The air in the room cools. Pops sucks in a breath, sitting straighter with a small wince.

"Oh, Ivy." Pops' hand squeezes impossibly hard and he tries to pull me forward but I don't budge. "It's not football's fault, sweetheart. He loved the game and the game loved him. But more than anything he loved you and your mom with everything he had."

Pops' words aren't helping. I feel too raw, too emotionally exhausted after this week.

I feel numb.

A chill spreads down my spine, flowing through my veins and numbing the fingers that are still clutched tightly in Pops'. My eyes sting and I try desperately to blink away the tears.

I hate crying about this in front of Pops.

"Ivy." His voice is low and warm and filled with sadness. "Ivy, my girl."

I look up at him, the tears still stinging behind my eyes. Pops' eyes reflect the same deep navy as mine just as much as they reflect the pain.

He quietly says, "I failed you."

"What? How could you say that?"

"I have. You have this idea that football is the reason your dad passed away but the drunk driver on the snow-covered, dangerous roads did that. Football is the reason he still lives." I begin to shake my head, trying to pull my hands from his so I can wipe my cheeks. He doesn't let me, holding tighter as he continues. "Your dad gets to live on, not just through you but through football as well."

As each of the salty tears drop down my chin, streaking a path down my neck and making my skin sticky, I feel the cracks in my heart slash open a little deeper.

He was my dad.

He was supposed to be mine.

But instead, football had him longer and it tore me apart every time the local news decided to remind me of that.

"Ivy ... please, you have to move past this. You're holding onto a grudge with no merit. I used to think it was just a teenage phase, that you'd eventually move on and start watching the game with me again. I wanted to tell you about your dad on that field and share that world he loved so much with you."

My vision blurs, my eyes sting, my heart hurts.

"You know, there are so many things I want to tell you about him before I die. I haven't because I know how hard this has been but your dad? He was one of the best. You can remember and cherish him as your dad *and* you can love the game he loved as a player. The two aren't mutually exclusive," Pops tells me.

I feel like there isn't any air in the room to suck in a deep breath and can't steady myself properly.

I am done talking about this.

"I don't want to lose you, Pops. You're all I have."

"Ivy." Pops' shoulders drop. There's a slight scold in his tone at my attempt to change the subject. His eyes search my face and his hand clutches mine as if he is worried I'll bolt if he lets go. At this point, I can't say that I won't. "Football can be a whole other connection to your dad. You just have to let it."

My lungs drain what little air is left. A weight settles on my chest, my body feels so heavy. I give into my heavy eyes and shut them. I struggle to inhale but with a moment, it comes easier. Pops lets me sit in silence. I can hear the rasp in his breathing as he waits and I focus on the slow, rhythmic pattern until I feel the heaviness ease a little.

"I really don't want to talk about this anymore," I beg in a whisper.

A thumb brushes over my hand, a gentle pull and Pops' hands surround my own, cradling them to his chest.

"Okay, my girl."

When he brushes a gentle finger across my cheek, swiping the tears away, I feel like a young girl again crying in my bedroom and asking how it is fair that all the other girls' dads turned up to the Father's Day event but mine can't. Crying because someone in middle school made fun of me for not having parents. Crying because every year at the annual pep rally to kick off the high school football season, they would honor my dad like he was theirs.

Inside I'm still that same little girl who discovered the home videos of my parents and stashed them under my bed, hiding them away from the world in an effort to keep my parents all to myself.

"Go home," Pops says after a few minutes of silence. "Get some sleep and I will see you tomorrow."

I don't have the energy to fight him on it. So I nod. Picking up my bag and Scott's sweatshirt that I've been living in, I make my way to the car.

I place my hands on the steering wheel, watching the slow movement of the other vehicles around me pulling in and out of parking spaces. My phone chimes from where it is sitting in the center console.

Scott: How is your pops?

Are you okay?

Ivy: He's okay. I'm heading home now.

I wait for his reply, watching the three little dots appear and disappear. When it doesn't come, I push the engine start button on the car. It hums to life beneath me and I drive home.

***

The black Mercedes SUV is waiting on the side of the road when I pull into the driveway. The windows are a near illegal tint and I can't tell if the man that owns the car is still sitting inside. I watch it out of my rearview mirror for a moment before collecting my bag from the passenger seat.

I don't see him sitting on the front steps of the house until I'm almost standing directly above him.

He wears the same gray sweats that he'd worn a week ago but the hoodie is different: a navy-blue Broncos logo stitched on the front. Seeing it brings the dull ache in my chest to life.

God, I am tired.

So done with today.

I need to curl up in my bed and sleep until next week.

Maybe I should. I've been at the hospital for more than a week. I can miss one Sunday. I can stay in bed tomorrow and sleep it all off. I can give myself a day to sit in my feelings and when I wake up on Monday, it will be all better.

But tomorrow is Sunday and on Sundays I play UNO with Pops and do the crossword puzzle with him. I bring him a pastry and coffee from Starbucks even though he isn't supposed to be having them and we'll half it as a compromise.

Tomorrow is Sunday and Sunday with Pops is tradition.

Whatever expression is on my face makes Scott pull me into his arms without speaking a word and I let him. I fall into his warm, strong embrace. His arms curl around me, locking me in place. My nose presses into his chest and I let the strong, masculine scent of him fog up my brain and chase away thoughts of anything and everything else.

"Hi," I mumble into his chest. He takes my bag from my hand and I burrow deeper into him.

"Hi, yourself." I feel his lips press into my hair and linger.

"What are you doing here?" I ask.

"You said you were coming home. I wanted to be here in case you needed anything. Is that okay?"

I am too tired to try and play it off as anything other than sheer relief that he's here.

"Yes. Thank you," I say. He pulls away from me, hands dragging lightly down my body until his fingers find mine. He pulls my house keys from my hand and unlocks the door, leading us inside.

Scott makes me a cup of tea and places it on the coffee table in front of me. He covers me with the throw blanket that is on the edge of the couch and fluffs the pillow behind my head.

He settles beside me and I curl into his warmth.

"You didn't have to do this," I say as I lean for the tea. He beats me to it, passing it over as I settle back into the couch cushions.

He only shrugs. "Wanted to."

I smile into my tea, sipping on it slowly. When I'm done with it, he takes it from my hands and places it back on the coffee table.

"So." He stretches an arm over the back of the couch, behind my head. "Your family is pretty much football royalty according to the local news."

The heaviness returns instantly and I lean my head back, resting against the strong arm he has stretched there. Rolling my head against it, I look over at him.

"Is it okay if we don't talk about my family? I think I'm all out of tears for this week."

He nods, the fingers of the hand behind my head lifting a strand of my hair and fiddling with it. "Family can be ... difficult."

I can't help the small scoff that leaves my lips. I let the smirk lift my lips. "Your parents sound amazing."

"My birth mother lives here in Boston."

Safe to say my sort of smile drops instantly and I sit up. "Oh."

"I understand that it can be hard to hear about people that are supposed to be in your life but aren't. I can't imagine what it would feel like to have to see *her* splashed across the screen night after night. I know it isn't the same, but I'm still sorry. It must have been hard."

My mouth goes dry as I try and find the words, any words, to reply with.

I can't, so I stay quiet.

He sighs, his eyes meeting mine and it makes me sit up a little straighter. There's a determined look on his face. Like he's come to a decision and he wants—no, needs to get whatever it is out.

I can't help it when my gaze drifts downward and I focus on the way his throat constricts as he swallows. The way his muscles tighten, the way his Adam's apple bobs and his jaw line seems to become even sharper.

He's so attractive it hurts and now he's baring his soul to me?

When I'm sitting here, feeling so sorry for myself and showing him how vulnerable I am a lot sooner into any sort of relationship than I'd like, he knows exactly what to do and ensures I know he's vulnerable too.

Fucking hell, this man is something else.

My body heats up the longer I stare at him. Sitting straighter, I press my thighs together.

"Ivy, I—"

I stop him, my brain suddenly going into overdrive. "Why did you tell me that? Just now, about your birth mother?"

His brows come together. "Huh?"

"Why did you share that with me?"

"I, um, well I guess I wanted to share with you. To let you know that I can understand missing a parent." He swallows hard and my eyes track every minute movement of it. "Now that I think about it, maybe it isn't relevant but you told me something really personal a week ago and I wanted to share too. You opened up. I wanted to do the same."

My chest heaves.

Just as I thought, he's hot and emotionally mature. He's rare.

I reach up, pulling his hand from my hair and bringing it into my lap.

By the time my brain catches up on the words I say, it's far too late. "What are we?"

Instantly I cringe.

In a moment, his fingers that are absentmindedly fiddling with mine pause and his eyes widen.

"Maybe it's too early and I'll probably regret this for the rest of my life if you freak out and run right now but," I suck in some air, pressing up to tuck my feet beneath my thighs. Now, it's me that fiddles with his hand. "I need to know what we are. I thought … I think, I mean I assume we're dating? I guess. We go on dates. I don't know … I haven't really done this in …"

Scott turns over his palm. He fits our hands together and pulls. I fall into his lap, my body twisting. My lips are inches from his. His forehead falls to mine.

"We're together," he breathes out. It's quiet but his voice still drips with decisiveness.

"Oh." I stare at his lips.

"Yes, oh." There's a tiny smile in his voice. I track his tongue as it darts out to run the length of his bottom lip.

"Good," I say, somewhat stupidly as I press my thighs together.

After today, after this week, feeling his body so close to mine feels nice. I feel small in his arms, on his lap. I feel safe and protected.

"Yes, good." He runs a thumb over my cheek and the heat rushing to my face follows it as if the thumb is personally pulling it from beneath my skin.

"You feel better?"

I go to nod, lean in and press my lips to his and formally seal us both away in the bubble where no one else exists but us. But I pause, glancing to meet his eyes. "Can you ask me?"

Scott looks confused. "Huh?"

I sit back on his lap, my hands come up to perch on his chest.

"Ask me to be with you."

He stares for a while longer, confused, until it dawns on him. "Ah." He shifts under me before cupping my face. "Ivy, will you be my girlfriend?"

We stare at each other. He stays perfectly still as I assess him, pretending to think it over. Eventually, the throb between my legs overrules my need to make him sweat a little and I let out a giggle.

"That was very high school of you. But, obviously, I will. Since you asked so nicely."

"You fished for that," he says, eyes shining with laughter.

I hold my hands up, pretending to throw out a fishing line and reel him back in. My cheesy joke is rewarded with a deep laugh.

"You fell for it," I giggle loving the sound of his laugh.

The echo of it wraps around us, warming the room, and the bubble seals off.

I feel the heavy weight of my grief and my tiredness dissolve. I relish the feeling, knowing it will only be until reality pops the bubble again.

Scott leans forward, catching my lower lip between his. He kisses me and I sink in, smiling. Against my lips, he murmurs, "I'm falling for you."

I freeze, the smile dropping from my lips and I go to pull back but Scott's hand finds the back of my neck and holds me against him. He kisses my lips again, lightly and attentively, a serious expression falling across his face.

"Ivy. I—" He sucks in a breath, "I have to tell you something. It's important if we're going to to—"

I climb off his lap, pulling him to his feet. "We can talk later."

I don't want the bubble to burst. The look on his face may as well resemble a giant, sharp pin. I'm not ready for that yet.

I want the bubble even for just a little while longer.

He towers over me, standing so close. "Are you sure?"

"Yes." I nod. My hand curls around his neck, pulling his lips down on mine.

"We should," he tries again. I cut him off with a kiss. "... talk ..." This time, he meets me eagerly, his words losing their conviction with every swipe of our tongues. "... first."

His hands drop to my ass, squeezing and pulling me tighter against his body. I roll my hips against his.

I groan as he bites down on my bottom lip before trailing a few hot, wet kisses down my neck.

"Scott, I get you want to talk but I swear to god if you don't take me upstairs right this minute," I say rolling my hips again, whimpering at the small friction I'm able to get between my legs, "I'll make you wait another four weeks and that tent in your sweatpants tells me you can't stand it either."

My skin is on fire, the throb between my legs aching and I so badly want his hands to move around from my ass to touch me. I know that if he stops this, probably for some stupid noble reason, I won't be able to keep the tears back. I need him. Now.

Then he groans.

"Fuck it."

Chapter Twelve

Scott

"Fuck it."

I all but growl as her smirk turns victorious. She's completely baited me into this but I cannot bring myself to give a shit.

Ivy presses against me. She's so close. The friction sends sparks through my body. I suck at her lips, learning every inch of her delicious mouth. My fingers need into the soft flesh of her ass and my dick thickens.

Fuck. Fuck. *Fuck.*

I should talk to her first. I should admit who the fuck I am and make sure she doesn't completely hate me for it after she knows.

I definitely shouldn't be burying my face in her neck and imprinting my fingerprints into her ass.

"Scott." Her breath coasts over my skin, warm and light. I only grunt in answer, my lips not leaving her neck as I suck and nip and bite a path down her jaw. "Please take me upstairs."

I know I should stop this.

I know I should tell her but my dick is in charge now.

Just once then I'll tell her. I need to get her the fuck out of my system and clear my goddamn head. I don't think once will be enough but this week has been a mind fuck. I haven't seen her or spoken to her all that much. I haven't worked on my strategy to come clean. All I have been doing is watching the stupid news coverage about her Pops and learning that her family is, or was, a big fucking deal in the football world.

It broke my heart to see her so heavy and defeated when she got out of her car tonight. She had this sad look on her face—broken, and tired, and grief-stricken—that had made me want to ensure she knew she isn't alone. She never would be again

We all have things that we should have let go of but still carry. That's why I shared about my birth mother.

I want Ivy to know that I'm just as vulnerable as she is.

I need her to know that.

Maybe if she knows that, she'll remember it when I tell her who I am.

When I tell her I've pretty much been lying to her for a little over a month.

She presses onto her toes and her hips press into mine, trying to close the distance. A small whimper echoes through the air as I gently skim my teeth against her pulse point and I've had enough.

All thoughts of stopping leave my head as the cinnamon scent of her skin fogs my brain.

I grab two fistfuls of her ass and lift. Ivy's legs wrap around my waist and tighten as I make my way over to the stairs.

Her grip is tight like she's scared we'll fall but she doesn't stop kissing me and she doesn't let me pull away. But when I readjust my grip on her at the top of the stairs, she unhooks her ankles and tries to wriggle free.

"If you're trying to get me to put you down, it's not happening," I say digging my fingers into her ass even harder. For a second, I get the urge to ease up so I don't mark her skin but then my cock twitches at the thought and I decide against easing up my grip.

I want to mark her.

To make sure that anyone who sees it—even though they fucking shouldn't be staring at my girl's ass—knows Ivy is mine.

From tonight, she's mine.

Hell, she was mine the moment I laid eyes on her in that stupid sports bar.

"Aren't I too heavy?," Ivy says breathlessly.

"Please," I tell her, tightening my grip as if to prove my point. "I bench two of you. Don't worry, baby. I won't drop you." I pull back and catch her gaze. Her cheeks are flushed red and her bottom lip is pulled between her perfect teeth. Then I wink at her.

Ivy erupts into a fit of giggles.

"You did not just *wink* at me?"

She digs her hands into my hair and I shiver at the feeling of her nails scraping against my scalp. Her fingers twist in the hair at the base of my neck like she has done in every one of our high-school-like make out sessions lately. Fuck, but it feels so good.

We edge into her room but I don't bother with shutting the door.

No need, we're the only ones in the house.

I lower her onto the bed, following her down and crawling over her body. Her chest is heaving and she's sucking in air like she's trying to calm herself down. I don't want her to calm down.

The fire I'm feeling reflects back at me through her eyes.

I stand up, eyes trailing down the soft curves of her body.

She's so ... real.

When the season ended last year, I had a fling with a cheerleader on the LA team. The girl was tiny, and blonde, and made of muscle. She'd been flexible but there had been nothing there. Nothing to sink my hands into, to massage, to *feel*.

Ivy is all curves, tempting and bathed in soft light.

Her bedside lamp is on and it's casting the same shadows across her bedroom I'd seen in the picture she'd sent me a few weeks ago. It's so pink if it was anyone else's it might actually hurt to look at but now all I see is Ivy.

Soft, sweet, football hating Ivy.

"Scott," she whispers, looking up at me from where she props herself up on her elbows on the bed. I realize I've just been staring at her for a beat.

"Sorry." I lean down, my fingers trailing down her body and finding the waistband of her jeans. I hook my fingers under it and follow the band until I reach the button, popping it open and sliding the zipper down.

I don't rush, slowly pushing her jeans over her hips and ass as I suck along the column of her neck. She stretches her head to the side to give me more access.

When I get her jeans to her knees, I stand back up to my full height over her. Her eyes flash with heat and she pulls her bottom lip between her teeth again as I pull her jeans off completely and toss them behind me.

I almost laugh because when I look down at her, all I see are her pretty, lace pink panties. So fucking her.

Ivy doesn't miss my smirk. "What?"

I trace the edge of the pink lace, around the curve of her hip and down her thigh, gently brushing over her center. She's wet. I can feel it through the lace.

My cock twitches again, reminding me that I want to be inside her. Badly.

I stroke her lace covered center gently and Ivy's breath hitches.

"Your panties are pink. Your room is pink." I press my thumb to her clit through the fabric. "You match." I can't help laughing at her small groan as my thumb rubs slow, gentle circles over her clit. She wriggles beneath me, trying to create more friction.

She wants to get off.

I take my hand away, laughing lightly when she whimpers a weak protest but it's silenced when I reach behind me to pull my hoodie and t-shirt off in one go. I drop them to the floor with her jeans and crawl over her body.

I trail a palm over each of her thighs, massaging her curves as I go. Reveling in the feel of her soft body. Fuck she feels good. It makes me want to see how many positions I can hold her in. How many times I can make her thighs shake as she comes.

I wonder if they shake. Maybe, the muscles in them tighten.

I want to find it all out now.

When I reach her hips, I push her body up the bed. She goes easily, fully pliant to my wordless command.

I hook my fingers around the lace of her panties and pull them down her legs too.

They make it to the pile of clothes.

Pink against the navy blue of my own jumper.

I hum as I settle between her legs, hooking my hands under her thighs and tugging until I'm inches from her bare pussy. "You even have a pretty pink pussy."

Then I dive in. Licking, and sucking, and kissing her clit.

Ivy squirms under me, her moans coming easily now. I revel at the fact I'm the one pulling those sounds from her.

"God," she moans. "Fuck. Shit."

She lets me eat her out for a whole minute before her hands are in my hair again, directing me gently to where she wants—*needs*—my tongue. I let her. I let her show me where she needs the pressure, the friction.

When I flick her clit with my tongue before pulling it gently between my lips and sucking, she bucks against my face.

"Is that good, baby?" I ask, pulling away to stroke her opening. She's soaking, my finger wet instantly. When she doesn't reply, I press my thumb to her clit, making her jolt again.

Her eyes snap open and meet mine.

"Feel good, baby?" I ask again.

"Yes," Ivy replies breathlessly. "Please keep going."

I smirk and dive back in.

Whatever my girl wants.

This time as my tongue flicks against her clit and my finger plunges inside her entrance, she isn't silent.

She moans, and whimpers, and swears. She lifts off the bed and grinds into my face, urging me on. Silently begging me to make her come and to hurry up about it.

I fucking love it.

My cock is practically weeping as I grind my own hips into the bed in time with her.

I suck hard on her clit, fucking her with my fingers. She starts to tremble and pride bursts in my chest. Her legs seize, thighs tightening and I feel her drag a heel up my back. When I glance up, she's got a hand on one of her own tits, sweatshirt pushed up to expose her soft stomach. Her forefinger and thumb are tugging at her hard nipple.

I don't stop sucking but I can't take my eyes off her as she comes on my tongue.

Her eyes closed, her mouth parts in a silent 'oh' as she grinds, and writhes, and squirms.

When she explodes, it's on my tongue and I can't help but be proud that I made her come like that.

I lick her clean and crawl up the bed.

She blinks at me through her dark lashes, her chest heaving and cheeks red.

"My god, you're good at that," she whispers, smiling shyly.

"Thank you," I chuckle.

I kiss her. She hums into my mouth and I know she can taste herself on my lips. I don't care. She tastes sweet as hell.

Ivy's fingers fiddle with my sweatpants. She hooks her fingers and pushes them down, nails scraping against my skin. My cock is finally free. I send the pants to the floor, along with her sweatshirt.

When I lean back over her, taking her mouth again, we're both naked and pressed up against each other. I can feel every curve now.

"Can I …" she whimpers as I bite down on her lip. She pulls away a little, pushing her hair over her shoulder. "Can I, uh, return the favor?"

God, she's cute when trying to be sexy. I can tell she's nervous at the idea. Her fingers wrap around my cock and when they barely meet, I hear the audible gulp of air she takes at the prospect of having my dick in her mouth.

Part of me wants to say yes.

Part of me wants to drag her off the bed and get her on her knees in front of me. Eyes watering, mouth filled, hair in my hands as she lets me fuck her mouth.

But that's for another time.

The other part of me, the weeping, throbbing, huge part of me needs to get inside her.

"You can." I stroke her cheek. "But another time. I need to be inside you."

I trace a path down her neck, and draw two fingers through the valley of her breasts. Moving a thumb over her hard nipples, I play for a while, taking in the silence of nothing but Ivy's breathing. Eventually, I lower my mouth and suck and I'm delighted to get the same reaction I got when I sucked on her clit.

Ivy arches off the bed, into my mouth, willing and wanting.

She's so damn reactive.

Her hand still slowly pumps around my cock but when I suck harder on her nipple, she reacts by tugging harder. Twisting her hand a little. Running a thumb lightly over my tip.

Nope, that's it.

I get off her, finding my sweatpants and digging for the condom I've kept in my wallet since our first date. When I join her back on the bed, she eyes the plastic.

"You just happen to be carrying one of those?"

"No." I smirk, tearing at the wrapper with my teeth. "I'm carrying at least five. Don't want to be caught needing to fuck you and be without a condom."

She giggles, the flush covering her body.

I roll the condom on and position myself between her legs. We both watch as I drag the head of my cock through her soaking pussy. I groan at how wet she is.

"When will you need to fuck me five times though?" Ivy tries to hide her whimpers beneath the words but I still catch them. "Seems excessive."

I slide my head from entrance to clit, soaking my cock before positioning myself. I lean in and the head of my cock notches just at her entrance. I'm throbbing, aching to get inside her.

"We both know …" I start edging inside, "… that just once …" I sink in a little further, her pussy stretching around me, clinging to me like it's been waiting for me forever and now that I'm here, doesn't want to let me to go, "… won't be enough."

I slide to the hilt, her warmth surrounding me.

Fuck. She feels better than I imagined.

God damn.

I'm so screwed.

I stay still, watching Ivy's face as I wait for her to adjust.

She stares at me, humming at the feeling of me filling her.

"Are you going to move? What are you waiting for?" she asks after a moment and I can't help the laugh that leaves me. She would still be asking questions in bed. I'm inside her and I'm laughing. I'm aching to move but truth is, I'm savoring the moment.

Somewhere deep in the back of my mind, the massive omission of what I do for a living flashes through my head like a brightly lit Vegas sign. But I ignore it. Glancing down at where our bodies meet, I push it aside and focus on her blue eyes, and her soft skin, and her beautiful curves.

Her thighs are splayed out on the bed underneath me, cradling me loosely. I run my hands over them, curling around them and lifting. I push her knees to her chest as I pull out of her, just so only the tip is in. I pause, smirking as she tries to lift up, trying to take me back inside.

"Scott," she whines, lifting her hips again.

"Yes, baby?"

"Please move. *Please*."

"You're so polite when you're so needy for me."

I slam back into her, fingers digging into her thighs as I keep her with me. I pump, in and out of her in a hard and fast rhythm, grunting every time I feel the walls of her pussy clamp down on my cock.

Fuck, she's tight.

I know I won't last long so I focus on Ivy. Her tits are bouncing. She lifts a hand above her head to push against the headboard and her bottom lip is back between her teeth, trying her best to keep the delicious sounds she makes inside.

"Ivy," I say wanting her attention. "Eyes on me."

The navy blue meets mine and I feel my cock pulse.

I fuck her harder, slamming our hips together. I want her noises. Her whimpers. Her moans.

I want them all.

"Does it feel good, baby?" I ask, repeating the same words I used when fucking her with my tongue. She nods.

Not good enough.

I pump in again, one hand moving from her thigh to play with her clit. I circle my thumb, timing it with my hard and fast thrusts.

"Tell me, Ivy. Tell me how good it is. Look at me and tell me who's fucking you."

She starts to tremble, her body shaking and her pussy clamps down. She still shakes her head, moans falling from her lips even as she tries to keep them back.

I grunt. "I want to hear you when you come, Ivy." She is so unbelievably wet. I know she's close so I keep pushing. I keep thrusting into her, I keep circling her clit.

"Who's fucking you, Ivy?"

"Oh, fuck. Scott," she cries. "You!"

She clamps down around me, pulsing, as she comes. I let go of her knees, falling into her as I keep pumping in and out, chasing my own release. I bury myself into her neck.

Her fingers tangle in my hair, and finally I get her words.

"God," she cries, ankles locking behind my back as I continue to pump into her. "You feel so fucking good. Don't stop, it feels so good." I don't plan to stop. I can feel my orgasm building at the base of my spine and I move harder, faster, erratically inside her.

I feel her start to tremble again beneath me. Her pussy is clamping down and she's so wet, I'm slipping in and out her body with ease. Like her pussy was perfectly shaped to fit only me.

I groan.

"Fuck," I grunt into her neck and her nails scrape down my shoulders.

"Scott," she cries. "Scott, I'm going to come again. Please make me come again."

And fuck if I don't rise to the challenge.

I slam into her, reaching between us to rub her clit. She is anything but quiet now and her moans spur me on.

My cock throbs, her pussy pulses, and we come together this time.

I spill into the condom, sucking on her neck. My hand follows her body to one of her tits and I squeeze.

Ivy huffs out a breathless laugh, squirming beneath me a little. She's so damn reactive, it's so fucking hot.

I'm still inside her but I lean back, pecking her lips. She gives me a sedated smile, her eyes fluttering closed as I roll off her to deal with the condom.

When I join her back on the bed, she curls into my side. I lift one of her legs over mine and entangle us together.

"You're right," she murmurs into my neck as she burrows in. Her lips brush my skin. "Once isn't enough."

***

The images from last night replay over and over in my mind like it is the best damn movie I've ever seen.

Waking up this morning, kissing her and slipping out of her sheets, had been pure torture. For the first time ever in my career I was begging for a sleep in on game day, wishing I didn't have the earliest report time than all my teammates because I needed a shoulder strapped before meetings and warm up.

We are playing in the primetime Sunday night football slot but the report time is still too damn early for my liking.

The corridors are quiet as I make my way back from the physical therapist's suites and toward the locker room. I need to get my head right. Ivy is still front and center and whilst I don't want to forget how it felt to slip inside her tight, hot body last night I also didn't want to play my entire game semi-hard.

Fuck.

This girl has me so distracted I almost laugh out loud.

I run through the list of my pre-game rituals.

A few songs from my pump-up playlist.

Call my mom and tell her which pair of socks she'd gifted me I've decided to wear today. She'd laugh, tell me where she'd found them, then wish me luck.

What? Tons of athletes were superstitious about shit like that. Mine just happens to be with my mom.

Then I'll grab a small plate of whatever catering has out and catch up with my O-line. The offensive linemen have my back out there but I'm new to this team and for us to be a unit, to meld and play like we've been together for years, I need to know them. To *really* know them.

So I'll ask about their families and their wives or girlfriends. I commit the information to my memory and I gain their trust, and in turn they'll gain mine. The results of this will show on the field.

In time.

I'm passing the passage that leads to the coaches' private offices when I hear her laugh.

My feet stop on their own accord and my pulse races.

Fucking hell, what is she doing here?

Ivy stands in front of Coach's office with another woman and Coach himself. She's wearing a mid-length pink dress that hits her mid-calf. It's tight on her waist, flowing freely from under her chest and all it does is push her perfect tits up to be the main star of the show.

Fucking pink, again.

My cock hardens and I reach down to adjust myself. My suit pants are fitted and they don't leave much room to hide anything let alone my dick if I get hard right now. Besides I was just trying to forget about her so this exact thing didn't happen.

Impossible now.

Seeing her here, with her long hair curled down her back and the straps of her dress so thin on her shoulders I could probably recreate the same path I'd kissed last night without even removing them.

My body hums with the want to go over there and wrap my arms around her.

To bow my head and press my lips into her neck. To inhale her sweet, cinnamon sugar scent.

Then I want to drag her into one of these empty offices, lock the door, and sink right back into her. Messing up her hair and making her moan just like I had last night.

The need is so powerful, I almost do it.

Instead, I stay rooted to the spot as I listen to the voices carry down the hallway. I lean against the wall, hidden behind the corner from their view.

"I appreciate the offer but I really need to get home. I go back to work tomorrow and I have so much to catch up on already," Ivy tells them. Her voice sinks into my skin like a soothing balm.

"Come on, Ives." The other woman with them whines. "When was the last time you came to a game?"

Her laugh rings out and carries my way. It wasn't as light, as musical as normal. She's forcing it as she replies. "Not since I was a kid. You know that."

"Are you sure you don't want to just watch from one of the boxes with Brooke? You can eat something and you guys can catch up, no watching of the game actually required," Coach replies. Their voices are getting closer and closer.

Shit, are they walking this way?

"I'm good. But thank you. And good luck with the game." Ivy's voice is quiet and reserved as she answers him. Surely, she's seen a game since she was a kid?

There is no way she can be a Booker and never watch football?

I'm still struggling to reconcile what I know about her family and her hatred for the sport.

I itch to turn the corner and beg her to stay, to tell her right now and ask her to watch me play. The cocky teenage boy in me wants to poke my chest out and show off. Show her what I'm good at, what I can do out on that field.

"Thanks Kiddo," Coach replies, so close they must be just on the other side of the corner now.

"Bye dad. I'll be back later, after we have lunch," Brooke, Coach's daughter I realize, says.

There is some shuffling, a few muffled hugs and then there she is.

Ivy turns the corner, heading in the opposite direction from me. They didn't notice me standing against the wall, hardly breathing. Ivy loops her arm through Brooke's and is led away.

The pink dress swishes around her legs. The same legs that I'd thrown over my shoulders just last night. The same that had locked around me when I'd slid inside her.

Shit.

No. Stop.

Game thoughts only.

No Ivy thoughts.

No. Ivy. Thoughts.

"Harvey? What are you doing, son?" I jump, flinching hard.

"I-uh." My eyes follow the girls, now so far down the corridor I can't even hear their footsteps echoing anymore.

"You see the physio?" Coach slaps my shoulder and jerks his head as he walks in the direction I'd been going. "Feeling alright?"

"Yeah. I—" I clear my throat.

I need to forget about Ivy for now and focus.

I have a game to win.

I recover, shaking my head and matching Coach's pace. "Yeah. I thought we could run over those plays we worked on for their O-line?"

"Let's walk."

Chapter Thirteen

Ivy

I missed cooking for more than just me.

When I was little Nan and I would cook all the time. I'd come home from school, run off the bus and into the house to find the ingredients for chocolate chip cookies or Pops' favorite red velvet cupcakes or double fudge brownies on the kitchen bench. In no time, the kitchen would smell like sugar and chocolate.

Eventually Nan taught me to peel the potatoes and carrots for dinner. Then how to marinate the chicken. Suddenly I was the one cooking while she sat at the island listening to how my day went.

It was my favorite time of the day, just being in the kitchen with her while we laughed and fended off Pops whenever he'd come to steal a taste.

I couldn't give it up after she passed. I felt connected to her when I cooked, especially when it was still in the same kitchen I'd grown up in. I imagined that other girls grew up learning to cook and to bake from their mothers. I guess I may have too. But it was special to me that I had something to hold on to with Nan.

I put the pasta bake in the oven when Scott texts that he's only about ten minutes away. It will be in there for at least twenty-five minutes but that gives us the perfect amount of time for him to give me a proper, delicious kiss hello.

I have missed him the last few days.

He has been away with the team and I am determined to finally find out his actual role with the organization. He still doesn't talk about his job much and, as he works for a football team, I'm not all that fussed about knowing the ins and outs of his role in the football world but I should at least know his role title. Right?

Yes. I need to know.

At the very least, I need to know so that when someone asks me what my boyfriend does for a living I can give them an answer.

I spent the last few nights lying in bed alone, dreaming up all sorts of different scenarios in my head. All of them involve Scott. All of them end up with us in bed, or on a kitchen counter, or the couch, or the back seat of his car.

All without clothes.

But some did involve meeting his parents, and a wedding and kids someday, and how we might celebrate birthdays and holidays.

Okay, I may have got a little carried away but without him physically here to distract me I let my thoughts run away with themselves. Just for a little while, I indulged myself in what a future with Scott might be like.

Not to mention, he gave me multiple orgasms the morning before he left on this work trip of his. I've never been so horny in my life.

Just thinking about him and his hands on body and his lips on my neck gives me shivers.

A knock at the door echoes down the front corridor, pulling me out of my day dream.

Scott leans on the door frame. Jeans tight around his thighs, black shirt stretched against his muscled biceps, faded black cap pulled down over his head. There are dark circles under his eyes and the ends of his hair poke out of the edges of his cap. He needs a good night's sleep and a haircut.

His tall frame invades my space.

"Hi." I breathe out. The hand clutching the door tightens, holding me steady. I glance up into his face, smile spreading across mine as the blush starts to heat up my neck.

I am weak for this man.

"Hi, you." He sweeps the cap off his head and dips down, his lips capturing mine. His hands creep around my waist, locking me in his arms and I let mine drape over his shoulders as I stand on my toes.

The kiss is soft and gentle and the perfect hello.

My body relaxes into his. He pulls back, trailing his lips along my jaw lightly before he drops down and buries his face into my neck.

I laugh as his hot breath caresses my skin, sending shivers down my spine.

"Missed you," he mumbles into my neck.

"Oh?" I tease, my fingers finding his hair and gliding themselves through it.

"Yeah." He pulls his face back, a feigned pout on his expression. "Say it back."

Shaking my head, I barely hold myself back. "I missed you, too."

He kisses me again.

"Smells good in here." He toes off his sneakers at the door, tangling our fingers together and letting me lead him toward the kitchen.

"It's the pasta bake. One of my nan's recipes."

"Fuck yes," he groans.

I laugh, pulling my hand away from his and walking around the island to check the oven. The cheese is starting to bubble and my stomach growls.

"Do you want wine? It'll be done in another ten or so." I open the fridge to pull out the bottle of rosé I picked up on my way home from seeing Pops after school today.

"I'm okay." Scott shakes his head when I look up at him.

He is still standing, hands on the back of the stool he stands in front of. He is clutching the stool so tightly that his knuckles begin to turn white. I tug on a strand of hair that's fallen over my shoulder. "Is everything okay?"

"Yeah, I—" He clears his throat. "Can we talk? I have to tell you something."

Dread drips into my stomach, slow and steady, weighing me down.

All my fantasies, all the scenarios I dreamt up over the past few days come rushing back through my head. One by one, burning from the outside in. The pictures I see in my head shriveling up and falling into a pile ash in the forefront of my mind.

God. I feel like an idiot.

My cheeks burn, my arms feel heavy at my sides, my stomach turns over, and over, and over.

"Sure," I choke out, swallowing down the rock that has lodged in my throat.

He goes over to the couch in the living room and I wish he didn't.

I am already emotionally invested in this man. I want him. If I can't have him, the decent thing to do is to stay standing and not soil the memories I have of him on that couch. Reluctantly, I sink into the couch cushions next to him. He drops his head and runs his hands over his jaw, rubbing at the same spot. He sighs, his voice sounding almost defeated when he speaks.

"I should've told you this from the beginning, but fuck did I love that you had no idea who I was when we met."

Confusion courses through me but I stay silent, letting him talk.

"My name is Scott Harvey; you already know that. I work for the Boston Broncos. You know that too." I nod, reaching up to play with the ring that hangs around my neck. "I have been avoiding work related conversations because the first time we really spoke, back at the bar, you told me you didn't like football. It made sense that you had no idea who I was when you said you didn't like watching it or like anything to do with it. I used that to my advantage and decided not to tell you the whole truth."

"You don't work for the team?" My brows crush together, the confusion surely written all over my face.

So he lied? About working for the team? Was that it?

"No. I do. I just ... I'm more involved than I've really let on."

"Okay," I say slowly. My breathing becomes shallow and my heart pounds in my chest.

What the fuck is going on?

"I'm the starting quarterback for the Boston Broncos." He stares at me but my vision starts to blur from the outside in. Just like the fantasies had, the sight of him is turning to ash as he keeps talking.

"I got traded to the team at the beginning of the year. When I walked into the bar two months ago, I'd been in Boston for a few days, and was miserable about being here and moping around. I saw you through the windows of the bar and I—I just had to meet you. When you didn't know who I was to begin with, I thought I'd got lucky. This line of work, we're told to be careful from the moment we get some level of success playing college ball."

I can't breathe.

I can barely register his words anymore. My throat is closing, my stomach still turning over and over.

"I should've told you that night I came to the party at the bar," he continues. "When I saw you again, I just ... I don't know. I wanted to know you. Then you told me you weren't a fan of football, that you pretty much hated anything to do with the sport. So, I played off my job as something minor with the team."

So he lied.

Dread fills me. My stomach is churning and my nerves are shot. All the questions he dodged. All the times he shut down whenever I asked about work. It was because he's lying to me.

Oh my god.

I barely see Scott still sitting in front of me. His voice sounds so far away now, my eyes unfocused.

"When you told me about your family and your connection to the game, I felt like shit. I don't want to put you in a position to be forced back into my world but then I almost ran into you at the stadium—"

"What?" I snap out of my haze.

"You were at the stadium last week with the coach's daughter. I almost ran into you coming out of his office."

"Oh my god." A little bit of bile rises in my throat and I struggle to swallow.

I feel sick.

"You should've told me." I get up from the couch, moving around it so that there is something between us.

My skin crawls and I feel like I should take a shower.

"I know." He stands too.

My head is pounding. I feel like I'm going to be sick.

"We slept together," I whisper, unable to look at him. "We had sex. Oh my god."

"I'm sorry. I know I should have told you before we—"

"You knew. You *knew* I didn't want anything to do with that world. You dragged me in regardless. I trusted you and you lied anyway." I feel like throwing something at him. My fists ball at my sides and I struggle to keep myself together. What kind of relationship begins like this? With lying and deception?

Even if we do this, what does that mean for me?

Do I have to go to games? Do I have to pay attention to his world?

No. *No.*

I swore to keep that particular box closed and I won't open it. I can't—*won't*—go there.

"I think you should go," I hear myself whisper.

"Please, Ivy. I'm sorry I didn't tell you but—"

"You should have. I can't trust … I would never have …" I suck in air, trying to keep my voice steady. I can't break in front of him.

Not now.

If I do, I will let him wrap me up and pull me close. I will let him kiss my hair and whisper promises he can't possibly keep.

If I let him in, I'll lose him. No matter how hard he'll try, he will suck me in then send me spinning. I don't even want to imagine the aftermath.

"Please don't regret me," I hear him beg. He moves around the couch, moving toward me slowly. "Give me a chance. Give me a chance to—"

"You touched me. You held me. It was all a lie. It wasn't real." Scott reaches for me but I step away. "Please, go. I can't do this."

Tears sting as we stand there, only at opposite ends of the couch but it feels as if the chasm between us grows with every passing second.

"Please go." My voice rings out louder, more defiant.

He has to leave before I break completely and I can feel it coming. His deception is only the beginning and I don't want to deep dive into the locked box of feelings tonight.

He nods, face falling in defeat.

"Okay. I'll go. But I'm going to text you later." He waits a beat before he stands taller. "I won't let you go without a fight."

"I won't ... I can't." I shake my head. He comes toward me, stepping into my space and crossing the chasm but he may as well be miles away.

"I am sorry I didn't tell you. It's my job and I should've been honest. But nothing I've said about you or about how I feel about you is a lie. It's real. Because, Ivy ..." He lifts my chin, his piercing green eyes seeing deep down into my soul. "Whatever this is, it's fucking special and I'll be damned if I give you up without a fight."

He presses a kiss to my forehead and turns to leave.

I don't stop him.

When the front door closes behind him and the oven timer beeps for my attention, I close my eyes. I take a deep breath, and then another.

I move over to the oven, turn the dials and use the mitts to pull out the dish inside. I place it on the stove before turning to the cupboard, pulling out some foil and covering the dish.

I go upstairs and pull back the covers on my bed.

I send a SOS text to Katie and crawl between the sheets. Pressing my nose into the pillows, I swear I can still smell him. Later I feel Katie crawl into bed and pull me into her arms.

That's when the tears finally come.

CHAPTER FOURTEEN
IVY

Mon, 23 Oct at 6:23 A.M.

Scott: Morning. Can I call you today? I have the day off practice so can talk whenever. Let me know. Have a good day x

Wed, 25 Oct at 3:33 P.M.

Scott: I'm heading out of town for a Thursday night game today. Just wanted to let you know. Will be in Florida. Call me or let me know when I can call you? We can just talk.

Tues, 31 Oct at 1:46 A.M.

Scott: Thinking about you, call me. Please?

Sat, 4 Nov at 9:23 A.M.

Scott: Heading to LA for a game. I'll be back late Sunday night.

Sun, 12 Nov at 9:23 A.M.

Scott: Will be away for a Monday night game this week then have stretch at home. We'll be in Denver.

Scott: Are you ready to talk yet?

Scott: Please Ivy, just call me.

"YOU CAN'T IGNORE HIM forever," Katie says from her place on the couch.

I grit my teeth and turn my phone over so that the screen is face down on the table. I glance up at her from the stack of letter writing books I'm going through. "Why are you even here, again? This is like the third time in the last week."

"I'm worried about you."

"I'm fine."

"I don't think you are. You're ignoring a man that is obviously very much into you and the reason you're ignoring said man is ridiculous, might I add." She waves her wine glass around her head. "Are you delulu or something? Scott Harvey is *fine*."

"You date him then," I mutter, closing one of the kids' books harder than necessary and tossing it onto my completed pile.

"I would, but I'm in love with Grant—" I make a gagging noise and I can practically feel her glare burning a hole in the side of my head. "Besides, Harvey is obviously in love with you. You should call him."

"No. He lied." The words feel like gravel pouring out my mouth. I pull the next book toward me, flipping to the pages where the child has been practicing their *J*'s.

"Barely a lie. He told you worked for the team, just didn't say what he did for said team."

"Still a lie."

She sighs sitting forward and putting her glass into the coffee table next to my own.

"Ivy, if this is because he plays in the NFL … you know this isn't the same situation as your dad. That had nothing to do with foot—"

"If you aren't going to be helpful then you should probably just go, I'm busy with this." I bite out. She slides off the couch to sit next to me.

"I just think you're being a little dramatic," she tells me softly, a gentle hand coming to pat my arm. "It's not the same."

I slouch against the couch setting my pen down. "You don't know that."

"I do." She snakes an arm around my shoulders. "And you would too if you actually faced the reality of what happened and saw it for what it was."

I shake her off, getting to my feet. "Do you want ice cream? I think I want ice cream."

"Ivy, come on," she pleads with me from her place on the floor.

"I don't want to talk about it. It's done."

"But he's still—"

"Ice cream or not?" I cut her off.

I can't think about Scott. I just … can't.

Scott

The amber liquid burns my throat on its way down.

I stare at my phone.

I have been staring at my phone for four weeks. I know she's gotten my messages. They all sit on delivered. Whether she actually read them? Who knows.

I don't understand this.

I knew she would be upset about the lie, but this seems more than that. I would be upset too, but I thought I had shown her who I was, Scott Harvey the man, not Scott Harvey the QB.

She looked like a ghost.

Her face went pale, her eyes glazed over. They sprung with tears like the more the information processed in her mind, the more upset and distressed she became.

I want to understand. I want to talk it through with her.

I just want *her*.

My hotel room is quiet. I always like playing in Denver. It is freezing by November but their fans are passionate and they show up to sell-out stadiums. We are a good match for them. The usual buzz that flows through my veins the night before a game is drowned out by the sense of dread that took residence in my chest the moment I left Ivy's house a month ago.

Two fingers of whiskey at a time. I have turned to alcohol to dull the pain.

Am I an idiot? Yes.

Will I regret drinking the night before a game? For sure.

Do I care when I haven't been able to sleep for weeks? Fuck, no.

I'm getting desperate.

For weeks, I've been walking past the windows of Pats trying to spot her behind the bar. Of course, it is the middle of a school semester. Logically I know that she won't be working at the bar over a Tuesday lunch shift but I check anyway. I've seen Katie a few times.

Only once have I walked in and begged to see Ivy. Katie just smiled sadly at me and shook her head. I'm not sure my pride can take another hit.

I miss her.

I miss taking her on dates, holding her during the movies she talks all the way through, kissing her.

I miss talking to her, hearing about her day and the kids in her class. Her updates on her Pops. Her stories growing up with him.

Fuck.

I throw back the rest of the whiskey in my glass. The headache is already forming but I push it away, pouring another shot into the glass. When I go to take a sip, my phone rings. The camera turns on and I stare back at my own reflection as I contemplate answering my mother's FaceTime request.

Eventually she wins. I swipe across the screen and answer the call.

"Hi, darling." Her bright smile fills the screen and I can tell by the bright pattern behind her she is sitting in bed already. "How's my boy?"

"Hi Mom." I lean over to the bedside table to put down my glass and adjust the phone in my hand. Her eyes narrow and it makes me sit a little straighter against the headboard. My mother can see right through me. I decide that deflection is my best chance. "How are you? How's dad?"

My dad's voice rang out from somewhere off screen. "Good thank you, son." I smile a little shaking my head.

Mom isn't fooled. "We're fine, pottering along as always. But how are you? How is Boston treating you? The team?" There is a pause and I watch her nervously glance to where my dad is sitting next to her. "How is Ivy?" She finishes quietly.

Immediately I hear my dad groan. "Annabel. You promised to leave it alone."

"I'm his mother, I'm allowed." She scowls at dad. "It's my god given right to meddle."

"Leave the boy alone."

I chuckle, pressing a hand to my chest as the dull ache starts to pound against my ribs at the mention of Ivy. I give my best noncommittal shrug, murmuring, "It's all fine. Everything's fine."

"Are you sure? I'm worried about you. I—"

"I'm twenty-nine, you don't need to worry about me."

"You're my baby boy. I will always worry about you. It's my right," she claims. There is a scoff from dad.

"I thought it was your right to meddle?" I ask her.

"I have lots of rights." She lifts a mug to her lips and takes a sip. We stare at each other in silence for a second, my mom's eyes narrowing just a little before she sighs, giving up her line of questioning.

Sometimes I curse how close I am with my parents. I tell them pretty much everything and anything. What socks I wear for a game, what I have for dinner if I try a new restaurant. I send pictures if I buy anything new.

And I told them about Ivy.

Big mistake.

My mom took the news that I met a girl and took her out a few times as a wedding announcement. I am wholeheartedly surprised that she hasn't booked a venue yet. Although I know her well enough that she probably thought about it but decided it's best to ask what Ivy would want first.

The images of Ivy in a white dress, walking down an aisle toward me, has my mouth feeling like sandpaper. I reach over to grab my glass and take a sip.

"Scott Bowman Harvey," mom scolds, making me flinch. "Please tell me that's not alcohol in that glass?"

I swallow the whiskey, letting the burn dull the pain in my chest. "Again mom, I'm twenty-nine."

"The night before a game, though? You don't drink normally but especially not during the season!" She looks at my dad. "Jason, say something to your son."

The phone tilts and my dad, leaning against their headboard with his glasses slid down his nose and a book in hand, comes into view. Without looking up from the book, I see his eyes roll and he replies in a dead tone. "Scott, do as your mother says."

I laugh, "It's fine. I just—" I pause.

"You just, what?"

"Ivy and I … we're having a break. Sort of. I think." I blame the whiskey for my blabbering. I promised myself that I wasn't going to say anything to them until I figured out what I'm going to do myself. I certainly don't want to tell them it was because I lied to her.

"Oh, darling. I'm sorry." Mom's features soften before she quietly asks, "Do you want to talk about it?"

"No," I say a little harshly. I sigh, putting my glass back on the side table. "I'm sorry. I just really do not want to talk about it."

"Okay." She takes another sip of her tea, dropping the subject.

"What's going on with you guys?" I ask, trying to move past the Ivy topic.

"We thought we might rent an RV. Go on a bit of a road trip." She glances at dad again.

"You aren't allowed to drive at night. And, dad has the worst sense of direction in the world." I rub a hand over my eyes. "You can't rent an RV."

"We can, and we will." Mom nods her head like the decision is final.

"Let me pay for a trip for you, please," I beg. "With a guide and a driver, and nice hotels where you won't have to listen to Dad complain about his bad back."

I've been begging them to let me pay for them to go away for years now. Ever since I received my first signing bonus. Their answer has always been the same—

"You save your money for your future. Your own family holidays."

Mom and Dad haven't met a girlfriend of mine since high school. Then again, it is hard to introduce them to someone when there isn't anyone to meet. Ivy's changed that.

Ivy's changed a lot of things.

Point is, I haven't taken a girl home to meet my parents in years but mom hasn't given up hope. Her sly comments every now and then confirms as much. When I told them about Ivy, back when I asked for Big Al's details so I could set up dinner, Mom's face lit up like a Christmas tree.

"Mom ..." I scrunch my face up, inhaling sharply.

"I'm not getting any younger here, Scott. I want grandchildren. You should talk to h—"

"Jesus, mom."

"What?!" Her feigned innocence paints a clear picture of the same look she's given me over the years whenever she's asked about the women in my life ... which is often.

Like she says, it is her god given right.

"Sue me for wanting to see you happy and in love."

"I'm busy. I'm focused—"

"On Football. I know," she cuts me off. I hear the deep mumble of his dad's voice again. His way of trying to warn her away from the subject again. It doesn't work.

"I just worry that you're lonely. I'd hoped when you told us about Ivy, things might change. Have you spoken to her lately?"

"I—" I don't have the strength to go into it right now with her. "I promise I'm okay, Mom. I have Flynn out here, and I've been getting to know the other guys on the team. Really, I'm fine."

"Have you ... have you thought about reaching out to ... *her*?"

Three months. That's how long it's taken my mom to finally work up the courage and ask the question I'm sure has been burning inside her.

I love my parents. Jason and Annabel Harvey are hardworking, uncommonly kind, caring people. My dad had been a criminal defense lawyer in his glory days but has since given it all up to work for a not-for-profit firm that helps kids in trouble all over California. Mom is a professor in environmental sciences. A scholar, with a hippie heart. I grew up never in want of anything.

I was given the best education, played any sport I wished to, and had tutors when I struggled. I always had a solid roof over my head, a hearty meal on the table, and a warm bed to sleep in every night.

My parents come from old money, add that to the family fortune through their own accomplishments, and they donate hundreds of thousands of it to charities every year.

They taught me the value of helping others, of money, of being grateful for all we had. My parents are always so full of life. I can't imagine that there might have been a moment in time that they thought they might not be parental material.

But there was.

They've told me the story enough times now. Never planned for kids, focused on their careers enough and they were happy with each other. Until one day they just weren't anymore. By then, Mom was pushing forty, Dad even older, and they struggled. It hadn't mattered, both were open to adopting. They'd started talking to adoption agencies, looking at their options and filling in the paperwork.

Mom told me that the process had been grueling. The deep dive these agencies did had taken a toll so they'd decided to take a break.

One weekend while they had been attending a conference in Boston, Dad had been brought to the emergency room at Boston General after slicing his hand while chopping onions. Dad's eyes were blurred on account of the tears he *swore* hadn't existed.

My parents had been bickering lovingly of course–about said tears and onion chopping when the emergency responders had wheeled in a five-year-old boy, high and sporting first degree chemical burns, that wouldn't stop screaming.

That boy was me.

My birth mother had been using our studio apartment to cook drugs and I'd been breathing in the fumes for months.

Mom and Dad like to believe it was fate.

The adoption process had gotten them down, tired. They had still been committed to adopting but every time they signed a new form, sat in another interview, Mom had told me it felt so transactional to her.

Then Dad slipped doing something he'd done a million times. Like someone calling the shots had nudged his hand and led them to the hospital at that moment. Mom's heart had broken, staring at the boy until she couldn't take it anymore. She moved to the side of the hospital bed, pushing her way through the crowd of nurses, picked me up and held me tightly to her chest.

Only then, in the comfort of her arms, did my five-year-old self stop crying.

My parents saved my life. I love them dearly, and I know there is nothing I will ever be able to do to make it up to them.

Except, maybe in Mom's mind, giving them grandchildren.

I shake my head. "You know I have no interest in meeting that woman. Why would you ask that?"

"Because you're in Boston now. She might still be there. You might get some sort of closure if you reach out. She is your birth—"

"I'm gonna head to bed. Think about the trip, okay? No RV."

Mom frowns and opens her mouth, looking like she might try to argue. Instead she simply nods.

"Fine. We'll talk about it. Maybe we can come see some of your home games in the next few weeks in Boston."

I force a smile, my hand itching to take another sip of the whiskey. "That'd be great."

"Scott?" I hum in response; the whiskey finally kicking in and sleep starts to take its hold. "I'm sure if you talk to Ivy it will work out. Do it in person, none of this texting crap you kids do these days. If you want her, you will fix it. I know you will. I love you."

"Love you too, Mom."

Chapter Fifteen

Scott

I DIDN'T SLEEP A wink on the overnight flight back to Boston.

We lost.

I played with a headache and felt like shit, my mind reeling with thoughts of Ivy, and Boston, and my birth mother. The briefest of mention of her and I was completely thrown off. I don't blame my mom. I could tell when the question had all but fallen out of her mouth the other night that she was worried and wanting to ask for a while. I avoided their calls after the whole situation with Ivy and I had no doubt that it had sparked Mom's anxiety. That's on me.

Ivy.

Fuck, I miss her.

I can't get her out of my head and it is messing with my focus. My throws are getting sloppy. I'm disconnected from the receivers, missing their route changes and their cues. The loss was entirely on me and everyone knows it. I am never one to scroll through social media, especially after a game, but in an effort to distract myself from my own thoughts on the way home I do exactly that. The comments from the fans are brutal.

Scott Harvey needs to get his head out of his own ass and learn the plays.

We want a ring; Harvey isn't the man to get us there.

Scott Harvey just played the shittest game of football in the history of the sport … trade him, please!

Football fans are savage but there is nothing they can say that could make me feel worse.

I'm the first to beat myself up after a loss.

"You okay over there?" I look up from my phone, slowing my pace as Flynn catches up with me on the way to the parking lot. His gaze flickers between me and my phone. "You shouldn't read that shit. It fucks with your focus."

"My focus is already fucked." I lock my phone screen and shove it in my pocket.

"You told Ivy, huh?" Flynn sighs, clapping a hand to my shoulder as we approach my Mercedes.

"Yep."

"What did she say?"

"That's the problem. I talked, she had some sort of silent reaction, told me I lied to her and then asked me to leave. No idea what happened in her head," I tell him as I dig in my backpack for my keys. Again the way her eyes glazed and how she looked like a ghost crossed my mind. I want to know what had gone through her head. I want to talk to her, and for her to actually talk to me.

"Do you think her reaction was because you lied about playing football or?"

"There's something else here. It cannot be just because I didn't tell her that I actually play for the team, not just work for them. She didn't seem mad. More like she was holding back? I don't know." I feel the brain fog start to take over as I try to remember every detail of her expression that day.

"Have you talked since?" he asks.

I shake my head. Before I can stop it, the embarrassing confession falls from my mouth. "I've texted her pretty much every week since I told her four weeks ago and she hasn't replied to a single one."

"Ouch." Flynn flinches. I open the back seat of the car, lifting my small case in and throwing in my backpack.

"It's whatever." It's not. But what else am I supposed to say?

"Well, you obviously know what you have to do now, right?" He leans against the car, staring at me like whatever he's talking about is obvious. I stare blankly at him. "God, women are not your forte," he mutters.

I frown. That pisses me off. Of course they aren't. No woman has caught my eye since college and no woman has held my interest since high school until Ivy.

And now she is fucking with my head.

"You have to talk to her. In person." He waves a hand out in front of him to lay out the steps for me. "Apologize, beg for forgiveness, and grovel."

"That's your advice?" I ask. Flynn just smirks and nods his head.

Idiot.

"I want to talk to her but she won't reply to me."

"So show up on her doorstep." He shrugs.

"Creepy much?" I shove my hands in pockets, thinking it over.

"If you really want to talk to her, you have to commit. Show up. Explain, say you're sorry, and grovel like your life depends on it."

"She's at school right now." I mumble, pulling my phone out of my pocket to check the time.

"So? Show up at the school. Ask to see her for a minute. Go knock on her classroom door." My head shoots up, seriously thinking the idea over. Huh. Show up at her classroom. She will have to talk to me. She won't want to cause a scene and I know she'll want to get me out of there. I can make her promise to meet me for dinner.

At the very least and even if she refuses, I get to see her.

And I really, *really* want to see her.

Flynn eyes me suspiciously. "Oh my god, you're gonna do it aren't you?"

I give him a light shove off the car before smacking his shoulder and opening the door to hop in. As I start the car, I roll the window down and call out to him. "Thanks for the advice."

He salutes me out of the parking lot.

I don't stop to think about how stupid this idea is. I focus on the road. My fingers tap along to the radio on the steering wheel.

Thirty minutes, ten songs, nothing but what I'm going to say to Ivy running through my mind.

I drive into the parking lot of the school, pull into a spot and make my way to the school's administration office.

"Good morning, how are you to—" The lady sitting behind the administration desk begins, looking up at me before finishing her sentence. Her tortoise shell framed glasses slip down her nose, mouth opening and the pen she holds drops onto the desk.

"Good morning ..." I glance at the nameplate on the counter. "Brenda."

"You—oh my lord, my husband won't believe me when I tell him. You're Scott Harvey."

"I am, yes." I nod. I tap my fingers along the counter top. "I'm looking for one of your teachers. Do you think you can help me out?"

"What are—who are you looking for? Here?" She rises from her seat, fiddling with the lanyard hanging around her neck.

"Uh, I'm looking for Ivy Booker." Brenda's eyes widen.

"Ivy? Our Ivy?!"

I chuckle. "You know her?"

"Well, of course I know her." She glances over her shoulder at the closed door behind her. "I can't just let you go wandering the school grounds."

My chest begins to tighten. The desperate need to speak to Ivy coursing through my veins. I convinced myself on the drive over that I would be able to see her now. I inhale deeply and plaster on my best, most charming smile.

"I promise to only be a minute. I really need to see her."

She purses her lips and her eyes track me from head to toe as if she's sizing me up. Then she lifts the phone on her desk to her ear, punching in numbers on the keypad. We both wait, her still sizing me and me just trying to keep my cool.

"Cheryl, can you please come and cover the office for a few minutes? I have to walk a visitor to Ms. Booker's classroom," Brenda says into the phone. She smiles and nods. "Thanks sweetheart."

Cheryl shows up and I notice that they have the same style tortoise shell glasses. I don't miss the not so subtle looks the ladies share before I follow Brenda out of the administration office and through the corridors.

I remember the way from when I was here in the summer but I don't let on. The last thing I want is to get Ivy in trouble and my guess is that Brenda and Cheryl don't miss much. Brenda slows down as we get to Ivy's classroom door.

"Thanks, Brenda." I smile down at her, pasting on the charming smile I muster up through my nerves. I glance through the window in the door and see Ivy's chestnut, honey hair swaying behind her as she wanders through the clusters of tiny desks.

"Not a problem, dear. Just a minute though, we didn't sign you in properly." She winks at me and steps away.

I steal my spine, suck air into my lungs and knock gently on the door.

Ivy whips around. Her hair settles over her shoulders, her cheeks flush and her eyes shine.

Fuck *me.*

How the hell did I forget how beautiful she is?

A small child tugs on her dress but her attention is locked on me. My heart races and I can feel the blood pumping in my ears. I want to burst through the door, thread my fingers through her hair and kiss her so badly. I want it more than I want my next breath.

Adrenaline spikes as she says something to her class while walking my way. I don't take my eyes off her.

The door opens, her body between it and the door frame. She glares up at me. "What the hell are you doing here?"

"I need to talk to you." I lean against the door frame and the position brings me a little closer to her.

"So you decided to turn up at my school? How did you even get in here during the day?" she whispers angrily. The flush begins to run up her neck, painting her soft skin red. She pokes her head further out the door frame, looking around until she see's Brenda lurking a few steps away. Her eyes roll.

"You didn't text me back."

"I know." She glances over her shoulder before sagging into the door frame opposite me.

"Can we please talk?" I ask.

"I'm literally at work, Scott. No. We cannot talk right now." Her words sting but I hear the strain, the sadness lacing them. It matches my own and that's enough to keep me going.

"Tonight? Can I come over? Can we talk tonight?" I press. I let go. I let the desperation seep into my words. I need her to see how badly I want this. How badly I want her.

She hesitates, chewing on her bottom lip. Out of the corner of my eye, I see Brenda step closer to us. She's doing a pretty shit job at masking her eavesdropping efforts but I'm past the point of caring.

"Please," I beg her quietly. "Please can we just talk?"

Ivy closes her eyes and I watch her chest rise and fall with the deep breaths she takes.

"Okay," she finally whispers. Relief floods me. "Tonight. Come by tonight and we can talk."

***

I turn up at Ivy's door armed with tacos.

And not just any tacos. The tacos from the truck we went to on our first date after mini golf. Am I trying to appeal to Ivy's sentimental side? Yes. Do I think it's going to work? Probably not but a guy has to try.

The front door swings open. Ivy stands in front of me, hair still hanging down her back and still in the dress she was wearing earlier. Except now, instead of the boots she was wearing, she wears a pair of thick fluffy socks and an oversized zip up hoodie that hangs loosely off her shoulders. I can't help the relieved smile that breaks out on my face when she looks up at me.

"Hi," she whispers, her hands clutching the door as if she is using it for support.

My body burns with the need to touch her but I keep one hand tightly wrapped around the handle of the take-out bag and then the other shoved deep in my pocket.

"Hi, yourself," I say. She steps back, giving me space to get past her.

"You didn't have to bring dinner," she says, glancing at the take-out bag in my hand as I step over the threshold.

"Of course I did." I hold up the bag as she closes the door and we start down the hallway. "I brought tacos from that taco truck I took you to. You said you really liked them."

She pulls her bottom lip between her teeth for a moment, chewing on her lip. When she looks back at me, her words are softer than before. "You remembered."

I feel a little offended that she thinks I could forget anything about her but then again, I don't think she really knows what she does to me.

How much space she's taken up in my head.

How in a little over two months of seeing her, she's pretty much become my central focus.

It scares the shit out of me.

For as long as I remember, football has been my focus and wetting my dick is something I did when the opportunity arose and I needed a release. Otherwise, I was content with my right hand.

That all changed when I saw Ivy.

When I saw her smile, and laugh, and when I realized she knew nothing about who I was or what I do. I relish in the fact that she seems to like me, for me. Not for the millions I make throwing a ball down a field.

But in my efforts to feel normal for once, I almost lost her.

I refuse to lose her again.

"You wanted to talk?" she asks as I place the takeout on the counter.

"You didn't text me back." I repeat my words from earlier.

She holds her hands clasped together, wringing her fingers. "I didn't really have anything to say."

"Ivy, I like you." I practiced a whole speech about why I lied and how I just want to feel normal but standing in front of her now, I only want to lay my heart on the table and pray she'll take it despite everything.

She doesn't say anything so I start again. "Ivy, I like you. For the longest time, I didn't care about anything else other than football and my parents. I lived in a bubble of my own making. Ignored the outside world and just wanted to play ball. But then I saw you through that dirty window at Pats and it was like the world titled and started to spin again. Or I guess, for the first time."

"I'm sorry that I didn't tell you who I really was but I'm not sorry for taking you on those dates, for getting to know you and telling you about me." I inhale, continuing as I cross the room and into her space. Ivy looks up at me, not moving away but not making a move to touch or get closer to me either. "I'm not sorry that I was able to be there for you when your pops went into surgery. I'm not sorry for kissing you. For touching you."

Ivy's breathing hitches and it's the only indicator I need to tell me she is as much affected by me as I am by her.

I take the gamble.

I run a hand down her arm, pushing the sweatshirt down her shoulders and exposing more of her silky-smooth skin. "And I am really, really not sorry for fucking you. I mean, damn it Ivy. I haven't been able to focus on anything else since you made me walk away from you four weeks ago."

"I didn't—"

"You did. You told me to leave. I would've stayed right in that moment if you had wanted to yell, and scream, and fight with me about it but you didn't. You asked me to leave. So I did. But I realize it was the biggest mistake I could've made." She begins to shake her head and that glazed look she got last time I was here starts to take over her expression again. I lift my hands to her face, stroking my thumbs against her cheeks and keeping her eyes on me.

"I can't claim to understand why you pushed me away. I know I lied. I'm sorry about that but I don't think that's the whole reason. Am I right?"

She nods her head, chewing on her lip again. I tug it from between her teeth with a thumb, stoking the slightly swollen pink lip.

"Give me a chance, Ivy," I beg her, my face so close to hers now, our lips inches apart. "Let's talk it out. Work through whatever is scaring you."

"I can't ..." Her words are rough, broken and she sounds terrified. "I can't have more of my life splashed across the news. In magazines. On gossip websites. Every time something happens to Pops, they run the story of my family and I am constantly reminded of exactly what I lost. What I have to share with the stupid, football world. I won't—I can't do that anymore. I just ... I want them to forget about me, about my family."

My heart breaks for her.

I lean my forehead against hers. "I don't understand Ives. Football has nothing to do with your mom and dad's death. How can you—"

She pulls out of my grasp, shaking her hands out by her sides before pulling the sweatshirt up and over her shoulders. She crosses her arms over her front.

A wall goes up between Ivy and I.

Her on one side, upset and grieving.

Me on the other, confused.

I need time. Time to understand her. Time to break the misconceptions she's got in her head. Time to change her mind about the game I love. I want to try and to try, I need more time.

"What if we just … keep it private?" I almost hate myself for saying the words aloud. There is nothing in me that wants to keep her—to keep us—private.

"You would do that? Private?"

"Yeah …" Something lodges in my throat, trying to stop the words leaving my mouth. "What if we just kept this between us? No public dates, no press or media, just you and me. See where it goes?"

I want her.

This isn't a permanent solution. I know that. But I need time to figure one out and walking away again isn't an option.

She gapes at me. "How can you want that?"

"I want you."

"No one could know, Scott." She throws her hands up in disbelief. "I won't risk it. I don't want my name, my face, my family history splashed all over *SportsCenter* night after night anymore. You are one of the most successful quarterbacks in America right now, you really think you can keep this—" She waves a hand between us, "a secret?"

"If this is how you'll have me, then yes."

Ivy scoffs, her hands running through her long hair. "I don't believe you."

I invade her space again, not caring about her walls anymore. I smash through, framing her face in my hands again and forcing her to meet my eyes.

"Look at me," I say. She does, navy eyes darkening as she gazes into the soul I bare to her. "I. Want. You."

The air between us turns heavy. I can feel her chest rising and falling against my own. I hold her stare waiting, and when her gaze finally breaks and she glances at my mouth, I dive in.

I kiss her. Hard and hungry. I kiss her for the last four weeks. For every day that I woke up wishing she was there beside me. I kiss her for every night that I wanted her in my bed.

Threading my fingers through her hair, I tilt her head, angling so I can go deeper.

Ivy whimpers, her mouth opens and she kisses me back.

Thank. Fuck.

Chapter Sixteen

Ivy

I can feel him playing with my hair.

The morning light starts to peer through the curtains. There's a gap in them and the beam of sunlight seems to cross directly over my face. I keep my eyes closed, listening to Scott's breathing as he gently twirls a piece of my hair around his fingers. I can't help the sigh of satisfaction and I snuggle further into his chest.

The last two weeks have been pure bliss.

I go to work, I go to the hospital to visit Pops, then I come home. Scott is normally waiting for me by his car on the side of the road, and we cook dinner and snuggle on the couch while watching *Friends* reruns. Then he scoops me upstairs and gives me at least two orgasms before I fall asleep in his arms.

Katie has been texting me non-stop with questions and demands that we go for brunch so I can spill all the 'dirty details'. Her words, not mine.

Deep down, I know that I'm terrified of bursting this blissful bubble if I tell Katie anything. So instead, I've been dodging her calls, and her texts, and blowing her off.

I know. I'm being a shit friend.

But the bubble! I just want to protect the bubble for as long as possible. As soon as Katie knows, she'll make me answer all the hard questions I've been avoiding since Scott agreed to keep this between us and I am simply just not ready for her brand of truth bombing.

Scott's finger trails down my arm. The sensation sends shivers along my skin. Another sigh escapes my lips as I feel him press a kiss to my forehead.

"Good morning," he murmurs into my hair.

I blink up at him, whispering, "Hi."

He smiles down at me, dipping down to press a kiss to my lips. I shift my knee hooking over his hip, turning into him so that our chests press together. My body relaxes on his and I bring a hand up to his chest, across his heart, and rest my chin against it. Beneath my palm, I can feel the steady thud of his heartbeat.

Contentment floods me.

I feel such a sense of peace. I wish this was how it could be all of the time.

"What time is it?" I ask in a whisper, eyes closing again.

"Just before six."

I groan and the laugh that comes from him makes his chest vibrate beneath me.

"So early. Back to sleep." I snuggle in deeper.

Scott's hands move up and down my arms. He draws a path from my wrist, over my shoulder and down my back. His fingers hitch on the thin strap of my top but it relents and slips, hanging off my shoulder as his fingers blaze a trail across my skin. I can feel the pulse between my legs begin to intensify and I do my best not to squirm on top of him.

I don't want him to stop but I can also feel sleep tugging at my eyes, coaxing me back to my dreams.

His fingers roam down my back, skim across my hips and over my lace covered ass. Scott presses his fingertips into the soft skin and I can't take it anymore. I whimper and my hips roll, searching for any kind of friction.

Scott lets out a soft laugh, squeezing my ass again. "This helping you wake up?"

I don't respond. I can't respond. He keeps moving, his fingers round the curve of my thigh and trailing lightly over my center. I sigh. Without really thinking about it, my leg hitches further up his waist, allowing more room for his hand between my legs.

I angle my head, looking up at him and the same heat and desire is reflected right back at me.

"You still sleepy?" he asks, slowly stroking me. I know he can feel the wetness starting to seep through my panties. He keeps going, every third or fourth pass he presses harder and he lingers on my clit.

What a fucking tease.

I nod in response to him, letting myself roll against his hand. He starts to toy with the edges of my panties and just as I think he's going to pull them aside and finally, *finally,* touch me, he stops.

I let out a whimper in protest and try to reach down, wanting to put his hand back in place. Before I can, he flips us.

Looming above me, he leans down, his nose nudging against mine before he pulls me into a sweet, loving kiss. Just as I settle into the kiss, he pulls away from that too.

Damn it.

His lips mark a hot, wet path across my cheek and down my neck. He sucks on the sensitive skin just below my pulse point before he moves on and down my neck. He reaches my chest, pulling the thin top I wore to bed down over my breasts.

He stares up at me as he takes each one in his mouth, swirling his tongue around the nipple and sucking hard on them. Heat floods me. I tangle my hands in his hair and tug.

God, that feels so good.

"Keep going, please." I breathe out.

But again, he pulls away too soon. I whine in protest but he just smirks up at me. "You're polite in the mornings."

I tug on his hair. "You're being a tease."

He laughs and his warm breath skims over the sensitive skin of my thighs. "Oh? Do you want me to touch you, Ivy?"

I hiss in response as he presses a gentle kiss to my clit through my panties. Squirming beneath him, I nod.

"Ah uh, let me hear you say it," he tuts.

"Please," I snap. "*Please* touch me." I'm a mess, fingers clutching at his hair, trying to keep his head between my legs.

The ache in my core intensifies as I feel Scott's warm breath. He reaches up for my hips, hooking his fingers around the fabric of my panties and pulls down. Tantalizingly slow, he removes them and throws them onto the floor.

His arms wrap around my thighs and his fingers dig into my skin. He's clutching me so tightly, there will probably be some light bruises left from his fingers and I can't say that I'm mad about the idea.

He stares at me, eyes hooded and a lustful expression marring his smirk. "Because you said please."

Then he dives in.

"Ah, fuck. Yes." I cry out, teeth sinking into my bottom lip to stop from moaning again.

Scott's wet tongue dives into my opening, licking, and searching, and playing. I grind shamelessly against his face, moaning and whimpering at every stroke of his tongue.

Fuck, it feels so good.

Heat rushes through my veins and I'm so impossibly wet. Scott pulls away, licking me from clit to opening before latching his lips around my clit again and sucking. I feel him release one of my legs and then, on another groan, he slides a finger inside of me.

I rock against him.

"Oh, don't stop," I gasp, hips grinding on his ever-welcoming face. "Please don't stop."

He laughs against my pussy, his tongue darting out to flick against my clit. He adds another finger and pumps harder.

"Oh, oh, god."

I can feel my orgasm building and my grinding starts to get frantic. I'm desperate to come. I'm desperate for Scott to make me come. With another suck on my clit, his mouth pops off me and he lifts his head, his fingers still pumping in and out of me in quick succession.

"I want you to come all over my face, Ivy," he rasps, and I stare down at him as he lowers his mouth to me again.

He swirls his tongues over and over. Sucking, and licking, and kissing me like he is a man starved and I am the first meal he's had in months.

My whimpers turn back to moans, my grip on his hair tightens and my legs start to shake.

I come with his name on my lips and my hands grasping at his hair.

His grip relaxes on my thighs as he licks up my orgasm, smiling and pressing his lips gently to my center one last time.

"Feeling awake now?"

I giggle, turning my head on the pillow. "Yes."

He crawls up my body and settles over me. "Good. Now, breakfast?"

I sit at the bench as Scott moves around the kitchen, pulling ingredients from the fridge and plates from the cupboards. He cracks five eggs into the fry pan and then adds some milk, leaning over for a wooden spoon and starts to stir. I gaze at his back, watching his muscles and sinking into my seat with a satisfied sigh.

"You good over there, baby?"

Warmth spreads over my cheeks at the nickname. He started calling me that after we got back together and it still makes me want to giggle like a teenager every time I hear him say it.

He turns off the heat, moving the pan to the heat protective mat he found in the cupboards a few days ago. He stretches up, twisting and making a face, I sit up.

"Is your back sore?" I ask, sliding off my chair.

He continues to stretch, his eyes on me as I move around to join him on the other side of the bench. When I'm close enough, he grabs at my waist and pulls me into him. Smirking he says, "A little, but nothing a good stretch can't fix."

"Is it because my bed isn't built for giants like you?" I stretch up on my toes, asking for a kiss. He obliges. "We never stay at your place. That giant bed is going to waste every night."

"I like it here. It's ..." He casts a glance at the room beyond the kitchen over my head before looking back down at me, "... homey."

"Homey?"

"Mm, yeah. Homey." He kisses me again, pulling me tighter against his chest. "I like your bed."

"Well *homey* is giving you back problems." I laugh as he drops his face into my neck and his hot breath starts to warm my skin.

I feel the shake of his head against my shoulder. "I like whatever bed you're in. Now, eat," he commands, pulling away from me and planting a light slap against my ass.

We've almost finished breakfast when his phone lights up, the screen coming alive with the camera and the piercing ring tone cutting through the air.

Mom shows on the screen. I immediately try get out of my seat and slip away as Scott pulls the phone closer. He shoots me a look, reaching a hand out and beckoning me back to his side.

"Hi Mom," he answers the phone, snaking his free arm around the back of my chair.

"Hi, honey. Happy game day!" His mom beams up at him through the phone. I can see the sun only just starting to rise in the windows behind her head. Being in LA, they run a few hours behind us. A rush of longing spreads through my veins at the thought. His mother gets up early just to ensure she catches him before he heads into the stadium for a game.

"Thanks. Just finishing up breakfast."

"Oh, that's nice." His mom narrows her eyes and I can see her looking at Scott's surroundings. "Where are you? That's not your apartment."

"I'm at Ivy's," he says it so easily.

Like it's the most normal thing in the world for him to be answering a FaceTime from his mother at my place. Suddenly, I am very aware of the fragile bubble that surrounds us. How easily it might pop. I shake the feeling away as Scott's arm leaves the chair and drapes over my shoulders. He tilts the phone and I see the same taken aback, shocked expression mirrored in his mom's face as my own.

"Scott Harvey, how dare you spring this on me? We'll talk about your timing later." The phone shakes in his mom's hand and just moves around in excitement. "Hello there, Ivy. I'm Annabel."

Annabel beams up at me from the phone and I have to give myself another mental shake in order to be able to reply. "Hi." I lift my hand to give a feeble wave and I feel Scott laughing by my side.

"It's so nice to meet you! Scott's told us so many lovely things." She looks over her shoulder and yells to whomever is lingering just out of frame. "Jason! Quickly, come meet Ivy."

"Who?" The voice calls back.

"Ivy. Scott's girlfriend!" My cheeks flush with heat and I watch myself blush a shade of deep, deep red on the screen. Goddammit.

Scott pulls the phone back a little so that he's in the picture too. "Hi, Dad."

An older gentleman appears, with a kind smile and even kinder eyes. "Hi son. Hello Ivy, nice to meet you."

"Hello." My voice is quiet and I know that everyone can hear my nerves. I clear my throat and plaster on my best smile. "Nice to meet you guys, too."

"Are you going to be free in a few weekends time? We're coming to town and would love to take you both out for a dinner on the—"

"I'll let you know, Mom." Scott cuts her off. Shame hits my gut as I realize going for dinner with his parents in the city would break our agreement to keep this thing between us quiet.

No dinners out, no public dates, no press.

I swallow the lump in my throat.

"Oh, okay." Annabel exchanges the briefest of looks with Jason before she recovers and looks back at Scott. "Anyway honey, we're going out on a boat today with the Palmers so I wanted to call for the pregame tradition before I get out there and have no reception."

Scott relaxes, smiling. "The yellow ones, with the tiny hot-dogs."

"Excellent choice, son." Jason comments.

"Oh, I loved those ones. Got them on sale at Target a few years ago. They were so cute, I couldn't resist." Annabel adds.

Scott's thumb starts to trace circles on my arm. "Thanks for calling you guys. Love you."

"Love you, sweetheart."

"Go get them, son. Good luck." Jason smiles and raises the coffee mug he's holding in a 'cheers'.

The phone goes dead and I wriggle out of Scott's grasp, picking up my plate and making my way back around the island to the sink. Scott follows, placing in his dishes after mine. Then as if he can sense I was planning an escape, he grabs my hips and twirls me to face him.

"Sorry," he says. "We don't have to go out for dinner. I'll tell them we want low key and we can have dinner at my place."

Guilt swirls in my stomach and I struggle to take a deep breath. "It's okay. We can—"

I go to tell him that we can go for dinner with them but the words get caught in my throat. I can't bring myself to make that promise to him. I wish I could but in the back of my mind, I still think about the paparazzi that showed up at the hospital, or how they followed me around that week.

Scott drops his forehead to mine and tightens his arms around me. "I love waking up with you," he says, changing the subject.

So I do my best to push the guilt away and meet his gaze. I press up on my toes and touch my lips to his jaw.

"I love waking up with you, too," I whisper.

He sways us on the spot. No music. Him in no shirt and sweatpants, me in one of the dress shirts that has found a home in my closet over the last week. We just sway.

Somewhere, outside the bubble, his commitments call and he slowly pulls away from me.

"I gotta go to work," he murmurs. I offer a hum in return, lifting my hands and running my fingers through his hair. "Wanna shower with me first?"

I smile, accepting the kiss he drops on my lips. "Yes, please."

***

I do my best to focus on the three cards left in my hand. It's harder than you think. My mind keeps wandering back to Scott and waking up with him and his tongue between my legs.

God.

I need to focus.

Pops puts down a red four and I sigh. I pick up a card and he smirks. With two cards to my now four left, I just know he's going to win. Damn it. I'm going to have to go get him the hamburger we bet on for lunch now. So much for sticking to his diet.

An alarm blares through the room. I watch as Pops hastily reaches across to his bedside table to turn it off.

I narrow my eyes at him. "What's that for?"

"Oh nothing." He tries to wave me off, tapping the table with a knuckle after he throws down another red numbered card. "Uno."

"What are you setting alarms for? Do you have someone else coming in to see you?" I ask, swiveling myself around to watch the door of the hospital room.

"Uh," Pops sighs before grabbing the TV remote that sits next to his alarm clock. "It's for the Broncos game this afternoon."

"Oh." I tighten my grip on the cards I'm still holding, game forgotten as I watch Pops flick through the channels.

"Playoffs are a shoe-in if they keep playing the way they have been." When he lands on the right channel, he turns up the volume. I keep my back to the TV but the commentators are speaking as clearly as ever and when they mention Scott's name, I jolt.

Pops stares at me, my flinch not going unnoticed. "You okay?"

"Yeah. I— um, well—" I wring my hands together. I want to tell Pops about Scott. He already knows I'm seeing someone and I waved off any questions about Scott during our little ... break. I put the cards in my hands down. "You remember the Scott guy I was telling you about?"

Pops eyes snap back to meet mine, the screen forgotten. He sits up. "Yes. How's that going? You haven't said much so I haven't wanted to push you but I can't lie that I haven't been curious."

"Curious?" I giggle. "You know, other grandfathers don't really want to hear about their granddaughter's boyfriend's."

He shrugs. "I like to gossip with the nurses. Sue me."

"You gossip with the nurses? About me?" I can't help the laughter that bubbles up. Pops has always been a character. Carefree, worldly, open. He always encouraged me to be open with him and Nan. That I was able to tell them whatever I wanted to tell them and they would never judge me for it. I guess that's why now, I actually want to confide in him about Scott.

I have to keep him a secret from the rest of the world, but Pops is the one expectation I'll make.

"The Scott I'm seeing is Scott Harvey."

"Harvey? Scott Harvey ... where have I heard—" The presenters on the TV cut him off, calling the starting lineup for the

Broncos. I don't turn around but I know enough about football to know that they are running out of the tunnels right now, screaming and cheering along with the crowd.

"You're dating the starting quarterback for the Broncos?" Pops practically jumps out of his bed as he shouts the question at me. "You said he was tall, his name was Scott, that he was nice but you failed to mention that he was a damn football player, Ivy."

"I—" I shake my head at him. I can't help the stupid smile that crosses my lips when I see how excited Pops has gotten. "I didn't know. He didn't exactly tell me at the beginning that he was a player and I'm so far out of that world that I had no idea who he was when we met."

"You have your head buried in the sand sometimes." Pops is shaking his head at me, pointing to the screen. "That man is the highest paid QB on a starting roster right now. He is a machine."

We rarely talk about sports so I've forgotten over time how animated and excited Pops gets whenever he watches football. Another pang of guilt hits my stomach as I think about all the time we probably could've gone to a game or watched on TV in the last few years but he's avoided the sport just for me.

"I ... I wouldn't know. I still haven't really watched him play or anything."

"What? Ivy ..." Pops gives me a disapproving look.

"In my defense, I didn't know he was a player for the first few months and he knows that I don't like the game."

"He does?"

"We spoke about it briefly, when you were in surgery. He came to the hospital."

"He did?"

"Yes."

"So that was the man the doctors said you were with." Pops nods his head, as if putting pieces together. "Why haven't you gone to his games? Or watched him play?"

I shoot him a look. "You know why. Besides, we're keeping things quiet while we get to know each other."

"Is that smart, sweetheart?" The concerned look Pops gives me has my chest tightening.

I don't answer. I give a noncommittal shrug and pick up my cards again. But I've lost Pops to the game playing on the TV at my back. From the sounds of it, they are well into the first quarter now and the offensive team from the Broncos are back on the field.

Something deep, deep inside me pressures me to turn and watch but I resist.

Separate.

I need to keep my Scott and that Scott separate.

Instead, I watch Pops as he watches the game. His eyes light up and he *ooo's* and *ahh's* at whatever is happening on the screen.

I hear the commentators call out a third down and Pops quietly speaks, so low that I'm not sure he realizes he's talking out loud. "He reminds me of Matty."

Tension races through me and I stiffen.

"He's good," Pops continues, his eyes following the play on the screen. "He's really good. The way he communicates with his O-line. So in-tune with each other. For a new QB to be so aligned with them already takes some major commitment to getting to know his boys. It's admirable."

"Mmm," I hum in return, pulling the cards closer and in a stack to shuffle them. I guess UNO is done for the day.

"The way he throws, how he hangs in the back of the pocket and can slow down the play when he wants. He reminds me of your dad. He used to be able to do that. He used to say that his O-line were his best assets as a player and because he trusted them so deeply, he had more control over the ball." Pops hasn't taken his eyes off the screen as he continues to talk. "Scott seems to have it too. Takes a lot of trust in the O-line to protect him like that."

Tears sting at the back of my eyes and I hold back the request for Pops to stop talking about my dad because the guilt in my stomach roars to life to remind me that he was his son. Finally, I turn towards the TV and my eyes immediately land on Scott, holding the ball above his shoulder, ready to throw.

His eyes are scanning the field, they find something and he releases the ball. It sails right into the hands of the tight end standing in the end zone.

The camera's cut back to live coverage and I realize it was a replay of the touchdown. God, I forgot how slow this game can be. The TV screen fills with Scott's face as they focus in and the world around me quiets down as he smiles, laughing with the player next to him. Flynn Reed, the tight end that made the touchdown.

They're laughing about something. Both sweat covered already.

Scott looks happier than I have ever seen him, truly in his element.

If I hadn't turned around, I wouldn't have seen it.

Pops sighs and I move to sit in the chair next to him. He reaches over, holding out his palm and I take it, wrapping my fingers around his as we settle in to watch the game.

"I miss it, you know. Nearly every day."

"Playing or watching?" I ask, ignoring the pain in my chest.

"Both," he whispers. "You know, I haven't been to a game since you were about six."

I nod, swallowing the lump in my throat. My heart hammers and I prepare myself because I know what's coming. Ever since the conversation we had after his emergency surgery, I've been waiting for it.

"Will you take me to one last game, Ivy? Before I die." I meet his gaze and tears spring to my eyes again. For the first time in a long time, I see the aged lines and the tired eyes. I see pale skin and uneven breaths. I face the facts and I nod. I agree because even though I know it will break my heart, I can't bring myself to break my pops' any longer.

"Sure, Pops."

Chapter Seventeen

Scott

I've started to think about my life in two ways.

There's everything that came before Ivy and then everything that's come after.

Before her I was a football focused, broody son of a bitch with resentment toward a whole damn city and no idea what would come next. Now, I'm still a football focused, broody son of a bitch but then I get to come home.

To her.

I come home to her and the world spins and the sun shines again and for the first time in my damn life, I feel like there's something for me beyond football.

The last four weeks, since I came clean and we decided to give it a go even if it had to be on the down low, have been the happiest of my damn life.

Ivy makes me smile, and laugh, and enjoy my downtime.

I used to spend it watching game tape and waiting for the next practice, the next game. Now? Now all I want is to go home and see my girl.

Which is why I am racing off the team plane and to the parking lot the moment we land back in Boston from New York. We defeated the New York city team 54 to 36 in a Sunday lunchtime game which means we are home in time for a late dinner.

Before, I would've gone to a bar with Flynn and some of the guys to watch the Sunday Night game. Now the decision to blow them off is an easy one.

I slide into the driver's side of my Mercedes SUV and as soon as my phone connects, I tap on Ivy's name on the screen.

"Hi," her breathy voice answers and it sends a jolt of heat straight to my groin. Damn it. Forty-eight hours away from her and I get hard just hearing her voice.

"Hey, you." I clear my throat, turning out of the parking lot and heading towards her place. It's become my unofficial home and if I didn't think she'd totally freak out, I would just suggest we move in together already.

"How was the game, you guys win? Land okay?" There's a small pang of hurt that she asks if we won. It means she hadn't watched the game, again.

Part of me had hoped that after the one she watched with Billy not too long ago would get her over her irrational fear of watching me play or whatever it is that stops her.

I guess I was wrong. I try not to let my voice sound too disappointed as I reply to her. "Yep. 54 to 36, was a decent game. I'm on my way to yours now."

"Oh ..." There's some shuffling and I can hear someone talking in the background. I listen closer and when I make out the sound of music, my heart starts to thump. She's out? Since when does my girl go out on a Sunday?

Normally, I wouldn't care less that she'd gone out with Katie or some friends but I just got back and it's not like she'll let me meet up with them at the bar.

"Ives? You there?" I ask after she doesn't answer.

"Yeah. Yep, sorry." She sounds out of breath.

"You okay?"

"I'm at Pats," she replies. A small smile tweaks the side of my mouth upwards remembering the old fashion sports bar where we first met. "Let's go to yours tonight?"

"My place? We never stay at mine," I say but I'm already changing lanes on the highway, preparing to make my way home for the first time in a week. If that's where she wants to be then that's where we'll be.

"I'm already here and I can't be bothered to get an Uber home now." I can hear the smile in her voice as she says quietly into the phone. "Besides, you have those big windows and the view and I think they could be a lot of fun given the right circumstances."

Yep. My dick is definitely hard now.

"Fuck me, Ivy." I reach down to adjust as I take the exit to my apartment. "I'll be there in fifteen."

"I'll tell Katie I'm leaving," she giggles. "Then I will *fuck you*."

I groan as she hangs up.

***

She flings her arms around my neck the moment I open my front door and all bets are off. I fuck her up against the giant, floor to ceiling windows. It doesn't matter that the sun only just set or that we barely say hello to one another before I rip her jeans down her legs.

Eventually we make it to bed, tangled amongst the sheets and breathing heavily.

"I missed you," Ivy murmurs into my neck, her face hidden. I look down at her and press a kiss into her hair.

"Missed you, too," I say. My hands trace a path over her skin and I feel her shiver beneath my touch. She's so damn responsive to me. My stomach growls and interrupts the silence that's fallen between us. She laughs, dropping her hand to my abs.

"Sorry. I haven't really eaten yet after the game."

"We better get some food into you then," she says. Ivy sits up, throwing her legs over the side of the bed. Her hair falls over her shoulder and down her back.

I reach out, twirling a piece around my fingers. She turns her head to look at me with a smile playing on her lips. I sit up and shift in behind her. My dick is semi-hard again and pressing up against her back but I don't care. I curl my fingers around the curtain of her hair and pull it to the side, pressing my lips against her pulse point.

I'm rewarded with a happy, content sigh before she leans back into me.

"There's nothing here to eat," I say against her neck. "We'll have to order in."

"Why do you have no food?" she asks.

I chuckle, threading a hand around her stomach and pulling her back into me a little further. "Because we never stay here."

"Oh," she hums as I press another kiss into her neck. This time I linger, sucking on her skin. "Right, yeah."

"So what do you feel like?" I say moving my lips up her neck. I bite lightly on her ear lobe and she lets out a whimper.

"Stop that, I can't concentrate."

"So don't." I try to pull her back into bed but she resists.

Shaking her head, she pulls out of my grasp. "No, we need food. Then round two."

I give Ivy a pout but as always, she wins. She orders Chinese food and we shower while we wait for it to arrive.

She's sitting on the couch in my living room, a takeaway box in her hand and a *Friends* rerun playing quietly on the TV. She's wearing a hoodie of mine from college and sweatpants she rolled the waist of multiple times. She's my fucking dream. One I wasn't even aware that I had. But as I stare at her, telling me about her day and all the things she did this weekend, I can't help feeling disappointed that not once did she think to watch my game.

I know she wants to keep our relationship quiet and I know she has a thing about football but come on, if someone told me I could watch her teach day in day out it would become my favorite fucking show.

It would probably be boring as fuck and nothing exciting would likely happen but I'd still jump at the chance to watch her do something that she loves.

"Ives." I start, interrupting her babbling.

She looks over at me, a sheepish smile curling her lips. "Sorry, I was rambling."

"It's okay, I like listening to you talk." I sit up, pulling the takeaway container from her grasp. When I set it on the coffee table I ask her, "How come you didn't watch my game?"

I hate how desperate and small my voice is.

She fidgets, her finger twisting together in her lap. "You know—you know I don't watch games ..."

"I know. I know you don't normally." I reach out for her hands, stopping her fidgeting. "But you did. With Billy. And I thought ... I thought maybe you'd start ... after that."

I feel exposed.

Heat creeps up my neck and suddenly I'm twelve again, trying to tell Sabrina Winkleman I want to take her to a school dance. Fuck, that was a rough day for me.

All through my high school and college careers, never did I lay my feelings on the line for a girl. I got close with my high school girlfriend but we broke up and I just ... let it go.

I was the silent, broody type.

Feelings aren't my strong suit and unless you count my parents, I've never said 'I love you'.

The high school girlfriend? She told me she loved me and I said okay.

There was a girl in sophomore year that I slept with for a few months. I thought it was casual; she thought we were official. When she sat me down to have the 'what are we' talk and told me how she felt, I stared at her dumbfounded.

Later after she stormed out of my dorm crying, I felt like an idiot because I actually liked the girl. But instead of just saying that and working the rest of my fears out with her, I let my thoughts go to football schedules, and classes, and exams, and not having enough time for her, and that she'd hate me because I never put football before her.

Again, I just let it go.

After that, I focused on football and didn't sleep with the same girl again twice.

Until Ivy.

Everything is different now.

Before I couldn't have cared less if a girl came to my games. Now, I am desperate for Ivy to sit in the stands.

And she won't even watch one on TV for me.

"I'm sorry," Ivy's soft whisper brings me back to the couch. Her eyes are starting to water and I can't stand it.

"It's okay." She shakes her head, disagreeing with me, and it only seems to make it worse because the first tear drips down her cheek and then the second. I pull her into my lap and wipe a thumb across her cheek. "Ivy, what's going on? This can't just be about me wanting you to watch my games?"

Her eyes close and she leans into my touch. Her voice is shaking and weak when she finally talks.

"Pops wants me to take him to a game. Before he ... before he dies."

"Oh, Ivy." I circle my arms around her, running my hands up and down her back.

"He asked the other week, when we watched you play. I'm sorry, I know it's a stupid thing to get so upset about and I would do anything for him. But take him to a game? I just don't think I can do that."

"Why? It's just a game, baby. It won't hurt anyone if you take him." I frown.

"It hurts *me*."

"Help me understand," I plead with her. "Please, Ives, I just need to understand this aversion. At first, I thought it was because you just weren't a fan but you won't even watch me play on TV."

I watch her face, the color draining. She squirms a little in my arms and I lean back, trying to give her space but without fully pulling away. My heart starts to sink. I feel close to begging on my knees.

"If I go, if I take Pops, the press will report it. And then, for the weeks after that, they'll parade my family history on every sports program, every local newscast. They'll talk about my dad as if they know him better than I do. They *do* know him better than I do."

Ivy's face scrunches up in pain and she sniffles before continuing, "I can't watch games because when I do, all I see is my dad running down the field. All I hear is the commentators calling out his name as he throws the ball. I—" She inhales and I tighten my grip on her hips, ensuring she doesn't move from my lap.

"I can't go to a game because the last time I tried with Katie a few years ago, a few people recognized me from the news stories that had been floating around and they were quick to tell me how good my dad was and how sad they were that they never got to see him play pro ball. *They* were sad. Imagine." She lets out a small scoff, like she's angry just thinking about it. "I had the worst panic attack of my life that day and I didn't even make it to my seat."

"Oh, damn. Baby, I'm sorry." I rub her back. "But this is Pops we're talking about here. I'm sure things will be different this time." She shakes her head so violently her hair falls around her face and her eyes glaze over. She's putting up walls behind those piercing blue eyes.

Fuck. Whatever is going on in her head is so much worse than I thought.

Logically, I'm still confused about how football and games are still a trigger for her. Her parents died when she was so young, I didn't think this kind of thing could still affect her so much.

But emotionally, the look on her face is breaking my heart and I can't bear it.

We sit in silence, her sniffles subsiding with time. She doesn't move off my lap at first but as if the wall she put up physically manifests in front of me she quickly scrambles off the couch and off me, getting to her feet. Ivy adjusts the rolls of her sweats, swipes at her eyes one last time and gives me a weak smile.

"Do you have any ice cream?"

I stare at her.

What the fuck? Ice cream?

How have we gone from opening up and finally getting somewhere to ice cream?

"Ivy, I—" I follow her into the kitchen and watch her dig through my freezer. Her hands are trembling but she doesn't stop.

"Seriously? No ice cream? Who the hell doesn't keep ice cream in their freezer?" She rattles off and I don't even think she's paying attention to me anymore.

I move to stand behind her. I pull her hands from the freezer and close the door. When I turn her in my arms, she avoids my gaze.

"What just happened?"

"I'm done talking about this," Ivy whispers, still not looking at me.

"But I'm not."

"What's there left to talk about? My inability to move on and get over it? This is just how my life is." She sucks in a short breath, obviously trying to keep her breathing steady. "I won't watch your games and I can't take Pops to one. End of story. It is what it is."

"No," I bite out. "It's not *is what it is*. Ivy, this is my job. My passion. I—" Three words sit on my tongue, waiting their turn to fall out but I don't let them. It's not the time. "How are we supposed to have any kind of future if there's this huge part of my life you refuse to be a part of?"

Silence falls around us and the air becomes stifling. Ivy is still trembling in my arms and my heart races miles a minute. The longer she doesn't answer, the deeper my fear sinks into my chest.

I wait, heart pounding and blood rushing and fear building, as I stare at her. When she finally looks up at me, her eyes are filled with tears and I feel like my heart cracks in two when she still doesn't answer me.

"Right," I whisper. "See the thing is Ives, I want you. I want all of you. But you don't want all of me."

"I—"

"You don't. Whether you like it or not, I play football for a living. It's my job. One that I love. If you can't get on board with that then you're not all in and I don't know where we stand." I cup her cheeks in my hands, stroking my thumb down her jaw line.

"I can't ... I won't make you a promise that I'm not sure I can even keep." She tries to wipe furiously at her cheeks but my hands are in the way. "I don't ... I can't ... please don't ask me to ..."

"I'm sorry, baby, but I have to," I murmur as my thumb swipes to catch a tear. I take a deep breath because the next thing I have to say is going to hurt us both.

"I'm going to drive you home, okay? I think we should take some space. Think about what we want." Pray she changes her mind.

***

When things start to feel so out of my own control, I sometimes think standing still will fix them. If I just don't move, don't change anything, don't make any waves, everything that feels out of my grasp will settle and make its way back.

Team dynamics feel off? I'll stop pushing and just let others move around me until we find our places and start to meld again.

In college when I would get overwhelmed with school work, and practice, and trying to keep up with a social life I would spend a few weeks staying in. Keeping to myself until I got some sense of balance back.

I'm so out of my depth with Ivy.

So out of control of my own actions. This secret relationship isn't sustainable. I want more from her, more *with* her. She's dictating the path and I am almost blindly following.

I'm officially torturing myself and I'm not sure if I'm even upset about it.

Two nights ago, when we had half an argument about her not coming to games and what the future looked like for us, I'd barely been able to go a night without her.

Ivy texted me the next morning before I headed to the gym for a workout apologizing. She hated the space as much as I did but it still didn't change the fact that she wouldn't open up to me.

She said she would think about the game with Pops and I accepted that.

Just like I'd accepted the secret relationship. I'd let my fear win and told her it was okay. I'd back tracked and caved and I felt like shit for it.

I want more. I want everything with Ivy. I just need time to break through her walls because there is no way in hell I am giving her up now I have her.

So today, as I sweated out the frustration in morning drills on the field, I made the decision to make it happen.

Ivy is scared, I get that. Why? No idea. I am going to make the game happen anyway.

I walk toward Coach's office, freshly showered and a Broncos gym bag over my shoulder. We've just finished Wednesday afternoon practice and everyone is heading home for the day. If I'm going to pull this off, it has to be now.

"Coach, got a minute?" I knock on his open door.

Jeff Brady looks up, his eyes narrowing at me standing in his doorway. His pen hovers above the notebook spread on his desk and the three TV's lining a wall of his office are all playing different football games with different teams.

"What is it, Harvey?" His eyes flicker back to his notebook but he waves at me to sit down, so I do.

"I, um, have a favor to ask."

"Hm. This wouldn't have anything to do with the fact you've been dating Ivy Booker, would it?" The look he levels me with has my mouth turning to sandpaper. I'm twenty-nine years old, sitting in front of my coach and I'm terrified.

"You know?"

"Billy and I are good friends. You don't think he'd call me and tell me his granddaughter, who also happens to be like a niece to me, is dating my new QB?"

"I guess he would." Fuck, this is not going well. "Y—yes, it is. Kind of."

Coach's expression is stone-like as he stares at me. I wait for him to say something, anything, but he just continues to stare. When I can't take the silence anymore, I decide it's better I get it over with so I can vacate Coach's office before he decides to murder me.

"Ivy's pops has asked her to take him to a game." I swallow the lump forming in my throat. "I thought since we are playing at home on Christmas Day, it would be the perfect game. I want to ask if I can use the executive suite for them. It's the most private, and has the biggest bathroom attached and closest to the service lift so if something were to happen, they'd be able to avoid the crowds. I know Ivy feels hesitant about coming to a—"

"Yes. Tell Meghan, she'll organize it."

"—but I think if I can sort out something private and completely away from the press she might be open to it." I finish slowly. I stare at Coach, who's already lowered his head back to his notebook.

"Anything else, Harvey?"

"I—uh, no, sir." I rise from the chair, tapping my fingers on the side of my leg as I hesitate leaving the office.

I've always looked up to my coaches. High school, college, LA. My QB coaches, offensive team coaches, my head coaches. They've all taught me something along the way.

Jeff Brady is a legend and when he called, asking if I'd come to Boston, I'd said thank you but no, thank you.

Then, he told me I'd regret it if I didn't. A week later, I signed a one-year deal.

I tap my fingers against my leg and grab my bag from the floor.

"Harvey," Coach calls after me and I pause in the doorway.

"Coach?"

"Ivy's ... not as okay and open as she pretends to be. She's happy and kind, but she's had a hell of a childhood." Coach leans back in his chair. "If you hurt her, Harvey, I don't care that you can throw a fifty-yard touchdown. I'll end your career."

I gulp. Then, nod, because there is nothing else to do but agree.

Yep, I'm terrified of my coach.

Chapter Eighteen
Ivy

"How was work?"

Scott's making dinner as I organize the mid-year reports for parents to take home with their kids tomorrow over the break. Most teachers in kindergarten don't bother with them normally, but I find that if there's a child that needs an extra hand in the second half of the year now is a good time to point it out. This week has been torturously slow. Time seems to have completely slowed down since Pops asked me to take him to one last football game a few weeks ago. Thinking about the promise I made to Pops makes my stomach turn sour because I'm a terrible granddaughter.

I haven't even begun to think about planning it.

Just like I have been avoiding thinking about the sort of fight Scott and I had about it. The one when he told me I wasn't all in.

Aren't I?

I barely slept that night without him next to me. Knowing he was in the same city yet not in the same bed drove me crazy. But every time I've tried to wrap my head around it, every time I try to break down my reasoning in my head that pain pulses in my chest and I can't take it.

It feels like I am being torn in two.

I want to open up, but I can't.

I look up at Scott, shrugging. "Last week of school before Christmas is always the same. Who asked for what from Santa and whether they've been good enough to get it."

"Did you do that Elf on the Shelf thing you were talking about?" I smile at his question because I love that he remembers the elf on the shelf idea I pitched him over a month ago.

"Yes," I laugh quietly. "And the kids love it."

I put my pen back into my bag along with the report cards and move it to the side. Getting off my stool and moving around the counter, I wrap my arms around Scott's waist and press my forehead into his chest.

He instantly wraps me up in his arms.

The past few weeks haven't been the easiest in terms of this 'private' relationship. We put a pin in the football conversation and neither of us are too keen to pull said pin out again any time soon. Scott also hasn't brought up the secret part of this secret relationship either, even though I know he's getting sick of having to hide away.

I overheard him explaining to his mom on the phone the other day that we couldn't go out to dinner with them next week because I'm not keen on being spotted by the paparazzi. I'm not sure what Annabel's reply was but it had drawn a lengthy sigh from my boyfriend causing the guilt to flare under my skin.

It's not like keeping things quiet is my favorite thing either but every time I imagine what it would be like if the world knew, I'm thrust into the midst of a minor panic attack.

So I've avoided both topics and when it seems like things are starting to get a little tense, I distract Scott by kissing him. Which usually then leads to him kissing me back, neither of us letting go, and after a couple of mutual orgasms the tension is normally gone.

So far, so good even if I was feeling guilty about it all.

"How was your day?" I ask, my question muffled into his chest.

"Good. Practice was good. Getting ready for the playoffs now we've clinched a spot."

"What?" I look up at him, my eyes widening. "I didn't know that. Congratulations!" I smile genuinely because I know that playoffs are a huge deal. I'm not a total monster when it comes to football.

Another pang of guilt hits me right in the chest. I smile wider, masking it.

"Thank you," he says quietly, leaning down to kiss me. "I also spoke to Coach today."

"Oh?" My hands start to itch and I feel like pulling them back from around his waist so I can wring them together but I keep them in place.

"I—Uh, I spoke to him and organized the executive suite for the game on Christmas Day. For you to bring Billy."

I flinch and my arms start to withdraw but Scott doesn't let me. He continues before I can tug out of his grasp. "I know you weren't sure when or which game, but I thought since it was Christmas Day it might be nice. And the exec suite is totally private with its own bathroom, fully catered in the suite and close to a service lift so you can get in and out without being seen."

He goes quiet, staring down at me.

I don't move for a moment, stunned by his confession. I can feel the anxiety clawing at the base of my throat but more than that, I feel the relief that floods my veins when he tells me it's all taken care of. All I have to do is pick up Pops and turn up at the stadium.

He's taken care of it.

All of it.

"Thank you," I whisper, standing on my toes to kiss him again. I ignore the anxiety building at the thought of the football game and focus on everything else. "You didn't have to do that for me."

"I did," he says against my lips.

"I'm terrified," I admit in a small voice, still trying to disappear into his large form. "It's only a game of football and I am terrified to take him. What kind of person does that make me? That I can't even do this one thing for Pops after everything he's done for me."

Scott reaches behind him and turns off the stove. He takes my hand and leads me to the couch to sit down. I pull a blanket over my legs, trying to ward off the December chill that seems to be creeping through the house.

It might be time to start lighting fires in the evenings. With Pops not here, I'd have to learn how.

"Ivy," Scott says, bringing my attention back to him. "I was thinking about this aversion you have to football and I just want to get through this without us having a fight or me making you cry."

I huff out a soft laugh, because damn he's right. I've been crying a lot lately. I nod for him to go on.

"When Jeff Brady called to ask if I would be open to signing a deal with Boston after my contract ended in LA, I originally said no. I said no because I couldn't stomach the thought of being in Boston. I couldn't stomach the thought of being in Boston because my birth mother still lives here."

I inhale sharply. Scott doesn't acknowledge the sound or stop, he just reaches for my hands and squeezes them between his own.

"I know who she is. I know where she lives. I know where she works." I gaze at him. His face is emotionless but his eyes are darkening and he looks almost angry. "I found her a few years ago after the details of my adoption became public and I was making my own money to be able to pay someone to look. I ended up telling my parents but they were just supportive, as I suspected they would be."

"Did you meet her?" I ask him.

"No. I never want to meet her. I have never had the urge to know her, to speak to her. I don't care what excuses she has or reasons she cares to give me. I found her because I want to avoid her. I hated walking through life knowing she's out there and could pop up at any moment. When I learned she was living in Boston, I started to avoid the city. When we played here, I'd fly in and out but I'd never linger. I never joined my parents when they travelled back here. I hated Boston. All because *she* chose to call it her home."

As Scott takes a few deep breaths, his thumb rubbing mine with our hands still clasped together, I watch as the anger fades in his eyes.

"I realized pretty quickly that I was meant to come to Boston. As much as I hated it and protested the move, something was drawing me here. *You* were drawing me here."

"Me?"

"I told Jeff Brady thank you but no thank you." Scott nods. "I only took the call as a consideration to his reputation; I was never ever going to say yes. But after I hung up the phone with him and went back to whatever I'd been doing there was just something tugging in my gut telling me that maybe I made the wrong choice. That feeling stuck around for a whole week before I called Coach back and told him we could talk. Even when I signed, it was no longer than a year because I was so sure that I'd be uncomfortable living so close to *her*. But something was still telling me that I should come here so I did. Then I met you."

Scott takes a sharp breath and reaches up to cup my face. His thumbs stroke across my cheek and his fingers splay down my neck. My body warms under his touch and I relax into him.

"If anything, *anything* in your gut is telling you that taking Billy to a game is the absolute wrong decision for you, I will respect that and we can make other arrangements to get him there. But I think if this is what he wants then you should try." Scott gazes at me, his eyes searching my own. I allow myself a moment to get lost in the pretty green, gold flecks swirling around and around the inner ring as he watches me right back.

His beautiful, grounding green. It's becoming a lifeline. A tether.

When he told me about organizing this for Pops I felt relieved. A little anxious and guilty because I hadn't been able to do it myself but overall, relieved.

I take a calming breath, shaking off the lingering anxiety still clawing at me and focus on the warmth of his body. "I can do this."

"You can," he agrees.

"It's just a game."

He nods. "And when you're watching that field, you focus on me. On my number. On my plays. On me."

"On you," I agree, leaning in to kiss him gently.

***

Scott took care of everything.

When I say everything, I mean it.

A week after I agreed to the Christmas Day game, the day itself arrives and I've been an anxious mess from the moment he left me in bed this morning. I dragged myself through my breakfast and morning routine to get ready. When I stepped outside at the sound of a car horn, I realized Scott had meant what he said when he whispered in my ear before leaving me with a kiss.

"Just get dressed and be there. Focus on me, baby."

Just before lunch, a car pulls up the curb outside the house. Blacked out windows, a huge SUV with so much space inside it I swear I could live in there comfortably. Once I'm settled into the seat, the driver informs me that we're stopping at the hospital. Pops is waiting, decked out in Boston Broncos gear, alongside one of the nurses, Sara.

Pops tells me that the only way Dr. Bryden is letting him do this is with the proper care, so his favorite nurse volunteered for the extra hours and outing. I'm sure the fact she gets to meet a team of NFL players has zero to do with it.

We turn up at the stadium and get escorted by a golf cart to an underground private parking lot.

"They didn't have this back in my day," Pops murmurs as he stares out the window at the giant painted tunnels. I watch him closely as a few security guards help him out of the car and wheel his chair into the elevator. Pops is speechless—not something that happens all that often—as we are let into the box suite overlooking the stadium and the field. Katie and Grant are waiting for us, drinks and snacks already in hand.

"You made it!" Katie squeals, hurrying over. "This is insane. Mystery football man did very well."

I only hum in agreement, my eyes darting around the room.

Pops sets himself up at the very front of the box, right against the windows that look down at the seats that are filling fast. Waves of white and navy move around below us, fans pouring in. I walk over to him, looking down at the green field. Players litter the field, warming up or crowding the sidelines.

I scan the field for the number eighteen but I'm too far up and there are too many people. I can feel the anxiety creeping up my neck.

"You okay, sweetheart?" Pops asks quietly. No one else can hear him, just me.

I swallow the lump in my throat. "Of course. You? Are you feeling okay?"

The smile he hits me with is so bright, so wide it lights up his entire face. He stares out at the stadium and nods.

"It's like coming home again." Pops takes my hand, squeezing it. "Thank you, Ivy. Thank you for making this happen."

"I—" The words get stuck and I blink away tears. "I didn't do anything. This was all Scott."

Understanding floods Pops' features and his smile softens. "He's a good man. Good for you."

I nod in agreement. Mostly because if I open my mouth the only thing that will come out is a sob. And once I start sobbing I won't be able to stop.

Others bustle in the box around us but I decide to stay by Pops' side to watch the game. If this is the last time he will get to see one, live and in person, then I want to make sure I'm here with him for it.

When the game starts and the players fall into their lines on the field, I finally spot Scott below. He stands on the sideline, a cap on his head instead of a helmet. When his face floods the big screens, my eyes track the movement of his jaw as he chews on a piece of gum. He's following what's going on out on the field but when he spots the camera tracking him, he flashes a quick smile and a wink.

My heart soars because I know that's for me.

Scott Harvey is a lot of things, but a football player that winks and plays up for the press? Absolutely not. The game I watched in Pops' hospital room proved it. He didn't bother interacting with the cameras that followed players around. He barely acknowledged them when he threw a pass into the end-zone other than congratulating the teammate who'd caught it.

The smile, the wink.

It's just for me.

As the game goes on, the attention Scott gives the camera becomes less and less but the game is close and even I can tell that he's focused in.

Every time I feel the familiar hand of anxiety start to creep up my neck, I find Scott down on the field and just watch him. I focus so heavily and intently on him alone that eventually the anxiety disappears, taking every fan in the stadium with it.

I see him glance up at the box a few minutes into the third quarter. He finds our box. I can't be sure he sees me too but it feels like our eyes lock. My body instantly reacts to being under his gaze, warming up.

Pops notices Scott down on the field too, turning his head to grin at me. "You're smitten, sweetheart."

"I am not." I so am.

"You're absolutely smitten over a football player." Pops reaches out to take my hand, tucking it between his own. "I'm glad. It makes me feel better knowing he will be there to take care of you when I die."

The tears sting behind my eyes instantly and my heart beats painfully in my chest. "Don't. Don't talk about that. Not to-day."

"Okay," he murmurs softly, lifting our hands so he can press a kiss to them. "No talk. Just enjoying Sunday football with my girl."

Guilt floods me. Pops gave up such a huge part of his life because I couldn't come to terms with the hand life dealt me. He's always done what is best for me even when it meant giving up the game he loves.

"I'm sorry we didn't do this more," I say quietly, resting my head on his shoulder gently.

"Don't be. We're doing it now." He sniffs. "I love you, Ivy."

"Love you, too."

Boston kicks ass and we win. The noise from the fans in the fourth quarter as Scott throws touchdown after touchdown is deafening. As the fans disperse from their seats around us, we remain in the box. The runner that's been in and out of the box tells us that Uncle Jeff wants us to all stay put while they finish up their press interviews and shower.

Pops starts telling stories from his own career on the field.

His face lights up as he speaks. Grant hangs on his every word. Just as he starts telling stories about my dad's pee-wee football days and himself as the coach, the doors to the suite opens.

For a second, my mouth goes dry and I forget where I am. Freshly showered with hair still damp and back in his game day suite, Scott follows Uncle Jeff into the room and heads toward me. He looks exhausted, moving slowly as he greets everyone.

"Hi." I look up into his face, noting the small cut on his hairline and the bruising coming up along his jaw. I reach up and gently draw my finger over it, murmuring a quiet, "Ouch."

"Hey, you." Scott brushes my fingers away from his face and leans down, covering my mouth with his own. God, I love when this man kisses me without being prompted. I hear a wolf whistle from Katie as we break apart.

"Good game." His eyes flash with pride as soon as the words leave my lips. Happiness floods his features and I'm a little bit flawed that I have that effect on him. Just by being here, just by watching him play one game I've made him so happy.

Warmth spreads through me and for the first time today I don't feel even the slightest bit anxious.

"Thanks baby." Scott's arm snakes around my shoulders and he pulls me into his side. "How'd it all go here?"

I look over at Billy, sighing happily. "He looks more alive than I've seen him in weeks."

"Good." Scott presses his lips to my hair. "Felt good having you here."

"Show off, did you? Played up for the cameras? Don't think I didn't catch that wink you threw."

He shrugs but the smirk that lifts his lips tells me all I need to know. We just stand there, staring at each other, smiling like idiots. Pops is talking to Jeff somewhere next to us, likely giving his notes on the plays. Katie and Grant are talking to Sara. No one's paying attention to us.

I lean into Scott. "Today wasn't as bad as I thought it would be."

"Yeah?" Scott moves me in front of him. His fingers slide down my arms, tapping lightly over the fabric of my jacket.

"Mhmm." I melt into his touch. "I don't know. Maybe I can watch one or two again."

The hope lights up his face and I melt even further. As I'd watched him down on that field today, everything I used to see, used to hear was gone. It was just him. I'm completely infatuated with him and it's becoming more and more obvious.

He leans down and kisses me again. Lingering this time, pressing gentle kisses to my lips. I smile and lift myself onto my toes.

The tether connecting us tugs and tightens. I let it.

Maybe I can do this thing with him after all, football be damned.

Chapter Nineteen

Ivy

"I THINK IT MIGHT snow tonight." His voice murmurs down the phone, deep and smooth. "Hopefully we're not delayed because of it."

I ignore the anxiety humming under my skin at the mention of him traveling in the snow. I fiddle with my necklace and ask, "When do you take off again?"

"A few minutes." Someone yells in the background and Scott groans down the phone. "I have to go now. I'm holding the team up."

I sigh. "Okay. Are you still coming here when you land?"

"It's New Year's Eve, baby." I practically hear the eye roll in his voice. "I wouldn't be anywhere else."

"Are you driving from the airport?" I can hear his teammates calling for him on the other end of the phone but I just need to be sure he knows to be safe. The sky outside is gloomy, and dark, and the air smells of snow. Boston winter is going to hit hard tonight and the thought of him driving in the snow makes me sick to the stomach.

"Yeah. The car's in the team lot." The line starts to crackle and I realize that he's walking out onto the tarmac.

"Drive carefully, okay? Text me when you land so I know you're on your way. Don't speed in the snow." My voice is dripping with nerves and I sound like a nagging girlfriend but I don't care.

"Of course, Ives. You okay?" he yells down the phone, over the noise of the plane he's probably walking toward right now.

"I—yes, just ... be safe. Drive safe." Those three short but huge words stick in my throat as a way of saying goodbye but I clamp my lips together.

Nope.

No way.

Not yet ... right? It feels too soon. I've only just started to watch his games, to dip a toe into his world. Saying those words feels like I would be jumping in the deep end of the pool not knowing if I could swim and without a floatation device.

"I gotta go." He pauses. "I'll message you when I land."

Then he's gone.

I tuck the phone between my legs, lean back into the couch cushions and close my eyes.

Deep breath in, deep breath out.

It's only a little bit of snow. It won't be that thick by the time he lands back in Boston. He'll be fine.

Did he get snow tires put on his car?

I didn't ask.

Fuck, why didn't I ask?

He probably does. He would know to put snow tires on the car ... right?

I reach for my phone, planning to send off a quick text to him and ask about the snow tires. I can't sit hit here for the next four hours whilst he flies home, thinking about whether or not he has the right fucking tires on his car.

Before I can start typing out a message my phone vibrates in my hand.

> Scott: *Scott has started sharing his live location with you.*

> I'll see you before midnight. Wait up for me.

Yep.

I'm in love with this man.

***

I watch his little blue dot get closer and closer to mine on the phone. It's almost midnight. I've been refreshing my phone since Scott landed an hour ago. I'm still in a small state of shock that he even turned the location on in the first place. Katie doesn't even have Grant's location on her phone.

It's like Scott heard the anxiety in my voice and knew, without asking, exactly what I needed from him.

I refresh the map and the blue dot jumps just as lights from a car turning into the driveway flashes down the front hallway.

Anticipation and excitement buzz through me. He only left thirty-six hours ago but it feels far too long to be apart.

I uncurl from the couch, toss my phone onto the coffee table and head down the hallway before I even hear the car door slam. Cold air rushes inside, making me shiver. I'm only in an oversized sweatshirt—one I stole from Scott—and fluffy socks.

Scott's hair is trapped under his signature black cap. He holds his overnight bag in one hand and his phone in the other, staring at something on his screen. When he gets close enough, I smile, rolling on the balls of my feet.

"Hey, you."

His head snaps up and his gaze locks on mine. He shoves his phone into the pocket of his sweats. A few more strides and he's standing in front of me, a few steps down so we're eye to eye. He drops a peck on my lips. "Hi."

Without dropping his bag, he reaches his free hand around my waist, skimming down until he cups my ass and lifts me up.

I squeal, wrapping my arms around him. I press my body into his and bury my face into his neck, giggling. He carries me inside, kicking the door shut with one foot and dropping his bag. He presses me into the wall near the stairs, wedging my body between him and the wall with my legs wrapping tightly around his hips.

He kisses me hard and messy. His tongue begs for entry and I open for him. I rip off his cap and my fingers sink into his hair. When he rips a moan from my throat, he swallows it.

We stand there, stealing each other's breaths for god knows how long before Scott slows things down. He drags his lips against my jaw.

"Fuck, but I missed you," he murmurs against my skin. He doesn't pull back or move away. He stays close, like he's trying to weld me to him.

"I missed you, too," I whisper, also not pulling away from him. "Good game, QB. How was your flight?"

"You watched?" His voice is muffled against my neck but there is no way I can miss the pride in his voice.

"I did." I pull back just a little because I want to see his reaction when I tell him. "Hell of hail Mary you pulled in the fourth. Way to give your fans a collective heart attack, Harvey."

Pride shines in his eyes. He doesn't reply, only kisses me again.

Eventually, he pulls back and I unlock my thighs from around his hips. I slide down his body and back to my feet. Scott lifts a hand, gently pushing a curl behind my ear. A quiet settles around us and as I glance over Scott's shoulder, I take a peek at the clock. It's five minutes to midnight.

I have never been kissed at midnight on a New Year's Eve before.

"What was going on earlier tonight?" he asks. "I could tell you were anxious. Was it because you watched the game?"

I clasp my hands in front of me and start to pick at my nails. The anxiety rushes back and my chest hurts from the force of it. I'm not really in the mood to talk about why I get so anxious in the snow. I just want Scott to kiss me, and take me to bed, and then not stop kissing me.

His hands slide into mine, fingers curling around and squeezing.

"I got worried that it was going to snow. I don't like traveling in the snow. Don't like anyone traveling in the snow," I tell him quietly. I trace my thumb over his skin.

"Why?"

"Just ..." I take a deep breath and steel my nerves. "It was snowing the night my parents died. They were driving home from New York City and there was a truck driver who decided to have too many at dinner and then get back behind the wheel. They were driving in a snowstorm and he didn't see them. They died on the way to the hospital."

My throat feels like sandpaper. Anxiety creeps up my neck. My chest begins to hurt and I squeeze my eyes shut, begging myself not to cry.

I really don't want to cry tonight.

Scott lets go of my hands. Then I feel the gentle caress of his thumb against my cheeks. He strokes my skin, waiting for me to open my eyes.

"I'm so sorry, baby," he says, still stroking my cheeks.

I only nod.

"Did having my location help?" he asks and I look up at him. His cap lies somewhere on the floor behind us and I can see the gold flakes amongst the green so clearly, even in the dim light.

"Yes. Thank you."

"You're welcome." His thumb swipes once more across my cheek before his fingers drop to my throat, finding my pulse there. "I'll keep it on. So even if I can't reply because I'm at practice or in meetings or doing press, you will know where I am."

"Okay." In the back of my head I know it's silly and I shouldn't need it but it helps. To be able to know that he's safe. Especially with all the traveling they'll be doing during the playoffs.

Scott dips his head, catching my gaze again before he gently kisses me. Then he presses another to my lips. And then another. Each one lingers a little more than the last.

My gaze wanders back to the clock. "We missed midnight."

"Happy New Year, baby," he hums against my lips.

"I've never celebrated a new year with a boyfriend before." I take a step up the stairs but Scott grabs my hand and pulls me back down the hall toward the lounge.

The fire is surviving but it's low and almost out. Scott presses a kiss into my hair before stripping his sweatshirt off and dropping to his knees in front of the fire. He adds a log and a few extra smaller sticks, poking and prodding until the fire comes back to life.

I sink back into the couch, watching him carefully. The muscles stretch across his strong shoulders and when he moves, I watch them bulge. Scott sits back on his knees, surveying his work. The fire is roaring now and the heat surrounds us.

Instead of coming to sit beside me on the couch, Scott moves the coffee table from between the couch and the fire, pushing it aside and out of the way. Then he takes the blanket that I normally curl up under and spreads it out on the floor. When he holds his hand out to me, I take it.

Scott pulls me to my feet before he takes a seat on the blanket in front of the fire. He leans against the front of the couch and tugs me down onto his lap, straddling him.

"Thank you for watching tonight. And for coming to my game on Christmas." He runs his hands up my bare legs, fingertips disappearing a little further past the hem of my sweatshirt with every pass.

I shiver.

"I don't think you know how much it means to me that you were there. That you watched me tonight," he murmurs as he pushes the hair from my neck. He trails his forefinger down the line of my neck, his lips following.

My thighs tighten around his hips.

"In the first, when I ran out of the pocket ten yards from the TD zone." His teeth graze along my shoulder.

"Yeah?" I urge him on. He nips at my skin.

"I knew we were going to win. It would be tight but I knew. Their defensive wasn't on their games—"

"You're right about that. They were actually in shambles. Did you see … what?" I ask when he pulls his face out of my neck to smirk at me.

"Mm. Nothing." He continues to run his big hands over my thighs. I love the feel of his hands. Rough and calloused. Big. They make me feel small. Precious. Breakable.

But only if he's the one breaking me.

He sinks his fingers in the soft flesh of my thighs. "I knew we were going to get the win. So, I decided something. Right there in the end zone."

"Oh?" I gasp when he grazes his teeth along my jaw, nipping at my skin gently as he blazes a path down to my pulse point.

"Want to know?" he asks.

I tilt my head a little and his lips latch onto my skin, just over my pulse. He sucks, marking me.

My heart pounds in my chest and my thighs become impossibly tight around his hips.

I want to roll my hips. I want friction. His tone, the way his lips are moving along my skin, he's promising something and I want it. So badly.

He's still waiting for my answer so I give him one. "Yes. Tell me."

"I decided that for every touchdown I got tonight, I'd give you an orgasm to match."

He thrusts upwards and I finally feel the hardness under me. Scott has me in such a trance, so distracted by the feel of him, that I didn't notice his cock straining against the gray fabric of his sweats.

My mouth goes dry and I bite down on my bottom lip. I roll forward and this time, his hands slide further up under my sweatshirt to take hold of my waist. He guides me. Slowly rolling me over his hips. Slowly enough that I feel every single inch of his hard cock.

Fuck me.

"You want to know how many touchdowns I threw into the end zone tonight?" he asks.

I whimper as he rolls me against him again, taking control of my movements and slowing them down a torturous amount.

"Six, baby." He kisses the corner of my mouth. My eyes close and his hands snake around my back and tug me closer to him. My nipples are hard and the friction against the fabric of my sweatshirt every time I brush against his chest is almost unbearable.

"Six?" I say breathlessly.

"Mhmm," he agrees. "Six."

A hand leaves my back. I follow the feel of his fingers as his hand snakes between our bodies and down. The tips trail lightly over my panties. Which are absolutely soaked. Ruined.

My back is too warm from the fire behind me and with him pressing me so close to his chest, I feel like I'm going to combust.

Everything is heightened.

His body is warm, the fire crackles behind us, and when he tugs my panties to the side and sinks two fingers inside me, I burn.

"Oh god." I drop my head into the crook of his neck.

"I played a hell of a game tonight. Like I knew you were watching," Scott murmurs into my ear. His fingers move in and out. A slow, controlled rhythm.

"I showed off for you." He strokes and plays.

I moan, trying to ride his hand to get more friction.

"Uh uh. We're going to go slow, get you there. One orgasm at a time," he scolds gently.

In. Out. His thumb brushes against my clit and I jolt.

"Should we count them out, baby?"

Fuck, fuck, fuck.

I want to come so badly. I'm about to beg, about to cry out, about to plead with him to go faster and get me there. I curl further into him, pressing my face into his neck, letting his skin muffle my moan. He builds up his pace.

"I feel so proud to play when you're watching. It means the world to me," he confesses in my ear. "You mean the world to me."

God, this man.

I want to reply. I want to tell him he means the world to me, too.

But then he presses a thumb to my clit, playing with me, and I forget how to use my words. Faster and faster. In. Out. My hands sink into his hair. My fingers curl around the strands and I tug.

He pulls back, staring at me so intensely for a beat I feel that tether again. Tugging me in, tightening the knots. Pulling us closer and closer into one another's orbit.

When I feel like I might combust just from the way he looks into my soul, I kiss him.

He ups his pace again, fucking me hard with his fingers as I ride his hand. When I come, my moans are swallowed right down Scott's throat.

Neither of us speak as he pulls my sweatshirt over my head and I tug his shirt off. I pull my ruined panties off and throw them over the couch. He tugs off the fluffy pink socks from my feet and they disappear too.

His gray sweatpants are the last to come off.

I move, kneeling beside him. He tilts his head as his hips lift and he drags his sweats down his thick thighs, capturing one of my nipples in his mouth. I gasp. I still feel the remnants of my orgasm sliding down my thigh. But his mouth is hot, and wet, and his teeth tug my nipple between them just enough I can feel myself dripping even more.

"That feels so good," I whimper. I feel him smile against my skin before swapping to the other. It doesn't last very long before he's kicking away the pants and pulling me back over his lap.

His cock sits hard, throbbing, the tip glistening against my soft stomach.

He's so big. The way it sits against me looks as if we're measuring whether it will fit. It does but I still eye it like it's gotten bigger and won't this time.

"Ivy." His soft tone draws my eyes up to meet his gaze.

Wordlessly, I lift on my knees. Taking his cock in my hand, I pump him a few times. I run a thumb across the tip and Scott hisses. I tease, just a little, before I position him at my entrance and sink down.

He fills me up so completely.

His arms circle my back again. He pulls me against his chest. When I start to move, slowly lifting up before sinking back down, his lips find mine and pull me into a passionate kiss.

This.

This feels different.

We're not fucking tonight.

Not with the fire, and New Year's Eve, and the way he handled my anxiety. Not with the way he was looking at me when I told him I watched his game. Not with the way he admitted how much I meant to him.

This is something more. More sensual, more meaningful.

I grind against him in an easy rhythm. We stare at each other, connected. Everything is slow and quiet. Just for a moment. He holds me closely, nibbling on my lips.

"You're so beautiful," he murmurs against my lips.

I close my eyes, my clit grinding against the base of his cock. I can feel my orgasm building. My thighs are aching. I love the slow and sweet with him but I need the fast and rough right now. I need more. I lose control of my movements, my slow grind picking up pace, as I chase the release.

As always, Scott knows what I need. His legs spread slightly and he pushes me onto my back.

I whimper when he slips out, mourning the loss of him inside me.

He's quick to follow, crawling over me and hooking a knee over his arm. He spreads me wide for him and sinks back into me.

He fucks me in front of the fire, deeply and without ever breaking eye contact. We know each other's bodies well enough that when he repositions himself and his movements become erratic, that he wants to come.

I reach up, resting my palm on his cheek.

"Will you make me come?" I whimper. He drops his head to my forehead. "Please. I want to come so badly."

"Yes. Come for me, baby," he grunts out.

"You feel so good. So big," I moan as he slams into me, hitting the spot inside me that only he can.

"Ivy," he moans, dropping his head into my neck.

A few more strokes, and when I feel his cock pulse inside me and the vibrations of his groan ripple over my skin, I fall over the edge too.

We're still for a moment. The fire has roared back to life, flames flickering and creating shadows that dance across the room. Chests rise and fall in unison. Bodies tangled and glistening with sweat. Lips find mine and words pass between us in complete silence.

He doesn't pull out of me when he rolls off of me. Simply switches our positions, so I'm lying across his chest with his softening cock still inside me.

The fire crackles. It's the only noise in the house. If it hadn't been, I may not have caught Scott's next words, whispered so quietly, they are almost lost.

"I think I'm falling for you, Ivy Booker."

CHAPTER TWENTY

IVY

"DAMN, SCOTT IS ON fire tonight," Katie comments from where she stands next to me in the box.

I arrived at the game late tonight, trying to avoid the press and excitement around the Broncos first playoff game. It's almost full time and Scott is on the field below us. The crowd is going wild, the noise deafening every time the boys make a few more yards but the game is a close one.

They want this.

Scott wants this.

The ring is why he came to Boston and why he works himself into the ground. Just last night I fell asleep curled into his side on the couch as he watched tape of the opposition over and over, studying them.

I watch as the offensive line sets up for another play down on the field. With only a few minutes left on the clock, the Broncos need to get a touchdown to secure their lead. Scott squats low behind the O-line center. The players are still for a beat, then another.

The ball snaps into Scott's hands and everyone's moving. Scott steps back into the pocket, eyes darting around looking for someone.

Katie grabs my arm at the same time as I see the gap but Scott is already running.

"Holy shit," I curse under my breath. Katie begins to jump up and down because Scott's broken through and is sprinting down the field. Forty yards ... thirty ... a defensive player from the other team is on his tail but he's too fast. Ten more yards.

"He's going to do it!" Katie screams, her voice matching the deafening noise coming from the fans all around us.

Scott runs into the end zone and slams the ball on the ground. His team mates catch up to him, circling around him and celebrating.

In the middle of it all, he points up into the stands. Towards our box. Towards me.

Katie slaps my arm over and over like I can't see exactly what she is seeing.

Heat crawls up my neck and I know my face is on fire.

Damn, I hope the cameras didn't follow his finger.

The moment passes and the teams swap over. I watch Scott rip his helmet off and scull some water. His hair is sticking to his forehead with sweat but he's smiling with his teammates, clapping them on shoulders and helmets. I watch as Jeff pulls off his headset as he walks up to Scott. Coach grabs his player by the shoulder and shakes him, smiling and laughing at the brilliant touchdown.

Pride floods me.

Scott is beaming and when the whistle goes to signify the end of the game, he throws down his helmet and cheers. The Broncos will progress through the playoffs. They've got a chance to be divisional champions.

Katie is jumping up and down next to me. Grant is yelling and cheering along with all the other fans. My eyes don't leave Scott as he's surrounded by cameras, giving his post-game interviews.

He's still sweaty, and still smiling, and damn, I cannot wait to celebrate with him tonight.

This is the first game I've come to since the game at Christmas with Pops. I've pushed down and ignored the anxiety in my chest pretty successfully. I stare down at the field. If I close my eyes, I could picture my dad running that same route Scott did today.

Not for the first time in the last few weeks, I wish I could have experienced this with him.

I wait around in the suite again. Katie and Grant left me an hour ago so I curled up on one of the couches in the back of the suite with a plate of fruit and have been there ever since.

I'm starting to doze off, bored of my phone and starting to feel exhaustion from the long first week back at school creeping in. The door opens as my eyes start to shut and Scott wanders in.

He's back in the same game day suit he left the house in this morning and his hands are shoved deep into the pockets. His bag is slung over his shoulder but he drops it inside the door when he spots me.

"Hey, you," he says, bending over the back of the couch to kiss me.

"Hi." I duck away, yawning as I sit up. "Sorry, I'm exhausted."

"Did we bore you?" he chuckles. He leans his arms on the back of the couch, eyes trailing down my body. His gaze pauses on the jersey I wear, his name across my back. A surprise that I didn't have last time.

"Where did you get this?" he murmurs, tugging at the shirt as I walk around the couch and into his arms.

"Gift shop," I shrug. I lift up on my toes and ask for a kiss. He obliges.

"You drive here?" he asks, running his lips against my jaw.

I shake my head. "I came with Katie. She's already left. Can I catch a ride with you?"

"Let me fuck you in that jersey as soon we get home and you have yourself a deal?"

I giggle and nod.

Obviously.

Why else would I have worn his jersey?

He tucks me under his arm and we walk through the quiet stadium.

Cleaners are about. A few players are getting treatment as we head past the locker rooms, and one or two coaches are still debriefing as we pass the offices.

There's a small group loitering outside but they pay us no mind. I curl further into Scott's side as we walk towards his car. He opens the passenger door and helps me into the SUV.

"Thank you for coming today," Scott says quietly.

I sigh, pressing my palm to his cheek and smiling. "You're welcome."

He rounds the car and buckles himself in. I watch as he turns on the car and fiddles with some buttons. My seat starts to warm up and I sink deeper into it.

I glance around the empty car park and a familiar guilt rises up in my throat. I swallow, turning to look at Scott. "Do you hate that we can't go celebrate with the team after a game like that?"

"Huh?" Scott looks at me. "What are you talking about?"

"I feel bad. That I can't ... we can't be seen together or you can't tell you teammates, or have me in the family room after a game. Do you hate it?"

He's silent for a moment. But then he reaches across the console and grabs my hand. Bringing it up to his lips, he says, "I want you in whatever way you'll let me have you right now. Like I said, if it has to be a secret for now then it's a secret." He leans in, beckoning me forward. "Besides, I don't want to celebrate with them the same way I do with you."

He winks and closes the gap between us.

God, I love kissing this man.

Later, we're curled up in bed and watching reruns of *Friends*, my phone rings on the nightstand. I groan, pulling away from where I'm practically burrowing into Scott's chest and turn the phone over to see the screen. Katie's name flashes up at me. I glance at the time and notice that it's almost eleven. She wouldn't call me if it wasn't important.

"Are you okay?" I answer the phone quickly.

"Have you seen it?" Her voice sounds panicked.

I sit up, Scott slowly waking up as I move away from his body. "Seen what? What is it, Katie?"

"I don't know how they got it. Or when? When would they even have had the chance to get it?"

"You're not making any sense. Slow down." I take a deep breath, hoping she'll do the same. Next to me, Scott picks up his phone and I see his brows come together.

"Shit," he murmurs next to me, staring at something on his phone. I try to look at his screen but my phone buzzes in my hand. Then, it buzzes again. And again.

And again.

What the fuck?

"Katie?" I prompt down the line.

"They have a photo of you," she says quietly down the line. "And Scott. Together."

"Who's they?"

I feel sick. My stomach turns over and anxiety floods my body. I look over at Scott. He's staring back at me. His features are full of regret.

"The press. A photo of you and Scott kissing after the game is all over the internet. Someone leaked it."

A sob crawls up my throat as she says her next words. "It's everywhere."

***

I scroll through my phone, looking at picture after picture of myself and Scott.

Me, tucked under his arm and walking through the underground tunnels at the stadium. His face is turned toward mine so you don't really know it's him but his name is clearly written across my shoulders.

Me sitting in the passenger seat of his car with my hand on his cheek.

Me leaning over the middle console of his SUV and kissing him.

Clear as day. Unmistakable.

It's all over Instagram. It's all over TikTok. His female fans didn't hesitate to start digging. My followers blew up in a matter of hours and I ended up making my profile private. I wish I had been quicker. My posts had been screenshotted and shared everywhere, people piecing together my history one post at a time. My high school yearbook pictures have popped up more times than I've probably ever seen them. I've seen comments from people I went to college with claiming to be my best friend. Katie lost her mind when I told her that.

As if on cue, *SportsCenter* also picked it up and started to take bets on whether we'd last.

Football princess and star quarterback finally reveal their secret relationship.

Sports royalty recluse shakes up with Boston's newest football star.

Continuing the D1 athlete line has never been so cute as Ivy Booker and Scott Harvey show off new love after last night's playoff game.

These headlines are starting to do my head in.

The television hanging from the wall across from the bed is on low but when I glance up and see the *SportsCenter* titles play, I groan.

Pops chuckles from his bed next to me. "You can't hide out here forever, Ivy."

"I can and I will," I reply, still scrolling through my phone.

"I think it's nice. All the reports I've seen are just commenting on how smitten you two look."

I look up, setting my phone aside and narrowing my eyes. "What reports have you been seeing?"

"Well ..." Pops runs his hands over the already smooth blanket. "They talked about it on the local news this morning."

I roll my head back to rest against the chair, my eyes shutting. "I don't want to know."

"All they said was that you make a cute couple." I crack an eye open to glare at him.

I try to ignore how pale he looks today, and how he's been complaining of being cold since I walked in. Still Pops smiles at me.

"And that you would make very cute, very athletic babies."

"Oh my god." I sink into the chair, covering my face with my hands. I burn up. The blushing is so real when I think about me and Scott, getting pregnant and having that kind of future.

Of course, that was before this relationship of ours—this very new relationship—was outed and became a media freak show.

"Jeff called me as well. Wanted to know if he should trade Scott effectively immediately." Pops tries to sound casual but I can hear his chuckle coming. I roll my eyes as he continues, "I told him no because I want my great grand baby to be a fourth-generation Broncos player."

Knew it.

The rollercoaster of emotions that I'm going through today is something else. I love that Pops is finding some joy in this going public and trying to keep my spirits up but I also know what the media coverage means. It means that I'm being thrust into a world I'm not fully ready to be in.

"What did Uncle Jeff actually say?" I ask after a beat.

"Well, he was concerned." Pops coughs, his face going a bit red. I move forward on my chair, reaching for the water on his bedside table. Pops sips on it before holding it gently in his lap. "He said it made sense you were keeping it quiet and he's concerned how you're handling the media attention now it's all out there. He is worried about you."

I feel my face heat. "He doesn't need to be worried. I'm fine."

"We both know you're lying through your teeth right now. But I told him there isn't anything to worry about. Scott is looking after you." Pops takes another sip of the water and sinks back against his pillows. He levels me with a stare. "How are you feeling about it?"

The question I've been avoiding all day.

The same question Scott asked me today before he left for practice and meetings that I wasn't able to answer.

How am I feeling?

I feel … disgusted. Exposed. Scared.

I feel itchy all over, constantly checking over my shoulder and terrified I'm being followed by some idiot with a camera.

I feel like I can't go more than a few hours without crying. I'd come to the hospital straight after school today, hoping to hide out from the rest of the world for a while.

It's as if I've been spiraling since the moment the pictures were leaked.

I can't control that my face is being posted across a hundred different gossip and social sites. I can't control that the sports media is making a connection between Scott and my dad. I can't control that my colleagues at work are already asking if I can get them tickets to games.

My head hurts and my heart aches. It feels as if an electric current runs just beneath my skin. My heart has been racing all day and I feel on edge.

Completely out of control.

Scott is still at the stadium, getting work on his arm done. If I'm honest with myself and admit to the pit that is growing in my stomach, I don't really want to see him when I get home tonight.

It just all feels ... tainted.

"Ivy?" Pops prompts, his gaze unwavering.

"I don't know."

I don't want to admit how I feel, not to Pops, or to Scott, or to myself.

Pops shifts on his bed. He's not been able to sit up while I've been here, instead he's just propped on some pillows. He's as white as a ghost and his movements are slow, sluggish. I know he's getting worse. I can see that just by looking at him.

The reality of being without him feels like it's getting closer and closer. The thought makes my stomach twist. I've been in denial for weeks, choosing to believe that Pops is going to come home soon. But even though he still smiles at me as brightly as he has my whole life, when I walk through the door to his room, I know he's in pain.

Pops is tired and it's starting to show.

Just another thing I'm not able to control or fix right now.

There is ache in my chest that goes along with the constant sting behind my eyes and nervous energy. One that I feel every time I think about my parents. One that just hurts more and more as Pops gets worse.

But, as with everything else going on, I decide to push the fact that he's not improving out of my mind and change the subject.

"Did you hear any more about whether nurse Sophie broke up with the boyfriend?" I ask him, shuffling my chair a little closer to his bed so I can hold his hand. He stares at me for a moment, the look in his eyes telling me he knows exactly what I'm doing. After a beat, he blinks and goes with the change of subject.

We gossip for a while. When they bring Pops' dinner in, I let him turn up the volume on *SportsCenter* and sit with him while the announcers replay the stats from this weekend's games. They ramble on about the teams, including the Broncos, who are moving into the playoffs.

Life for Scott is about to get more hectic, more pressurized, more intense.

My stomach turns over as I think about whether or not I even want to be a part of it.

After the nurse drops off Pops' night medication and warns me about visiting hours, I finally get up from the chair and collect my coat from the small couch in the corner of the room.

"Ivy?" Pops says as I pull my coat on. I look up at him, waiting. "Don't let the press ruin what you and Scott have."

Ice runs under my skin and my lungs tighten. I feel like crying. Again. I swallow the lump in my throat. "I ... I don't know, Pops. It's been a lot."

"You and him ... you just remind me of your mom and dad." He takes a sip of water after popping another pill in his mouth. He swallows before continuing. "I just don't want you to throw that away because you think you can't handle something as insignificant as the press."

I don't know what to say.

The press is nowhere near insignificant. Not to me.

"You're stronger than that, Ivy-girl. I promise." He lifts a hand, shaking a little as he does, and reaches for me.

I move over to him, wrapping his hand in mine and squeezing gently. I lean down and press a kiss to his cheek.

"Love you, Pops." I blink back the tears stinging in my eyes. "I'll see you tomorrow, after school."

"Love you too, sweetheart."

Chapter Twenty-One

Scott

WITH EVERY TWIST OF the steering wheel, my shoulder tweaks. Pins and needles spread through my nerves, buzzing under my skin. The wild card game tonight killed me. My arm is half way to numb; my shoulder in pieces. The Pittsburgh defenders played the game of their lives tonight and made it their mission to sack me every chance they got.

I'm a wreck, exhausted and in pain, and the only thing keeping me upright is the idea that any minute now, I'll be kissing my girl.

I haven't been back to the apartment since before Christmas, when Mom and Dad were visiting. I'd let them into the apartment when they arrived. Ivy and I had dinner with them a few times, but when it had been time to call it a night Mom and Dad had gotten into my bed there while I'd gone home with my girl and gotten into hers.

My home is wherever she is and she is most comfortable in her own bed, so that's where we sleep.

Playing the Sunday night football spot means we stayed overnight in Pittsburgh last night and got through morning physical therapy before flying home this morning. Tomorrow, a Tuesday, is a day off meaning when I get into bed with Ivy tonight I get to wake up to her too.

Normally, I'm up and dressed before she's even fluttered an eyelid. I'm kissing her goodbye before she's fully awake. But tomorrow, I get to stay. I get to watch her morning routine, pick out her outfit, listen to her talk about the day she has planned.

Life before Ivy was different: football, my parents, and more football. My Tuesdays were another day of reviewing game tape, and stretching, and training at the gym.

Now, Tuesdays are about slowly waking up with her in my arms and lazy mornings. They're about cleaning up the house while Ivy's at school, about going to the grocery store to get her favorite ice cream if we're out, about visiting her Pops over lunch to get to know him and talk football with him.

My career used to be everything.

Now, Ivy is everything. Football is a bonus.

As the Boston brownstone comes into view, I relax back into my seat. Somewhere in the last few months, I fell hard and fast for the Boston born girl that lives on this tree covered street. I've been hooked since day one. Football feels almost like it's nothing if she isn't there cheering me on, too.

I park in the usual spot alongside the street lamp lit sidewalk in front of her house. Her car sits in the driveway and there's light filtering out of the front window and illuminating the small garden. I grab my bag from the back seat, wincing as I throw it over my shoulder and head toward the house.

Something flashes behind me, lighting up the dark street. Then another, and another.

What the fuck?

I turn around to find two people carrying large cameras, extra lenses hanging around their necks, stepping around a car a few yards away from my own. They continue to snap pictures. The continuous flashing blinding me as I'm rendered motionless.

The fucking paparazzi?

What the hell are they doing here? Do they really have nothing else to do?

I've seen the posts. The constant stream of those three photos that got leaked and continue to get posted over and over. A few of Ivy's Instagram photos got reposted on gossip sites but following me home? Surely not.

"Hey, Harvey," one of them shouts. "Rough game. Glad to be home? How's the new relationship? Working out?"

I grit my teeth. None of that is his damn business. I hold my tongue, ignoring them and pulling my cap further down to hide my face. I've been through enough media training to know that I can't answer them otherwise they get what they want but that doesn't stop me tightening my grip around the handle of the bag thrown over my shoulder to stop myself swinging at the slimy idiot.

Does Ivy know they're here?

Did they follow me home or were they already here?

I'd been so lost in my own thoughts; I didn't notice until they started taking pictures.

I turn the key in the door, the feeling still new. After the Christmas day game, I noticed the new addition to my key ring. We didn't speak about it but now, instead of knocking, I let myself in. I keep the door close to my body, shutting it as soon as I slip inside.

I kickoff my shoes and turn the lights out. I can hear the studio laugh track of what I think is a *Friends* episode echoing down the hallway. I leave my bag at the bottom of the stairs and make my way into the living room.

Ivy is sitting in her corner of the couch. She's curled into the cushions and covered by one of the many blankets she keeps on the couch. As suspected, *Friends* plays in the background but Ivy's attention is solely on her phone as she scrolls.

I'll bet my Mercedes SUV that she's scrolling through those pap photos.

"Hi, baby," I say, keeping my voice quiet so as not to make her completely jump out of her skin. I fail and Ivy flinches anyway. I laugh but it feels hollow. "Sorry, didn't mean to scare you. I thought you would have heard me come in?"

She sits up, her hair falling over her shoulder as she stretches. The t-shirt she's wearing lifts, giving me a nice view of the curves I love to trace endlessly in bed, or when we're on the couch, or whenever I get my hands on her.

There aren't any lights on. Just the reflection from the TV and the low light coming from the bright flames that flicker in the fireplace.

Ivy stares at me for a moment. Her navy-blue eyes look almost black in the low light but I can see her tracing my features. Like she's taking notes. Committing me to her memory. I do the same when she falls asleep before me and I find myself not believing she's actually real.

"Hi," she whispers finally. She puts her phone down on the couch cushions beside her.

I move toward the couch, wanting to touch her. I feel her slipping. Like ever since those fucking photos got leaked, something's been off and she's pulling away. Becoming distant.

I feel helpless. Her hair is tired on top of her head in a messy bun. There are dark circles beneath her eyes. She's tapping her foot against the edge of the couch in a random rhythm. I know she's spiraling but if she doesn't let me in, there's nothing I can do other than watch from the outside as I lose her. It only makes me want to grab a hold of her tighter, lock my arms around her, do whatever it takes to convince her that we can work through this.

I kiss her but she doesn't melt into me in the way I'm used to, in the way she normally does, like the weight of the world washes away when my lips touch hers.

"Did they follow you here?" she asks quietly.

Goddammit.

"I don't know, baby." I take a seat on the couch next to her. "They'll get bored eventually. Someone will get done for drinking too much or a newbie will get in trouble for their celebration dance and they'll move on."

She shakes her head the tiniest amount.

"I'm sorry," I say. Because there really isn't anything else I can say. Her walls—the big ones I spent months breaking through—are back up and this time, they're a few extra meters thick.

She's staring at me again. Or, staring through me.

Then she's moving. She flies off the couch, the blanket that was wrapped around her body falling to the floor. Ivy moves around the couch and into the kitchen, away from me.

Her hands wring together in front of her. It's like she's itching her palm, scrapping her nails over and over the skin. I stare at the movement. Her anxiety is flowing off her in waves. I slowly get up from the couch and move around it to stand with her in the center of the space between the living room and the kitchen. It feels so fucking familiar.

It feels like the night I told her about playing football and she told me to leave.

Except this time, there's an edge to her movements. My bet is on her feeling like she's losing control of the emotions she keeps locked up inside. All the stuff around her parents, losing her pops, the way she blames all of it on football.

She's unraveling right in front of me and there is nothing I can do about it.

"Ivy," I say. I don't move toward her. I don't reach for her even though every bone in my body is begging to touch her. The tension ripples between us and I fight with myself about what to do here. How to handle this. She's pushing me away. She's soft sand falling through the cracks of hands desperately trying to stop something as inevitable as gravity. I can't help it when the doubt starts to creep in.

Have we been headed here the whole time?

Was I fucking naive to think we could work this out?

After Christmas, after she started watching the games, I thought maybe there was a chance. Get through the season, see how we land in the off season and figure it out.

Contract talks and deals are being put on the table and I haven't touched any of it because I've been terrified of this very moment. The one where she tells me to leave and I won't be able to change her mind.

If deep down, I thought she really was done and really didn't want me, I'd leave.

But she doesn't want this to end either. It's a hunch but my gut is telling me there's more to whatever is going here. That this grudge about football, the anxiety around the press is only surface level. That they are masking feelings much deeper and much more unresolved after being left to simmer for so long.

She's blinded by the past, and the unresolved feelings, and the hurt she's been carrying around for so, so many years. I want to shake her. I want to make her talk to me. To talk about it all. If she got it all out, we could have our chance to make this work.

Instead, I am helpless. I stand on the other side of her walls simply praying for her to build a door to the other side for me. I can help her tear the wall down from the other side, but here? I'm stranded.

"I told you ... I told you I can't do this ... I don't want to deal ..." she hiccups. There's no tears on her face. Her eyes are glassy and the firelight is reflecting back at me as her chest heaves with the words. But she's not crying. Not yet. Like she's holding herself back

"Baby." I start towards her. She takes a small step back but I decide that I need to touch her. I need to remind her that we, public or not, are still us.

I reach for her face, cupping her cheek in my palm.

"Please don't call me that right now," she whispers.

"Don't do this," I plead with her. My thumbs stroke the soft skin of her cheeks. I memorize her beautiful face and commit her every expression to my memory.

Silence falls around us. A single tear runs a lonely path down her cheek.

I don't move away or remove my hands from her face or break away from her gaze.

If I do, she'll close herself off entirely. She will hide away from the world until all the delayed grief that seems to be bubbling to the surface is back in a neat little box. I will lose her to her own mind.

"Are you breaking up with me?" I ask quietly, my thumb catching her tears.

She shakes her head, her eyes closing. Another few tears drip from the ends of her lashes where they rest against her cheeks. I wipe them away, too.

"It hurts," she says shakily, "It hurts so much."

"What hurts?" I have my suspicions yet I want her to say it out loud. To admit it to me.

She's grieving.

"I can't ... I ..." She sucks in air like the mere thought of vocalizing her pain only causing her more. I take a deep breath.

"Can I kiss you? Please?" I ask. I wait until she nods before pressing a gentle, lingering kiss to her lips. When I pull away, I rest my forehead to hers. She sniffs and it makes me smile, just a little.

My girl is trying to be so strong right now.

"It's okay to be scared, Ives," I murmur. "You're working through a lot in that head of yours. I wish you would let me help you but I know that sometimes, admitting you need help is hardest even to those closest to you. Do you think talking to someone who isn't me might help? I could do some research. Find someone—"

"No. No, I won't ... I don't need to do that." She is shaking in my embrace now. Shivering in my arms. "Maybe ... maybe I just need some space."

My stomach lurches. No.

No way.

"Are you breaking up with me?" I say through clenched teeth and try to remain calm. This girl is beautiful, and funny, and I'm pretty sure my soulmate but fuck she is infuriating.

I stroke my fingers down her throat, finding her pulse point and counting silently to ten in my head. Her pulse is racing. Beating so fast under the tips of my fingers. I wrap my arms around her and pull her into my chest.

If she isn't ready to talk to someone, then I can't force her.

"I don't want to lose you," she says into my chest. "But every-thing is too much. I can't … I feel like I'm not strong enough to handle this. I'll figure it out and then it will be fine."

I can't be sure if she's talking to me or to herself so I stay silent, holding her close to my chest. The chest she fits so fucking perfectly against. Like she is custom built to fit me, in every way.

Yeah. No. We're not breaking up.

"I'll go sleep at my place," I say quietly. The decision seems to break her resolve and I can't be sure if it's because she's upset that I'm doing as she asks or just relief in not having to make the decision herself. "But we're not breaking up. So no ignoring my texts for weeks this time, okay?"

She manages a small, broken laugh that muffles straight into my chest.

"We're not breaking up," I repeat. I pull back a little, my hands snaking up her arms to gently wrap around her neck, holding her head in place so I can say this while staring directly into her eyes. "You can have as much time as you need to get your head around it all. You can have your space. But we are not done. I'm not done. And when you're ready, if you want, I am here to help you figure it out."

Then because it's probably the last time for a while that I'm going to get to, I kiss her.

Thoughtfully, and long, and sealing of a future that I will fight on both sides for until she's ready.

***

Waking up in the king-sized bed this morning felt all wrong.

I searched for her the moment I woke up and the events of the night before came rushing back to me the minute my hands found a cold, empty bed.

Fuck.

My chest hurts already and it's been less than twelve hours since I was with her. Not for the first time today, I rub at the pain as I wait in the hospital room. I'm early today. The bag of cheeseburgers from Shake Shack sits on the table beside me and I fidget with my phone.

I lean back on the couch and close my eyes. Ivy's face fills the black behind my eyes and I rub my chest again.

Just as I decide to send her a text—something I refrained from this morning even though it almost broke me—the door to the hospital room opens and Billy is wheeled inside.

"Aren't you supposed to be walking around?" I ask, getting up to help him back into bed. When he's settled, I shake his hand.

His grip is weak and his hand falls limply into his lap when I let go.

"Not today," the nurse that wheeled him in answers for Billy. "We're a bit tired today so only one cheeseburger and lots of fluids." She eyes me sternly, pointing a warning finger at the bag before leaving us alone.

"How are you feeling?" I ask, pulling the chair Ivy normally occupies closer to his bedside.

"Like I'm dying," he says dryly, I try not to laugh but I can't help but crack a smile. The fact he still has some sense of humor at the end of his life astounds me. He shifts on the bed, trying to get himself comfortable. I itch to help him but after I tried the first time I came for a Tuesday lunch and he all but barked at me to sit back in my seat, I refrain. Ivy is the only one he'll let fuss over him.

"So," he says once comfortable. He reaches for the grease-stained bag and I pass it over. Gingerly, he takes out a burger and unwraps it. "How's our girl?"

"She tried breaking up with me last night."

Billy shakes his head. "I was afraid she'd try to do that."

"We're not. Breaking up, I mean."

"Didn't think you would be," he says, mouth full of his bite. "Have you seen you around her? You're obsessed with my granddaughter."

I laugh, lounging back in the chair and grabbing a burger of my own. I unwrap it and take a bite. Billy and I just sit in silence, enjoying the fast food and the company. When he's done, he places the wrapper on the roll away table hovering over the hospital bed.

"I'm dying, Scott." I swallow my bite without chewing and cough. Goddamn, this man has no filter. He stares at me hard as he continues, "I need you to look after my girl. No matter how hard it might be, I need you to stick with her. Have a bit of patience."

I can only nod.

"I'm serious." He shakes his again, eyes closing as the ghost of a smile crosses his face as if he's remembering a fond memory. "She's so stubborn. Just like her mother."

"What were they like?" I reach for the bottle of water I brought with me, needing to clear my throat.

"Matty was my son so of course I loved him. But Sara? She was the daughter we never had. I remember when they came home one weekend in their freshman year and told us Sara was pregnant. I've never told Ivy this but Sara was out of her mind scared at the idea of being a mother."

"Really? Ivy speaks as if she was a natural."

"She was. We used to tell Ivy that all the time when she was little and it's true. But at first, Sara was spooked. Matty was the one to calm her down, to convince her they could do it. He was smitten with his daughter from the moment they found out Sara was even pregnant." He reaches for his own water on the side table with one shaking hand. "Sara had a plan. Being pregnant in her freshman year of college wasn't part of the plan. She was convinced they wouldn't be able to handle it."

I dip my head, thinking of the walls Ivy puts up when I try to get her to talk about football and the connection.

"I love my granddaughter, Scott," he says. "She's the light of my life. But she's stubborn. She has been holding a grudge against an entire sport her whole life and along the way, I think she's forgotten what a connection it could be for her to her dad. She needs some time to come to that conclusion on her own."

"I have no intentions of going anywhere," I confirm. I clear up the burger wrappers and place the remaining burgers in the bag back on the couch with my coat. I'll likely eat them later.

"I was so happy when she told me about meeting you. When she told me you were a football player, I was ... well, happy." He takes a small sip of his water, the straw shaking as he tries to capture it with his mouth. "You are her gateway. To move on, to let go, to find the connection with her dad and finally just start living."

"She's been watching more of my games. I think it is getting easier for her," I say in agreement. "If only those photos hadn't leaked ..."

Billy rests his head against the pillows, exhaustion flooding his features. He looks more and more fragile every time I see him. Today is the worst he's been.

Fuck.

"I love her, Billy," I tell him quietly. My elbows rest on my thighs as I lean forward in the chair and watch him.

His eyes close and exhales in a sigh of relief. "I know you do."

"I want to marry her. One day," I add. "She's it for me."

"Good." He nods with his eyes closed. After a moment, a tired smile spreads across his lips. He cracks open one eyes and glances over to me. "She wears Matty's ring around her neck but Sara's engagement ring is in the safe in my bedroom at the house. The code is Ivy's birthday."

"The ... what?" He tells me all of this so casually that I do a mental double take when processing his words.

"You can buy her something new if you want to. But just in case you want to use her mom's, I'm telling you where to find it." He pauses again, shifting in the bed and his face screws up in pain. It's only for a moment and when the moment passes Billy finally opens his eyes again. "We both know I won't be going home."

His words today continue to hit me like tidal waves. Over and over, they keep coming. I'm starting to think he's being blunt on purpose, like he knows something we don't so he's hammering his points home.

Eventually, I nod.

"Okay. I'll keep that in mind." Billy only nods in answer. He leans back into his pillows before pointing to the remote and I take the wordless command to turn on the game from Sunday. He loves to walk through the plays with me.

We watch half the football game, keeping our conversation on the routes and the plays and the touchdowns.

Sometime in the fourth quarter, knowing my visit with him is coming to an end, I look over at him.

"I'll look after her, Billy. I promise, I will."

"I know you will, son."

Chapter Twenty-Two

Ivy

I CAN BARELY MAKE out the usually lush, green field. It is covered in snow and patches of ice. As if the cold is reaching through my TV, it seems to wrap around me in a tight fist as I watch the players on the field run warm ups. It didn't matter that the fire has been going since lunch or that I'm wearing a sweatshirt that is two times too big for me. Nothing about the heavy blanket covering me helps warm the chill spreading over my body.

They are being careful. The whole team, all the players. I may be watching through a screen, tuning out the annoying commentators, but only an idiot that has never watched a ball game in their life wouldn't be able to see the running backs aren't going full out when they start to warm up their legs down the side lines. Or that the defensive linemen aren't desperately trying to break through the top layer of ice and snow with their cleats, looking for a way to dig their heels into the ground.

The broadcast cuts to the commentators in their cozy box and I groan.

I don't care about the fucking commentators.

Katie blows up my phone as the game begins but I don't need to look at her messages to know what she's texting me about. She's at the game—with Grant, in a season box because Scott got them both the same season passes so I would have people to attend the games with—but I can tell just as clearly from my cocoon on the couch that Scott is playing recklessly.

Unlike the others out on the field of ice, he's running full out and he's not taking precautions. He's not watching his teammates, not communicating, he's not playing their game.

He's playing his.

Whatever game this is, it's not a safe one.

He gets taken down by the opposition's defense time and time again. Each time is a direct hit to my nerves the moment contact is made. By the end of the first half of the game, I've worn the nail on my thumb down by anxiously chewing on it and I'm curled into such a tight ball in the corner of the couch that there is a really big possibility that I may never be able to get out on my own.

I twirl my phone between my fingers, itching to call him and tell him to pull his head in.

I can't. But boy do I want to.

There's no way he would pick up between quarters anyway. I know that his phone is currently tucked in the side of his bag in the depths of his locker and even if there is a chance he is nearby and did hear it, I am absolutely certain that Uncle Jeff would be ripping into him right about now.

Jeff is like Pops—he believes hard in the team game and hates players that think they are bigger than that.

I almost hope that Scott is getting ripped into by Uncle Jeff. Maybe it will make him start playing safer in the snow.

It's in the middle of the third quarter when it happens.

The Broncos offensive team is on the field and his former deep blue and white uniform is covered in mud and, from what I can tell, a bit of blood.

It happens so quickly I almost miss it.

I'm not paying attention, my eyes on my phone screen typing furiously to Katie.

"They're down!"

"Woah, where did that come from?!"

"Ouch! That had to hurt."

My eyes dart up to the screen in time for the broadcast to switch from the live feed to a replay. I don't catch the two players' numbers that are on the ground, but I know it is a Broncos player that got hit.

My legs uncurl from beneath me as I lift myself out of the corner of the couch, phone slipping from between my fingers while the blanket drops to my feet.

In slow motion, they play it back.

Scott hesitates after the snap, just barely, and the left tackle digs in as Scott takes his moment. I see it in the replay, the moment it all goes wrong. The left tackle—Connors I think his name is—takes the brunt of a defender but his back foot jerks, slipping on a patch of ice before sliding through the mud underneath. The defender barrels through him and collides with Scott.

Arm still lifted, ball still in hand, shoulder-hitting-the-hard-ground-first type of collision.

My heart is in my throat. My empty stomach seems to churn over and over. When the live broadcast comes back, I inch closer to the TV. The crackling fire licking at my skin is burning me but I can't step back.

"Get up," I beg him. "Get up, Scott. Please, god, please."

I can't hear the commentators anymore.

My heartbeat thuds in my chest. Blood rushes in my ears. A distant ringing starts to echo as if an explosion has gone off right in front of my face.

Only it has, hasn't it?

I am watching the only casualty in live time. Still on the ground. Not moving.

"Scott for fuck's sake, get up!" I scream at his still body on the TV screen. My body begins to shake and I can feel the tears stinging behind my eyes.

I can't shut them. I can't—won't—look away.

Not until he gets up, not until he moves.

"Please, please," I beg again, waiting.

Finally he moves and oxygen fills my lungs again. My breathing is shallow and the air feels thin, but it's something.

The shill ring of my phone cuts through the air and I'm stunned momentarily as I watch medics rush the field. Scott waves them off, slowly getting to his feet.

My hand makes contact with my phone, which is buried in the blanket that had pooled at my feet in my haste to be closer to the TV.

"Ivy? Ivy? Are you okay? Are you there?" Katie yells down the phone as soon as I answer the call. I can hear the crowd in the background but her voice comes through, shaky and concerned. She sounds out of breath.

"Yeah—yes. I'm here. Am I okay? Is he okay?" I question, my voice crackling. My chest hurts. I press the palm of my hand to the ache, trying to soothe it. Something catches in my throat and a small sob escapes. I feel a few tears finally rolling over my cheeks, making my skin feel sticky. "He—I can't—what if he—"

"He's okay. He got up. Are you watching? He's walking off now. No help. He seems okay. He's okay."

"The hit—oh my god, Katie I—I can't breathe." She curses on the other end of the line as I desperately try to calm myself down. It doesn't work. I watch Scott disappear from the field. He doesn't accept any of their help but the entire team's medical staff follows closely behind him.

The benched, second-string QB runs onto the field. I watch as they reset and play begins.

The clock restarts in the corner of the screen and I feel my lungs constrict.

Nothing. No comments. No cutting away.

What's happened to him? Why aren't they saying anything about him?

"I'm trying to find someone from the team. I don't know—Ivy, who should I ask? Who would know what's happened to him?" I didn't realize I spoke out loud but Katie's panicked questions cut through my spiraling thoughts.

"I—" My eyes finally close. *Think.* "Meghan, I think her name is. The PR girl. She usually sits in the players box with the owners for home games. She'll—she'll know."

"Meghan, player's box, right." I can hear Katie trying to push her way through the crowds.

I close my eyes again and focus on the background sounds I can hear through the phone. Zoning in on the muffled voice of my best friend seems to help and the tears begin to slow down. In any other situation, at any other moment of my life, hearing Katie argue with different members of the staff at the stadium would be downright comedic.

Maybe one day, we will marvel and laugh at her ability to tear through what is probably a six-foot something security guard and into the player's box.

I glance at the TV. The commentators are filling the time between plays and the same time I hear my name coming through the phone I have pressed to my ear, they comment on Scott.

"—Harvey didn't even see it coming. Did you see how he landed on his right shoulder? That can't be good for the throwing arm, no sir. Hopefully it's superficial, otherwise the winning trade that was speculated to take Boston to the Super Bowl may just have ended his season."

"Ivy? Can you hear me?"

"Yes," I whisper in reply.

"He's heading for Boston General. He's okay but the physio isn't convinced and wants more scans. Meghan asked if you want her to put your name on the list for security to let you through?" Katie speaks so quickly my brain takes a moment to process her words.

He's okay.

Not convinced. More scans.

Security.

Lists.

Boston General.

"He's okay?" I ask, needing more certainty.

"That's what they're saying."

"Okay. I ..." My head is spinning but I'm already moving, my body making the decision for me. My keys are in my hand before I answer Katie. "Yes. Please. Ask her to put me on the list. But, Katie, they can't tell him. I don't want him to be disappointed if I can't—it's just that ... it's snowing."

"Fuck ... do you—I can come get you?" she asks. I love her. I love her with everything I am. Because in the moment, regardless of the crowds, and the game, and the hordes of people she'll have to drag Grant through just to get him to leave before the game is over, she would move mountains so I didn't have to drive in the snow.

Not this time.

This time, I will be okay.

"No. I will be fine. I think—will you tell her?"

"Yes. Of course I will."

"Okay. Thank you." I hit the garage door button the moment I close the driver's door behind me.

The snow falls lightly beyond the cover of my garage. The phone connects to my car's Bluetooth and Katie's goodbye echoes around me.

"Text me when you get there. You'll be fine. It's not heavy and should be stopping soon. I'll follow your location as well, okay?"

"Okay," I whisper back, eyes locked on the almost transparent specks of snow through my back windscreen.

"Drive safe. Love you."

"Love you, too."

I take a deep breath, put the car into reverse and slowly back out.

***

The main lobby of Boston General is wall to wall filled with reporters. I regret not at least putting a pair of jeans on as a replacement for my workout leggings. I fold the ends of the oversized sweater over my hands, keys clutched in one hand and my phone in the other. I can at least be glad for the cap left on the back seat of my car.

Another item of Scott's.

I ignore the sharp pain to my chest when I pull it on and down over my eyes. I'm thankful he left it, for more than it being helpful to just hide my face.

The fact that I was likely to be in the background of multiple news outlets' sports reports this evening looking like this was another thing that I need to file away to laugh about with Katie in the future. When it's less painful.

I keep my head down and slip down a corridor to the left. Thanks to Nan, I know this hospital like the back of my hand, and thanks to Pops' stories, I know that they have a suite of private rooms for VIP patients. If Scott is anywhere, he'll be there.

"Sorry, miss. Can't let you back there." A large, stern looking man stops me at the main doors. I imagine this security guard looks similar to the one Katie barreled through back at the stadium.

Despite knowing my eyes are puffy and red, that I'm practically drowning in the sweatshirt I'm wearing, and I'm seconds from sobbing all over the poor man, I do my best to give him a confident smile. "Uh, Ivy Booker. I'm on the list to see Scott Harvey."

The security guard blinks, staring down at me as understanding crosses his features. He glances at his phone, most likely to the approved list of names and nods.

"Of course." He puts one large hand on the door to open it for me but stops. "Uh—will you let your Pops know we're praying for him to pull through? My old man is a huge fan."

Another sob crawls up my throat but I manage to gulp it down again. The image of Pops this morning when I visited him—in bed, and pale, and barely able to manage a laugh without coughing afterward—floods my vision. I blink a few times before looking back to the guard. "Thank you. That's very kind of you. I will pass it on."

Tears are threatening to spill over again and I do my best to keep the weak smile I managed just moments ago on my face. The guard nods, not saying anything else, and pushes the door open. I slip through.

The noise of the reporters and hustle of the main lobby dies significantly. It's calmer, but not really all that much quieter. Replacing the reporters are team officials, coaches and assistants, members of the PR team roam around with phones to their ears and iPads under their arms.

No one looks up at me.

In fact, as I take a few steps down the busy corridor, it seems no one takes any notice of my quiet entrance. Feeling like it may be best to keep it this way, I edge down the hallway ensuring to stick close to the white walls. I've only taken a few steps before a few people shift, moving past me as they keep their phones to their ears, clearing the path for my eyes to find him.

Scott's sitting up, legs thrown over the side of the hospital bed in a small recovery room. The doors are pushed open so I have an uninterrupted view of him. His fingers are filthy. There's mud on his neck and caking around his hairline. But at least he's out of the mud stained uniform and in a clean set of sweats. I freeze, eyes roaming him carefully.

He's okay.

He's fine. He's sitting up. He's moving.

The words repeat in my head over and over again as I watch the physiotherapist and doctor examine his arm together. They start taking him through the basic shoulder rotation exercises.

I watched him do them time and time again in the living room while I cooked dinner and he stretched out his muscles on a mat while I took the opportunity to unload my entire day with the kindergarteners onto him.

In the gym, on a day he opted to join me for a workout instead of going to the Broncos facility.

In the bathroom, wearing only a towel and standing behind me, watching intently as I cleaned my teeth or brushed my hair or did something completely mundane yet never getting bored and looking away.

He's okay.

I wrap my arms around my middle, holding myself back as the urge to go to him washes over me with the power of a tsunami.

I want to check him over myself. I want to run my hands through his hair, mud and all. I want to check his shoulder, his arm. I want to kiss him and press myself into him. I want him to wrap his arms around me and tell me himself that he's okay. I want to lose myself in him and never be found.

Watching him, assessing him from a distance, it's not enough.

Not enough.

I broke us.

I broke us and because of that, halfway down the corridor and pressed against the wall is as far into his world that I can allow myself to come anymore.

My world tilts when he looks up and I get lost in the green kaleidoscope.

I can hear my heartbeat in my ears, my chest heaves and my lungs fill with air. I've been underwater from the moment I made him walk away from me. Again.

Colors have dulled and sounds have muffled and everything I've touched has felt rough.

But now as our eyes meet, it all reverts.

"You're okay," I mutter, speaking quietly to him knowing he knows without needing to hear me. I take a hesitant step toward him. Scott moves at the same time, gingerly pushing off the bed, shaking off the doctor's hands gently.

The doors to the corridor open with a bang.

Noise from the reporters in the lobby muddles with the noise from the members of staff. Camera's flash and questions are thrown from all directions. Uncle Jeff strides down the hall, eyes so fixated on Scott that he doesn't notice me. Flynn is next, uniform still covered in dirt and sweat. Connors limps behind him, shaking off the defensive team's physio as all three men make their way towards Scott.

Back flat against the corridor again, our eyes stay connected.

It's as if he is my lifeline.

Everything feels richer, deeper, brighter again now that he's looking at me.

I don't want to blink in case the connection breaks and I am shoved back into the depths of the dark world I've been living in lately; a world without the green I so desperately crave.

I'm shoved back anyway.

Scott glances at Jeff and his teammates and the connection is broken. Everything dulls again and the pain in my chest throbs. Again I press a hand into my chest, watching him for only a moment more before I turn away. Slipping through the door, eyes watching the floor as I weave through reporters, and cameramen, and hospital staff alike. It's the least I can do to keep the tears from clouding my vision.

I fail and hot, sticky tears spill down my cheeks in quick succession.

My sneakers slip over the ice-covered parking lot. The last of the air that had refilled my lungs when I'd been looking into his eyes escapes me as my arms shoot out, attempting to catch my balance. A few more feet and I'm pulling the driver's side door closed and engulfing myself in the silence of my car.

I attempt to control my breathing as best I can but, as I should have expected, my phone chimes and cuts through the silence.

Scott: Don't Leave.

My resolve completely crumbles and I let the sobs take over, wracking through my body, taking me over as the waves wash over me one at a time.

Scott: Ivy?

Pain slashes through my body.

My parents. Pops. All of it.

I lost all of them and I thought tonight I was going to lose Scott too. Weaved amongst it all is this fucking game, and the fucking attention, and all the goddamn, fucking press. But as the sobs wreck me and my tears run hot and salty down my cheeks, the locked box I have been keeping buried away bursts open and I feel as if I might pass out.

I was safe in my world before him.

Safe from the heartbreak, and the time lost, and the worry, and the spotlight.

Safe from grief.

It would be so much easier if I wasn't completely and utterly in love with him. Maybe then I could just go back to the way it was but now? Now, no matter how much it hurts, I want him more than I want to hide away from dealing with my past.

Ivy: I needed to see you were okay with my own eyes.

Scott: Come back inside, baby.

Not yet.

First, even though I can't be sure I'll even survive it, I have to deal with my shit.

***

"Ives, are you sure you're okay?" Katie sets a cup of tea on the coffee table in front of me. My phone lights up again, buzzing as it rings next to the tea. "And are you sure you don't want to answer him?"

The *him* she is referring to is Scott. He hasn't stopped calling since I left the hospital last night. Katie was waiting for me when I got home. I hadn't been able to explain anything, my body tired and my nerves shot from driving in the snow, but she'd stayed and was still here when I woke up this morning. I didn't deserve her.

I shake my head. "I'm fine. I don't ... I can't talk to him yet."

"Ivy," Katie drawls on. I can tell she's disappointed in me but I need a second to catch my breath before I can figure out how to do what I need to do.

To move forward. To be better.

So instead, I fall on old patterns. "I have to get to work."

"No, Ivy." Katie grabs the bag I was about to pick up from the counter. "You aren't going anywhere until we talk about this."

"I don't want to talk yet." I say. My chest is beginning to ache.

Last night officially drained me of all my emotions. I woke up this morning feeling numb. My eyes are itchy and I blink a few times, trying to bring back some of the moisture. I have been crying all night. I'm officially sick of crying.

"You love him," she says stating a fact rather than asking a question.

"I—"

"You do. And you're being so fucking stubborn about this. You love this guy but because you have some weird grudge, you're not going to be with him?" If I had anything left to give, I would likely flinch at her words. Instead, I just let them wash over me.

"It might never work," I reply, my voice sounding almost robotic.

"Say's who?" She steps back, arms out and palms up, like she's asking me to point something out to her. "Because from what I can see, Ives, he's trying to make it work with you. And do not try to tell me he isn't because the man has been calling and texting you non-stop for weeks!"

Anger rises in my chest. An emotion so hot and powerful, that I'm almost shocked by it. I feel my face flush and my hands shake.

All the decisions I made on the drive home last night—getting help, working through my grief, figuring out how to control my anxiety better—feel as if they are crowding around me and sucking the air from the room.

Too hard.

It all seems too hard in the light of day.

"Says me," I all but yell back at her. My best friend just stares at me with a sad expression. "I say, Katie. I have spent my whole life having people tell me how great my parents were. What a great couple they made, that they were great parents when I was a baby. I have been told over and over and over about how *incredible* my dad was on the football field, how he would've been inducted into the hall of fame with Pops, how it is such a shame that *we* lost him so soon."

"We," I snarl, desperately trying to keep calm and not allow the angry tears that wait in the wings out. "There shouldn't be a *we*. *I* lost him. I lost them both. They were away because of that stupid game. Maybe if they hadn't been so god damn invested, him such a fucking prodigy, I would still have them." My voice cracks and I feel as if I'm going to be sick. "Don't you think I'm allowed to be a little hesitant of throwing myself back into that world for a man. A man that they feel like they own? Just because he is in the NFL?"

Because what if I lose him too? What if I have to end up grieving him too?

My head pounds. My stomach rolls.

Katie stares at me, her eyes glassy. "Ivy, your mom and dad didn't die because of football. You … you know that right?"

Memories flash through my mind.

Except, they aren't memories. They are memories in the form of stories. Stories that my Nan told me of a time when Pops was on the road playing football back in the sixties. Stories they'd told me of my parents. My dad dedicating his time and his energy to playing ball growing up, to the struggles my parents went through when they fell pregnant with me because how could my dad focus on going pro when he had a daughter he wanted to be home for? How would they possibly make that work?

And then, suddenly, the faces in my head morph and it isn't my parents but Scott and myself.

Scott being gone all the time.

Scott missing birthdays and holidays.

Scott being more famous than my pops or dad ever was.

In every scenario, I am left alone. Every single silly fantasy I have thought up since meeting Scott rises from the ashes and morphs into my personal nightmare.

I squeeze my eyes shut trying to make sense of all the emotions swirling around inside me.

Sadness, confusion, numbness, anger, years old grief.

They're all there, mixing together like one giant, confusing cocktail.

"I just ... I'm angry. I miss them. I wish I had more time with them. I don't know who else to blame," I say quietly after a moment. "Scott is ... I don't know. What should I do?"

"I don't know sweetie. Maybe it's time to talk to someone about all this." Katie steps forward and wraps me in her arms, hugging me tightly. "You can find someone to help you work through it, if you're ready. And, Ives, I love you. I do. But not being with Scott because of his literal job? The only people that you're punishing are you and him."

I turn my head, resting on her shoulder. If I had any tears left, there is a good chance I would cry.

"I miss him," I murmur.

"I know you do."

"I don't know how to be all in," I admit out loud to her. "I'm so scared. Of facing that world, of all the things that come with it. Of losing him to it."

"He'll help you, you just have to let him," she tells me quietly, her hand running soothingly over my back.

Something in my resolve crumbles. A brick from the endlessly high wall comes crumbling down. She's right. I know she is. I knew it last night, and I know it now.

I'm still angry. I'm still confused.

Maybe if he never walked into the bar all those months ago, I would spend the rest of my life living in the football free bubble that I made for myself, perfectly content. But he did. And now that I know him, now that I love him, I don't want to go back.

I just need to figure out how to go forward.

He's told me he isn't going to give up, that he'll fight for me. I think it's time I step in the ring.

My phone rings again. This time I pick up.

"Ivy? It's Dr. Bryden." A chill takes over my body. "I think you should come to the hospital."

Chapter Twenty-Three
An ESPN Newscaster

"Sad news in sport today. Reports have confirmed that William 'Billy' Booker passed away in a Boston Hospital late last night. A representative for the family has released the following statement:

Billy was battling poor health after a minor stroke six months ago. We sadly lost him overnight. His granddaughter, Ivy, was by his side. Billy was a big personality and loved by many. He will be dearly missed. The family requests that you respect their privacy at this time.

The Broncos will be holding a celebration of Billy's life next Saturday morning at their home Stadium. It'll be open to the public and tickets can be reserved on their website now for free. Our hearts go out to his granddaughter Ivy and Billy's close friends. He was a one-of-a-kind player that had captured the hearts of many a football fan. We pay tribute to the illustrious career of Billy Booker, next on *ESPN*."

Chapter Twenty-Four
Scott

Snow covers the church and its surrounding grounds.

Brown stone, red brick and stained windows look dull under the storm clouds that circle above. Rain is coming but for now, the only sound is the bells echoing in the air.

Black cars line the road in front of the church and I kick the gravel path as I move quickly toward the front doors. I'm running late.

My shoulder is torn and I'm sitting on the sidelines. If we make it to the Super Bowl, there's a chance I can get cleared but Coach confessed to me through the week he isn't confident we will. The draft pick straight out of college that replaced me on the field after I got injured was good, but isn't NFL ready. The boys held onto a lead we already had to win the game but the gap closed pretty quickly.

I was angry. I was annoyed. I hate being hurt.

But then Billy died.

Being hurt hasn't mattered so much since I found out the news. Nothing has mattered all that much since then.

Except Ivy.

I look up at the church as I get closer to the front steps. My heart pounds in my chest and my eyes itch. I'm man enough to admit that when Coach called to tell me the news, I cried. Billy was special.

He meant a lot to the Broncos organization.

He meant a lot to Coach.

Most of all, he meant a lot to Ivy.

It kills me that I have to sit on the sidelines right now. Ivy asked for space and I have to give it to her, as much as I fucking hate the idea.

When she walked away from me in the hospital on the day my season ended, it crushed me. I don't know where we stand right now. I don't know if I'm someone she wants to see. To talk too.

But fuck do I want to see her, comfort her, be there for her.

There isn't a reason on this earth that would keep me away from being at this church today. Not the shitty weather, not the fact I haven't had a full conversation with my girlfriend in weeks—and yes, she's still my girlfriend regardless of how she walked away from me or tried to break up with me.

I hurry up the stone steps of the church and through the heavy wood doors. People are everywhere, finding their seats. Everyone is dressed in black suits, black dresses. There isn't a color in sight. Well, except the crisp navy and white jersey draped over the coffin in front of the altar.

Booker is in large, white letters.

A few heads turn my way but I pay them no mind. In the corner of my eye, I notice Coach standing a little out of his seat when he sees me but I don't stop and I don't turn to him.

My focus is on the girl sitting in the very first row. Her hair falls in loose curls down her back. I see Katie sitting next to her, body turned into her friends so that she can speak quietly into her ear. Grant, and two other elderly people are sitting on the other side of Katie.

I slow my steps as I come to the end of the aisle.

Even in her grief, she's beautiful.

"Hey," I say. I keep my words low, not wanting my voice to carry too far back over the crowd. I'm not here for them. I watch Ivy's eyes close and her shoulders rise and fall as she takes a shaky breath. But she doesn't look up or give me her eyes.

"Hi, Scott." Katie gives me a kind smile. "Thank you for coming."

I only nod at her, glancing briefly at the people sitting next to Grant who are staring at me with approval in their gaze. They must be Katie's parents.

I take the empty seat between Ivy and the edge of the pew. Our thighs press together. She's wearing a simple dress under a coat and black stockings. On her hands, she wears black leather gloves.

My eyes don't leave her face as I take her hands in mine and gently remove her gloves. I place them on the seat beside me and tangle my fingers with hers. Eventually, the ice cold of her skin warms up in mine. Her head turns, just a little, and her body sinks into mine. Her cheek rests gently on my shoulder and her fingers tighten around mine.

I don't let go.

The minister that performs the service is respectful, reflecting on Billy's life with ease and a little bit of humor. I didn't get to know him for very long, but I think he would have kind of hated it. Billy was always smiling, always going around telling jokes and laughing. There's not enough color in the room.

Ivy's hands are still wrapped up tightly in mine when Coach and a few others carry Billy from the church to a Beatles song. She doesn't make any indication that she intends to follow them out, so we stay put. Over her head, I give Katie a subtle nod and she takes my hint.

The rest of the guests follow Katie's example and start exiting the church.

Quiet settles around us. Ivy doesn't move.

I turn and press my lips into her hair, inhaling the rose scent of her shampoo. The arm that's wrapped around her shoulders gently guides her to stand and turn to face me. For the first time since sitting down, our hands drop and I instantly pull her against my chest. My arms wrap tightly around her and she sags into my chest.

Ivy presses her whole body into me, shaking a little. I tighten my arms.

"I'm so sorry, baby," I murmur quietly into her hair. "I'm so, so sorry."

We stand there in silence. I rest a cheek on her head, arms still around her, keeping her pressed against me.

"It will be okay. I promise," I whisper into the empty church. Ivy makes no effort to reply and I don't push her too. After a few more silent moments just holding her, I glance up. Feeling eyes on us, I look around and find Katie standing at the entrance of the church, watching us with a sad smile on her face.

I pull back but don't take away my touch. I don't want to let go. I never want to let her go.

"Do you want me to take you home?" I ask, staring down into her face. I expect tears. My girl is a sensitive soul and she cries at commercials if they're even remotely sad. I stoke a thumb over her cheek, desperately wanting her to give me a sign of what she may want here. No answers, no tears. She simply stares ahead. She's numb.

When she doesn't reply, I nod at Katie and she makes her way toward us.

I press another kiss to Ivy's forehead, lingering as I revel in having her in my arms again.

"Okay. Katie's going to take you home." I kiss her again, hoping with my whole heart that she can feel what I'm trying to tell her.

I love you.

I miss you.

I'll be here when you're ready.

"I'll see you soon." I wait again for any sign from my girl-friend. There is a beat of silence. Then she looks up. She rises on her toes, silently asking for a kiss.

As always, I oblige.

Her lips are soft and just as I remembered them. *I love you.*

Before I know it, she lets Katie remove her from my embrace and guide her toward the entry of the church. Everyone is wait-ing to say goodbye to her so I let her go.

I watch her walk away.

I'm getting so sick of watching her walk away.

"Hey, man." Someone clears their throat beside me. I realize Grant followed Katie and is now standing in front of me, hands in his pockets. "Thank you for taking the night shifts this week at the house. Katie is so worried about Ivy and scared to leave her alone. Naturally, I worry about Katie." He chuckles a little and rubs the back of his neck. I just stare blankly, waiting for him to get to his point.

"Anyway, pretty sure Katie would've moved in by now if you weren't sleeping at the house with Ivy each night. So, yeah, thanks."

Ah.

He's talking about the self-induced torture I've been par-taking in every night since Billy passed away. Sneaking into the dark house and sleeping on the couch just in case Ivy needs something. Making her breakfast and then leaving before she wakes up.

I haven't spoken to her. I haven't touched her. It's killed me.

But I've been there. Just in case.

"Does Ivy know?" My throat feels like sandpaper.

"I don't think so. Katie says she's not been talking all that much."

Katie calls Grant's name, the sound echoing off the high ceilings of the church. Grant nods at his girlfriend before holding his hand out to shake mine.

"Thanks again. Oh and hey, good luck with the game tomorrow night."

***

"A lot of people turning out for this." Flynn glances around at the fans filing into the stadium. We stand close to the center of the field as a team. All the boys are dressed in suits. The wider organizational staff have joined us. A few players from Billy's old team sit on the opposite side of the stage.

"Everyone's turning up to say goodbye." The words almost get stuck in my throat. I shove my hands deep into my pockets, trying to not fiddle or reach for my phone. My eyes wander over the crowd on the field, once again looking for her.

"How's Ivy doing?" Flynn asks. "You still sleeping there every night?"

"Mostly. Sometimes Ivy stays up later or even all night and Katie tells me not to come." I shrug, the ache in my chest intensifying. I'm pretty certain Ivy knows that I've been sleeping on her couch the last week but she also hasn't spoken to anyone other than Katie.

Everyone's worried.

I am too, but fuck if I don't miss her more than anything else right now.

The crowd is almost completely full and they fall into a silence I have never heard in all my time playing in stadiums all over the country.

A video is broadcast across the big screens of Billy's career. They play a highlight reel of his life. They show his laughing, smiling face. His eyes crinkled when he was younger the same way they did when I knew him. His smile was just as infectious. He had a big personality, it's obvious. They show him as a player, they show him as a teammate. As a member of the organization.

And they show him as a father.

The videos are home videos. Billy with his son: throwing a football in the backyard when Matty wouldn't have been more than one or two, Billy running the sideline of a pee-wee football field yelling encouragement, Billy at a high school football game and showing off the Booker jersey with his son's number.

Something catches in my throat as I watch a young version of Ivy's father wrap his arms around Billy and smile for the camera. He's pointing at his Harvard jersey.

Number eighteen.

"Holy fuck," Flynn swears under his breath. "Did you know he wore your number?"

I shake my head. "No. I mean, I saw him play once. But I didn't remember his number."

"Ivy never mentioned it?"

"Ivy doesn't talk about her dad."

My eyes search the crowd around us, desperate to find her. Coach told me she was going to be here, so I switch up my aim and look for him instead.

Toward the end of the video, I see him walking out of the tunnel and to the stage.

His arm is thrown over Ivy's shoulders.

To my surprise, she is wearing my jersey. The number eighteen is navy on the white jersey. She's got a pair of blue jeans and knee-high boots, with a white long-sleeve shirt poking out and covering her arms.

My heart soars at the thought of her wearing my number on a day like today but as she gets closer, I notice the small differences. The subtle changes that have been made to the Broncos uniform throughout the years.

She's not wearing my number.

She's wearing her dad's.

Coach presses a kiss into the side of her head, patting her shoulder like any father would before leaving her by the edge of the stairs to the stage. He takes two at a time and heads for the microphone.

"Broncos fans, thank you." He pauses, waiting for the cheers of the crown to die. "Billy Booker was a legend. A hall of fame player. A father. A grandfather. Most of all to me, he was a friend. I had the pleasure of knowing him for the last half of his life. I was his son's college football coach and I was close with his family after Matty's passing."

My eyes drag back to Ivy. She's twisting her fingers over and over as she clasps them in front of herself. Coach goes on, talking about the life Billy had. His involvement in the organization, his love for football.

I keep my eyes on Ivy though.

She keeps flinching. It's as if the words Coach is saying are physically hurting her.

"Billy was a proud grandfather. And today, to pay special tribute, his granddaughter Ivy would like to say a few words."

My head snaps back to Coach and then quickly back to Ivy. She steels herself with a deep breath, her shoulders rising and falling, before she takes the stairs onto the stage.

Her face is duplicated over and over across the big screens. It's zoomed in and her features are as clear as day. The cheeks I so love to stroke with my thumb while I hold her at the perfect angle to drop a kiss onto her lips. The hair I absently fiddle with in the mornings as we slowly wake up. The lips that are mine, and mine alone, to kiss.

Something like jealousy rises in my chest and suddenly I don't love the fact there are a million cameras pointing at her for everyone to see what's mine.

I'm caught up in my cave man like thinking as she starts to speak. Her voice breaking through and tugging at me as if she herself pulled on the invisible tether that seems to exist between us.

I'm already walking toward the stage when she leans into the microphone.

"Pops was … he was my everything." Ivy starts, her quiet voice amplified throughout the stadium. "When my … my …"

I take two steps at a time and stride out onto the stage. The crowd starts cheering and yelling and making enough noise that Ivy pauses and glances over her shoulder.

Coach, who is standing a few steps away from Ivy, looks back at me too but I don't bother with taking in his expression.

Just like when I walked into that church a week ago, I am not here for them.

I am here for her.

Ivy's eyes widen, the glassy look she gives me breaking my heart right down the middle. I don't pause. I don't hesitate. I simply cup my girl's face in my hands, stroke my thumb across her cheek and dip my head so that my lips can touch hers.

It's a gentle, quiet peck. Something to simply tell her that even though this thing between us scares her shitless, I am not afraid. I will stand by her side in every way. I will hold her hand, support her, kiss her when she needs it. Even in front of a stadium full of people.

For her.

Only for her.

The crowd erupts around us. The sound of their cheering is dull and muffled. When Ivy is in my arms, the world quietens. It's been far too many weeks since she's been in my arms.

"Let me help," I say quietly to her.

Ivy stares up at me, blinking rapidly and lips trembling. The moment feels monumental for us. Here I am standing on my side of the wall, and her on the other. I am waiting, yet again, for her to decide if letting me in, if letting me help is something that she is willing to do.

In the past, I've not succeeded. I've been pushed back. I've made small progress but the door never appeared for me to walk through and join her.

This time though, in front of thousands of people and the world she hates so goddamn much, I decide to not take no for an answer.

I lean down and press my lips to hers again, speaking quietly just to her. "You don't have to be alone in this. Let me help. Please, baby."

My thumb swipes her cheek again and if it weren't for my hold on her, I would've missed the nod she gives.

I remove my hands from her face. A hand slides around her shoulders and I tug her into my side. She reaches up, threading her fingers through mine and curling into me. With Ivy pressed into me, exactly where she belongs, I step up to the mic.

"Billy was a special man." I begin, not bothering to wait for the crowd to pipe down. "He was more than just a Hall of Famer: he was a force of nature, a father and a grandfather. His larger-than-life personality lit up the room, and his laughter was infectious. On the field, he was a leader and a teammate. He was a pioneer. A role model to my generation and the one that came before me. He was a part of a team that helped shape the game. And when he retired, he helped shape this organization."

Cheers and clapping echo through the crowd on the field, those who work for the team adding to the crowd.

"Most of all though, he dedicated his life after football to his family. To his late son, Matty Booker, and his wife Sara. He was a devoted husband to his late wife Marie and with her they raised Ivy, their granddaughter."

Ivy presses her face into my chest, curling so far into me that it is as if she is trying to burrow her way through me.

"I didn't have the pleasure to know Billy for very long personally but for the time I did, it was obvious that football came a very distant second to his family. He spoke of getting out and living life. Having fun. Laughing. He taught me that even in the hardest of situations, life will surprise you. To move forward with passion and joy. To have patience for the things we really want and to put in the work where it's needed."

I run a hand down Ivy's spine, keeping her close.

"I don't know about everyone else here. I can only speak for myself but Billy always said to have patience. We would go over my game tapes every Tuesday—"

I feel Ivy lean away from me, peering up through her dark lashes.

"And he would point out all the plays that I moved too quickly, when I didn't look up and missed an opportunity. He would tell me to have a little bit of patience and the play would open up for me as it should."

I glance down, meeting Ivy's eyes. The navy sucks me in and the world quietens again around us.

"I think everyone could have a little more patience, be a little more like Billy. Move through life laughing and cheering on the ones we love. Step back once in a while and be present, not to miss what might be right in front of us."

I don't take my eyes off the girl curling into my body like I am the only thing keeping her standing right now. I lift an arm out to the side.

"To Billy."

The crowd repeats it back, erupting in more cheers, and screaming, and shouts but I hear none of it. My gaze is solely on my girl. Coach steps up to us, clapping a hand on my shoulder and nodding a head toward the tunnel.

It's permission to leave an official team event.

"Come on, baby." I guide Ivy off the stage. "Let's go home."

Chapter
Twenty-Five

Ivy

My body hurts and I have a headache.

As in, my whole body. I've felt the aches of the flu, and the aches of being exhausted out of my mind. This is something different entirely.

And I can't cry.

Is that weird?

I'm a self-confessed oversensitive girl. I am a crier. Stressed out? I'll cry. Sad? Crying before I even know why. Having an argument? So many tears it frustrates me more.

But I haven't shed a tear since Pops died.

Ouch.

My chest explodes with pain and I close my eyes. It hurts so badly.

Scott drives with one hand on the wheel and the other on my thigh. His fingers are digging into my jeans and his thumb stokes the fabric absentmindedly. He hasn't stopped touching me since that kiss in front of eighty-thousand people.

The kiss. Oh god, the kiss.

I have no idea what on earth made him think that would be okay and I felt sick watching him stride toward me, the determination painted all over his gorgeous face. But when his lips touched mine for the first time in weeks, the world started to turn again and a little of the ache I had been feeling in my heart healed.

I don't care about the photos that are probably circling by now.

I don't care about the gossip columns, or news reports, or social media posts.

It hardly matters. I should've realized that I wouldn't just be able to move on from the man sitting in the driver's seat. Not when he's spent the last two weeks showing me exactly where I rank on his list of priorities.

He's tied himself to me and wrapped my life around his.

Football and I ... well, we will probably never be friends. I still hate the reminder of what I lost every time I look down at the field. Every time I hear an announcer talk about my family. Every time I feel like I have to share a piece of my dad with the rest of the world.

So no, we won't be friends. But we can be *friendly*.

Because Pops is gone. My worst nightmare has come true and I'm on my own. At least that's how I viewed it before this summer. Before Scott.

Now, I see the man sitting across the console from me, his hand holding my leg as if I'm a lifeline and he's scared I'll ask him to leave again. The man that has been sleeping on the couch downstairs for two weeks because he didn't want me to be alone.

Yes, I know.

Of course I know. He's not exactly quiet and I haven't been sleeping nearly as much as he and Katie think I have been. The home movies they played today? I've been playing them on repeat since I came home from the hospital that night. I've been watching Pops games, my dad's games. I've been listening to them talk. To each other, to my mom and nan. To me.

I look down at the jersey. An old but hardly worn Broncos jersey that has been sitting in a sealed box for almost twenty-two years. My dad's draft day jersey. The one that he would've been given when drafted to the Broncos if he hadn't died before he made it.

I hadn't even known the box existed two weeks ago.

I left the hospital the night Pops passed with Katie on one side and Dr. Bryden on the other. He gave me a hug after walking us to our car, then he pulled out a crisp white envelope with my name written in Pops' neat scrawl across the front.

There wasn't some big confession inside. No huge plot twist that may have set my life on a different path the moment I read it.

It was simply a reminder from Pops.

You need to live a little.

Remember me, remember your dad, but don't forget to live.

My heart constricts and my nose stings as I remember. I'd read his words over and over, hearing them in his voice and then again in my dad's.

He is right. Of course, he is.

Pops also told me about the box of football things in the back of his cupboard. He'd been saving them until I got over my resentment which in his letter he hoped would be any day now, now that I was in love with a quarterback. It was full of game tapes, and play diaries, and notebooks, upon notebooks that my dad kept. I've been obsessively pouring over them the last few nights. He was good, really good. The Broncos jersey was neatly folded inside, along with a few others. All with my dad's number and name stitched into it. Pops mentioned in his letter that it was the one they gave him after Mom and Dad died. The same one they had been planning to give him when they got him in the draft that coming April.

I left the box sitting open on my bedroom floor after pulling out the jersey and deciding to wear it.

I fiddle with the hem, glancing down at the large number eighteen on the front.

Scott's hand pulses on my leg and I look up. He's staring at me, his other hand resting on his own thigh. I furrow my brow and turn to look out the window. The brownstone looms over us, bathed in afternoon light painted in pretty patterns from the shadow of the trees.

"Want to go inside?" he asks gently. He doesn't move, waiting for me to decide.

"Sure." My voice sounds like gravel. I haven't been talking much lately. No crying, and no talking. Two things I normally excel at are the two things I haven't really felt like partaking in.

Scott waits for a beat and then makes his move. He's out of the driver's seat and at my door before I can even unbuckle my seat belt. He opens the car door and extends a hand. I take it and step out of the car, he keeps his fingers threaded through mine. As we get to the front door, he uses the key I gave him at Christmas to open the door.

Fair enough. I never asked for it back.

Although, I don't think he would've given it to me anyway. According to him, we never broke up. And I guess we didn't.

I was being a fucking idiot.

I strip off my coat and sit down on the small bench by the door so I can peel off my boots. Before I can reach for the zipper, Scott bends down onto one knee and reaches for my calf. He pulls the boot toward himself and gently takes the tiny zipper between his large fingers, tugging it down. He slips one boot off my foot and then repeats the action with the other.

I can only stare at him as he carefully puts them to the side and stands again, holding out his hand. I let him lead me down the corridor, into the living room and over to the couch. He sits down, pushing back into my usual spot of the couch so he's nestled right into the corner cushions. Then, he pulls me down onto his lap.

I mold myself to his chest and he covers us with a blanket.

With every breath, every intoxicating inhale of him, I feel as if a tiny surgeon sits in my chest with a tiny needle and thread, stitching the cracks in my heart together one tiny stitch at a time.

An hour passes. Or a minute. I'm not sure. We just sit in silence. His hand runs a soothing path up and down my back and my cheek presses deeper and deeper into his chest.

"I'm sorry," I whisper, finally breaking apart.

He doesn't stop or change or move. He simply replies, "You have nothing to be sorry for."

"I do. I was a stubborn idiot." I close my eyes, my stomach churning a little with anxiety. "I should never have pushed you away for something as silly as you playing football. You just weren't—"

"Part of your plan?" he finishes for me.

I'm not exactly sure how to describe the feeling that washes over me at this moment. It's something new.

Scott, for all that I have put him through the last few weeks, continues to work, and to fight, and to want me. The feeling settles me. Like roots are starting to anchor me down but those roots are intertwined with his, twirling and twisting around one another's until they're tied together with no hope of ever coming apart.

And I'm not scared.

Not like I was.

When Scott looks at me, he sees all of me. Every flaw, every imperfection, every delusional grudge I keep. He sees through the happy mask I have on and into the anxiety, and the fears, and the vulnerability I try so hard to keep inside. He looks at me with acceptance and understanding.

And love.

"No. You weren't part of my plan," I murmur back.

"I know, baby." His hand continues to stroke my back, the soothing circles lulling my exhausted body to relax against him. "Plans don't always go the way we want them too. I know that scares you. But I'm here. To help. I'm not going anywhere. If you let me."

My eyes sting and my throat feels scratchy. My stomach twists and turns.

But no tears so instead, I close my eyes.

***

I must have fallen asleep.

I wake up with my body tucked under the heavy covers of my bed and my arms circled tightly around a pillow. My bedroom is dark, the only light coming from the lit hallway lamps where the door has been left open. I sit up, letting the covers fall off my body.

Scott changed my clothes. I'm no longer wearing the jeans or the jersey I'd picked out. Instead, just an oversized Broncos t-shirt. I run my fingers through my hair, pushing the strands out of my face as I yawn. My body still hurts but my headache has gone and the pain in my chest has eased, if only a little.

This morning I left my bedroom in a state. Clothes every-where, video tapes scattered all over my dresser, the box of foot-ball memorabilia open in the center of the room. It's not a mess anymore. The clothes are gone, the tapes are stacked neatly on the dresser alongside the sealed box. The jersey I wore today is hanging from the curtain rod over my window.

I look at it and I think of my dad.

He would approve of Scott. I know deep down that he would.

Throughout the years, there've been so many times when Pops would try to tell me that my dad would've wanted me to love football like he did. To enjoy the game and the connection to him it gave me. I ignored him. Stupidly. I'd ignored a whole part of my dad that I could've had before now and even though I know that it's ridiculous, part of me still hates football.

Still hates that it got him first.

My chest squeezes tightly as the push pull continues inside my head. I can't move forward and I can't go back. I know that it's something I need to work through. Considering the man that's downstairs probably sleeping on the couch. I can't let him go, even if I really wanted to. He is a part of me now.

I lean over, opening my bedside drawer and fish out the card Katie gave me last week.

A therapist's office number is printed neatly under a picture of the older woman with gray hair and a kind smile. I turn the card over in my hands and practice taking some steady breaths.

I pull out my phone and set a reminder to call the number first thing on Monday morning.

Just as I'm placing the card back on the bedside, a small knock comes from my open bedroom door. Scott stands there, hair messy and black t-shirt wrinkled. He's also changed from the suit he wore today. He holds a mug, steam drifting from the top.

"Hi." I smile shyly at him.

"Hi, yourself." He moves toward me, placing the mug on the bedside table next to the business card.

"What time is it?" I ask, reaching for my phone realizing when I picked it up before I hadn't even glanced at the time.

"Just after six. Not late." He rounds the bed and gets in next to me. As if my body is on autopilot; when he holds an arm out, I crawl into his lap. "You were only asleep for a couple of hours," he finishes.

"Oh." He finds a strand of my hair and begins to twirl it around his fingers.

"I made you some tea but if you're hungry, we can order some dinner."

"Okay," I whisper. My heart hammers in my chest.

"What do you feel like? Pizza?" Around and around, my hair is twirled and twisted before he lets it go loose just to repeat the process.

"I don't know."

"Are you hungry?" My stomach answers for me with a growl. Scott chuckles and the sound seeps into my skin, chasing away some of the chill I've been feeling for weeks now.

"Ivy?" he asks. I hum in response but don't look up at him. Gently he asks, "What's the business card for?"

"Oh. A therapist," I say. I push away from his chest and the strand of hair he's holding drops around my face. "I'm going to go and talk to someone. A professional someone."

"If that's what you want to do, I think that's a great idea," he says softly. No judgment. No curiosity. No further questions. Just unwavering and unquestioned support.

I stare at his handsome face. There are questions I wanted to ask him before Pops passed. After I went to the hospital the night Scott got injured and then he wouldn't stop blowing up my phone, I made a list of all the things that were still unsettling me.

Where was he playing next year?

What happens if it's not here?

Do I have to just follow him around as a football girlfriend? Do I want that?

Yes. Maybe. Who knows.

What about the paparazzi? What do we do about them following me home?

Even if I get the help and work through my issues with football, and my dad, and my past, what if I still can't stand being a part of his world? What happens to us then?

I am so far in love with this man that I want so badly to move past the anxiety and the fear and make a plan—a new plan—with him but what if it's too hard? What if he decides it's all too much to be with me?

"Ivy." His voice jolts me from my thoughts. I feel like I want to cry again.

"I have ... there are things we need to talk about. To go through." I take a deep breath.

"What kind of things?"

"Well ... where are you playing next year?" I ask. Anxiety turns over and over inside me and my eyes itch and I blink a few times, desperately trying to get rid of the feeling.

"Here." Scott sounds so certain but surprise floods me.

"You signed a new contract?"

"No." He shakes his head, lifting a hand to tuck the stray piece of hair behind my ear. "But I will. If you want to be here, then I'll play here."

"And if Uncle Jeff can't offer you anything?"

"Ivy." He invades my space, coming so close that I think he might kiss me. I won't be mad if he does. I miss kissing him. Touching him. Being with him. His green eyes darken, swirling with the gold flecks that give them so much depth it's as if I'm starting straight into his soul.

"I love football, but I love you more."

Relief. Pure and utter relief floods me. Like a river breaking a damn, my eyes well with tears, and my body hums, and the waves crash over me. It runs through my veins, warming me and raising goosebumps all over my body.

Scott doesn't look away. He doesn't back up. He just stares at me as I stare at him.

"You love me?" I whisper.

"More than anything."

"Even when I'm being unreasonable, and stubborn, and letting my fears get the better of me."

"I can handle it. I want to handle it." He drops his lips to mine in a gentle kiss. "You have changed it all for me. You're *it* for me. If Coach can't find me a deal, although I'm pretty sure he will, then I'll take a break until I get one. Or I'll go play for a team nearby. Or we can talk about what happens if I do get offered something else further away. But the point is that whatever happens now I want to make the plan with you. Only with you. *Always* with you."

Hot, wet tears run down my cheeks so fast I don't bother trying to catch them.

"Please don't cry, baby."

"I'm overwhelmed," I sob and it's so ridiculous that I begin to laugh. I choke out a laugh through the never-ending tears that just keep coming. Weeks and weeks' worth of tears. "I haven't been able to cry since they called me about Pops."

"You haven't?" He swipes his thumb across my cheek and I sniff. Shutting my eyes, I take a steadying breath. "But you love crying."

I laugh again. God, this man.

"I know." I breathe deeply through my nose and exhale, opening my eyes. The endless green is waiting and I sink into it. Sink into him. "You love me?"

"I love you," he confirms, his hands cupping my head. His fingers curl into my hair and I relax into his touch.

"You love me more than football?" I ask. I hold back my smile, because I know it's his job, and I am going to work through my issues, and I did decide to call a truce with that world but it's still nice to hear that I get to win.

"I love you more than football." He smirks at me, lips hovering inches away.

I lean toward him, closing the gap and falling into him. I kiss him, pouring how much I missed him the last few weeks into the kiss. I sink my hands into his hair and wrap my legs around his waist until he falls back on the bed and I'm straddling him. His tongue fights with mine and his arms circle me, pulling me against him so tightly that there's no space left between us.

When I pull back for air, I whisper against his lips.

"I love you, too."

Chapter Twenty-Six

Ivy

"So, how's therapy going?" I almost choke on the soda I've just taken a sip of. Katie is staring at me, her serious expression unchanging.

"Oh." I clear my throat quickly. "It's good. Great, actually. Early days but she's really nice."

Katie just nods, like it's exactly what she expected to hear from me. I cock my head, a small smile playing on my lips.

Today is Super Bowl Sunday. It also happens to be Scott's thirtieth birthday. So we're having our friends over to watch the game. A few players from the team, Flynn of course, and Katie are all here. Grant is not, surprisingly. I haven't been able to question Katie about his absence because every time I do, she asks me something else to change the subject.

This time, it is my therapy session.

I have been seeing Dr. Karla for a month now and it's the best decision I ever made.

Well second best.

"I'm working through everything. It's a slow process and I cry a lot—"

"A given with you," Katie interrupts, smirking.

"Shut up." I hit her arm lightly, taking another sip of my soda. I stare at my friend for a moment, questions about Grant on the tip of my tongue but I decide to hold them back. She will tell me when she's ready.

"But it's good. I'm feeling … calmer. About everything." Katie only nods in response and goes back to arranging the crackers along the edge of the cheese board she's preparing.

My sessions have been overwhelming for the most part. I'm exhausted after every one and my eyes are always red and puffy. But when I get home, I walk straight into Scott's waiting arms and I remember exactly why it's a good idea to go. Not just for him, but for me and the future I know that I want.

The point is I'm finally working through the endless pit of grief I haven't been able to get rid of since I was old enough to know what grief is. Finally working through my parents' death and coming to terms with Pops'. I miss them the more I talk about them out loud—opposed to keeping them to myself like I used too—but I also don't.

It's weird.

Like now that I talk about them more, now that I am starting to accept that they're gone in a healthy way, I feel more connected to them than I ever have.

Scott is nothing but supportive. With the season over, he spends his days at the gym and doing odd jobs around the house.

He's moved in. Officially. That happened not long after Pops' memorial. He didn't sleep at his place anyway so it made the most sense. I came home after my first day of leaving him home alone after he moved his stuff in to find a to-do list sitting on the kitchen counter.

Fix the back deck.

Hinges on the shed door.

Retile downstairs bathroom.

Paint the office.

Paint the main bedroom and redo the bathroom.

Hang Matty's jersey.

One by one, he's slowly trying to tick things off. The first was painting the office upstairs that hasn't been used since Nan passed away. The second, hanging dad's jersey in said office.

The office is mine now. Every evening when I store my work bag, I brush a gentle hand over the glass encasing the Broncos jersey hanging across from my desk. The bookshelves are filled with photos of my parents and my grandparents. All the ones I kept locked away on a hidden album on my phone when I was pretending to be okay without them are on display.

And every day looking at it hurts a little less. Thanks to therapy.

I'm watching Katie strategically place the three different types of cheeses around the board when an arm snakes around my waist. Scott pulls me back into his chest and I sigh, leaning into him too.

"How much cheese does one board need, Katie?" he asks with a laugh. Pressing his face into my neck, he presses a soft kiss against my skin. I shiver.

"Hush. Perfecting a cheese board is an art, Harvey," she retorts, not looking up from the board. "Don't distract me."

Scott's arm loosens a little around me as his hand starts to play with the waistband of my jeans. His hand dips and I feel the warmth of his palm press against my bare stomach. I only pulled on a sweatshirt this morning because with the amount of people in this house right now, it's warm enough not to have to layer up. His fingers splay across my stomach, his thumb slowly moving back and forth over my soft stomach. I turn my head toward him, looking up into his gorgeous face. He's decided to grow his beard out a little and I am more than supportive of the decision.

The feel of it between my legs last night was next level.

The hand on my stomach slips up and I feel his thumb brush the lace of the bra I'm wearing. Heat floods my cheeks and I bite down on my bottom lip. His eyes lock on mine as his thumb takes another swipe, higher this time, closer and closer to my hard nipple.

An ache starts to pulse between my legs and inch my hips back. Scott grunts.

"You two are gross. Get a room." Katie scowls, gagging as she rolls her eyes at us.

I laugh but Scott's hand tightens around my waist. He leans down and I shiver when his warm breath coasts over my skin, whispering his quiet words into my ear.

"Should we? Get a room?"

Despite myself, I cock my head a little to give him more room. He presses a gentle kiss to the base of my neck as his other arm wraps around my body. I rest a hand on the forearm that isn't tucked underneath my sweatshirt.

"No," I murmur, leaning to look back up at him. "We're quite literally in the middle of hosting a party. *Your* party."

"And for my birthday, I want to fuck you in the bathroom upstairs."

Katie makes another loud gagging noise, making it known she heard his comment, before she picks up the cheese board and walks toward the dining room table.

Scott doesn't let up.

"Please," he begs.

I shake my head but the ache between my thighs is screaming for me to say yes. He brushes a thumb over my nipple, his forefinger coming up to twist it. Just a little. Fucking tease.

I press my hips back and feel the bulge growing behind his jeans and I feel the little willpower I had seep out of me. I turn in his arms, lifting on my toes.

He meets me halfway and kisses me.

Like always.

The word 'yes' is on my lips when the front door opens and closes with a slam and I hear laughter coming down the hallway.

"It's fine, Jason. They won't mind." Scott stiffens at the voice before he crumbles against me, burying his face in my neck and reaching down to adjust himself.

I look up just in time to see Annabel and Jason reach the end of the hallway. Holding out her arms full of gift bags and groceries, Annabel's face lights up in a smile as she sees us.

"Surprise, Sweetheart!"

Scott just groans against me. I laugh, untangling myself from him and spinning toward his parents.

"Hi." I plaster my best smile on my face and stay in front of Scott a little longer, giving him a chance to calm down. Poor man. Cockblocked by his parents. "I didn't know you guys were coming."

"I wanted to call," Jason says. He places the bags he's carrying—two small overnight bags—down and moves around the counter. "But your mother wouldn't let me. She wanted it to be a surprise." He rolls his eyes as he opens his arms to me for a hug.

"Mom," Scott grumbles behind me. "You should have called first."

"It's fine," I say as Jason tucks me under his arm. Annabel presses a kiss to my cheek in greeting before moving to wrap her son up in a hug.

Scott hugs her back just as fiercely.

"I wish you'd told us you were coming," I say, looking from Annabel to Jason. "Scott decided he *has* to paint the guest room so there's only my old bedroom to sleep in."

"That's okay, love." Jason squeezes me to his side. "We're just happy to be here."

"I'll take your bags up. Grab a drink and some food." Scott moves to grab his parents' bags and head upstairs but Annabel stops him.

"No! Presents first. I found the funniest pair of socks for you." She starts unloading the bags she is carrying onto the kitchen island. "And I found something I thought you might want to see."

Jason lets go of me and I move to stand next to Annabel, examining all of the beautifully wrapped parcels she spreads over the island. She pulls out an old shoe box and sets it carefully on the bench.

In the corner of my eye, I see Jason move over and clap his son on the shoulder. Scott turns to his dad and hugs him. My heart thuds against my chest. They love each other so deeply. Thinking about how Jason and Annabel chose to adopt Scott, chose to love him, makes my eyes sting with tears. I'll be forever grateful to them for raising the patient, kind man that loves me just as deeply as he loves his parents.

"So, did you hear?" Jason asks his son.

"Yep." Scott holds up three fingers. "Signed for a further three years."

Jason smiles so brightly; I can't help my own blooming. He fist pumps the air, crying out, "Yes! Knew it."

"So, you're staying?" Annabel is watching for her place beside me.

"I'm staying," Scott says, his eyes finding me. "We're staying. That's the plan."

"Oh well then." Annabel taps my hand gently. "We'll have to come out here more often. Don't want to miss any ... milestones."

Scott groans, shooting a playful smile at his mother while shaking his head. My cheeks heat. We haven't talked about our future much, but when one of us brings it up Scott doesn't speak in 'what-ifs'. He talks in definitives. With certainty. After all we went through—all that I put him through—a future with Scott Harvey is the only plan I need.

God, I hope our kids get his eyes.

"What's with the old shoe box, Mom?" Scott asks from across the island.

Annabel pushes the box to the center of the four of us and peels the lid off. Inside is what must be hundreds of pictures of Scott as a kid.

"Oh my god," I laugh as I pick up one from the top. Scott is young but his bright green eyes are just as they are today. They must have only just brought him home from Boston because he's nothing but skin and bones. He sits in the middle of a bathtub, surrounded by bubbles. Jason leans over the tub, a beard made of bubbles on his face, trying to make the younger version of Scott laugh.

The next one is just as cute—napping on a picnic blanket with Annabel.

His first day at school, getting older in each one I pick up.

His life, from the moment they found him, is documented in pictures.

"These are gorgeous, Annabel. Thank you for bringing them with you." I smile even with the tightness in my chest making it a little hard to breathe. I think—I know—it's jealousy.

I want this. I want memories with my parents.

I take a breath, inflating the invisible balloon in my chest until it's close to popping. Then, I exhale, letting go of the negative feelings that started to creep in. Just as Dr. Karla taught me.

"They are." She shuffles a few photos in the box until she finds one particular picture. "But this is why I wanted to bring it with me."

She passes me the photo of Scott, dressed in a football jersey much too big for him. No older than six or seven. He's standing with the game ball held up in front of him, the brightest smile on his boyish face.

And next to him, an arm around his shoulder and a smile just a big, is my dad.

"I don't … how do you have this?" I ask, looking up at Annabel. The photo falls through my shaking fingers.

"Mom, what is this?" I glance at Scott as he picks up the photo.

"It's a UCLA versus Boston game. I believe it's one of the only ones Matty Booker played in. When we saw the video reel from your Pops memorial, I knew his face looked familiar but I wasn't sure why. So I went looking."

"That game … you were at that game?" I ask Annabel, looking between her and Jason. Annabel's brow furrows but she nods.

"We took Scott. He was just starting to show interest in football and we were donors to the university. We got free tickets and thought he would enjoy it. He watched Matty the entire time. Wouldn't take his eyes off him. So when we were let onto the field after the game I caught him after the media interviews to get a picture of Scott and him."

"I don't—I don't remember that game," Scott replies quietly, still clutching the photograph in his hands.

"You were just a kid, son." Jason places a hand on Scott's shoulder. We're all silent, just staring at the photo still in Scott's hand.

"I was there," I murmur quietly, the memory flooding back in. Scott's head whips to me.

"What? How?"

"I was only a baby," I say quietly, more to myself than anyone else as I pull out my phone from the back pocket of my jeans. I scroll through my photo albums, looking for the private one I kept my parents hidden away in for all these years. I click on the album and unlock it.

There it is.

The very last photo I saved.

The one Uncle Jeff sent me the night of the party at the bar where Scott and I talked in the alley.

It's from the same day. Sitting on my mom's hip and staring at my dad. It is my new favorite picture of the three of us.

But there is no mistaking it. It's the same game, the same day.

"Matty is the reason Scott asked to play football. After that game, as soon as he could he begged us to get him into peewee." Annabel wraps my hand up in her own. "Scott, pass the picture."

He does and she holds it up to me.

"You see there?" She points to the figures standing just behind Dad's shoulder.

A woman in a football jersey and jeans, holding a baby on her hip, smiling gently at her husband taking a photo with a young fan.

It's a little blurry, a little smudged, but she's there.

My mom. And me.

"Oh my god." Tears well in my eyes and blink them away, not wanting to get the photo damaged.

Strong, muscled arms circle my waist again and Scott pulls me back into his chest in this kitchen for the second time today. He rests his chin on my shoulder, staring down at the picture.

"Look at that," he whispers.

I swallow, closing my eyes. My hand is shaking but I don't let go of the picture. When I open them again, Annabel and Jason are quietly moving away from the kitchen, giving Scott and I a moment of privacy.

"You were there," he says.

"I can't believe this." I turn slightly, looking at where he's resting on my shoulder. "What are the odds?"

"Oh, I dunno." He retreats from my shoulder and spins me in his arm. "Maybe, somehow, your dad had a hand in driving me here. To Boston. To you."

"What? Like fate?" I scoff, unsure if I want to laugh or cry.

"Yeah, baby." He drops his lips to mine, pressing a gentle kiss to my lips. "Like fate."

The tether I felt weeks ago when my head was still waging war against the idea of being a part of his world and dragging up my unresolved grief, tightens and draws us ever closer. I look back down at the picture as Scott's arms lock around my waist.

Maybe it is fate.

What are the chances of this? Of my dad inspiring a young fan at a game between two teams who hardly ever play one another. Of that young fan taking a picture and my mom and me being in the background. Of that young fan becoming the best quarterback the league has ever seen—and no, I'm not biased.

Scott showed up in my life exactly when I needed him too.

He was drawn to Boston for whatever reason when he had sworn off the city for so long. But he came anyway. He felt like he needed to be here.

Then he walked into the bar.

Into my life.

"I think he sent me to you." I look up, my lashes wet with the inevitable tears. "I think your dad sent me to you exactly when he knew you were ready. Is that stupid?"

"No." I shake my head. "Not stupid at all."

"I love you, Ivy."

He brushes a tear from my cheek with a thumb. I lean up on my toes. "I love you, too."

385

EPILOGUE
SCOTT

Eighteen Months Later.

"Fᴜᴄᴋ. Fᴜᴄᴋ. Fᴜᴄᴋ." I riffle through my gym bag, pushing clothes, and cleats, and gym towels out of the way. Why the hell do I keep so much shit in this bag?

Fuck.

If I've lost this ring, Billy is going to haunt me from the grave.

The sound of the front door opening and closing filters upstairs. I freeze, listening. Ivy's voice drifts my way and I go back to furiously rifling through my bag. My fingers brush against the velvet box just as Ivy appears at the top of the stairs with the phone pressed between her shoulder and ear.

She spots me and smiles. It still flaws me even after a year and a half together.

I tuck the box into my pocket as Ivy pulls the phone from her ear and then puts her bag in her office. I take a seat on the end of our bed and kick my bag away from me.

"Hi," she says. Ivy comes down the hallway into our room. She's still smiling as she saunters over to stand between my legs. I part them, letting her settle between them easily. Her fingers brush over my shoulders and she leans down to kiss me.

"How was your day?" I ask her, placing my hands on her waist.

"Boring," she sighs, leaning into me. "What did you do today?"

"Started the deck outside," I say as I dig my fingers into the fabric of her dress. I've slowly been working through the list I started when I moved in. A list that is never-ending. I finish one task, two more get tacked on. The back deck is the biggest project so far. I can't do most of the building myself so the contractor will take care of it while we're away.

It will be good to finally knock it off though. Just in time for Summer.

And when the weather turned so did Ivy's outfits and I don't hate it. She wears these summer dresses that show off her legs and I've enjoyed having the easy access.

"Mmm," she hums. "How many barbecues can I expect to arrive or did you pick just one from the website?"

"I narrowed it down to two." Ivy narrows her eyes at me and I smirk. "Okay, it's three. But I want to make sure I get a good one. We're going to be having all the guys over for the fourth."

"Oh. I get it. You want to make sure you have the biggest and best toy to show off to your friends."

"Stop it." I know she's teasing me. The tension that's been building since I made my decision this morning eases a little. "It's the off-season and you're at school all day. I'm bored. Sue me."

"Well, thankfully, I'll be done with school in a week."

"You, me, a villa in Italy for three weeks." I tug her closer to me.

"You, me, and ... Katie." She leans away and pouts at me. I stare at her blankly, processing what she's just told me.

"Katie?"

"She was talking about Grant and being alone this summer, and that he had been messaging her again." Ivy sits on my thigh, wrapping her arms around my neck and sinking in. Buttering me up. "He's an ass to her. I don't want her to go back to him just because she's sad. So I invited her to come with us for the summer."

"You think that will stop her getting back with him?"

She shrugs in reply. "Maybe not, but it'll be fun anyway. She's my best friend. Please?"

I smile, shaking my head a little. She doesn't need to say please. "Of course, Ives. You want her to come then she can come along."

"Love you." She presses her lips to mine again. Her fingers toy with the hair at the back of my neck. She kisses me once more before getting off my lap. I already miss her. "Oh, hey. You should invite Flynn. That might be fun!"

"Sure. I'll ask him," I agree. As much as Katie has become a staple around the house lately, bringing Flynn might keep her occupied while I spend some much-needed alone time with Ivy.

"I can't wait to get on the plane. The kids this year are exhausting." She moves around the room, chatting about her day as she changes out of her work dress and into her workout clothes. Our afternoon ritual is a run around the neighbourhood. We run together, and then we shower together.

That's my favourite part.

She takes a pair of my shorts out of the drawer and throws them my way, silently asking me to change. The velvet box burns a hole in my pocket as I carefully change out of my pants, making sure it doesn't fall onto the floor.

I've been a nervous wreck this past week, since I pulled the ring out of the safe. Every time Ivy goes near my gym bag my heartbeat becomes erratic and my stress levels skyrocket. I was planning on stashing it as soon as she pulled out the suitcases to start packing. I've been emailing with the villa owner in Italy for over a month trying to set up a proposal dinner.

The roses.

The candles.

The moonlight.

All of it.

But I woke up this morning and looked over at Ivy. Her hair was fanned out behind her. Her face adorably pressed into her pillow and an arm thrown over my stomach. The golden morning light was casting a warm glow over her and I just knew.

I glanced down at her left hand and was annoyed there wasn't a ring on it.

So I'm going to change that.

I need to change it.

I need to not only remind her that this is forever, but let the world know she is all mine.

Tonight.

I will ask her tonight.

"Come on." Ivy tugs on my hand to lead me out of the room. I glance back at my pants on the floor where I've left them, ring box still tucked safely in the pocket.

"What are we doing tonight? Do we have plans?" I ask her.

"I want to finish the new season of housewives." She smiles at me over her shoulder. "The reunion episodes are the best."

Tonight.

Ivy

I sink back into Scott's chest, giggling. The housewives are so dramatic and I love them. I feel the gentle shake of Scott's body against mine and I look up.

"You love it," I accuse him. To be fair, I didn't ever force him to watch them with me. He just got hooked one day and now he's begging me not to watch without him.

"I blame you. You got me addicted to these silly reality shows." He shakes his head, glancing down at me. His eyes soften instantly and it makes my heart jump.

I'm so in love with him.

The last eighteen months has been the happiest of my life. Losing Pops was devastating. Therapy was—*is* rough. I'm still working on myself and getting through my grief. But I sometimes find myself thinking back on the months that I'd kept Scott and I a secret and I mentally kick myself for it. I needed to heal, I needed to move on from the stubborn grudge I kept. And I have.

I'm even a football fan now.

But fucking hell, I was an idiot back then.

The thing I love most though is now, after a tough day mentally or physically at work, I get to come home and crawl into bed next to Scott.

The love of my life.

I couldn't imagine keeping this a secret now. No way.

Scott shifts, moving from behind me to stand.

"Do you want some ice cream?" he asks, already halfway to the kitchen. He knows the answer.

"Of course." I turn back to the TV, sinking into the couch cushions.I pay attention to the screaming match the housewives are having over yet another dinner table. I let out another genuine laugh. They are ridiculous.

"These people have everything yet they still find stuff to complain about. Fifteen seasons and they're still having the same fights," I tell Scott. He gives a noncommittal grunt in reply.

I turn my head in time to watch him round the corner of the couch with a food tray in hand. On the tray are two bowls filled with ice cream.

A single red rose.

And a box.

A small box.

A box only big enough for a ring.

"Oh my god." I don't mean to let the words slip from my mouth but they do anyway.

Scott sets the tray down on the ottoman in front of me. Then he gets on one knee.

Tears well in my eyes. Goosebumps spread over my skin. Nerves and excitement mix and mingle in my stomach, turning it over and over again. I shake my head, staring at the man in front of me in disbelief.

In the background, the housewives are still screaming at one another.

I can't help but let out a laugh, leaning over to bury my face in my hands. Holy shit. Is he actually doing this?

"Ivy," Scott begins but I look up and launch forward, nearly toppling off the couch. I reach for the remote and shut the television off.

"Okay, now go." I sit back on the couch, but I'm at the very edge now with Scott kneeling in front of me.

"Ivy. I love you."

"I love you too," I interrupt, smiling like a fucking idiot.

"Baby, you have to let me get through this," he chuckles. He picks up the small box from the tray and holds it in one hand. The other covers my knee.

I stay silent, nodding my head to urge him on.

"I love you. So much." Scott's thumb begins to trace a pattern on my skin. "I have been falling for you from the moment I saw you in that bar. Just catching a glimpse of you through the window had me walking in the door and taking a seat. It's like my body knew what my heart didn't yet. The last year and a half with you has been the happiest of my life. Watching you grow, and heal, and fall in love with what I love. I couldn't ask for anything more. I know it wasn't easy but I want you to know how proud I am of you. Of how far you've come. Pops, your mom and dad, they'd be so proud of you, too."

He takes a deep breath, stares up at me and opens the box. I resist the urge to glance down at it, not wanting to take my eyes off him.

The deep green with the gold swirling flakes. The same eyes that captivated me that day in the bar and had me curious to know more. My anchor. My tether.

"Now that I know life with you, I don't want to know a life without you," he says. A sob crawls up my throat and I try to take a deep breath, holding in the tears that threaten to spill over in waves. I fail.

"Will you marry me?" Scott asks.

He lifts a hand, swiping at the steady stream of tears making their way down my cheeks. I blink as I try to clear my vision.

I glance down. My vision is blurry and I blink again, trying to clear them. The ring is simple. Timeless. Elegant. The smooth, white gold band glints in the light from the lamp beside us. At the center is a round, sparkling diamond, held in a simple setting that lets the stone catch the light from every angle.

"But this is ..."

"Billy told me where to find it before he passed." Scott takes the ring from the small cushion it sits on inside the box and reaches for my left hand. I let him pull the hand toward him, his thumb gently stroking over my trembling skin. "You already wear your dad's every day, I thought you might like to wear your mom's too."

"I—" My throat feels like sandpaper. Tears are still falling freely over my cheeks. I watch myself shake as Scott holds my mother's engagement ring out to me.

"You okay?" he whispers. Just the sound of his voice brings my eyes back up to meet him.

"I don't remember the last time I pulled this out of the safe to look at it." I glance back at the ring. I glance back at the ring. "I used to as a kid all the time. And then I just stopped."

"So you don't want to wear it? I can get you something else?"

"No, I ..." I swallow, still staring at the ring. "I forgot how gorgeous it is."

"Your dad had good taste."

Where before I may have felt pain and longing, I only feel love. I miss them every day. My dad. My mom. Nan and Pops. The family I lost. But as I've dug through all of my resentment and grief over the last year to deal with them, the feelings have been replaced with ones of love. Hoping I make them proud every day. Hoping that Pops is looking down on me and sees how far I've come. Hoping that Mom and Dad approve of the choices I've made that led me here.

More and more, I believe they had a hand in bringing us together.

Like fate.

"Yes," I whisper, covering the ring in his fingers with a hand and holding on. I lift the other to curl around his neck and I tug, pulling his lips to mine. "Of course I'll marry you."

Acknowledgements

Thank you for reading my debut novel, Play The Last Card! This has been a journey that's taken over a year and I am so excited for it to be out in the world. I wouldn't have succeeded without those closest to me and those who have helped me get to this point.

To my family, thank you for the endless support on this journey. For always asking for updates and getting excited with me.

To my best friends—Grace, Laura, Hollie, Shanè, Giorgie, Kiera and Taylor—for listening to me talk about this book endlessly for the last two years. Thank you for giving your feedback where I needed it. For allowing me to bounce ideas off you and guiding me to make the right decisions where I needed it. And to Eileen and Sophie who read the roughest first draft and helped shape Scott & Ivy into who they are today.

To my editor, Ash, thank you for holding my hand and guiding me through this process. This experience would have been a thousand times more stressful without you.

And finally to you, my readers. Without you I wouldn't be able to make this dream come true. I am so grateful to you all for choosing to read my book and I hope you love it as much as I do.

About the Author

Olivia is a romance indie author living on the east coast of Australia with her miniature spoodle, Scotland. She's been writing since high school and is doing her best to live out her dreams—becoming a published author. Her hobbies are snuggling with her dog, reading all sorts of romance books, and hanging out with her family.

OTHER TITLES

The Boston Broncos Series

Play The Last Card
Play The Last Track

Standalones

A Misstep Of Fate

WANT MORE?

Turn the page to read the first chapter of *Play The Last Track*, which follows the love story of Flynn Reed & Katie Murphy.

PROLOGUE

KATIE

"Who am I supposed to talk to? Eight hours stuck next to a stranger."

"You will be fine." Ivy laughs as she leans back into Scott's chest. The sight only makes my scowl deepen.

Ugh.

My best friend and her fiancé are absolutely sickening.

Well, not really. The two of them are perfect together. Made for each other. Fate brought them to one another, and I promise you, I'm not even a little bit jealous.

Okay. Maybe, like, ninety-five percent happy for them and five percent jealous.

Ten percent jealous, ninety percent happy.

Fifteen percent, but that's really it.

I used to be happy. I used to have someone to lean on when I was tired. Someone I would sit next to on flights. Someone I looked at with that kind of love.

I think.

That's been my problem the last few months. I think I was in love, but I'm not certain.

Grant says he was certain. He says he was in love with me. That he wanted to spend the rest of his life with me. He tells me all of this over and over again.

But he doesn't show it. I don't think he ever has.

The longer I went just hearing those words and not feeling them, not seeing them, the more I think I fell out of love with him. Or, maybe, I just woke up to what I settled for.

Ugh.

"Can't we all just sit in coach? That way, you can sit next to me and Scott. Everyone wins." I beg my best friend, but it's completely futile. The tickets are paid for, and we've checked in.

Still.

"My knees and my back will pay for it," Scott mumbles. His face is pressed into Ivy's neck as he tightens his arms around her waist. My heart clenches. See? That's loud love.

I groan and mumble, "Old man."

"It's eight hours, and then we will be in Rome. Watch a movie and have a nap," Ivy says.

"Scott, swap seats with me. I need entertainment, and Ivy will gossip with me. I have to tell her about the mess Doug and his cronies made in the bar the other week." I clasp my hands in front of my chest, hitting him with my best ever puppy dog eyes. "Please."

"Not a chance, Murphy," Scott replies instantly. He doesn't even look up. Dammit.

"Don't worry, Rockstar. I'll keep you entertained."

A shiver rolls through me, and I have to work not to let it show on my face. I look up. Standing over me, broad shoulders stretching a crisp white T-shirt to breaking point, and a smile that would make even the devil fall to his knees, is Flynn Reed.

Tight end to the Boston Broncos and Scott's best friend.

And my secret, totally off limits, but definitely in my dreams, football crush.

Fuck, yes.

www.ingramcontent.com/pod-product-compliance
Lightning Source LLC
Chambersburg PA
CBHW050959210726
48287CB00004B/1288